I0760499

Quest *for* Kwifon

Quest for Kwifon

Book One

Martin Fusi

Spears Books
Denver, Colorado

Spears Books
An Imprint of Spears Media Press LLC
7830 W. Alameda Ave, Suite 103-247
Denver, CO 80226
United States of America

First Published in the United States of America in 2025 by Spears Books
www.spearsbooks.org
info@spearsmedia.com
Information on this title: https://bit.ly/4gxe7bS

Library of Congress Control Number: 2025941426
ISBN: 9781957296579 (Paperback)
ISBN: 9781957296586 (eBook)

Available in Kindle, Google Play Books, & Apple Books

Designed and typeset by Spears Media Press LLC
Cover designed by D. Kambem

Distributed globally by African Books Collective (ABC)
www.africanbookscollective.com

Contents

One

Whisked to Tikari

The house was silent, the only noises coming from Kajere's video game on the television. Suddenly, he stopped.

"I'm bored," he said, "let's do something exciting." Though his voice sounded tired, there was something bullish about it.

At first, Nintai did not hear him. She was on the phone with a friend. Then, after he repeated himself, she looked up.

"Did you say something?" She asked.

"Yes. I said I am bored. Let's do something exciting," Kajere said.

"Like what?" she asked casually, not looking up from her phone.

He shrugged. "I don't know. I'm just tired of video games and today's Friday. We can't sit here doing nothing."

"Why don't you visit some of your college mates?" Nintai asked, her eyes still on her phone.

"Those? They'll all just want us to go drinking and to smoke weed. I don't feel like doing either. Plus, I need to stay home with you, or else you know what mom will say," Kajere replied.

"Well, I'm not bored. I'm chatting with Jessica, and she's telling me about her new boyfriend." Nintai continued texting her friend furiously, not caring to look up at Kajere.

"I know what I'll do," Kajere said, getting up from his seat and stretching.

"What?" Asked his sister without looking at him and still focused excitedly on texting her friend.

"I'll be right back," he said, disappearing into the house. Moments later, he returned with his father's black box.

Nintai, still focused on her phone screen, did not see it. Eventually, when she casually looked, her eyes caught Kajere's loaded hands. Her eyes opened and widened in shock. Her phone dropped from her hand.

"No! You can't touch that, Kajere!" she shouted. "Dad will get mad. Return it, or I'll call dad and mom," she said, picking up her phone.

"I want to see what's inside. Of course, nothing will happen," Kajere said, smiling mischievously and already trying to prise open the box.

His persistence and casualness somewhat relaxed Nintai's fiery start, but she spoke up: "Mom and dad allow us to get away with a lot, but what dad always says about that box is more than a warning. He told us ever since we were kids never to go near that box. He repeated that almost daily. Just how did you come by the key in the first place?" As she spoke, her voice lost its steady firmness and became hysterical as he dangled a key in front of her face, grinning.

Just then, Nintai's friend Jessica distracted her a little with a phone call. She did not answer it. The matter at hand was of the utmost importance, and she took a moral stance to have things right.

However, Kajere too meant business. "I don't need to tell you everything," he said mischievously. His eyes were beginning to twinkle at the thought of opening the box. "I think it's a pistol inside. Maybe dad has always lied to us that he does not like guns. There's a gun inside. I just want to see it, that's all. That way, I can call his bluff and tell him how he's been lying to us for so many years about not having a gun in the house."

The new curiosity again brought down Nintai's worked-up temper and her tone became discursive: "A gun?" she asked rhetorically. "Maybe there's one there, but maybe there's none there. We've never seen mom and dad with a gun, and we know what they think about guns." Her mood still had panic and concern, but anger seemed to be in the offing at Kajere's antics.

Disregarding her angst-ridden frustration, Kajere simply continued his investigation, announcing: "Let's find out. I want to see what kind of gun dad has. That's all."

"I'll call them now if you attempt to open that box," Nintai threatened again. "Go return it, or I'll call mom now!" She pretended to dial their mom.

This only pushed Kajere to mock: "Uh-oh, you're so scared of everything. It's just a gun. I want to see what kind of gun it is. I won't touch it. I promise. Unless, of course, a thief walks in on us now." Kajere sounded calmly jocular, but he did feel shivers going through his body. For one thing, he had never touched or still less, held a real gun before. So, the thrill of anticipating the discovery was thrust with tremors of what the actual encounter with reality might mean. Yet, bravado was on the outside of him as he looked at her comically.

"This is no time for jokes. I'll text mom now." Nintai actually started texting this time around.

Kajere sensed the authenticity of the threat and upped his cajoling skill. "Okay, Okay. But don't you want to know what's inside?" He played up her curiosity, but the trick did not work.

Nintai kept typing and did not look up at him. "No, I don't want to know anything, "she said, furiously texting their mom.

Kajere was desperate, too. "I'll just say I did not do anything," he said and then quickly proceeded to open the box. Nintai paused her typing. She capitulated, being tangled in the web Kajere had spun for her. Curiosity overcame her. She moved closer to Kajere to peep into the box. Kajere noticed this and smiled scornfully and sardonically.

He had succeeded in prizing open the lock after a few failed attempts. The lock off, they looked at each other, fear and foreboding enveloping them, Kajere's fingers trembling. Nintai's observant femininity did not miss his restlessness. So, she tried to backpedal on her initial curiosity now that the lock was no longer a barrier to the final spectacle. "I don't think you should open it. I don't feel good about this," she stuttered, breathing heavily.

Although he was also suddenly scared, Kajere was of the mind that, having already come this far, he had to complete the venture. He did not want to show her how frightened he was because he needed to play the man as most men were known to do. So, slowly, certainly slowed down by fear and the caution it inspired, he carefully peered inside the box. He saw no gun. In the box was a tarantula with a chain of white cowries around its upper part.

"There's no gun inside," he said blandly, half whispering before gaining his voice: "Hey, what's that? Looks like a tarantula with cowries ringing it. I thought dad had a gun. What's he doing with a tarantula?" Not groomed in the background of superstitious awe of the tarantula, Kajere was disappointed that there was nothing that fearful or novel in the box. He let his guard down, and fear left him for the moment.

"Now that you're satisfied, close it quickly and let's go," Nintai said as she too looked at the contents. She, too, was not impressed. She mocked: "Oh well, that's your excitement for the evening." She mused, "But why would dad stop us from seeing a dead tarantula?"

The idea of the tarantula being dead and intact all those many years did not impinge on their sense of how things worked. They missed the mystery. Was it a shimmer, or did the tarantula actually move? Kajere was sure it actually moved; its over-hairy skin and tentacular projections stirred the air, he was sure. He did not wait to have a second signal. "It's not dead; it's alive!" Kajere said, his fear returning.

Nintai looked closer. The tarantula was motionless. "It's dead. It's not moving. It's impossible for it to move, not after these many years in a box without food and drink. Is it a virus or of the theraphosidae family we all know?" Nintai said, daring to examine it closely and thinking of the 30,000-year-old giant virus of the Siberian permafrost she had read about a while before. Her mind reverted to viruses of infamous virulence, including the Ebola and hantavirus. But this was no virus, just a creature of the Arachnida class.

"You remember what mom said about the tarantulas she saw in her office and how they disappeared? I saw this one move," Kajere said, and Nintai thought he was trying to scare her. Visions of the kids Kajere had seen close to their home rapidly flashed through his mind as he mentally groped for ideas on what to do next.

Nintai still did not notice the creature's movement even as she peered closer a second time. "I think you're already insane or still going bananas, Kajere. That thing is dead and dead, final," she said.

Kajere conceded in order to end the glamor of expectation. "Well, the excitement is over. I wanted to see the kind of gun dad had, not a tarantula," Kajere said, trying to shut the box.

Nintai too wanted the chapter closed. "I'm out of here," she said, even though she still expected something exciting.

Kajere virtually stopped her in mid-thought. "Hold on! Hold on! I think it just moved once more. I swear!" Kajere affirmed, swearing to impress his conviction and excitement.

Now, this was weird and fear was engulfing Nintai as she said, "I think you should close the box and put it where it was."

"What kind of tarantula is this, in the first place; one with cowries ringing its neck?" Kajere looked closer and picked it up so they could both look closer. As they saw, the cowries tightly wrapped the tarantula. Kajere tried to move them, but the cowries were firmly secured. Before they could comment, the tarantula bared what looked like fangs. They were white, human-looking teeth.

"Hey, it's got teeth like humans. How strange! O do tarantulas usually have humanoid teeth? You know things like this better, Kajere. I have never known that tarantulas have teeth that look like ours," Nintai said, alarmed at the unnaturalness of what she saw. "Put it back. I don't like this. I don't like what I'm seeing." As she spoke, she started stepping back from Kajere and the box, which heightened Kajere's fear too.

"Me too," he said, instinctively moving backward. But before he could put it back, the tarantula bit him hard, the kind of bite a teething infant delivers.

"Aaiee! It has bitten me," he yelled. "And it's painful! Aaiee!" He screamed, trying to drop it, but it wrapped its long legs around, clasping itself on his fingers, not relenting.

"Kajere, what's happening?" Nintai shouted in alarm. "Throw it away, throw it away," she screamed in panic.

Kajere too screamed, while Nintai tried to pull off the tarantula from his fingers. "I can't. I can't pull it off. It's attached itself to my fingers, and it's terrible. Help me, Ninatai." Kajere was now sounding desperate. "Remove it, Nintai. Please, remove it. Help me," Kajere screamed out his apprehension.

"I can't," Ninati said, pulling as hard as she could. "It's not moving."

Kajere tried using his free hand to pull it off, but it would not come off. Nintai came to his help, but their combined efforts were no match.

"Remove it, Kajere, I can't do anything. Put it back in the box," she said in desperation.

"I am trying, but it's not moving. It's stuck like glue to my fingers, and it's excruciatingly painful; can't you see?" he replied.

"Aaiee! Help me, Nintai! Help me!" As he said, he suddenly noticed that he was beginning to shrink, to grow smaller in size.

Nintai too noticed this and screamed at the very top of her voice as if calling him from the dead: "Kajere! Kajere!"

Not comprehending the entire scope of what was going on, Kajere rather noticed that Nintai was getting bigger and bigger. Panic struck him. “Nintai, what’s going on? You are growing huge! Are you okay?” he shouted full-throated and uncontrollably, sweat and tears mixing in a rush down his face and brows.

Nintai’s embarrassment was total. “I’m okay. It’s rather you shrinking,” she said.

“Oh! Oh! Oh! Please, help me! I feel weird inside! I feel dispossessed and emptied.” Total disbelief confronted his fright.

This was, from the outside, matched by Nintai’s panic-stricken wail: “Kajere, you are shrinking!”

“What do you mean? What are you talking about?” His disbelief did not convert the mesmerizing reality to unreality.

“You’re shrinking!” Nintai heard herself screeching through tears. She still had her sense of the present in control and dialed her parents. None of them picked up the call. “Where’s mom?” she worried, anxiety making her stamp her feet in disconnected strikes on the floor.

“What?” Kajere became discombobulated. “What’s happening to me? Nintai, help me! Call dad now! Call dad now! Tell him what’s going on. Call dad now!” Kajere was hysterical in his desperate iterations but continued growing smaller and smaller.

Nintai made more attempts to call their dad before dropping the phone in panic and haste. The phone rolled and disappeared under one of the couches in the room. She bent to retrieve it, but when she took up her head, Kajere had shrunk to an unbelievable minuteness. He barely measured up to her knees and was still shrinking. As if she could stop the process with words crafted by fear, superstition, and formulaic magical hints, she shouted further: “No! Stop! Stop shrinking! No!” her apoplectic voice cantered. Again, she tried calling her parents, but her phone dropped the second time. She, however, refused to take her eyes off Kajere, fearing that perhaps out of her sight, he might simply disappear.

She had heard that the dying could be kept back by being recalled to the present by loved ones. "Kajere! Kajere!" she kept calling out. Her words did nothing, being totally ineffective as he kept on shrinking. Before long, he was barely a few inches in height. His voice shrank with him. So, hard as he screamed, Nintai could scarcely hear him. Then Kajere simply disappeared right in her sight.

"Oh my God, oh my God! Mom. Dad. Oh my God! "Kajereeeee!" she cried, desperate for a glimpse of her beloved brother. "Where are you?" Silence greeted her, the kind that can be described as dead silence. Reality was being remade for her. A human being, her own brother, just became nothing right in front of her eyes.

For his part, Kajere kept screaming, his eyes closed to maximize the volume of his meager voice. When he finally dared to open his eyes, he found that he was falling through clouds and could see the heavens, stars, and the night sky beneath him. So, although he was falling through the clouds, he was falling towards the sky. Topsy turvy describes inversions and convections in phenomena strange. Here he was in a never-imagined convection, as it were, of unreal reality.

"What's happening?" he mused and again shouted, "Help! Somebody help me, please," knowing that the shout was to somebody who had to be a nobody or even nothing in the new reality sphere he was thrust into.

It was becoming clear that he was alone, and that no one was there to help him. No one seemed to hear him. He hurtled and spiraled down the night sky in the spatiality of huge stars. On one side was what he thought had to be the moon. On the other side, he was swooping in a plunging direction into nothingness. Then everything seemed churned, stars dancing in every direction, in no direction in a rhythm that should be described as nothing but cacophony. Land, tens of thousands of feet below, was but a small round ball. There was nothing to lean on in this rapid lunge in swift descent, brushing past clouds and spinning without pattern or control. The earth rose to meet him rapidly.

Closer to what was earth and an end to his gyration and chute, a volcano was spewing red-hot lava up thousands of feet skyward. He was plunged into the lava, but the mesmeric reality continued; deep inside the red-hot lava, he felt the heat but was not burned. And the red, hard heat enveloped him, the red-hot bubbles of the molten heat swirling with measured power, unruffled. Additionally, weird, indescribable animals were right in it. They clawed for him, for their food, but each time they came close to him, they suddenly shied off. A hidden potent force protected him and repelled them, it seemed. He kept screaming, though.

Then, the volcano stopped spewing its lava, became dark and darkness came. He could see nothing but heard unearthly sounds well up from deep in earth's bowels. He was still contending with the meaning of the darkness and the disorienting sounds when a compelling light replaced the darkness. So bright was the light that it almost blinded him. Abruptly and rapidly, a powerful force propelled him up towards the light and then let him go into a freefall, a backward fall, so to say. Try as he could, he had no control of the fall. He tried to turn around, but could not. Great fright held him, especially as he could not see where he was going.

Rushing past him were so many things – buildings, skyscrapers that soon became other types of houses, smaller, and became adobe huts. Then came cars, trucks, and various kinds of vehicles flowing by. These yielded way to horses and myriad forms of transport common in past centuries. All whizzed past as he kept moving backward, his mood a feeling of time in suspension. Before long, their mood and ambiance changed, and he felt that he was definitely moving slower. The direction was still backward, and different kinds of animals went in the opposite direction. Such were dogs, cats, wild cats, some looking so remarkably aggressive that fear overtook him.

Particularly when a lion loudly roared not far from him, actually coming a scary close to him. Of the many birds that also flew past, he could recognize some but some he could not.

Without warning, all of a sudden, there was a lull, no animals or birds coming. The lull did not last long, for shortly after, the same animals, birds, reptiles, and many other creatures recommenced their drift in one direction. This time, he no longer recognized anything. For the animals and birds were now all strange. Too scared to look, he closed his eyes in the hope that he would survive the dream. For even now, as far as he was concerned, he was only in the midst of one big dream.

As if to wake him up to reality and to prove that he was in no dream, one of the animals hit him. It was like a wake-up jolt. He opened his eyes wide and passed his left hand over his eyes as if to help them wake up to reality. Slowly, he began to take in the kind of creatures that floated past him – dodos, Mascarene parrots and coots, Ascension flightless capes, broad-billed parrots, and DeLand's coua that kept sailing by. He screamed out, not in fright anymore, but in wonder. Animals too were in the flow and float and in the same direction. He stared at the creatures in awe. The mussin too kept coming. At last, one of them carried their curiosity far and came close to him, paused momentarily, and stared at him.

Kajere gawked back and noticed that it had an inviting look in its eye. The message was clear, and Kajere got it, sprung to its back, and they floated away. The mussin flew with him, high and fast. Animals materialized in the flight line. Particularly, he noticed and recognized quaggas, flying foxes, red gazelles, blue bucks, aurochs, and atlas bears. As he took everything in, he nearly fell over a Saddle-backed Rodrigue's giant tortoise. It had approached him silently. He gasped at the sheer size and beauty of the animal. And it was not just one rare find, for hundreds of them floated by, uttering sounds he could not reproduce, sounds he had never heard before. He tried to talk to the strange bird on whose back he was riding.

"Where are you going?" he asked, wondering how it came about that he was trying to talk to a bird. The bird looked at him in a bemused but not arrogant squint, but said nothing in reply.

"My name's Kajere, and thanks for the help," he continued, hoping that expressing gratitude would bait the creature into a conversation. His confidence rose with this, but the bird simply continued, although he thought he saw it nod. He decided to confirm his guess that the bird communicated in echo to his words:

"Can you hear me? I am Kajere. I don't know where I am or where I'm from, nor do I know where I'm going, but thanks for the help," he said. His elaborate words fell on deaf ears, it seemed. The bird kept flying. Shortly, dark stones and giant boulders charged towards Kajere, the mussin and other birds or creatures. Each creature skillfully maneuvered itself about and away from the boulders.

Kajere wondered whether the threat of the boulders was the cause of it ignoring him. He ventured once more: "If you can hear me, please tell me where I am or where we're going." It was as if Kajere was sending out feelers in his quest, just trying different ways to understand his new experience. He was lost and already giving up.

Around his neck, the gris-gris dangled. For that was what it was. The cowries and tarantula were *gris-gris* meant to protect him. However, he did not know it just yet. His hands toyed with it as they moved on. Just then, he noticed a boulder coming straight at him. Panicked, he quickened to scream, in the process, letting go of the bird and falling through the sky. The bird went for him, diving in a successful chase and catching him.

"I did not mean that. I'm scared. Thanks for the help," Kajere said. It was as if he was begging for friendship or seeking notice. The bird did not answer, and to him, it was as if the creature was snubbing him. Yet he continued trying to converse with it as they kept flying. Kajere could not tell how long they had been flying. He was not exactly gaining confidence. There was something like stoicism in his decision to trust that if he had to die, he ought to have died earlier. He chose not to be scared anymore.

After what seemed like many years, he decided once more to engage the bird in a conversation.

"Who sent you to help me?" Kajere asked. It was not so much the need for information he was aiming for. Mainly, he was trying to keep his sanity through what might be termed a talking cure. Undeterred by the creature's silence, he went on to ask:

"Where are you from?" He expected no answer, of course. Yet, when it did not answer, he was disappointed and smiled ruefully, feeling bored. It would have been great to have some fun with his rescuer. He employed self-pity, victim, the needy, and the vulnerable as schemes to evoke the bird's attention and help.

"I'm thirsty. I haven't had anything to eat or drink in a while. Where can we find some water?" he asked. He might well have been speaking to the wind or a rock, for the bird made no reply. On, it kept flying.

Just then, another boulder came rapidly at them. This time, he was knocked off. But unlike earlier on, the bird did not dive for him. It kept flying. He screamed for help as his fall accelerated rapidly. As despair made its throttle hold on him, darkness gave way to daylight. For the first time since he found himself in the odd trip, he saw the earth. It was rising rapidly to meet him. He crash-landed on the top of a very high tree in the middle of a jungle. So tall was the tree that he could barely see the ground. Also, there were so many trees, and the jungle was so dense that light did not penetrate the forest floor. For a good while, he stayed up, sitting on the branches that had caught him and wondering what to do next.

All around him were strange bird and animal sounds, none of them familiar. Then it started raining hard. It was a blessing for the rains provided him with water. He was dying of thirst. Using leaves from the tree, he funneled the raindrops into his mouth and drank to his satisfaction. From the height, he saw no humans at all; there was nothing he recognized as far as his eyes could see except the green of the leaves. The tops of the trees stretched far into the distance, smelting at the blurry edges with some mountains.

Yes, there were creatures he could place in categories. Thus, there were insects, which, however, looked like Saint Helena earwigs. He was unsure of his eyes for Saint Helena earwigs, which were definitely already extinct. Since he had lost his communication chances with the mighty mussin, he sought relevance with the entire ambience.

"Where am I?" he wondered aloud, his mind wandering. The typical interpretation of speaking alone he had known was that the speaker was insane or overburdened with psychological stress. Here, he was alone and doing what he knew carried degrading impressions where he had come from.

"Hello. Can anyone hear me?" he called out loudly. For all the force he gathered and put in the loudness, all his voice did was rustle a colony of strange-looking insects. These flew up into the air, some flying towards him but just passing by as they reached close to him. Otherwise, everywhere looked virgin and uninterrupted.

A few twigs from where he was, hung a strange-looking fruit to which hunger pushed him. He did not care if it was poisonous. When he made to get at the fruit, stretching his hand to pluck one, several branches gave way, and he hurtled down. It was a rapid flight down with a loud scream for the revving engine of the otherwise noiseless plane. He landed with a massive thud as his momentum careened him into a muddy river that swept him down towards a waterfall. He reached the edge of the waterfall and tried to stop himself by hanging onto some stones but was thrust down with great force. He finally landed a few thousand feet below, sinking right to the very bottom of the water before resurfacing in a rebound. It was a moment to take stock of the training he had had without thinking of when it would come in handy. He thanked his mom for forcing him to learn to swim. He had been extremely reluctant and had asked himself what he would ever have to do with swimming. His mom, no-nonsense in the spirit of most well-meaning moms, had insisted. He and Nintai had thus been imposed upon and taken swimming lessons. As he gained flexibility, he occasionally went swimming with his friends. It was their companionship that he valued and not the contact and mastery of the water, for he never really enjoyed it. He tried unsuccessfully to swim against the current, sweeping him downwards, towards a swift-spinning whirlpool. In one massive decisive sweep, he was sucked deep into the entrails of the whirlpool, a maelstrom in which he noticed weird fish and crustacea, till then, not something he had imagined. However, the creatures suddenly disappeared, the water becoming thick and milky.

Still, he felt himself descending to the endless depths of emptiness while the thick and tasteless liquid kept spinning and pulling him in one direction. In the distance, he saw faint, weird lights. Meanwhile, he felt enveloped and covered by a semi-transparent canopy of colossal proportions. It is right in the middle of the maelstrom, consisting of an unimaginably potent substance. He had no way of contemplating the potency of that magnitude. It was both ethereal and physical, a meeting point of physics and spirits, so to speak. A powerful jet of air merged with the thick liquid. It swung and flung him to the top of the canopy. He could be said to have splashed rather than landed there. The liquid burst open. He screamed, landing on something he could not recognize at first, but which felt warm and comforting.

Two

The Tumenta Tarantula

Time had a way of defining the past, present, and future, recoloring the past to connect with and establish the end with ease. Los Angeles appeared to be a vast city, especially for a migrant from Africa, surrounded by smaller towns, each unique in character. The Inland Empire was that one neighborhood in Los Angeles that remained closely tied to the family of Dr John Tumenta. Some said it was named so because of how far the so-called 'Empire' was from Los Angeles and its proximity to the desert.

Among the many small cities in the Inland Empire was the beautiful Upland, located about an hour east of Los Angeles. In this small, lovely town, little occurred. Nothing extraordinary ever happened there. The houses were similar, all constructed within the last decade or so. The lawns and driveways all looked the same.

That is where Kajere lived. Kajere, who had graduated from university several years before, had nothing peculiar about his appearance, nothing to raise the eyebrow of the curious or even keen observer. He had decided to stay at home rather than on campus as his parents had desired. There was nothing peculiar about his family either. True, he was born in Los Angeles, but his parents had migrated to the United States from Cameroon, and his father became a professor at one of the universities while his mother taught at a middle school. Kajere had a sister a few years younger than him. He loved her but sometimes found her annoying. Generally, he considered her a prattler.

Like most kids in the neighborhood, Kajere played basketball and soccer when he wasn't studying. He wasn't the best, but he wasn't the worst either. He mixed well and was welcomed among his peers. His upbringing was so ordinary that no one who knew this family would expect anything extraordinary from them. From all appearances, there wasn't anything to set him or them apart. The only problem people had was pronouncing the name *Kajere*—a rather superficial issue, though he sometimes worried about it. His sister's name was Nintai, and not many people could pronounce it easily. Often, he wondered why he had to have a name like that. Nintai was a sophomore and had attended the same high school as her brother.

Kajere could be described as handsome, though he did not particularly feel it. Girls thought he was handsome, but he showed no interest in them. He was a rather intellectual person, interested in becoming a biologist. He majored in biology, loved everything about birds and animals, and could name any bird or animal any time. He knew their common names and their scientific names; no one knew how. Perhaps it was 'in his blood' as some wryly put it.

Why he cared to know things like that bemused many of those who knew him, and his parents were no exception. But he cared for and liked it, puzzling his lecturers with his wealth of information about animals, plants, and other natural species. He never actually realized that girls liked him the more because of how intelligent he was in class. He just seemed to wade through class and life daily, mixing fairly well. He did not need to go the extra mile to be likable. Suffice it for him to enjoy video games, study biological things, and play basketball or soccer.

The peculiarity which escaped many was that he was deeply

reflective and perhaps wiser than he should have been for his age. However, he was not very much the expressive type. He fitted the description of being always taciturn, except perhaps towards his mom and dad, with whom he 'flowed' freely. As far as his friends were concerned, he went by as quiet, almost shy, and nerdy, a big contrast to his younger sister, who was an outgoing, prattling extrovert. A stoic introvert, when Kajere thought something too complex or puzzling to understand, he would become reticent and analyze the phenomenon from different perspectives. His shifting perspectives nearly always ended with the right solution to just any of the puzzles he encountered.

His camaraderie with his father meant that he brought up any nuisance that struck his fancy. Thus, he would often challenge his father to justify such an odd name, which was like a punishment for him in the setup. His father would return the conviviality and tell him to be proud of his name instead, considering the profundity of its meaning and extended implications.

His father had left his country of origin many years before, initially coming to America to study and return home. When he completed his studies, a university took a liking for his dissertation and asked him if he would like to become a professor there. It was both flattering and a financial boost for him to accept the offer. He did, hoping to acquire experience, return home to his people, and teach students of his native country. He was in Kentucky then, and before long, twenty years and more had elapsed. The convolution of happenings was easy to explain away his failing to keep to his initial plan, but that could only be a kind of casuistry. But so it was. He met his wife in the process, got married, and they moved to California. There, his children were born, and life treated him well. For a while, he visited his country of birth often. Recently, however, he had mentally and physically decided to become an integral part of his adopted country.

Growing up as a young boy in Cameroon had been different. In the city where he grew up, he spoke English, learning his vernacular language only later. Early in his teens, his father had sent him to a Catholic boarding school for boys. There, and even at that young age, he knew that he had to learn his language and experientially understand the traditions and culture of his people. Thus, he both learned to speak the language of his people and understood the history, culture, and behavioral patterns of his people. He learned to work on the farms, plant, harvest food, and work in his uncle's coffee plantation. He developed a passion for chasing bush rats through the grassfields. He made time to climb the high mountains in the village adventurously, from where he could look down with exquisite excitement and admiration of the beautiful plains below and beyond. Rustling streams played delightful music to his ears, and the golden sparkle of springs and rivulets delighted him. Water was like air, and he felt as if he was at a feast of nature when he fetched and drank water from the open waterways when he went hiking or working in the fields.

He learned to set traps for small game and to work in the rice farms. The work on the rice farm hyped the value of the food he would eat ravenously, for he realized how much work went into cultivating the tasty food. Learning to tap palm wine was another exciting new skill that he valued and was proud of. His uncle, Abong, introduced him to it on his first trip to the village, explaining as a primer or introductory that he needed to differentiate 'raffia wine' from 'palm wine.'

"You climb for palm wine, and dig for raffia wine. You can say that palm wine is better because raffia wine often has much water. But palm wine, which you climb up to tap, is less watery for the most part."

Uncle Abong taught Tumenta to tap raffia wine from the raffia trees. First, he demonstratively dug around the tree roots usually growing in swamps. He learned to slice into the stem of the plant carefully. The angle of the cut that pierced to tap the raffia wine was a delicate skill. There had to be a burning of the area and proper placement of a funneled calabash to trap the wine dripping out. It was nectar so sweet that sometimes when he came to collect the wine with his uncle the following day, they found bush babies drunk near the tree. The delicate application of the manual skills of tapping and their mental directives came in handy in later life when Tumenta faced life's adulthood pressures. He applied patience and meticulous forging for exact slants (physical and metal) and was encouraged by the expectancy of a mellifluous outcome.

He remembered that one beautiful rainy season when, with his uncle, he had gone to tap palm wine. There hadn't been rain that day, and the sun shone brightly. The brilliance and heat of the sun did not hurt them because they were well sheltered by the leaves of the raffia trees. As they worked, a slight breeze swayed the leaves, its shadows dancing across his uncle's hunched back as he chipped away at the stems of the raffia trees. From nowhere, a creature, a tarantula, moved a couple of inches from his feet.

"Pa," he whispered, trying not to stir with a loud voice and trying to stay calm, "Some tarantula dey near my foot." His uncle did not flinch. Because the kid was afraid, he had to be careful how he proceeded. Fear was not the kind of thing you taught kids without taking strictly the context and implications.

"I've seen it. No, don't do anything. Do just what I tell you. What foot?" His uncle whispered back, "right or left?"

"Right," he answered, his breath quietly coming out of his nose and mouth simultaneously, and in short rasps. Before he knew what was happening, his uncle swiftly turned around and sliced the tarantula in two with his machete. The aim was perfect, the timing so exact.

Then uncle picked up the arachnid, still writhing in its death throes.

"This is a bad sign," he said, shaking his head pensively and trying not to frighten the little boy. He knew how grave the situation was and explained to the young man, "We have to *wash* you quickly."

That was many years ago. Those who came to Dr Tumenta knew him as a fine gentleman. Perhaps this was down to the skills he acquired as he grew up in the hills of his village. Not only was he never angry, but he seemed to have answers to all problems. Within, however, guilt burdened him.

His wife, Edwina Tumenta, knew very little about the deep pressure he put on himself. She was also blank on the strange dreams he was having, dreams of his late father appearing to him. Strange it was because he had never dreamed of him before, not since he died. In the dream, the old man kept trying to warn him about an impending but imprecise happening of magnitude. Usually, the figure would dissolve slowly and evaporate when the warning came. And the dream was recurrent. The last time it occurred, it was more vivid, so intense that he had quite a scare from it. When he woke up, he forgot about it and forgot that he had even dreamt. The dream was most luminous and so real.

His day had begun like any other beautiful Southern Californian morning. In fact, you could not have asked for a better day from the free hand of nature. Besides, it was a Friday and, with Edwina, his wife, he planned an evening out. That was not a common thing with them. More uncommon, perhaps, was the spectacle of magnificent birds that graced the morning sky, flying towards the mountains. They were long-feathers, and he had no idea what they were called. He stood watching them momentarily through the window but was interrupted by his wife's voice with a jolt.

"John, why are you looking at the birds as if you have never seen them before?" Edwina signaled him back to life.

They mostly spoke to each other in Pidgin, being from different ethnic groups and not understanding each other's mother tongue.

Their American children understood Pidgin because of the frequency of their parents' use of it.

"If you continue this way, you will be late for work, and they will be late for school," she added, looking at him and wondering why her husband was becoming more absent-minded than usual.

He apologized, gave her a peck, and sat at the breakfast table. Kajere and Nintai were already there, devouring pancakes. They mumbled good morning to him, their lips full and holding the bounty in their mouths. At the same time, they were fidgeting with their phones.

Dr Tumenta cheerfully sat down at the table, acknowledged their greetings, served himself some coffee, and hummed Humpty Dumpty. He wore a big smile, the day being a promise of weekend and relaxing time out with Edwina. The children exchanged glances and Nintai shook her head comically. Kajere, looking at his dad pensively, asked,

"Dad, can I ask you something?"

"Yes, my man," Dr Tumenta replied, noting the rather severe expression on his son's countenance and trying to dissolve it with the light mood.

"Why is it that when we hear you sing, you sing songs we learned in nursery school here or other songs we are familiar with here? I never hear you sing anything African. Didn't you have songs there when you were young?" As he spoke, Kajere helped himself to some cereal, but kept an eye on his dad's face as seriously as he could. The face spoke as much as the mouth, he was convinced.

"Poom! Answer that," Edwina jubilated.

"That's true," Nintai chimed in, not relaxing her munching on a peanut butter and jelly sandwich. "Are there no songs from there, dad?"

It was a little disconcerting, and Dr Tumenta swallowed hard. He did not know how to answer them, but he had the mental presence to note that they said 'Africa.' That indicated ignorance, ignorance of the vast and differentiated lands and peoples, cultures and climates of mother Africa. Of course, it could be simply due to the bad practice of hearing others talk that way, but those others too were likely to be influenced by ignorance or deliberate willingness to distort. "Did these kids not know about Cameroon? Why was it always Africa?" he mused.

Kajere, anticipating his victory, continued, "Even when we were kids, you read stories like *Cinderella, Snow White and the Seven Dwarfs, Beauty and the Beast, Little Red Riding Hood, Goldilocks and the Three Bears*, and *Hansel and Gretel* to us—lovely stories. Yet I also would like to hear stories about where you grew up. Did your father not read you stories, dad?"

His son's spate of questions caught Dr Tumenta off guard; he could not immediately think of an answer. His father had never read him any bedtime stories, and neither had his mother, but he did not think about it. Things were done differently where he grew up.

Worse, Edwina stopped what she was doing and came to the table, which gave greater weight to what Kajere sparked. Dr Tumenta looked at his wife, and she looked back at him. No word, no voice, no sound was uttered, but the looks spoke.

And then Nintai also picked up the questioning trail: "It's true, dad. Even now, you make me read *Gulliver's Travels, Robinson Crusoe*, and Shakespeare. I don't mind, but I don't see the likes of you in those works. It was only by mistake that I read *The White Man of God*, which I found quaintly interesting." As she spoke, she did not pause her work of mastication and ravenous swallowing of peanut butter blended with jelly. Her father was up to his neck in the deluge and answered with definite silence, which Edwina interrupted. She rescued him. She always did:

"Well, time to get ready for school. Finish your breakfast. Dad will be dropping you guys off today; don't let him be late for work.

I thought you liked the stories he used to tell you about growing up in Cameroon." Though she addressed the kids, her eyes were on Dr Tumenta as if to say, "I won't rescue you next time; you need to do your homework and make them understand your country and upbringing, hubby."

Behind the kids, Dr Tumenta mouthed a big thank you to his wife, who just shrugged and hastily left the room. She also had to prepare to leave for work. It always frustrated her that her husband hardly ever addressed the issue, which could partly be accounted for by the speed of life and work in that hemisphere. She had the awkward dissatisfaction of feeling that the kids would grow up ignorant of their home culture to lean on or fall back on.

Edwina had done the trick, but Kajere would not relent. Looking at his phone, he said, "We still have some time; let dad talk about this. He told us his experiences but did not seem to have read anything about his country. And why did you punish me?" As he spoke, he ate his cereal, trying to sound and appear non-committal to the questions he was posing to his dad.

Dr Tumenta looked at his son, nonplussed. "Me? Just how did I punish you, son? When exactly did I do such a thing? You and your sister know, and as far as I can tell, I've never touched you by way of punishment." Even as he spoke, he began to sense where his son's accusation was leading. He needed to end it before it reached there. So he started looking for his briefcase.

His comment led to a frontal remark from his son on just what he was dodging away from: "Dad, we've talked about this many times. It's my name. It is awkward and not exactly the kind of name I am comfortable with among my peers. Why such a name? Why did you give me a name like that?" The central issue at stake and at hand, was that Kajere did not have the luxury this time to pretend to concentrate on eating cereal. He stopped eating, placing his spoon on the serviette, and looked full-faced at his dad. It was a checkmate, the way he looked.

"Haven't I told you many times that it's because your name has an important meaning? … You know that."

Kajere joined his dad in saying the last part of the sentence, indicating his boredom with the punctual response that made little sense to him.

"Yes, Dad. By now I know it like the back of my hand that the name means someone who brings eternal joy and strength. I also know that Nintai's name means magical beauty. But just how do we represent those names? I do not feel it." He looked at Nintai as if to make her have his back in the matter, but she didn't say anything.

"You are right. It's true," Dr Tumenta said in an unsuccessful attempt to turn attention from himself to something else. But that was inviting Nintai in.

"How?" Nintai spoke, taking her cue from her brother. She placed her peanut butter sandwich away from her direct setting but still on the table. It was an indication of greater interest in what, to this moment, was Kajere's concern. "Tell me, dad; tell me how we represent our names, not even knowing from where we are rooted. Even if we did know, what would be the relevance of such names in the US, given its myriad cultures, all different from the culture of where you grew up? Our names have no meaning here except that you call us by them to make you think of your home, isn't it, dad?"

"A lot of things only get clear with time. As you get older, you will understand better," Dr Tumenta said, his tone one of resignation and virtual defeat. He finished drinking the last gulp of his coffee, tasting nothing of it because his mind was in turmoil.

"And don't you both understand Pidgin?" Edwina, who had sneaked into the room unnoticed again, tried to defend her husband. "Isn't that something that makes you and your brother feel different here?"

"But didn't you and dad say that even in Cameroon, Pidgin is for those who are not educated?" Kajere countered.

"How come we never learned your African language?" Nintai asked.

The spate was raging again. Dr Tumemnta looked at his wife, guilt all over his face.

"Tell them the truth," Edwina said. "It's because we speak two different languages, and we did not know which one to teach you. Also, we don't even speak our languages that well."

"But how can you grow up in a place and not speak your language? You speak English so well that one would think it started in your home village," he pushed. It was the first time he had heard his parents' explanation.

"Let's go. It's late. We can talk about this in the evening during dinner," Dr Tumenta found his tongue and spliced in to escape excuse from his children's torrent of prying questions. And he acted with his voice as he grabbed his suitcase.

The house was left silent as they departed, the sun's rays filtering through various crevices. A whiff of wind blew in, nudging the quiet house before disappearing toward Dr Tumenta and Edwina's bedroom. The blinds swayed to the nudge and gently flapped to acknowledge the friendly brush from the breeze.

About superstition and psychological insights, Dr Tumenta could be described as bland. He did not even seem to notice anything out of the ordinary. With the weekend and day out with Edwina in his mind, the morning conversation did not dampen his day. Instead, he had a brilliant work day, contributing brilliantly at the faculty meeting. He contributed several new insights, much to the dismay of his colleagues. His students, too, noticed that a more cheerful Dr Tumenta attended to them during office hours. It was a hectic day, but he did not feel stressed. Yes, and he did think about his dream about his father that night, but he didn't dwell on it.

If Dr Tumenta had put his emotional and mental feelers out

and had been sensitive enough, he would have noticed a giant black tarantula close to his car that morning. But he was not of that kind of mind frame. He did not see it; if he had seen it, for that matter, he would not have thought anything odd about it, not even if he had caught it. He had simply started his car and with the kids, driven off. The tarantula was strange-looking, having cowrie beads ornately wrapped around it. It had ambled to the house and slowly disappeared into it through an open window.

A more discerning person would have noticed the other signs, signs that would otherwise have been ominous to the perceptive. He would have seen that his phone rang more than usual, most of the calls coming from Cameroon, even though the callers hung up whenever he picked up the phone. That was not new since it was understood that the attempted callers wanted him to call them back. They could ill afford the phone bills. He planned to call them when he got home, away from the busy noise and haste of the workplace. However, the sheer number of times his phone rang should have raised his eyebrows, but it did not.

He should also have noticed that there were more stars visible in the bright summer sky, competing with the sun high in the deep blue sky. He missed that. People did not generally look up into the bright sky because the sun's rays would hurt. That excuse did not hold for Dr Tumenta, not seeing that there were far too many children in the streets that day.

Not so with Kajere. He noticed the number of kids on the streets as he walked back home from his university. Unlike his dad, he thought it highly unusual. Something was burning deep within him, something vague but ponderous and accompanied by a weird feeling. An acrid taste rushed to his mouth as he immersed himself in the surreal scene. He had the odd feeling that everyone was directly gazing with blame for what was going on.

When his friend, Alan, walked towards him, things became more convoluted. He had been friends with Alan since grade school, but Alan attended a different university. But Alan was their next-door neighbor, one of Kajere's best friends. Being friends did not mean that he did not sometimes get under Kajere's skin. But though he feared his rebukes, Kajere liked being with Alan.

"Hey, what's up, Argu?" he teased, calling Kajere by a name he knew he abhorred.

"Don't call me Argu. You know I don't like being teased with that name," Kajere retorted, a moody crease forming on his brow.

Alan, however, persisted. He ignored Kajere's protest: "Not again; we can't just go around calling you Kajere all the time; my mouth will get tired. It's your name, so you don't have to call your name all the time. We do," he spoke, smiling confidently as if daring Kajere to stop him.

Kajere rather seemed to be looking beyond him and asking hesitantly, "What's going on? Why so many kids around?"

This took Alan by surprise. He looked around him. "Where?" he asked before looking closely and noticing that Kajere seemed a little too severe. It was no joke, judging by his expression. Again, he surveyed the environment but saw no one. The pieces were fitting in as he had always had his suspicions about Kajere, not least about his name. He had noticed several times before that Kajere moved around trance-like. His thoughts were in the direction of whether he had some mental issues, whether his trance-like absentmindedness presented as a telltale sign of a cracked mind. Just now, Kajere's comment about kids around beat his past awkwardness. Where was Argu picking up the vibration or notion of many people around when there was, in fact, no one but the two of them on the spot? Was it time for him to do something more intensive and extensive about his friend's situation? Alan wondered as he peered at Kajere.

But Kajere was in no relenting mood. "What do you mean, where? Don't you see all these kids playing?" he asked, a baffled and somewhat angry face accompanying his question. From his side, Alan was again up to his witty banters, rebukes, and charades. Yet, Alan's face showed that there was no joke in the back of it. He was dead serious and truly worried, for once, Kajere decided.

Alan shook his head, then shrugged and said, "I see no one else but you." Then he tried to change the subject, hoping to relax and clear the confusing atmosphere. His tempo of concern was on the upbeat as he worried about his own safety amidst the weird insinuations. Thinking and action were in sync as he immediately took a few short steps away from Kajere, hoping the latter would not notice his action. He stopped in his own steps and rethought. Perhaps a leisurely distraction would help instead. "Wanna shoot some hoops?" he asked, troubled that Kajere could see things in his imagination.

Kajere was visibly worried, but while he contemplated what to do and how to explain what he saw to Alan, the apparition vanished. Just he and Alan were in the street right then. "This cannot be happening to me," he thought, rubbing his eyes in a bid to come to terms with what he had just experienced. Everyone disappeared along with their noisy voices, leaving the moment deadly quiet. He exchanged glances with Alan, and Kajere looked around again, nonplussed. Bare and quiet, the street stretched the same as it always was. Not a single sign of anyone having been present could be detected. There was just nothing to show that kids had recently populated it.

"Was I perhaps dreaming?" Kajere wondered. He knew that Alan would not believe him. He had not missed out on the doubt that painted Alan's face.

"Maybe you were dreaming, indeed," Alan replied sarcastically. He tried to appear calm, but his general demeanor announced confused worry. It troubled him that Kajere was oblivious to his own peculiarity. He quickly bounced his ball, and Kajere joined him in the distraction.

It was not Dr Tumenta and his son alone having weird happenings.

Edwina Tumenta was also having an exciting day at work that day. Unlike her husband, she had noticed some things out of the ordinary. She had come petite and beautiful from Cameroon to study, just like her husband. However, she returned to Cameroon and taught for a few years before returning to the US for graduate studies. Although she intended to return home with much to offer his students back in the country of her birth, fate changed her plan. She met Dr Tumenta and fell in love with him this time around. After graduate school, she took up a teaching job, which she enjoyed.

Life as a couple with Dr Tumenta began. Then Kajere was born, and the choice of the name her husband made for him surprised her, but she did not complain. When Nintai came along, she decided to be the one to choose a name for her. She was liked and praised by all who knew her. Meticulous, she was quick and deep in thinking before speaking. She spoke from a background of deep insight and rarely lost an argument. Her mellifluous voice, with the clarity of a well-tuned guitar string, added to this. Her gait, too, was gentle yet deliberate and dignified. You instantly felt she had a major place to be and that she was purpose-driven.

Her friend, Mrs. Joan Wright, who was also a teacher and had two kids, lived a few houses away from her. She, too, was meticulous, but her children did not follow her in this. Her kids had fallen into nasty drug habits in high school. However, they were older now, graduates from university and successful careerists. Their mother felt Edwina was the most extraordinary person ever since she helped her.

Although more observant, Edwina, just like her husband, was not superstitious. But that day, when she got to her class some thirty minutes before her students would come in, she got her notes ready, but something caught her eyes: two giant tarantulas only a few feet from her. She shrieked and jumped in frightened shock. However, when she tried to move out, the creatures moved towards her, seeming to preempt her every move. They followed her to the left and the right.

Edwina had not been afraid of tarantulas or any such arachnids. However, one day, as a little girl, she went to the farm with her mother and father. Her father cleared the grass while Edwina and her mom tilled the soil with hoes, making rows and rows of ridges of earth in which to plant corn. She did not see two tarantulas approach her until they were almost on her. Her mom, who was close by, saw them and shrieked. Edwina jumped up and landed on both tarantulas, which stung her and she screamed. Her father rushed to her aid and with her mother, they took her to a traditional doctor who healed her. However, it took days for her swollen feet to return to size.

As she glowered at the tarantulas, thoughts of that unpleasant first encounter ran through her mind.

"Are you okay, Mrs. Tumenta?" a voice interrupted her thoughts. It was the janitor, Mr. Patrick Stewart. He could see something was troubling the usually composed teacher.

She pointed at the tarantulas.

"Those are tarantulas. Mr. Stewart, can you do something about them?" Though she tried to steady her voice, it sounded strained, and Patrick could tell she was agitated.

"Well, yes, Mrs. Tumenta; I sure can if I see them," he replied. "What tarantulas are you talking about?" He saw nothing and started getting alarmed that Edwina was tense and getting more agitated. But he did not wish to frighten her more than she already seemed to be.

"Right there," Edwina said, pointing to the floor.

Again, he looked but saw nothing. "I don't see anything, Mrs. Tumenta. Are you alright? Are you sure you can see tarantulas over there?" he asked, frightened and concerned that Mrs. Tumenta could be having a schizophrenic episode. He had encountered people behaving like her at his other job in an asylum where he was also a janitor. Some of them were dangerous, he thought.

"Don't you see them," she asked, recoiling from her table and quickly walking towards the classroom door." She was guilty, angry and frustrated that she could see something he could not. What would he think of her?

Again, Mr. Stewart shook his head. "I don't see anything, Mrs. Tumenta." He walked to where she stood, but saw nothing. "You see, there's nothing." He had seen caretakers react this way when they spoke to patients at the asylum, and he had learned that you had to proceed calmly. "If there's anything there, maybe it left," he continued, unsuccessfully trying to convince her that there was nothing. He knew he sounded unconvincing.

Edwina peered again. The tarantulas slowly dissolved into thin air right before her own eyes. She wiped her eyes and again looked. They were gone. All she could see was Mr. Stewart staring at her, a worried expression on his face.

"They're gone," Edwina said. "Did you see that?" They just melted before my eyes and disappeared into thin air."

Patrick stayed silent, wondering exactly how to react without appearing impolite to her.

"You do believe me, don't you?" Edwina said, and her words rebounded to mock her; Patrick nodded.

"Yes, I do believe you, and I believe that the tarantulas melted and disappeared into thin air." He knew something was wrong with her but did not know how to help.

"I've got some work to do, Mrs. Tumenta, but if you need me, please holla. Maybe you do need a break," Patrick said, trying to calm her while trying to keep his distance and sanity. Maybe something was wrong with this sister from Africa, he thought. He hoped it was not serious, though.

"Thanks, Patrick. I know you think I see things. I do apologize, but they were there. Maybe I do need a break," Edwina said with a chuckle that did little to make her sound convincing as Mr Patrick Steward walked out. Alone, she tried to take in the events that just happened. Moments later, her students started streaming in.

So, the day that had started pleasantly ended gloomily for Edwina and Kajere, more because they all had their minds on the inexplicable phenomena each had witnessed. Dr Tumenta could also have been in a similar disposition had he been more discerning of the wonders around him. But, for him, the day was beautiful. No one knew whether he chose not to notice the usual or unusual things around him or that he saw them, but he decided not to talk about anything, hoping they might just go away.

Over dinner that evening, each told of their experiences.

"Today, I saw two large tarantulas in my office," Edwina said as they ate. What was scarier was that I was the only one who could see them. No one else could."

"OMG, mom, what did you do? I hate tarantulas," said Nintai, frightened, even though no spiders were around.

"I screamed, but when the janitor came, and I told him about the tarantulas, he could not see anything," Edwina said, her body shivering as she recollected the experience.

"Are you serious?" Nintai asked, looking around her, suddenly scared.

"When he said he could not see anything, I thought I was losing my mind. I became ashamed of myself. How could I see things others could not see?" Edwina told them.

"What did you then do, Mommy?" Kajere asked. He had been reticent as he listened to his mom. His mind was going through his own earlier experience that day.

"The tarantulas disappeared," Edwina said.

"What do you mean by disappeared? Tarantulas can't just disappear," Nintai said, again looking around, wide-eyed. "Did they not get into your bag or something?" she asked, deadly serious.

"Don't worry about that," Dr Tumenta said. "Tarantulas, don't bite." He unsuccessfully tried to brush the matter under the carpet. What he meant was that although they bite to hurt, they deliver 'dry bites,' which means not injecting venom along with the bite.

Edwina thought her husband, in his attempt to be reassuring, had missed the context: "Did you hear what I just said?" Her interjection was quite forceful, drawing attention from all of them. "I said I was the only person who saw them; no one else. By the time the janitor left, he surely thought I was losing my mind," she said, concealing her mounting concern.

"I never heard you talk like that about snakes," said Kajere, laughing drily, trying to hide his own fear of the vision he had seen earlier. However, his laughter quickly faded when he perceived the severe expression on everyone's face.

"As I said," Edwina continued, "the question is why I was the only one who saw them," she asserted and tried to eat, but put her fork down because appetite and worry walk parallel ways.

They looked at her nonplussed, especially Dr Tumenta, for whom the whole thing sounded simply comical. He dared not utter a word, though, because he knew that it would not amuse Edwina if he made light of the matter that way. When he found the right words he thought he could use, he asked rather casually, "Are you sure this all did not happen in your mind?" He had the face of someone with interest, empathy, and understanding of his wife's situation. He definitely could not tamper with her feelings about the episode.

"Most certainly; I am very sure I saw the two giant tarantulas; they came straight at me. Mr. Stewart entered when he heard me scream and found me visibly shaking. When he asked what was wrong, I told him, pointing to the tarantulas in my office. He looked but saw nothing. Then, while I looked at them, the spiders rose into the air before my eyes and disappeared like a burst bubble."

"Tarantulas don't disappear into the air. There is no science to support that. Anyone in their right mind knows this too well," said Dr Tumenta, but he was finally taking in the gravity of the situation.

"Are you insinuating that I am insane, that I see things in my head?" Edwina was enraged by the insinuation, as she noted her husband's refusal to accept the abnormal.

Kajere saw his chance. "I think mom's right," he quickly interjected upon noticing the acerbic disagreement between his parents. "Something strange happened to me today, too. I did not want to say anything because I thought you would all think I was crazy."

While his parents still wrestled with their minds and hearts against each other's views, Nintai was the one who first expressed interest in Kajere's narrative. "What happened?" she asked, adding, "Don't tell me that you too saw tarantulas that disappeared!"

"No, not tarantulas. When I was returning from the campus today, I saw many kids playing on the other side of our home. Some could barely walk, but I did not see any parents, caretakers, or the police with them. Nothing," Kajere said, trying the same way his mother had done to appear calm. "More bizarre, and to my shock, all the kids were talking. How could kids that young speak so fluently, I wondered. I began to think that I was probably going insane."

"Are you serious?" Edwina asked. Terror was in her voice even as she tried to hide it.

"Yes, mom. Honest. I only said this because I heard your story. How can two such strange phenomena happen on the same day?" Kajere asked.

"What is wrong with kids playing on the streets?" Dr Tumenta asked, again, a little absent-mindedly, away from context. He had started getting annoyed at the narratives of apparitions his family claimed to be seeing. He did not have much patience with anything that lacked a concrete physical reference.

"Dad, how many times have you seen toddlers who can barely walk or talk play on their own in the streets? To make matters worse, no adults were there with them?" Nintai challenged his dad. "Maybe the world is coming to an end," she added, still frightened at the thought of the spiders her mother had seen.

"But when Alan came to play hoops with me, he saw nobody; he heard nothing. That was when I began to think I was either dreaming or going mad. When I asked whether he saw any toddlers playing, he shook his head and looked askance at me." As he spoke, Kajere looked at his mom as if to invite support and confirmation. "Now that I have heard mom's story, I think I was neither insane nor dreaming."

"Things like that don't happen. That's impossible," Dr Tumenta said sarcastically. He was adamant, but did not offer any explanation for what his son and wife claimed. Rather, he took a few mouthfuls of his food, but stopped short when he noticed the others were watching him.

"For you, they don't happen. For me, they did happen, and I know what I saw. You are not oblivious to the fact that I do know a little about the sciences, and that is the subject I teach," Edwina said, calm on the surface but pulled in multiple directions by inner dilemmas.

"Dad, did you notice anything weird today?" Nintai asked quietly in a bid to refocus his father's lenses.

"That is not in his build. Even if anything happened, he would not remember; he would not even be aware of it. Your dad is too blind to mysteries. He notices nothing until it physicalizes in his presence," Edwina said sarcastically.

Dr Tumenta shook his head, "No, I saw nothing. My day was like any other day."

"Ever since we got married, you hardly notice anything, John. You live in your world inside your head all the time. I don't think you've ever noticed what happens around you," Edwina said. "When Kajere started teething, you only noticed three months later. That was when he already had a mouthful of teeth. Then, you started asking if he had all of them at once," Edwina laughed dryly. This was the lone time she had forged a kind of smile since the conversation began.

Everyone laughed and shook their heads, and the tension in the room lessened, diluted by the incongruity of Dr Tumenta's perceptive lenses.

"Is that true, dad?" Nintai teased, more to get a better laugh than for information. She was speaking between mouthfuls of food.

"Yes, yes, it's true. That does not mean that a tarantula can appear and disappear or that toddlers can appear playing and eloquently talking to each other in the streets. If that happened…" He stopped short to emphasize the impossibility.

"Something strange did happen," said Nintai. "First, mom saw tarantulas in her classroom which, we all know, don't just appear, dad. Then they disappeared, and other people could not see them. Next, Kajere saw toddlers playing on their own. Toddlers don't walk without adults to watch over them. It happened that only Kajere could see them. One thing I know for sure is that neither mom nor Kajere is lying." She inwardly admired her own logicality and sprayed her look of satisfaction with herself across the table to everyone. She was rarely this serious about anything. It was different this time, and she looked deadly serious, which seemed to unnerve everyone.

Later that evening, while Dr Tumenta and Edwina were getting ready to go out, they were still discussing earlier events.

"John, take us seriously when you hear us talk like this. What Kajere and I saw was real," Edwina said as she pulled her clothes over her head.

"I know, I know. I am sorry. Just that the whole thing is hard to put into a logical grid," Tumenta replied apologetically. He did not want this disparity of opinion to influence the planned evening out with his wife. Belatedly, he was coming to terms with the fact that his dismissive attitude towards the subject had upset his family. He sought ways to make amends. He had not yet told her his own dream. In fact, he had forgotten about it.

"When you hear us talk that way, it is nice to listen, even if you don't believe us. Things like that don't just happen. I also realize that even though I maintain or try to maintain the same rationale as yours. Yet, I know what I saw," Edwina pressed home her advantage.

"I heard you and believe what you said. What do you think I should do about such happenings, and what do you think they all mean?" he asked.

"I have no easy answers, dear. Perhaps you could call home and find out if anything needs your attention there. You might get insights about the happenings," Edwina suggested, knowing that he would do no such thing.

"You know I don't do that. Moreover, who can I call? Everyone's gone. I've been out too long and forgotten by the few remaining relatives," he replied. Then he paused, putting on his tie, deep in thought, melancholic.

Edwina noticed his sudden mood swing. "Eh eh, you know that's a lie. You have a big family who text and WhatsApp you all the time." She smiled as she spoke, trying not to make him feel bad. She actually knew that what he said was true. Like him, she knew she was alienated from her people. Sometimes, this hurt, especially when she dealt with situations that could have been handled differently. "Have you considered how some of the problems we encounter here can be resolved from back home?" There was no way to separate this line of thought from some form of superstition, but she tried not to sound too concerned. Yet, she had to make him realize how seriously she took whatever occurred to her earlier.

"Why don't you call your mom and tell her what we told you? Maybe she can help. What Kajere and I saw should not be taken lightly. Maybe it's a message." Edwina was pushing up her luck now that he seemed open to a solution.

Dr Tumenta paused, looked at his wife, and decided not to take the fight. He yielded. "I will do as you suggest when we return." His voice sounded resolute, but Edwina knew he was being pushed to it.

As they rounded off their preparations, she noticed a slight frown on his face.

"We can't abandon our ways and enter another culture we don't understand. Sometimes, let's look for solutions in places we understand," Edwina said, smiling sweetly.

In the dream which Dr Tumenta had the previous night and which he promptly forgot, he could fly without wings whenever he jumped. He would jump and hop from one place to another. One such hop was a big one, and he passed, suspended in the air until he landed in an extraordinary place. It was a place which I had no recollection of having visited. As he jumped and hopped around, trying to figure out where he was, he heard a powerful voice that stopped him in his tracks. He had not heard that voice in a long while. It was his late dad's. It sounded angry:

"Ngong, Ngong, what brings you here, and where are you going?" The voice was full of passionate anger. Few people ever called him by his middle name, and apart from his dad, Dr Tumenta couldn't remember anyone who consistently called him by that name.

"Dad, is that you?" he asked, terrified, fearing to speak, his voice trembling with anxiety.

"Yes," the powerful voice replied.

Dr Tumenta felt the earth tremble with the vibrations of the voice. He looked around him, saw nothing, recognized no one. Then, his dad's figure slowly morphed into view. Dr Tumenta rushed towards him, but the closer he got, the more his dad receded. "Dad, why are you running away from me?" he asked, almost out of breath with exertion, sweat already pouring down his face.

"Because you don't deserve to be near me. You've greatly disappointed me, Ngong. I trusted you, but you've become a big disappointment," his dad's raspy voice replied.

"But what did I do, dad? I went to school, worked hard and got degrees as you wanted. I got a job, I got a wife, and I have had children, as you wanted. My wife is educated; my children are doing well in school," Dr Tumenta listed. "It looks like high scores, dad.

Aren't those the things that you wanted? What wrong did I then do that you should be mad at me?"

He kept trying to inch closer to his dad throughout his answer as he receded. When it seemed he would catch up, his dad suddenly receded with unnatural speed, forcing Dr Tumenta to redouble his efforts. No matter how hard he tried, his dad kept shifting away from him while they conversed.

"I know you worked hard, Ngong. I've been watching you ever since you went abroad. You have a family, which I know you love, and that's good. But you must remember that I was not the only one who sent you abroad. The whole village did. You were to return home and help everyone you could."

"How can you say that everyone sent me, dad? You sent me abroad. You paid my fees throughout. You sent me abroad. How can you say the village sent me?" Ngong asked his father.

"And that's the problem I have with you," his father said sternly. "Your eyes have never opened even though you are a grown-up man. You don't know how to see things the way they are."

"But papa…" Ngong started, but his father interrupted him.

"You had to return home with knowledge acquired abroad and to make your home a better place."

He noticed that Ngong had stopped trying to catch up with him because he was too tired and barely able to move. Papa stopped and watched his son's every move.

"You have lived in the West, and nobody here knows you are from a big and important family, a family which, for many rainy seasons, made decisions on other people's lives. You are just a face in the crowd now. No one respects you the way you deserve. What good have you done with all the education you have, eh Ngong?"

Ngong was lost for words.

"My child, some of the people in the country where you are now do not like or appreciate your presence there. They don't want you there."

Ngong was quiet.

"Look into my eyes and tell me if I'm lying."

"You aren't lying, Papa," Ngong replied at last, quietly.

"If you had returned home, maybe the story would have been different," his father said, his voice and tone softening.

"But papa, what kind of home could I have returned to when so much had changed? There's not much I could do. You know I tried my best," Ngong said, sounding defeated.

"I know," his father replied, "but who do you think could have helped change it? Your best is not good enough. You grew up among a proud people, but in your new home, nobody knows this except your wife. Your children do not know who you are. You grew up where the people were a proud and ever happy people," his father added. "You meant something. Now you are nothing."

Ngong could see that different emotions beset his father.

"Papa, what exactly do you want me to do? I can't return home and leave everything I have worked so hard for behind," Ngong protested, knowing that his protest would lead him nowhere. His father always had a strong personality.

"And why can't you do that? Are you afraid that so much time has passed and no one will recognize you if you return home? Are you afraid of that?" His father continued.

"Yes, papa, I am afraid of that. I would not know what to do if I return. I would be lost," Ngong replied.

"Ngong, your father, your grandfather, your great-grandfather, and those before him were fighters. You know that. Your child's name means strong, but he does not know anything about his people and the kind of powers he has. We know how to fight, and we know how to lead." His dad's voice rose with every statement.

"Remember that because of you, your children have no sense of history. They don't have a past, a present, or a future. You don't have to have children if you cannot give them a sense of value or worth. If you don't do anything about it, they will be lost forever." His dad now suddenly appeared too tired.

"But my children don't know exactly where I am from, and it will be hard for them to adjust to life if we return home," Ngong said, desperately trying to protect his children and himself.

"And whose fault is that? Do not hide behind the children, Ngong. Your life is not yours, and you know that. You came to this world to serve and to lead. You did not come to this world to be an unknown imbecile."

"You know the story of our family, but you've never told anyone, not even your children. How do you expect them to know who they are or what they are worth? Your grandfather fought against the Germans during the great war and was captured by the British. When I grew up, I thought I was clever, so I fought for the British, but the Germans captured me." At this point, his father broke out into paroxysms of laughter, the only time Ngong had seen his father laugh since their first encounter.

"That's how you used to laugh whenever I told you that," he said.

"Yes, I remember how you used to tell me that story," Ngong said.

"Then why did you not tell your children that story? Are you ashamed? That's a story your children can write books about, and it's a story that will make each of them proud," his father scolded.

"I don't like to talk about it," Ngong replied, much to the dismay of his father, whose mood got back to being serious.

"I brought you up to lead and not to fight a war, but you've become comfortable where you live. You have become so comfortable. You've forgotten who you are and where you're from." His father's exhaustion was now relayed in the fact that he could only whisper, and Ngong strained to hear his every word.

"Papa, I can't hear you. What are you saying?"

His father had stopped receding from him, yet when he tried

hard, he could not get close to him while they talked. Some invisible force prevented him from progressing.

"Papa, why don't you want to come and live with me? It's been a long time since I left home. So why don't you want to come and see me? You know that when I left home, you were still alive, but since you went to the land of our ancestors, I have not seen you. Papa, I need you, don't leave me," Ngong said, straining futilely to reach his father.

His father's mood softened a little, and his voice rose a little from the whisper. He said, "My child, I can't be with you any longer. I came with a message for you."

"What do you want to tell me, that you can't stay with me? And Papa, who sent you?" Ngong asked.

"Your ancestors have seen something terrible about to happen to your family here and your people back home. So many centuries have passed, and they want you to return home and send away some people who have invaded and owned our land." His father's voice was now a mixture of strength and softness.

"Who are these people, Papa? What do I have to do to send them away? I am not a soldier like you or my forefathers were," Ngong replied, tears streaming down his cheeks and sweat on his brow.

"Something strange will happen, and you will have to read its meaning, so you have to pay attention to what happens in your daily life. When you see the sign, you will know that our medicine is telling you who your enemy is," his father replied.

"What is this sign? How will I know it? How will I know that it's the sign?" Ngong asked, afraid to hear the answer.

Once again, his father drifted away from him, and Ngong struggled in vain to close the gap between them. Once more, an unseen force stopped him from closing the gap, which got bigger and bigger. His father also realized that the distance between him and his son was getting bigger, so he started talking louder.

"Do you remember the black box I gave you the first time you traveled?" his father asked, his voice coming out in deep gasps as he struggled to breathe, as if in the throes of death.

"Yes, Papa. I've never opened it. You told me that unless I found myself in a situation where all the *mungang* in the world could not help me, I should not open the box," Ngong said, straining his ears to hear every word from his father.

"The time has come for you to open it. Immediately you return home, make sure you open the box." His father was now speaking faster. His breath seemed to be failing him, and he was taking bigger gulps of air. Before he could utter any more words, a powerful force that looked like the wind in whitish dust had formed around him, hurling him away. He struggled to fight against it, but the energy was too powerful and seemed angry.

"Papa, Papa, don't leave me again! I beg you, Papa, don't leave me!" Ngong screamed emotionally and tried to grab his dad, but the wind was so mighty. It swept his father away, knocking Ngong to the ground.

"I told you never to visit him, but you would not listen to me. You want to show me how headstrong you are," Ngong heard a deep, strong voice say. He looked around, but all he could feel was the wind. "I am Chumbo, and your father is a bad man. He's done what he was never supposed to do, and he will be punished for it," Chumbo said.

"What kind of creature are you? Are you the wind?" Ngong asked. "I did not know the wind could speak."

"I am Chumbo, and I am the guardian of all who went before you. However, because your father wants to show me how clever he is, you will suffer, and he will not be able to do anything to help you because you won't even remember what happened. You won't even remember that you saw your father," Chumbo asserted. Then, with supernatural strength, he blew Ngong's father away into the open skies.

"Papa, father, where are you?" Ngong was hysterical, frantically searching for any sign of him.

"Your father has left," Chumbo growled. "Soon, it will be your turn. After that, you won't remember anything and will even forget who you are." His voice was big, much more powerful, and severe than anything Ngong had heard before.

"Who are you?" Ngong asked anew, panic-stricken. "Where's my father? What did you do to him?"

Chumbo again laughed loudly and hit Ngong hard. At the brunt of the punch, Ngong slowly fell, asking in fear, "What kind of person are you? Why did you hit me? What have I done?"

"Just like your father and his father before him. Too scared to stand and fight for yourself. You are all weak people," Chumbo said. "I hit you because I don't want you to grow up and be like your father. You have to learn." He hit Ngong again, and this time, Ngong collapsed half-conscious, no longer able to see Chumbo but hearing the voice.

Swaying in and out of consciousness, Ngong said, "You won't get me." He struggled to move away from the wind, but its force got more robust; he knew Chumbo would soon be on him. He struggled hard, though the strength was leaving him, and he could hardly move.

"I can see you already have acquired some of your dad's head-strongness. I will show you that you are all beneath me," Chumbo said.

"I am not scared of you; you can kill me for all I care, but you don't frighten me," Ngong asserted, struggling to get to his feet. He felt afloat each time he thought he had an advantage over Chumbo.

"Since you think you are smart, take this," Chumbo said, and the wind again hurled Ngong up. He saw himself sail through the air and land somewhere so dry and hot that he immediately felt thirsty.

"Where am I?" he wondered.

"You're on your way to meet your father," Chumbo's voice

announced.

"You lie," Ngong protested and struggled, but he only heard Chumbo's deep guttural laughter getting closer. He screamed, trying to move away, but he could not. Hard as he tried, he did not budge. He struggled. The next thing he knew, he woke up in his bed, cold sweat coming down on one side of his face. Edwina lay fast asleep to his side. He briefly looked around and then slowly went back to sleep. He was surprised she did not hear him, for she was usually awake during his nightmares.

He never told anyone his dream, and he did not remember it. He looked at Edwina as she got dressed. He was dressed and ready to go.

"Why do you always take longer to get dressed?" he asked playfully, adjusting the sleeves of his shirt and suit.

"I have to look good for you," she replied with a wink, adjusting her own dress and looking into the large mirror.

"You always look good," he said and kissed her.

"And you always know how to get your way when you use those words," she replied.

They kissed and stepped out, Kajere playing a video game on TV in the living room while Nintai toyed with her phone. None of them bothered to look up.

"We're going out," Edwina announced, and the two young people nodded without looking up.

"Okay, mom," they both said nonchalantly.

"We are going to the Ndop party at the home of the Kumets." Both children only nodded, not looking up. "Do call us if anything happens," Edwina continued. She knew she would not get any response, and indeed, again, both kids only nodded, not looking up.

"What kind of kids do we have nowadays? They only answer with their heads when we talk to them. Can you imagine when we were growing up, and you answered your parents with your head? I can only imagine what they would have done," Edwina said, but she did not look as angry as she sounded. The joy of her husband's presence made anger impossible.

"We raised them, so they are our trouble," Dr Tumemta said, smiling.

"See you," she announced to the children as she and her husband closed the door behind them. The only sound heard in the room came from the TV as Kajere played his video.

Three

Tikari's Hope Comes to Woe

In the land of Tikari, on a bed in a home, lay Prophetess Ngounso, comatose for hundreds of years. She was gorgeous; the passage of time had done nothing to age her appearance or spirit. Nevertheless, she lay there, breathing but motionless. Beside her sat Yafon, the chief attendant to Princess Zasheri, the ruler. In the background, three other female attendants sat, watching Ngounso closely for signs of life. They had been doing this for centuries. The room was silent, eerie, yet beautifully ornamented. Many unrecognizable paraphernalia adorned it.

In the middle of the room, a small firewood fire smoldered. It was known as *tringeh*, an essential part of Tikari life. There was respect and appreciation for everything natural and necessary there, and the fire was known to have healing and cleansing properties. The fire in each home told the community a lot about the people who lived in it. All respected fire as the source of life for every living creature. Not only fire but water as well. Both fire and water had more uses here than would be imagined. Vegans, Tikari-landers did not cook. Almost everything they ate was raw, as they lived on fruits and vegetables from the land, an assortment of which was in abundance.

One of the attendants got up, picked up a gourd with water and gave Yafon, who used some leaves to wipe Ngounso's face with. Still, she lay motionless. It was silent; no one said anything, and everyone in the room was young, although they had been watching and waiting for hundreds of years. Like Ngounso, they stayed young, the years and centuries doing nothing to make them old. As it seemed, they all possessed eternal youth.

Suddenly, Yafon's eyes grew bigger as she watched Ngounso's body, on whose upper arm, near the shoulder blade, there seemed to be swelling. She wiped her eyes and stared again; the swelling grew bigger and bigger. Finally, she smiled broadly and motioned to the other assistants, who also perceived the bump. The excitement among the ladies was palpable.

Yafon said, "Go get Princess Zasheri now," doing little to conceal her glee. Her face and eyes were radiant with joy and happiness.

"Okay, madam," the attendant replied and quickly left. The swelling grew to about the size of a tennis ball and then started to blacken. When the assistant returned with the princess and another attendant, Princess Zasheri saw the swelling, a zit that was about to burst open.

Everyone in the room bowed as Princess Zasheri approached the sleeping figure. To say she was beautiful would be an understatement. Her beauty radiated throughout the room, her eyes large and clear, giving her face a glowing beauty. Her high cheekbones made her face seem to smile all the time, even though many knew how tough as concrete nails she was, especially in matters concerning her people. She walked with the grace of a gazelle because her long legs carried her beautiful frame effortlessly. Her neck was as graceful as a cattle egret's, and her teeth symmetrical, white as pure melon seeds. Her body was a mixture of chocolate and olive oil. So pristine and lustrous she was, it seemed she had been dipped in it. Her well-plaited hair fell right over her shoulders and down her back. She looked like she was in her early twenties, yet she was three centuries or more old.

Before her father had been taken away by the Ketummites, she had been anointed to lead her people. Her poise, strength, and the fact that she was very calm and calculating, always seeming to make the right decisions, always pleased him. Most of the men wanted to get married to her; her beauty and character to boot, they were gunning for the princely rank. However, before her father went away more than a century before, he had said there would be a sign and that prophetess Ngounso would bring someone who would help her lead her people against the dreaded Ketummites.

Her mother had been taken away by the Ketummites long before she even grew up. So, she never remembered who her mother was. She was the calm and quiet type, but many knew the power of her wrath if things were not going well in the land. She was thus tranquil but fierce, understanding but firm, kind but unrelenting in her quest for peace and justice. Both humble and assertive, she would listen to the thoughts and ideas of everyone in her clan. She knew that each one had important things to say, and she only had to make decisions after consultations. Zasheri was thus a balance of power and cool, vigor and poise, justice and empathy.

Her sister, Princess Suliya, was different, more erratic and singular in her decision-making. She always wanted things her way. She could not understand why Zasheri had to consult to make decisions. For her, power had to be exercised in an absolute manner. That they were royalty and had the right to rule defined her mindset.

When Prophetess Ngounso announced that Princess Zasheri would take over the throne at their father's departure, Princess Suliya was furious. With 'prophetess' Nabangua, who had been Prophetess Ngounso's assistant, she broke away, taking some clans with her to form her own community. Though she never directly fought her sister for the throne, she did many things over the centuries to usurp it, but failed. Thus, she conspired with the Bafungieh clan to challenge her sister in riddles, but her sister put everyone to shame, solving all the mysteries before anyone else could. In watching her sister solve the puzzles, Princess Suliya discovered she had to be more meticulous and more calculating in her destructive plans if she would usurp the throne. Deciding to fight her sister for it, she amassed a plethora of crafty people she knew would individually beat her sister and her cohorts in given competitions.

Princess Zasheri came in and uttered a loud ululation. Everyone else, including Yafon, ululated with her. Complete silence followed, then the zit popped open. From it, Kajere jumped out, the liquid gushing out with him. He carefully cleaned and wiped himself, trying to be calm but apprehensive. He realized that he was only a few inches tall and that everyone else around him was a giant. He looked around, wondering how he had become so little.

"Where am I?" he asked, finally, feeling his lips move, but there was no voice. He could not even hear himself talk. No one answered. They all stared at him nonplussed. He felt they could not hear him. So, he asked again, this time as loudly as his voice could go. Everyone seemed suspended in time, and the surreal nature of the situation quietly dawned on him.

"Where am I?" he asked again. "What country is this?" He was trying to make sense of his new surroundings and of the humans he was now seeing after such a long time. Then, he resolved to conceal his fear and panic and to go where the situation took him. Whatever the case, he knew something special had just happened to him, something perhaps phenomenally disastrous and scientifically untenable. The question was, why him? Again, he tried to communicate.

"Who are you? Can you understand me?" he asked quietly, this time with a sense of both calm and foreboding. Still, he was voiceless; still, no words came from anyone. All simply gave him a blank stare, observing his every movement. It seemed they were waiting for someone to arrive or for something to happen.

He did not realize that he was standing on someone. So small was he compared to everyone and everything around him. But then, the silence began to affect him. He could feel their eyes watching his every movement and felt like a mouse trapped by a cat watching it before pouncing on it for supper.

He lost all memory of who he was and of his previous life. All he remembered was his journey to this new land, nothing about his past life. Everything was fresh and strange, a clean slate. He decided to go with the flow and to play his cards close to his chest.

"I am hungry and thirsty for something to eat and drink," he said quietly but firmly. Even so, he could not hear himself; he had no voice. No one budged. But their looks softened at last, and he knew something was about to happen.

As he walked around, he realized he was trampling on someone. He could see the eyes and face of this person. He shrieked in fright and jumped, but got entangled in the person's hair. He fought to disentangle himself. Still, everyone stared, and no one came to his aid.

Then the body stirred, and there were oohs and aahs from those watching. Kajere tried to use this distraction to make his rapid escape, wherever he imagined he could escape to, but the watchful eyes of the assistants were on him instantly. They barred him from moving. He still could not make out where he was or what was going on, but could follow the proceedings as they presented themselves.

Ngounso, the prophetess from whom Kajere had emerged, stirred, and slowly sat up. Princess Zasheri watched her come back to life; a glint of joy and happiness sparkled in the eyes of the princess. Everyone, including the princess, bowed, almost touching the ground with their foreheads when Ngounso rose from her sleep. She looked around, taking in her surroundings very slowly and carefully as if trying to regain her bearings and consciousness. Then, everyone, led by the princess, ululated, and from the outside, Kajere could hear massive ululations coming, and that was when he knew there were many others outside.

"Ulilililililili," Princess Zasheri ululated. "Ngounso is back.

Welcome back. Welcome back."

"Ulililililili yah," everyone responded. "Today is when we start to count the beginning to the end of our troubles," they added.

"Ulililililili," again the Princess wailed, "Do we all see what Ngounso has brought back with her?"

"Ulililililili," they again replied, "Yes, we see it."

"Ulililililili Ngounso has returned with the man with the gris-gris. Today is the day Tikari knows the end of its problems is in sight," the Princess said, sweat forming on her forehead as she sang.

"Ulililililili, let's get ourselves ready for change," everyone present answered.

"What have I got myself into?" he thought. He struggled to remember who he was but could think of nothing. His mind was blank, enveloped by nothingness, desolation, and despondency. He decided to suppress his hunger and thirst and see where this would take him. At least he could understand these needs. The mystery of his circumstances needed exploring.

Then, the figure spoke. Kajere knew she could communicate. Miraculously, he could understand the language spoken. Kajere's mood brightened up a bit, though he decided to stay quiet until he knew what was unfolding in front of him.

"How long have I been asleep?" Ngounso asked, stretching and yawning, her voice sounding quite tired.

"Ngounso, welcome. You've been asleep for over five centuries," Princess Zasheri replied quietly but assuredly, happy to see the prophetess back from her long nap.

"Chei, I am glad I did not sleep longer than that. It felt so long. Whatever I was sent to do was of great importance. They allowed me to achieve my objective and return in record time," she replied joyously. "I am glad to be back. The journey was hard, and finding our savior was even harder. How's everyone doing? And how is Tikari?" she asked, looking around.

"Everyone is fine," the princess replied. "Only Wubangeh is giving us trouble, but now that you've returned with the man with the gris-gris, I think that will shut him up for good," she added.

"Princess Zasheri, I am delighted to see you again," Ngounso said, gesturing for the princess to come closer. Both ladies hugged each other warmly and tearfully.

"Welcome back with good luck, prophetess," the princess said, enthusiastically hugging the prophetess. "We are happy to see you return safely."

Finally, her eyes softened, and so did Ngounso's eyes, as they began to figure out how to approach the people of Tikari with the news each had.

"So, what's been going on since I went away? Is Suliya back yet?"

The princess shook her head. "No, she's still with her people. Nothing has changed. Everything is almost as you left it. At one time, I tried to get her to return, but war nearly broke out, and I decided not to pursue it," she informed Ngounso.

"I see. You said Wubangeh is a bit of a troublemaker?" Ngounso asked.

"Yes," Princess Zasheri answered, nodding. "He still insists on marrying me, but I have refused. I told him to wait for your return, and if you did not return with the gris-gris man, then I will think about it, just as father said before he was taken away," she said.

"Good to know that everyone's fine," Ngounso said, trying to sit up. "My journey took me to places I never knew existed; not even in my wildest dreams could I imagine them. Chei! I can't tell you everything at once. It will take years for me to narrate them. I will tell you bit by bit," she added.

"I know what you mean, and I still must know how you found our gris-gris man," Princess Zasheri replied. "Take your time."

"What my eyes saw was incredible. My feet took me to places that I can't even describe. I came across people doing things I wouldn't know how to explain. Indeed, to find the gris-gris man, I was told that the person must have the strongest mungang in the universe," Ngounso informed her attentive listeners.

"Where did you finally find the gris-gris man?" Princess Zasheri asked pointedly, her whole attention riveted on the prophetess.

"If I were to answer that question, I would be lying," Ngounso said. "I don't exactly know where and how I found him. He found me," she said, and everyone adjusted themselves upon hearing that.

"What I saw was unbelievable, and I am only too glad to be back home. We should be happy to be what we are because there are so many terrible things your mind cannot understand out there in the universe. We are blessed to be in Tikari, and I don't know how the gris-gris man found me," she reiterated.

"We are happy you returned safely, Ngounso," Princess Zasheri interjected.

"Me too, and I am most happy that I returned with the man who will eventually marry you, as your father wanted. He who wears the gris-gris has the most powerful mungang in the universe. He is here to save us all. He will marry you and rescue us from the Ketummites as your father prophesied," Ngounso said. She then stopped to regain her breath, looking at the princess excitedly, and then continued. "Where's my man with the gris-gris? The man I returned with to take care of our problems. Where's he?" Ngounso asked.

They all started making way for Kajere.

"Bring him here so my eyes may see him, and I know my work is over. From this point, Princess, you know you are taking over everything," Ngounso said.

They all pointed at Kajere, whom, at first, she could not see. When she finally saw him, she gasped, horrified, before quickly regaining her composure. She also noticed the melancholy in Princess Zasheri's eyes. After that, the whole room was silent. Even the crowd outside, who were not witnessing anything directly, could sense the tense atmosphere within.

Prophetess Ngounso got up, walked to Kajere, and stared at him for a long time. Kajere stared back, neither of them saying anything to the other. Princess Zasheri watched them closely, trying to figure out what would happen next. They both stared at each other without batting their eyelids.

"Kajere, welcome to the land. I am Princess Zasheri. On behalf of the people of Tikari, I am thrilled to make your acquaintance," she added.

"I am glad to be here," Kajere replied. He found himself going along with events as they unfolded.

Deep inside her, Ngounso felt a powerful force envelope her whole being as she stared at Kajere. Kajere felt the same. He felt an indescribable energy overtake his whole being. Ngounso laughed, and so did Kajere, though he did not know who she was. Their joint laughter seemed to diffuse the tension and suspense in the room; everyone, including Princess Zasheri, visibly relaxed.

"He will bring peace, strength, honor, happiness, and joy for all of Tikari," Ngounso said, her voice exuding a force hitherto unfelt. "Before I went to sleep, I had been told that I would return with the person who would conquer the Ketummites when they next invade our land. He will eliminate them once and for all." Ngounso continued calmly but forcefully, her whole being glowing more and more radiantly as she spoke.

"Today, I give you all Kajere, the gris-gris man with the power to finally terminate the people of Ketum."

"Thank you all," Kajere replied.

"Kajere, I want to present to you Princess Zasheri. She's our princess and ruler over all the lands of Tikari," Ngounso continued.

Kajere, for the first time, had a moment to look at the princess. Everything around him had been too fast and kaleidoscopic for him to focus and to look at her. Now that he did, he could say that there never was anyone so beautiful he had seen. He was literally breathless, looking at her beauty; for a moment, he forgot everything about his surroundings. He could not help but stare at her as time stood still with that ecstatic gaze. Despite his size, his fixation could not go unnoticed.

"Has something gone wrong with him?" Yafon said. "Why does he not speak?"

Ngounso alone knew what was happening and was over the moon with joy at it.

"Don't you all worry," Ngounso reassured them with an understanding smile. She had been to many places and understood what was going on. She knew Princess Zasheri and the others could not get it, at least not yet.

Kajere slowly got out of his reverie, beginning to realize what lay in store for him. He was beginning to understand why he had to survive the journey to this new land. Then, as everyone seemed to understand, they all, including the princess, bowed in front of him, saying,

"Welcome to Tikari."

Considerate by nature, Princess Zasheri said to Ngounso, "You've been asleep for a very long time, while we waited for your return. Why don't you rest and regain your strength? When you wake up, we'll decide how to welcome Kajere."

She turned to Yafon, too, and said, "Get everyone informed about Ngounso's return and that she has returned with Kajere, the man with the gris-gris. After that, prepare everyone for the traditional welcome ceremony."

"Yes, Your Royal Highness," Yafon replied and was gone in an instant, urging the rest to go along with her. At the entrance, she stopped and looked back at the princess and asked,

"Suppose Wubangeh says anything; what will you want me to reply or do?"

"Leave him to me," Princess Zasheri replied, and Yafon bowed before quickly and excitedly going out. Everyone else eventually left the room to Ngounso, Kajere, and Princess Zasheri. Then Nguonso beckoned to the princess to come nearer and conspiratorially said,

"Princess Zasheri, I want you to go as well. Give me some time to talk to Kajere; lots he needs to know, … why he's here and what might happen."

The princess nodded her assent, "That's true."

When Ngounso looked at Kajere and smiled, he smiled back quietly. Princess Zasheri looked at both curiously, shook her head, and left the room. Then Ngounso clapped her hands, and one of the assistants came in.

"Give him something to eat and drink," she said.

"Yes, Your Highness," the assistant answered, moving to do as she had ordered. She brought him a lot of fruits, the likes of which he had never seen, and a lot of vegetables as well, all organic.

"Delicious, very delicious," Kajere said between attacks on the food. "Won't you have some?" he asked Ngounso.

"Thank you. It's all yours. I'll have mine later," she replied, noting and admiring the generous gesture. Kajere ate and drank ravenously, and in silence, Ngounso watched him eat. When she felt he had eaten enough, she said, "Time for us to talk."

"Yes," Kajere replied, smacking his tongue and turning his attention to her. "I listened to everything you told the Princess, but perhaps I should first of all know what is going on generally and where precisely I am."

"That's right. I am Ngounso; you are in Tikari, and I brought you here."

"I guessed that much already. I am interested in the why," Kajere asked, sucking a giant mango he wasn't letting go of because of its sweetness.

"We have been invaded over the centuries by the Ketum people.

They take our leaders and the best of us away," Ngounso began. "The last time they attacked, the strongest King in our history was ruling us–Princess Zasheri's father. That was a time when we thought we could not be conquered. Yet, the Ketum people came again and did just as they wanted. We all felt so weak, so vulnerable. Worse, they even left their mark among us so that we lack even the energy to know what they want in our land."

"These Ketum people you talk about, who are they really?" Kajere asked, puzzled at the invincibility of the attackers even when a formidable ruler was on the throne.

"They are a powerful people and possess the most powerful mungang imaginable," Ngounso replied. "So powerful, theirs dwarfs our mungang so that they overcome, capture and take away our elite squad of people.

Still lost and impatient to fully understand the situation, Kajere asked, "So, why am I here, really? My role, what is it? And the whisper about me marrying the princess, how does that add up?"

Ngounso couldn't miss Kajere's attempt at being neutral about marrying the princess. "Let me explain," she said with a chuckle.

"In my position, you would understand my impatience," Kajere said to explain himself.

Ngounso nodded and began telling her story: "Many centuries ago, I had a powerful dream in which I was instructed to sleep for centuries. It would be a means of a mystical and sophisticated journey to places unimaginable and find the person chosen to save the people of Tikari."

This intro entranced Kajere; he sat still.

"I was told that the said chosen person would have a gris-gris with the strongest mungang in the universe, one that would be powerful enough to send the Ketummites away the next time they would come to Tikari," Ngounso said. She watched Kajere's demeanor for any changes that could be interpreted as a contrary motion. Instead, an overpowering affirmative sensation met and gladdened her. She knew she had made the right choice. Instead of providing further details, she said, "There are still many things that need to be explained, but you will grow in understanding the more you live among us."

All Kajere said was, "I see," and did so while toying with his gris-gris.

Ngounso noticed this and said, "That gris-gris around your neck has that most powerful mungang that would save this land."

This just made Kajere ponder on all he was hearing and understanding. But he asked, "So only I can wear it?"

Ngounso nodded, "Even if you try to take it off, it would not come off. Try if you like."

Kajere resisted the temptation to test Ngounso, but curiosity soon overcame his resistance, and he pulled at the gris-gris. Hard as he pulled, he was unable to detach it from around his neck. At last, breathing hard, he looked at Ngounso and asked, "And will everyone here do as I want?"

"After you have been officially welcomed into the land," Ngounso informed him. "But, first, we will teach you the ways of the land; because of gris-gris, you will understand everything quickly. The time will come when you will have to use your powers."

Thinking about what she just said, Kajere raised his head, looked at Ngounso, and asked, "When do I get to start?"

Ngounso's face lit up with radiance at this readiness and assurance that he was the man to lead them against the Ketummites. She knew he would solve the riddles and overcome the hardships and obstacles to come his way. Her satisfaction was that she had done her part properly, even if it did not look so colorful on the physical plane. In spite of that, she knew that Kajere had the psychological, moral, and intellectual attributes to be Zasheri's prince. The time was not far from expecting all to fall in place. Both Kajere and the princess needed to be ready for it. Even as she thought, from outside came loud cheers. She told Kajere, "The people have been informed about your arrival, and you will soon be presented to them. We have to get you attired for the event," she said, rising and motioning for him to stand up. Then she added, "Soon, the princess will return and present you in person to the people of Tikari. Time to get you ready in the right regalia."

Kajere, rising to the occasion, nodded as Ngounso slowly got up, and before Kajere knew what was happening, she attacked him, saying, "Time for me to test you," she said. She was on him trying to wrench the gris-gris necklace from around his neck. Hard as she tried, the gris-gris did not come off and failed to move. Her superhuman exertions made no difference. She went one further step, rubbed some seeds on an amulet that hung around her waist, and tried again. Kajere could tell she was reinforcing some powerful munging, but it made no difference, for she could not even move Kajere from where he stood. Sweat gathered on her brows from the exertions, but she got nothing for it.

Then she spoke some incantations and transitioned into a trance, saliva gathering at the sides of her mouth as she spoke. She reinforced this by anointing herself with some ointment from an amulet that hung around her torso. Even this had no effect. At last, she collapsed in total exhaustion. Exasperated, she breathed out, "You are indeed the chosen one; no doubt about that." She was reassuringly glad that she could not remove the necklace from around him.

Kajere was still lost, and from his position in one corner of the room, he repeated the old question, "Who are these Ketum people?" adding, "Where do they come from?"

"We don't know," Ngounso replied, her energies not yet fully recouped.

"You have no idea where they come from, at all, and they just would appear and do as they please?" Kajere persisted.

"Yes, and they usually would leave their markers. Some of us even carry their names, though we don't know who. No, we don't know where they come from," she said slowly, deliberately. "Usually, they stay long enough to change us; then, they disappear and then return, and the cycle continues."

As she spoke, Kajere watched her closely, silently absorbing the gravity of the situation and the enormity of what lay ahead of him.

Nguonso continued, "Apart from their powerful mungang, they are smarter and extremely cunning. That adds to why we feel useless without mungang that is more powerful than theirs. For without such a mungang, there is no way we can overcome them." She was strained with tense emotions as she talked on.

"So much suffering here!" Kajere said.

Ngounso, smiling as if to avoid discouraging him, nodded. "Indeed, nothing is worse than being a stranger in your land. That's what we are here. We're strangers in our own land. It is an abomination which we want to erase. You come with our hope of reversing this sad story. As our great one said, we would know when we find the man with the powerful gris-gris." Ngounso's tone bore finality.

"Your great one, who is he?" Kajere inquired.

"Princess Zasheri's father, the one who was our mighty *Fon* before. When the Ketummites started their incursions, he proved too recalcitrant for them. On their last storming of this place, they took him along with his wife and all those who governed with him. That is when Princess Zasheri started ruling."

Kajere was quiet. Sometime later, after he had changed into the ceremonial regalia and was preparing to meet the people, Ngounso informed him about some problems he could face. "I warned you about the Ketummites, but there are other challenges here in Tikari. There's nothing your gris-gris can't take on, however," Ngounso cautioned and assured him.

"What is the nature of the problems I am to expect?" he asked.

Ngounso began with a pacifier: "Many people here love Zasheri.

The men, you know... They well know that the one with the gris-gris is destined to marry her, but they will put up a fight." She allowed him to figure out the details.

Amorous jealousy, Kajere thought, and let the new information sink in with a smile. "We'll see," he said pensively.

Ngounso added details cautiously. "Some have very powerful mungang and would do anything for her hand, so be careful," she said.

Kajere smiled and touched his gris-gris, which made Ngounso smile, happy with his confidence.

"A bit of history before you go, Kajere," Ngounso chose to add. "Princess Zasheri is the princess of the whole land of Tikari. A while back, Princess Suliya, her sister, got into a big fight with her that ended with Princess Suliya moving out and forming her own community. With her, she took my closest confidant, Nabangua. They ought to have been here too to welcome you, but they did not come because Princess Suliya thinks she ought to be the heiress." Quiet anger informed Ngounso's details, and Kajere could feel it, but he remained silent as he listened.

"Is there some more background to the rift between them?" he asked.

"I will fill you in with details after your presentation," Ngounso replied, even though Kajere wanted her to spill some more information. However, she decided it was not the time yet and quickly switched to a related but different subject. "Princess Suliya has fifteen quarter heads backing her up, while Zasheri has twenty. Each quarter has a chief who rules under orders from each of the princesses. Suliya, however, wants to take over the whole land."

"And what is Zasheri doing about it?" Kajere asked.

"When you look at Princess Zasheri, you would think she knows nothing about this, but she knows everything that's going on in the land of Tikari. To her, leadership is destiny and not something you create out of conflict," Ngounso replied.

Kajere was about to say something when Princess Zasheri, Yafon, and her attendants walked in. The Princess walked up to him and Ngounso, her steps slow and dignified. Kajere would only gradually get used to her dignified bearing in the years and decades ahead.

"It's time, your highness," Yafon said.

"Are you ready?" Ngounso asked Kajere, and he nodded.

"Everyone is in attendance, even Wubangeh," Yafon continued. Ngounso did not comment even though she knew that mentioning Wubangeh was for her information.

"Kajere," the princess said, her voice clear but husky, concealing the butterflies of worry that danced in her stomach, "You ready?" He could feel she was not entirely confident in him and knew he had to make her believe he was the chosen one.

"Yes," Kajere replied, trying to sound as firm and confident as possible.

Princess Zasheri's chest heaved. She took a deep breath, and Kajere noticed how even more beautiful she was. It took all the resistance he could muster for him not to tell her so. He knew the time was not yet right.

"You realize that you are about to fulfill the purpose of your destiny," Princess Zasheri said, and Kajere nodded, looking at Ngounso, who smiled despite herself.

"I am ready," Kajere said in a confidently quiet manner. His tone of voice reassured Princess Zasheri. Then, she stood up and clapped her hands to prepare everyone for the occasion. "Wonderful," she said, turned to Yafon and said, "Yafon, get the traditional stool so he can stand on it during the presentation."

"Yes, your highness," Yafon replied and made to scuttle away, but Kajere's words stopped her in her tracks.

"I don't want to stand on anything, your highness. I want everyone to see me for who I am. I will want everyone to recognize me as Kajere of Tikari, brought here by the most powerful mungang in the universe with the destiny of this land in my hands." Kajere again spoke with quiet dignity. Everyone felt the power of his voice and the message behind it.

The room went silent. Kajere had challenged the princess, something no one had yet done in the presence of others. Princess Zasheri looked at Kajere, smiled, and the tension in the room eased.

"If that's what you want, so it should be," the princess said, much to the relief of everyone present. It was clear that not only was Kajere going to get on well with Princess Zasheri, but that he would also be her ally; also, it was possible that, as her father had predicted, he would finally become the prince. Outside, a festive atmosphere rang with drums, xylophones, and flutes.

"We are ready," Princess Zasheri told Ngounso. That was Ngounso's cue for everyone to get in place with her in the lead. Kajere and the princess would bring up the rear. When Ngounso entered the arena, it erupted in a frenzy. It was the first time they had seen her in centuries. The rest of the procession entered one by one, Princess Zasheri and Kajere going in last, exciting the already hysterical population into wilder celebrations.

Everywhere people danced, several jujus in all corners of the arena which was a large field. The different jujus dances thumped, and in some quarters of the crowd, there was panic-tinged excitement as people saw some jujus that had not come out in époques. Some did not even recognize many of the jujus because this was the first time some of them had ever made their presence known.

It was the first time Kajere had a view of the new land, and it was a sunny afternoon, with a blue sky and cloudless. From the raised dais, Kajere had a panoramic view of the virgin green stretches that merged with distant hills and high mountains. Grasslands spread around him as far as the eye could see, only partially obstructed by the many bopping jujus. This did not cloud the fact that the land was beautiful, its mountains, rugged hills, and cliffs ringing the land with security. It was as if he had always lived there.

"Are you okay?" Princess Zasheri's words interrupted his savoring thoughts of the beauty before him.

"Yes, your highness," he replied and commented, "Tikari is a beautiful land. I did not know it was this beautiful."

"I'm glad you like it," she whispered back. "The beauty is beset with problems that test the very nature of who we are," she said as they walked towards the throne.

"Sometimes infinite beauty needs some form of ugliness to highlight it," Kajere replied philosophically. Zasheri appreciatively understood the implications of the statement. She decided the royal train would walk through the crowd before going to the throne. Informed of this, Ngounso quickly obeyed. The people realized what was happening, and their excitement and joy hit the sky with ululations from the cardinal points of the setup.

"Today is a great day for Tikari," they sang in crescendo, bowing as the train passed by. Some stretched their hands to touch Ngounso in excitement as they also sang, "Welcome," to the princess, adding, "We are happy you have brought us the man to save us and rebuild Tikari. Thank you for bringing him."

The train soon reached the throne, and everyone took their seats. The clan leaders sat in front, behind them, their clan members. To one side sat members of the *ngumba* house. They were those whom the princess consulted to make secret laws that governed the land. They were compelling, their mungang rivaling anyone else's anywhere. They were all attired in different colorful handmade clothes. Members of the ngumba house, along with the clan leaders wore bright caps with red bird feathers stuck in them. Ngumba house members had two feathers, which showed their importance and influence.

Nkukanteh, the only person who survived abduction the last time the Ketummites visited Tikari, was not in the crowd. Zasheri had been very disappointed when she learned he and his clan would not be present. However, he was apologetic, and his message stated that he had some matters to attend to. She felt she needed his support in a moment like this. There were other clan members around, some of whom conflicted with her.

"So Nkukanteh could not make it?" Princess Zasheri whispered her anxiety to Ngounso, who took her place just behind her throne.

"No," Ngounso replied. "He sent his message of support, though."

"Is there a problem?" Kajere asked when he heard the conversation. Ngounso and Princess Zasheri looked at each other.

"Tell him," The princess spoke.

"You remember how I mentioned that because you were the gris-gris man, you would marry the princess? You remember how I said there were people opposed to it?" Ngounso asked, and Kajere nodded.

"Well, all the suitors of the princess are right here. Nkukanteh is the only chief who supports the princess. If those suitors decide to cause a commotion, that would mean potential trouble," she cautioned.

"I see," Kajere said, and Ngounso decided to be more detailed:

"That man over there is trouble," Ngounso said, indicating with her chin in the crowd. "Now, Nkukanteh is the father of Tikari; his word always carries weight. For him to be absent on this occasion is a slap on Zasheri's face. She takes it in her stride, though."

The risks feared did not delay the activities. Princess Zasheri got up from her throne and walked to the front of the dais. The crowd hailed her even louder, and as she approached them, the drummers beat the drums louder than before. Then, as she reached the front, they all quietened and waited for her to address them.

"Fellow Tikaris, welcome. I am glad you all could make it to celebrate this unforgettable day with me."

The crowd ululated, with spikes of sharp screams, and then

quietened.

"As you all know, Ngounso is back." She stopped and motioned for Ngounso to join her, the crowd cheering her on with each step she took, and bellowing loudly. The chiefs, however, only sat quietly in front, taking everything in.

"As you can see, she returned safely," Princess Zasheri added, smiling.

Again, the crowd interrupted, welcoming Ngounso back with more music, dance, shouts, and screams before getting quiet.

"Ngounso, we are glad to see you back," they said. "We missed you, especially me," someone in the crowd said and some in the crowd laughed louder.

Among the chiefs sat Wubangeh, who passionately loved and admired Princess Zasheri. He wanted her for his bride, and for over two hundred years, he had tried and been repelled. This was his chance to try again, he decided. And to be fair to him, he was handsome indeed. Yet he had a quick temper. Of his other claims to her affection, his father had been one of the most trusted lieutenants of one of Princess Zasheri's father. The Ketummites took him away with Princess Zasheri's father.

Fighting among the Tikari was quite critical, although it never came to actual physical confrontation. Mostly, it consisted of agility, dexterity, and the ability to surmount obstacles placed on one's way. You needed craft, wit, ruthless cunning, intelligence, and tricks to make it past the wiles of the enemies. In these, Wubangeh was an outstanding victor, much like his father before him, and he was dreaded for it. Conscious of his excellence, he was determined to apply himself to it to take Princess Zasheri as bride. Anyone interested in her was to him a pest to be eliminated. This was not affected by the fact that Princess Zasheri had spurned him many times.

***

"We all know Ngounso left us because she had work to do," Princess Zasheri said. "There comes a time in every land when it has to fight for itself; a time when a people need a strong leader with powerful mungang to help defend itself. Ngounso left us because she had to find and bring onto us the person with the gris-gris that would help to save our land. Today, that person is here."

The crowd cheered and roared, the sounds of drums rending the air and scaring the birds to fly in disparate directions of imagined security.

She watched Wubangeh, the clan leader, who listened as she spoke, a devilish smile slowly creeping up his face. His plans were already underway to undermine her and seize her throne. From her corner on the dais, Ngounso also watched Wubangeh and knew he was up to something.

"Today I present Kajere," said Princess Zasheri. Again, the crowd loudly screamed and ululated, "Long live Kajere!" Shouts came from multiple directions in the arena, and Wubangeh's face darkened in response.

"For many decades, we've waited for the person with the gris-gris. Today, he is here with us in Tikari. We can now be confident that the next time the Ketummites dare to show themselves here, we will defeat them," Princess Zasheri's face glowed with proud radiance as she explained.

As she said, "Today, the man with the gris-gris is among us," she looked in the direction of Kajere. He stood up to acknowledge her reference and bowed to the crowd.

The crowd cheered. As he walked around the dais, the cheering rose louder, even if those seated far back could not see him. All felt the aura of his august and powerful presence, nonetheless. But not all.

"Which is he?" Wubangeh's voice loudly interrupted her. "Where is the person I hear is coming to free the people of Tikari? I can't see him. Where is he?" His loud voice rumbled across the arena, and silence fell on the scene. Wubangeh stood up and, pretending not to see Kajere, peered here and there, climbed up the dais, and even there still pretended not to see Kajere. "Where is he?" he thundered again. Still acting blind, he turned around and defiantly stared at the other clan leaders and members of the ngumba house. He did not frighten everyone, for some of them defiantly stared back at him. Some averted his look and even crouched, however, trying not to be the object of his contemptuous and searing gaze.

A physically big specimen of a man, his booming voice matched his physique. He not only had an elongated and large torso, but his extremities were also large–his hands, legs, and feet. These reminded people of the "black" trees everywhere. His large body was also matched by his rather rowdy temperament, which both dominated and scared many, but not Princess Zasheri.

"Who asked you to say anything?" she challenged him. "Who asked you to open your stinking mouth here?" she insulted, holding down her temper with as much calm as possible, given her disaffection towards his entire bearing and actions.

Much to Wubangeh's infuriation, the crowd laughed. He had to cover his shame by attempting a civil answer to Princess Zasheri's challenge: "I was asking where this gris-gris person is," he said, trying hard to retain the leftovers of dignity in his shame. He knew that the public was seeking to see who would gain the upper hand, and he also knew that Zasheri's calm disposition put him at a disadvantage.

"Then you wait for your turn. I will let you know when to speak," Princess Zasheri said. "For now, take your seat and listen quietly," she added, her tone stern and cold.

Wubangeh simmered with vengeance as he looked at Kajere, who returned the stare without flinching. He was slow at it, but Wubangeh eventually sat down, defeat all over his person. The crowd clapped in appreciation of his discomfiture, and he stared back at it, but no one really cared, and none was scared.

From her corner, Ngounso smiled with satisfaction at the coup de grace Zasheri just served Wubangeh.

Unperturbed, Zasheri continued, "Today, I present you Kajere the gris-gris man with the most powerful mungang in the universe. He is the one my father spoke of and has chosen to lead us and defeat the Ketummites." She pointed at Kajere, who once more stood up to a rapturous applause and music. Wubangeh bided his time, seething.

"As you can see, he is wearing the gris-gris, and you all know what that means," Princess Zasheri continued.

"Yes, yes!" the crowd roared in unison. They cheered, and Princess Zasheri motioned Kajere to move closer to the masses, which he did.

Wubangeh was no longer able to hold back himself, his voice rang out: "What is this nonsense? Who is this little joker? Am I the only one seeing that this nanus, this *pumilus* is an impostor? Is this the thing that has the power to lead the great people of Tikari?" he asked angrily, appealing to their sense of pride and dignity, but the arena only went quiet.

He continued, "Am I the only one watching this unrealistic drama unfold in front of my eyes? Why is the princess presenting us with a little joker we can hardly see? Are you all so fickle, so gullible? Do you just go believing without questioning this scam of a gris-gris man?"

One of the ngumba men mildly rebuked him by asking, "Wubangeh, how can you say that?"

But he came on him like a thunderbolt in a loud rumble: "Be quiet! Did anyone ask you to talk?"

However, this rubbed Princess Zasheri on the wrong side, for Wubangeh had only bashed in without permission to speak. "You be quiet as well!" she barked. "Did anyone tell you to open your mouth? If you intend to ruin this presentation and dirty the ritual we are about to perform, you will fail. As princess and ruler of all Tikari, I speak, and you must not forget that, Wubangeh. Be quiet, or I will throw you out myself. Who do you think you are?" Her forehead furrowed in a frown of rage.

Wubangeh would not give up, however. Perhaps he had been ill-advised to challenge the princess in public as a way to her heart, which was certainly bad counsel.

"You cannot deceive me like everyone here?" he said. "This Kajere has no mungang that can match mine. No mungang in this world can match mine."

One other person in the ngumba house retorted: "Princess Zasheri deceived no one here. We all know that whoever wears the gris-gris is the ordained emissary."

"Fools all! You are all fools!" Wubangeh shouted hotly with contempt. "Just because the princess said so does not make it right or true," he said.

Much to Wubangeh's embarrassment, the crowd booed, but he sniffed with a dry laugh, "So this Kajere has the gris-gris? Hahaha!"

Princess Zasheri spoke back, "Yes, he has it, and he's wearing it. You can see for yourself if you want. He came out of Ngounso's body after her journey. My father's mungang predicted it. Do you think we are insane when we believe he's the person?" She stared directly at Wubangeh, daring him, and Kajere watched, taking all in.

Gently, Ngounso whispered that Kajere should take no action. He had learned to listen to her and the princess.

Wubangeh continued his mockery, not in any way trying to disguise his contempt: "But he's a nobody. We can't even see him. We can't even hear him talk, so what kind of power does he possess?" This way, he managed to coerce some people in his entourage to see in his direction and to mock Kajere and the princess. Others, however, were apprehensive and uncomfortable with the entire callous irreverence he portrayed. Then, before anyone could consider it, Wubangeh leaped onto the dais where Kajere, Princess Zasheri, Ngounso, and the others stood.

"You have no respect for the law and order in the land, Wubangeh. Do you think you can bully me because you can't have your way? Get back at once!" Princess Zasheri ordered, but Wubangeh would not budge.

Instead, he continued challenging her: "We've never seen anything like this in Tikari. You keep saying he came out of Ngounso. Did anyone see it happen?" Several attendants tried to counter this assumption, but he disregarded them. "How do you know if it is not some bad witches with bad mungangs that have sent him here, and he has come here with evil mungang to destroy Tikari. How do you know that?" In spite of evidence against Wubangeh's rants, some in the crowd began to nurture doubts, and Wubangeh noticed it and pressed on: "Maybe it's even the Ketummites who have sent him here to create confusion and chaos among us. How do you know?"

No one answered him, but a few in the crowd laughed in agreement with him.

"Ngounso brought him here," Princess Zasheri made herself heard above the dissenting voices from one side of the arena.

"That is what you want me to believe!" Wubangeh exclaimed.

"If anyone here should know the power of the gris-gris, I am the one, Wubangeh. You do know that it's the most powerful gris-gris in the universe," Princess Zasheri said hotly.

Then, Wubangeh took the matter from another angle: "That joker does not even look like us. A foreigner like that comes to rescue us from the Ketummites! Go tell the mariners that," Wubangeh mocked, ignoring everything the princess had just said.

"You are talking as if he's absent. You have no respect, Wubangeh. He's standing right here. You don't really think our forefathers sent him here to take us to the land of the Ketummites, do you?" Princess Zasheri asked Wubangeh, a slight rise in her tone betraying her frustration with his obstinacy.

Wubangeh had only begun, however. "Why do you make it sound

like he's one of us? First, he is so little. See what a nanus he is. Then, check his head and shape, all so different from ours. Who in the land of Tikari remotely looks like him? Show me. I think the gris-gris around his neck is fake. How do you know it's the real gris-gris?" He pushed up what he considered a psychological advantage over Princess Zasheri. Those who followed the taut exchanges knew the implications for both of them and the community.

"We don't want trouble in this land. Foreigners always end up bringing us trouble, and we all know that. This joker is a foreigner and will not be different. We need to stop this right now. He is a Ketummite, and they've used their mungang to deceive us as usual. How can you marry one who does not look like us?" Wubangeh's last statement showed the source of his passion, and to further illustrate its force, he grabbed Princess Zasheri and said, "I will marry you sooner or later. You are too headstrong. And after I marry you, I will get that gris-gris away from that..."

He let go of Princess Zasheri and grabbed Kajere, pulling hard at the necklace, but it would not come off. Try as hard as he could, the chain did not budge, but he kept trying, hours going by. Then he began to run out of breath. Still, the necklace would not come off, and Kajere offered no resistance throughout the drama. Everyone perceptively observed and noted this. They waited for Wubangeh to pull off the gris-gris. No music or dance sustained this gripping drama, during which the entire arena stayed quiet.

Hours had passed, and Wubangeh poured some liquid and other potent mungang from the amulets that adorned his waist. These he rubbed all over his body, much to the horror of the crowd who all knew the power of his mungang. As he did, he smiled confidently, believing it would get the job done. Then he attacked Kajere again, but there was nothing to show for his mungang reinforcement. Kajere uttered no word even while the earth rumbled beneath Wubangeh's thumping feet.

It was Princess Zasheri's turn to mock now. "I thought you said it was fake gris-gris. Take it off." She was not concealing the triumph in her voice, while her face was severe and stern, and no smile of victory showed on her countenance.

The assembly remained quiet as Wubangeh, frustrated and angry, flung the little Kajere in all directions. The necklace would not come off. In final and exasperated anger, he picked Kajere up, swung him several times, and flung him high, so high that he disappeared into the cloudless skies, everyone staring.

When, after some reasonable time, Kajere did not return, Wubangeh announced victory. "Who said my mungang was not powerful enough? The joker is gone now. We don't need creatures like him here. We did not wait all these centuries for a nincompoop like him to tell us what to do. We need someone with a strong vision and the most powerful mungang in the world to lead Tikari against the Ketummites and other invaders. You need me." Wubangeh started portraying himself as the redeemer, a tone of confidence in his voice. A section of the crowd shouted acceptance of him, but Princess Zasheri stood, unfazed by his antics.

"Some usurper came here trying to deceive us all that he is the person with the gris-gris, and you all believed him. After this fake ceremony, I want you all to return home, and my men will go into the land seeking out those who believed in him. You are not true Tikari patriots, and you should be severely punished," Wubangeh said. The crowd began to get restive as he continued: "Why did you believe that an outsider who looks nothing like us would be the chosen one? Are you all blind with belief in her?" he mocked, pointing at Zasheri. "A thief has come to betray our own Tikari, and many of you believe her?"

Princess Zasheri's wisdom kept her upbeat, however. "You think our forefathers did not see you before sending Ngounso on that journey?" she asked. "I am warning you, Wubangeh, step aside now, or you will start new trouble in this land," she said acidly.

"Be quiet now. I will deal with you later," Wubangeh said, his confidence rising with the disappearance of Kajere, but Princess Zasheri laughed back at him, "And how do you intend to do that? With the mungang you have?" she asked, without words, reminding him of his failure to overpower Kajere's gris-gris.

Wubangeh was adamant, focusing his attention on the crowd instead: "You all know that the Ketummites have always come and controlled us. Even though we've always fought bravely, we kept losing. We don't need that impostor to help us. We can do it ourselves," he said illogically as he walked around the dais.

"Then why have we not done so since?" someone in the crowd dared ask, indicating his broken mindset.

"Who asked that question?" Wubangeh turned around, appealing to fear on the ready with an argument to the cudgel, or as the Latinists would put it, *argumentum ad baculum*. "Who said that?" he roared, and the crowd went dead silent, but the courageous voice was not.

"Why is it now that you think you can do it? Why did you not inform us about this some other time? Why did you choose this time to let us know we can fight for ourselves without any help?" The voice continued. "It's because you can't; your mungang is not powerful enough."

"Who is saying that?" Wubangeh still threatened, and his consortium of men got up and joined him in the bullying trick.

"Whoever said it is right." Kajere had suddenly appeared beside him, unseen by anyone. Everyone, including the princess and Wubangeh, had not seen him return and were stunned. But what stunned them more was Kajere's voice. It was big and deep and echoed and reverberated throughout the four corners of the whole arena.

"That person was right. Tikari needs someone to lead it against the Ketummites, not an impostor," Kajere continued and walked around the dais, ending in front of Wubangeh and staring at him squarely.

An angry and humiliated Wubangeh faced him defiantly.

"Tchongwa arena in one week," he said with frothy lips and all the force he could muster before walking away. The crowd gasped. No one had challenged anyone at that arena in centuries; in fact, no one had even gone that way in ages. All were surprised when Wubangeh challenged Kajere to a duel on those terms.

"Okay, I will be there," Kajere replied.

The members of Wubangeh's clan followed him out of the assembly. Midway out, he turned and walked back to Kajere. It was as if he felt he had missed out on some detail in the attempt to wrench the gris-gris from his neck. So, he went for it again, but there was no difference. He gave up for the moment and left, his clan strung behind him to cushion his very evident embarrassment. In horror of what happened and what to expect, the rest of the assembly stood waiting.

Although Kajere did not know what the Tchongwa arena meant, the look on Princess Zasheri's face told him it was heavy news. Everyone was waiting for him to respond. A rush of pure energy, strength, and knowledge from deep inside him surged up, and in a deep voice overloaded with power, he called out, "Wubangeh!" The sheer potency of the sound stopped Wubangeh and his clan in mid-course. "We all know what you will get if I lose, but what are you willing to give up if I win?" Kajere asked.

"What do you want?" Wubangeh asked, smiling confidently, his swaggie posture announcing his confidence.

"When I defeat you, do you agree that Princess Zasheri is the rightful ruler of Tikari? And will you give up trying to marry her?" Kajere asked, his voice still powerful and carrying his confidence to jolt Wubangeh's. It was only after moments of hesitation that Wubangeh responded with a question:

"And what do I get when I defeat you?"

"What do you want?" Kajere asked.

"Your gris-gris," Wubangeh said.

"I thought you said his gris-gris is fake?" Princess Zasheri asked, but Ngounso quickly silenced her.

"Okay, if you defeat me, you can have it," Kajere replied without hesitation.

Wubangeh laughed a hoarse laugh, and although it was already evident that he was up against a formidable force, he was blind to his own weakness and said on his way off, "This is one of the easiest duels I will ever take part in." His attendants, blind to the reality he was not looking at, also laughed. The rest of the audience stood watching Kajere.

He addressed them, "Fellow Tikaris." Again, the boom of his voice brought the crowd to its feet, and drums called out joy and enthusiasm from all. "Fellow Tikaris, I am glad to make your acquaintance and humbled to be chosen to help send the Ketummites away. We will do it as a team: you, your Princess, and I."

The crowd hooted its approval.

"I thank you all," he rounded off his crisp speech.

Then Princess Zasheri took the opportunity to reemphasize what Wubangeh had distracted her from clarifying: "We all know that Kajere came from Ngounso's body, despite what you've heard today. My father's words have come true. He has been vindicated by this coming of Kajere. Join me to make him feel welcome and at home."

She was greeted by loud ululations and screeching screams while Kajere took everything in stoically. Ngounso quietly watched the unfolding. She knew she had a lot to inform Kajere about.

Four

Kajere Gains Tikari Ways

Wubangeh's challenge accepted, Kajere set about learning Tikari ways. He went to his new abode, which Kajere noted was mainly stone-built and typical of the people. Apart from responding to challenges or offering them, the men did the construction of homes and gathered food. Although diligent, the people were a relaxed lot. They built at a fantastic speed, engaging supernatural abilities. Strikingly, everyone was about the same age: no older people, no kids, no younger people, and no middle-aged. Everyone was like Kajere and remained that way, time seeming to stand still.

Ngounso visited Kajere that morning and as they walked, he took everything in, focused on understanding rather than being excited.

"How long have the Tikari been settled in this place?" he asked as they walked along.

"Since time began," Ngounso replied. "We used to be somewhere else before our ancestors came here following a giant rat with extremely potent mungang that told them to settle here."

"So, you were led here by a giant rat?" Kajere asked.

"Yes," she replied.

As they walked along, she greeted many people on their way to the farms. Most recognized her and Kajere and paid their respects, wishing him the best in his fight with Wubangeh.

Meanwhile, Princess Zasheri, grappling with the challenge, needed the counsel of her chief attendant, Yafon, as she applied camwood to the feet of her princess.

"I think Kajere will make a good husband for you," Yafon said, beginning an interesting gossip line. "He's got all the qualities for a princess like you."

"Why do you say that?" Princess Zasheri unsuccessfully tried to conceal the anticipated happiness in her bosom.

"Just gut feeling," Yafon said, a wink and a smile on her face. "Your father prophesied well."

"But there's nothing about him that I have not seen in Tikari," Zasheri said to tease out more from Yafon.

"Chei! Princess, how can you say that?" Yafon answered playfully. "Don't you see how he behaved yesterday? He made Wubangeh look like a child," she added with a wry smile.

"Do you believe he has it?" Princess Zasheri asked.

Yafon nodded enthusiastically. "Yes. There's no way he could have done what he did if his gris-gris were not genuine. You saw what he did to Wubangeh. He will unite Tikari. He even has the power to bring your sister back. That is different from Wubangeh, who is all self-centered and divisive. He hasn't got what it takes to be a leader," Yafon elaborated, her mirthful demeanor increasing Zasheri's happiness.

"Yes, and that's where my worry lies," Zasheri said. "Anything can happen now that Tikari is at the crossroads, given Wubangeh's antics. I don't think Kajere is taking in the full impact of his presence and the reason he's here."

"Princess, how can you say that? You think he knows nothing?" Yafon asked, surprised by Zasheri's insinuation.

"I think we need to explain a lot more to him," Zasheri replied, noticing how disappointed her attendant was at her lack of confidence in Kajere.

"Princess, do you doubt the power of the mungang of his gris-gris and what your father prophesied?" Yafon asked, disappointed. "You know that whoever wears that gris-gris has the mungang will defeat the Ketummites, and whoever has it will marry you. Wasn't that the last thing your father said before being taken away?" Yafon was so animated that she dared to question her princess.

"I know. I know," Princess Zasheri said, melancholy in her voice.

Yafon, sensing the sadness of the princess, inquired, "What's wrong, my Princess? Are you concealing something from us?" She was genuinely concerned, all flickers of playfulness gone from her voice.

"Just that I am perturbed about Tikari," Princess Zasheri replied. In fact, she was experiencing emotions which she had never felt before, and was too embarrassed to admit that to Yafon, who edged closer to her. "Do you love him or are you worried about his coming duel with Wubangeh?" Yafon hit close to the mark.

"No, no," Zasheri replied rather quickly, too quickly, for she realized that Yafon could see through her words as she noticed her cunning smile. Considerably, Yafon kept quiet for a moment and continued applying the camwood on her feet. She knew that whenever Zasheri was ready, she would open up.

Smiling and pretending to be taking care of a few things, Princess Zasheri paused and did not answer immediately. When she did, she tried to change the subject: "Father had said he who wears the gris-gris will come among us, now, I know we have trouble coming. Lots of it. Beginning with this fight," she said pensively. "Even if he defeats Wubangeh, we still have Suliya to deal with. We can't defeat the Ketummites if she doesn't return. You know that." A deep frown creased her brow.

"Princess, how can you even doubt Kajere?" Yafon asked.

"I know Kajere will be successful, but I feel uneasy about the peripherals. You see, we have been too idle in this land for so long. With idleness came complacency and increased superstition," Zasheri said. She was astonished by how much Yafon believed in the power of the gris-gris and in that Kajere was indeed the chosen one. She decided to follow with Yafon's enthusiasm and faith. "Let's get ready to celebrate *kalangu* welcoming Kajere," Princess Zasheri said, trying to breathe some fun into her own demeanor. "Tell my *chindas* to let the word go round."

"Yes, your highness," Yafon replied, noticing the change in Zasheri's mood and smiling to herself. She knew the conversation was over. She stepped out, leaving behind a pensive princess.

At this time, Ngounso and Kajere had walked far out, and he was asking, "Where are the boundaries of the land?" The serene scenery in front of him was breathtaking.

"Tikari extends to where the sun touches the earth. It will take you years to reach the ends of our land," Ngounso informed.

They walked through a bulrush and ascended a hill, Kajere following her. The combination of the grassfields and the various animals and birds seen had a calming effect. The rugged beauty impressed Kajere. Deep within, he desired to belong here.

"This is paradise! It makes sense that the Ketummites should be interested in it to the extent of invading the land. They surely intend to one day come and take over here."

"I've also thought that way myself," Ngounso supported his projection.

"That's why you need me," Kajere said.

They reached the top of the hill. Kajere longingly looked at the beautiful green plains below, Ngounso watching his reaction. She smiled, knowing she had indeed brought the redeemer. The journey was yet long for that redemption, and she wondered if she could prepare him enough for it.

"You see that?" Ngounso said, pointing to some rocks.

“You mean that huge rock?” he asked.

“Yes. That’s the Ngoketunjia rock,” Ngounso said. “It’s always been there, and that’s where all our most powerful mungang reside. We perform our secret rituals underneath that rock.”

“So that’s where you pray?” Kajere asked.

“Whenever we have major decisions to make, everyone in the ngumba house goes there for the ritual,” Ngounso informed him.

“Could you not stop the Ketummites with these rituals?” he asked.

“Their mungang is not earthly,” she said.

“I see,” Kajere said and lingered for some minutes looking at the rocks before they moved on.

“You see that lake?” Ngounso was pointing at a lake.

“Yes. I wanted to ask you about it,” Kajere said.

“That lake is in the center of Tikari and although it looks close, it can take months to get there. It’s called Nkorta. Sometimes Zasheri goes there with those in the ngumba house to make decisions that affect the land, especially when we fear an attack.”

“Are there other lakes?” Kajere asked.

“There’s a smaller one that way,” Ngounso replied, pointing east, “but it’s in Suliya’s land,” she added. They continued their walk around the land, and then, suddenly, Ngounso said, “Hold on a moment.” They both stopped and listened. Can you hear something?”

Not hearing anything at first, Kajere continued to look around. Though it was daytime, he could see a couple of full moons and some stars. He turned and looked at Ngounso, who said, “That’s kalangu preparing to welcome you. Look at the moons and stars? We’ve not seen that in a long time. Can you see it?” she asked.

Kajere nodded, but wanting to be sure, Ngounso asked, “How many moons do you see and how many stars?”

“Two moons and thirteen stars,” Kajere replied.

At this, Ngounso leapt into the air with unbridled joy.

"What does that mean?" Kajere asked.

"You're the chosen one," Ngounso replied. "Only you would be able to see the moons and stars during the day."

Kajere nodded, still trying to get used to the enormous power and authority attributed to him in spite of his size. Spontaneously, his hand went to his gris-gris.

"We have been too passive recently, and I fear trouble is brewing," Ngounso began. "Things that mean nothing have suddenly begun to take on different perspectives, and people are growing restless over things which don't matter."

"What are you getting at?" Kajere asked, after briefly hesitating.

"What Wubangeh did the other day was no mistake. He has some powerful Fons who support him and believe they know the right direction to go in this land. They believe they have powerful mungang, but the fact that you saw the moon tells me you are more powerful than them."

"He wants to overthrow Princess Zasheri, you mean?" Kajere asked.

Ngounso nodded. "He considers himself the rightful ruler. But it is easy to see through his selfishness," she said. "That's why he wants to fight you, and I think he has something up his sleeve. I cannot exactly tell the nature of his game."

"We shall see," Kajere said. "Essentially, he thinks himself clever and that his mungang is more powerful than mine. Do I have any reason to believe him?" Kajere asked her.

"No!" Ngounso said emphatically.

"Why then are you worried?" Kajere asked to indicate the non sequitur of her fear.

"Because I don't want us to appear weak in his eyes," she replied.

"Then, you should not worry at all," Kajere said. "You brought me here, and that means whatever you and the princess have in mind is what is good for Tikari."

"I want you to be aware of the secrets of the land," she replied. They rounded a corner, and Kajere found himself in what to him was new land.

"Where are we now?" he asked, noticing nothing familiar about the place.

"I want to show you those," Ngounso said, pointing at some vast structures. At first, Kajere did not notice them because they were so big and imposing.

"Those are the carvings of Munka," Ngounso said. "Can you try to touch them?" she asked.

"Yes, of course," he replied. "Why don't you lead the way?"

Ngounso hesitated, and although Kajere noticed it, he said nothing. Moments later, the reason for hesitation became apparent. The moment she tried to touch it, she screamed in agony.

"I can't," she shrieked.

"Why?" he asked, scared at first.

"Because I just can't." Again, she tried and again screamed in pain. The effort was too much for Ngounso and Kajere realized that she was sapped of all her energy. Her mungang became powerless. Kajere quietly walked to the carvings and touched them, however. The moment he did, the ground around them rumbled powerfully and the statues began to move. Kajere looked around; Ngounso was nowhere to be seen.

"So, you finally made it," a statue said. "I told you it was a matter of time," it continued and Kajere found himself in a mysterious place. It looked nothing like Tikari.

"You see, he's not scared of the rumbling," the other statue said. "I told you it was him."

"I was not expecting someone like him," the first one said.

"Why? Is it because he's a little man?" the second statue asked.

The first did not reply. Instead, it looked at Kajere and said, "I am Bondong, and this is Awundong."

"I am Ka...."

"We know who you are, and we know why you are here," Bondong said. "We've been waiting for you."

Though it was daylight, Kajere noticed no sun, moon, or anything lighting up the heavens.

"You took longer than we thought," Awundong said.

"Come closer," Bondong said.

"I think we can see him clearly from where we are," Awundong said. "Why do you insist that he come closer?"

"Who are you both, and how do you know who I am?" Kajere asked. "Why am I here, and where's Ngounso?"

"You're here because we have to cleanse you before you start your duties here," Bondong said. Before Kajere realized what was happening, he found himself between both carvings, and they started squeezing the life out of him. He tried to shake them off, but he could not. They were big, strong, and possessed superhuman powers.

"Tikari is about to encounter problems. If you cannot get out of here, you cannot solve them," Awundong informed him. The gris-gris began to blink, turned bright red, and Kajere's breathing became harder to control. He felt his hands beginning to push apart the carvings; with superhuman effort, he struggled, freed himself, and found himself at the feet of Ngounso.

"What are you doing on the ground?" Ngounso asked, perplexed. Kajere quickly stood up and stared at her, too shocked at first to say anything. In front of them stood the carvings. Kajere did not answer her. He stood staring at the carvings.

"I was saying they contain powerful mungang, but we don't know how to get to them," she continued. "I wanted to let you know about them," she added as they continued. "Over there is Tchongwa, where you will meet Wubangeh," she said, using her head to point at the grassy arena. "It used to serve for major celebrations, but recently, after Wubangeh began to force himself to the forefront of affairs in the land. It has now become more of a place of disputes than for joyful celebrations," Ngounso informed him.

"Why do you think the Ketummites are your biggest enemy when, from what I gather, you have lots of cracks in your very own land?" Kajere asked.

"You're right, and we need to take care of these cracks. We can't even begin to think of taking care of the Ketummites without taking care of the cracks," Ngounso said.

***

While Ngounso introduced Kajere to the land of the Tikari, far in another section of the community, Wubangeh was in council with Kuriyango, Kamesu, and Asabuna, his advisers and mentors. He looked angry and aggressive.

"You know he has the gris-gris," Kuriyango said defensively. "You cannot defeat him; Kajere is not fake. He's the real deal. So why couldn't you take the gris-gris off him?" Her eyes were blinking fast as she spoke.

The others agreed with her. Wubangeh did not say anything but kept staring at the earthen floor. Finally, he looked at Kamesu, who quickly began to talk.

"You know how much we believe in you, Wubangeh, and you know we've sworn our allegiance to you. We will stand by you until the end of time. However, we are worried that Kajere has mungang that is unmatched. If you try to take him on at Tchongwa, you will fail. We have to think of something else." Kamesu was resigned to the fact that Wubangeh would lose, and the others nodded, but said nothing. There was tension and fear in the air.

"Bad! Bad! Bad! There must be something we can do. I have defeated anyone who dared come up against me for many centuries, and you believe this little man can defeat me? No way. I must beat him. We cannot allow foreigners who do not look like us to come and take over here. That's plain wrong. There must be something we can do to get him out." Menace and icy coldness wrapped his last words and set them all thinking for a while.

"Think!" he growled. "Think! Think!"

Urged to think, someone had to come up with something. "I think there's something we can do, but it's a very long shot," Kuriyango said. "If we can pull it, you can defeat him," she continued, drawing all eyes on her.

"Go on," Wubangeh said, his excitement barely concealed from behind his cool urging. He always respected Kuriyango's opinion, even if he was extra-careful not to let it go into her head.

"The idea is to set him in search of the Kwifon of Mekan," Kuriyango said slowly. She was testing her own words against reason and possibility.

The suggestion drew a group gasp that quickly gave way to total silence. No one ever thought of going that far. They all looked at each other, each tongue-tied. Even the ordinarily boisterous Wubangeh was jolted by the suggestion and shook his head.

"That's impossible," he said. "Kwifon is the most powerful spirit in the universe. Even the supernatural power and mungang of the Ketum pales to insignificance when compared to Kwifon. Besides, none of us really knows if Kwifon exists," he added, more to himself than the others.

"That's true. We only hear about Kwifon. Even those with the strongest mungang don't know whether Kwifon exists. No one has ever seen or known what Kwifon is. It might be right here among us, but we don't know," Kamesu said, his fright evident.

"But, but...Mmmm the Kwifon of Mekan. That's a big deal. What plans do you have in mind? Looks like an impossible request?" Wubangeh was visibly frightened.

"Do you want to rule Tikari or not?" Kuriyango asked coldly.

Her rhetorical question had only one answer, which everyone was aware of.

"You know how much I want to rule Tikari," Wubangeh stuttered.

"Then we are in for it. We will have to trick Kajere and his gris-gris," she said acidly. "That has to be before the duel," she clarified.

"Let me have the light of what is in your mind?' Wubangeh said.

"Tringeh! Kuriyango said. "We can use tringeh to get him out. I can use my mungang, which is powerful enough if we do not let Ngounso on it. Before she can react, he will be gone. That will leave you with the throne and the princess as well," Kuriyango explained, and the silence of bafflement reigned a while.

Asabuna voiced the question everyone had in mind: "What if the princess goes in search of him? A revolution will ensue. Does Tikari need that now?"

But Wubangeh was already in for it. "It won't be a revolution," he said. "You all know I am the right person to rule this land. I am only taking what is rightfully mine."

I see the point. "If we succeed, Wubangeh won't fight in Tchongwa anymore, and Kajere may never come back to Tikari." Kamesu looked at Wubangeh to gauge his emotions.

"That's it!" Kuriyango exclaimed. "It will mean that he will never return to Tikari." Everyone breathed deeply, considering Kuriyango's plan. Their attention was now riveted on Wubangeh who saw his chance paved with gold.

"I don't want to see him in this land ever. He has come to divide and make us foreigners and enemies to fight each other. Let him go away forever," he said.

Asabuna had to draw attention to the obstacle. "Let us not forget that there is no power stronger than his gris-gris." The reality of the situation needed to be stated without flourishes. But ambition blinds with its own arguments.

"Did you not hear what Kuriyango said?" Wubangeh asked

gruffly. He was an impatient man and disliked slow people.

"I heard her," Asabuna replied cautiously.

"Then what's your problem? Don't you want to be a new part of the chambers that will rule this land?" Wubangeh asked.

"I do," Asabuna answered.

"Then be quiet and listen!"

Even so, Kuriyango needed to elaborate on her plan. "We can achieve this without much fuss if we send Kajere away from Tikari without Zasheri being able to help him. The saving twist is for Kajere to have no assistance from anyone," Kuriyango informed everyone.

"Are you sure about this?" Wubangeh asked.

"The way I see it, you stand to gain whichever way it goes. If Zasheri decides to look for him and help him, she too would forever be lost and never return. If she decides not to go for him, then you can marry her even without her consent, and become the rightful heir of the land," Kuriyango detailed.

Wubangeh was between the horns of a dilemma he understood would weaken him if he tried to explain to the others.

"Furthermore," Kuriyango continued, "even if the princess decides to look for him, she will need very powerful mungang to find him. Only Ngounso has that kind of mungang, but if she uses it to help the princess find Kajere, she will have nothing left with which to challenge you. She will be weak, vulnerable. Tikari would then be yours." Kuriyongo had it all laid out and spoke with excitement.

Wubangeh's face broke into a wide grin. Asabuna and Kamesu could not believe how far Kuriyango really would want to go to usurp Ngounso's position in the land.

"You have thought this over, haven't you?" Wubangeh smiled behind cold eyes.

Kuriyango nodded. "They will spend centuries looking for Kwifon, and Zasheri will never return here if she decides to look for Kajere," she added, confidence affirming her words.

Precautious Asabuna had one more objection: "Suppose he disappears, and everyone says you feared him. What will you say? Is that what you want?"

"Who cares what people say? I have the mungang and power, which I will use without hesitation on anyone who tries to question my motives," Wubangeh said. His voice was intense. The prospect of full powers moved him deeply.

Another voice of caution was Kamesu's: "There's no way we can exile him without everyone knowing that you orchestrated it, and that could sow the seed of chaos and confusion in the land."

By this time, Wubangeh had become his own lawyer. "When he leaves, we will make them follow our lead. Those who refuse will suffer the consequences of the new rules we will set." He already had absolute dictatorship in his reigning program.

"This is how it will go," Kuriyango, the evil genius explained. "We will bring palm wine, and you will pretend to make peace with him, making him think that you are ready for Tchongwa. My mungang will be working in the palm wine to keep Ngounso from being able to act in time."

"You will tap that palm wine," Wubangeh said, his eyes on Kamesu. "Everyone knows the excellence of your palm wine. Too frightened to object, Kamesu nodded. He did not want to antagonize Wubangeh and bear his wrath.

Wubangeh also needed to engage others who might not otherwise support his scheme. "Asabuna, you will engage Kajere in pleasant conversation until Kuriyango does her job."

Also too scared to object, Asabuna simply nodded.

***

"The Kalangu festival is ready for you," Ngounso informed Kajere. "There's going to be a sacred ritual for you during the festival," she added.

Kajere nodded.

"There will be many people there, including all the dignitaries in the land. Many already see you as one of us. There are also many enemies led by Wubangeh. We need to tread carefully. It wouldn't surprise me if he's up to something," she cautioned.

"Why would anyone want to harm me when I am here to help?" Kajere mused loudly.

"Because we have become too intelligent for our good. We believe that Ketummites excluded, we're better than everyone else in the world," Ngounso replied.

They kept walking along the tiny stone-built homes of the community, beautifully built homes with carvings, gorgeous lawns, and other forms of aesthetics that adorned the homes. When they arrived at the reception, where many people awaited them, everyone started clapping in rhythm as they walked towards the front of the reception. Kajere could not miss out on how serene and organized the setup looked. Princess Zasheri with Yafon and her attendants sat on a raised dais, Wubangeh conspicuously absent. Kajere sat beside the princess, and the crowd shouted loudly, drums beating even louder. Then Princess Zasheri proceeded with the ceremony.

"This kalangu today is an exceptional one. Special because we will use it to welcome Kajere." To this, the crowd called out and ululated as she pointed at Kajere. Then she clapped her hands, and some *nyinben* dancers came in, in accoutrements of leaves and different kinds of raffia. Their dance set the occasion in motion and ushered in the fire eaters, whose powerful amulets and mungangs adorned their bodies.

Before they ate, the princess led them all in the ceremony of thanks.

"Today is an important day in Tikari because of the presence of the man with the gris-gris." The crowd was silent, Kajere lost in thought, his eyes riveted on the princess whose regal *kontri ndise* was ravishingly radiant in the gentle evening. As the people would say in their ways, evenings like this one were made for Kalangu.

"We know Kajere has come here to help us, and we thank him for the work he has already done," Princess Zasheri continued, but was interrupted by loud ululations.

"Ulilili," Wubangeh's dancers sang as he made his way to the front. Around him were amulets, which caught the attention of Ngounso, who wondered why he wore amulets to a Kalangu. She had the uncanny feeling that something was not right, that something would go wrong. Exactly what was not right, she could not fathom, and so she watched them like a hawk as they took their seats.

"Continue your merrymaking," she heard Wubangeh's loud voice over the din. "We're here to pay our respects to Kajere on such an important occasion."

When Ngounso saw Kuriyango, it was most certain in her mind that what she only suspected was at hand. She therefore fixed her lookout on them, all considering various possibilities. Meanwhile, the feast and merrymaking commenced. A little later, Zasheri engaged her in a conversation that only confirmed her fears.

"I don't like Wubangeh's relaxed looks," Zasheri said. "He has to be up to something."

"Yes. His being friendly with Kajere on the eve of Tchongwa does not add up," Ngounso said.

"Has he perhaps finally realized that he cannot escape tradition?" Zasheri wondered.

"Tradition and cultures mean nothing to zealots. They use them for their convenience only and discard them when they feel like it," Ngounso said. "I met many like him during my trip."

"Something dangerous is in the air. Perhaps you need to put on the outfit you wore during the centuries when you were seeking Kajere. Put it on and return as soon as possible," Zasheri said, urgency suddenly featuring in her voice.

"Yes, your highness," Ngounso replied and quickly exited the scene. Hawkeyed Kuriyongo did not miss her departure. She knew their plans should be put into action right then.

Straightaway, Wubangeh accosted Zasheri and Kajere, milk in his voice. "Princess, thank you for this ceremony to honor Kajere. I have thought about it, and I believe you are doing the right thing."

"It's part of our culture to do this," Zasheri replied guardedly, her mind racing in many directions to figure out why Wubangeh had suddenly started acting like an ally of the tradition.

"Though we will meet in Tchongwa, I recognize the power of gris-gris in our desire to conquer the Ketummites," he said to Kajere, to Zasheri's surprise at the unusual humility.

"My role is to do as the leadership of Tikari desires," Kajere replied intelligently. But intelligence was nothing to the wily cruelty of the schemers. For right then, Asabuna edged closer to them. They constituted a noose narrowing on Kajere's neck. Ngounso returned from her errand when the enemy plan was already in motion. First, Wubangeh and his clan returned to their places, but kept watch. Then, not long after, Kajere drank *ningreh*. He disappeared directly as he drank, and Princess Zasheri screamed, causing Ngounso to return to her side immediately. Looking at his cup, she immediately knew what had happened and directly confronted Wubangeh.

An elephant in the house, Kajere's disappearance was immediately noticed by all. Commotion set in as everyone tried to figure out what had happened—everyone, except Wubangeh and his cohorts, who sat silently and nonchalantly watching the spectacle unfold. Zasheri's chindas were scouring the festival arena. Kajere was nowhere to be found.

Zasheri became frontal. "Where's Kajere?" she asked Wubangeh, suddenly appearing beside him.

"You brought him here, look for him. Am I his keeper?" he replied with acidity and sarcasm, his eyes in a squint.

"What did you do to him?" Zasheri asked in a hysterically cold tone, anger flaring at the edges in her voice, the type no one could remember seeing in her. Silence fell on the crowd as they watched.

"Me? What do I know?" Wubangeh asked, a wry grin on his face, as if he had an inner celebration. Then he took a long swig of palm wine from his elaborately carved bull horn cup.

"You made him drink ningreh, right?" Zasheri asked.

"Me? Why do you accuse me of something so serious? Don't go around making accusations without proof. I will take you in front of the ngumba society for wrongful accusation," Wubangeh countered, his eyes in mock anger.

The feast came to an instant end. Chaos and confusion ensued as people tried to figure out what was going on.

Ngounso tried to make sense of the action. "You did it because you were afraid of fighting him. You're a coward; you always are." She was as incensed as anyone had ever seen her. Wubangeh took one last long swig from his cup and handed it to Kuriyango, who exchanged hostile glances with Ngounso.

When Wubangeh stood up, his entire entourage stood up with him. He marched to the center of the arena, looked at everyone, and announced, "I want you all to listen to me." His voice was loud and harsh, commanding silence.

"That impostor who came here looked nothing like any of us here. He has been ostracized," he stated. "He has been eliminated from this land. He will never return."

"What?" A voice asked, horror-struck.

"That's not possible! Kajere is the gris-gris man," some in the crowd persisted.

"Do you think we would like to litter Tikari with liars and impostors? Anyone with pure Tikari blood should be incensed and not be a part of the big lie," Wubangeh continued, newfound air of authority effusive as he spoke.

"What are you saying?" Zasheri counted, unflinching.

"The little impostor creature with the gris-gris is gone," he said hoarsely, "Unless he returns with the Kwifon of Mekan, Tikari will never accept his presence."

The moment Wubangeh said this, a hush descended on everyone present. They realized the seriousness of what he was saying. Even Zasheri and Ngounso were spellbound.

"Kwifon is the most powerful spirit in the universe, and only the true gris-gris can find it," Wubangeh basked in glory. "Only if he returns with Kwifon can we know his gris-gris is genuine," he laughed sarcastically.

Princess Zasheri was so stunned she could not think of anything to say. She had not realized just how far Wubangeh was willing to go. How could he want Kajere to return with the Kwifon of Mekan, something they all had heard of and knew was powerful, but of which no one knew what it really was? Her heart and mind competed in a stationary race of rhythm and distracted shifts.

Ngounso looked at Wubangeh incredulously. "Did I hear you mention the Kwifon of Mekan?" She was barely able to control her anger and hatred for Wubangeh.

"You heard me," Wubangeh replied rockily, eying her mischievously.

"You want him to return with Kwifon?" Ngounso asked, stupefied and petrified.

"If his gris-gris is genuine, he will return with Kwifon," Wubangeh said and exploded with laughter.

The situation was dead serious. How was Princess Zasheri to deal with it? The occasion of merrymaking had been disrupted by the greed and selfish ambition of Wubangeh.

"What did you do with him?" Zasheri asked again, still incredulous.

Wubangeh's confidence rose with every minute. "I made him drink ningreh. What can you do about that?" Wubangeh now said defiantly.

"Whatever plan you have will be fruitless," Ngounso said, foaming at the side of her mouth. "You do this to Tikari after what I have been through to find him?"

"He's either an impostor or he finds Kwifon," Wubangeh replied gruffly.

"Coward! You were so afraid of what he would do to you at Tchongwa that you decided to blaspheme. You preferred to drag Tikari through the quagmire with you? You're a disgrace," Zasheri said, her rage uncontrollable.

"Be careful how you address him," Kuriyango said. "He's in charge now."

"Shut up, ugly witch!" Ngounso attacked and walked up to Wunbangeh and, in a cold and heartless voice, said: "He shall return. You cannot destroy the power of the gris-gris. He will soon understand the full extent of his powers. He will return and get you. You better vanish before he returns because he will not be forgiving." Ngounso was stern, deliberate, and threatening.

"It's time for you to leave this place," Wubangeh said, pointing at everyone. "All the land now belongs to me."

"And just who has made you ruler?" Ngounso asked. "I did not see anyone from the ngumba house installing you."

"Who needs ngumba house?" Wubangeh asked. "Who needs it, corrupt as you and Zasheri are? I will create my ngumba house to help me oversee this land," Wubangeh said. "Take her away," he said, indicating Zasheri, who was still lost in the unexpected turn of events. A bunch of Wubangeh's men appeared from all corners of the place and quickly bundled Zasheri away.

Ngounso walked up to Wubangeh and squared herself in front of him. "I did not take that long journey for nothing. You've even helped us because he will return with Kwifon. When he does, if I were you, I would run. The combined power of gris-gris and Kwifon is something you will not want to face."

"Take her away," Wubangeh said.

Sometime later, when it was already night and dark, Ngounso and Princess Zasheri took a long walk. Wubangeh had granted them that opportunity. They reached the hill where Ngounso had been with Kajere some hours before. From there, they could see and feel the whole land.

"Why did you bring me here? Do you want to join the rest in mocking me?" Princess Zasheri asked, inconsolably heartbroken about Kajere's disappearance.

"How can you say that, my princess?" Ngounso was disappointed that Zasheri should nurture such negative feelings even towards her person. "I brought you here because all's not lost."

"I lost my people, and now he wants to marry me, or Tikari will suffer," Zasheri complained. "How did this happen?"

"That's not going to happen?" Ngounso said.

"His mungang is more powerful than ours, and I know he will force the members of the ngumba house to do as he wants," Zasheri said.

"That's where you're mistaken," Ngounso said confidently. "You will help bring Kajere back."

"And how do you think that will happen? He drank ningreh, and his gris-gris could not stop it. In a way, Wubangeh might be right," Zasheri stuttered. She found it difficult to understand what Ngounso meant, primarily as she knew that not only did no one know where he disappeared to, but that getting the Kwifon of Mekan was impossible.

Ngounso did not immediately reply as she tried to swallow her anger at Zasheri's doubt. This delay prompted more confusion on Zasheri's part.

"How can that work? If he's gone, he's gone! He could not even fight it." Zasheri was heartbroken. Her hope in Ngounso's words was faint.

"Princess, listen to me," Ngounso began, but Zasheri was still inconsolable and ranting: "Now I am forced to make a decision which I don't like for the simple reason that I love Tikari and because Suliya and the Ketummites will attack and defeat us."

"Will you just listen to me?" Ngounso screamed at Zasheri, stopping her in her tracks. Her prophetess had never before raised her voice at her. Never! The silence of shock held her awkwardly.

"There's something you can do," Ngounso began, "but you will need help."

Zasheri listened.

"Kajere can break the spell, but he will need you with him. And that's the only way he can find Kwifon. Both of you have to do the search for Kwifon." She looked at Zasheri for any sign of refusal.

Zasheri took in the full impact of what she had just heard. "That will mean I have to leave Tikari for I don't know how long," she protested.

"That too will mean halting Wubangeh from trying to marry you," Ngounso said, and Zasheri quietened.

"You do realize that everything will fall under his authority with me out of the way. Even you as well," Zasheri said.

"Princess, what do you prefer: bring back the man with the gris-gris and Kwifon, or stay here as Wubangeh's vassal and another capitulation from us when the Ketummites come again?"

"You know how much I love Tikari," Zasheri said.

"Then you must leave! Now!" Ngounso commanded.

"What? Now? This very moment?"

"Yes!"

"I am not quite ready...the right mungang to guide me...." Zasheri could not complete her excuse.

"Time for you to go," Ngounso stated. "Before your father left, he gave me these." She showed Zasheri three brown seeds. "These are *neken* seeds."

"What are they?" Zasheri asked. "You kept them all these years?" She was incredulous.

"No time for answers," Ngounso said. "Take them and go."

"But I can't just leave like that," Zasheri said, aware of how feeble her protest was.

"Yes, you can, Princess," Ngounso said. "The power of the neken and your mungang are enough to guide you till you to find Kajere and continue the search."

"But how about you?" Zasheri asked. "You will have no powers, and you won't stand a chance protecting yourself in the new Tikari."

"I know. I will have enough to keep me alive till you return," Ngounso said. "You have to leave now. When you're ready to leave, mutter a prayer, pull your belt with the neken seeds, and jump." Her voice was urgent. She wrapped the neken seeds in a belt and tied it firmly around Zasheri's waist. A moment of silence followed during which Princess Zasheri took in her circumstances.

"You know you can't leave on a journey without my knowledge," a voice said behind her. It was Nkukanteh, the most reviled Fon in the land. She was relieved to see him.

"My Lord Nkukanteh," Zasheri exclaimed, surprised. "I thought you were rather engaged and could not make it to the welcome festival," she added hastily.

"When I heard what happened, I had to come quickly," Nkukanteh replied. He was the lone survivor of the inner ngumba ruling house, the last time the Ketummites came. Seeing him that moment gave Zasheri a feeling she had never experienced.

"Ngounso told me everything, and don't worry, I am on your side," he said. "And of course, you cannot go on such a journey without a ritual from me," he added. She could see that he was trying his best to keep a smiling face.

"Come here, princess," he said, his voice suddenly having an icy edge. He spat on Zasheri's hands and then rubbed the hands together while muttering incantations. When he was done, he threw the rest of the substance into the air. "Your journey will be long and hard, but you will be successful in your quest. The whole of Tikari is behind you," he said.

"Thank you, Nkukanteh," Zasheri said emotionally.

"I know Ngounso has given you neken. Go in peace, and don't worry about us. Focus on the reason for your trip. We will do the best we can," he added.

"I have heard you," she replied. "I am glad you came."

Ngounso and Nkunkanteh wished her a safe trip, turned around, and left without looking back at her. But she watched their receding figures, her heart heavy. If they turned around to bid her goodbye, it would be a sign of weakness and might mean bad luck for the venture she was getting into. She was armed and powerful, but a feeling of emptiness dug at the pit of her stomach. Perhaps it was fear. In addition, her deep feelings for Kajere were not supported by sufficient knowledge of the kind of man he was. She longed to find out, to know him more, and wondered what she would discover.

Five

Tough Picks in Distant Lands

It had happened so unexpectedly. Kajere did not have an idea how he got here. He vaguely attributed his transportation to Wubangeh, and that it had begun with his drinking and feeling dizzy.

He was in another land, hundreds of years back in time. Everything looked different, lush green everywhere. He could not recognize any of the plants or animals. Strange animal noises filled the otherwise quiet countryside, and he picked his way carefully through the virgin forest whose carpet of fernlike grass was like downy.

Around his neck swung the gris-gris necklace with which his left-hand kept toying as if groping for strength. He smiled stoically, picking his way along. Yes, the gris-gris had power. He had sensed it when going through the dark tunnel. He had come to no harm during the projection as the gris-gris had pulled him towards a plant the likes of which he had never heard of or seen. The plant stood alone, starkly contrasting with every other plant around it. Gris-gris impelled him to approach and start digging down to the plant's tuber. He dug faster and furiously, hunger urging him. When he reached the tuber, he realized that it was a fruit. How could a fruit grow so deep under the earth, he pondered. It was a fruit he was looking at. It looked dirty yellow and was the only one in the vicinity. He plucked it gingerly, and as soon as he ate it, a sharp sound emanated from the gris-gris, and it got scalding even though it did not burn him. Before he knew what was happening, he had grown up somewhat. He was still small, a few feet shorter than any other person he thought of, but he was satisfied that he had risen from the thumb-size figure to something more sizeable. After initial shock and surprise at having grown, he got used to being bigger and physically stronger.

He walked for several days, seeing no form of life except vegetation. He lived on wild fruits and berries and kept moving forward, even if it meant moving in a vast circle that felt like progress. He sought a way back to Tikari. Unfortunately, no one told him that the further he walked, the more he got away from Tikari.

After many weeks of wandering, he walked into a strange-looking town. He had no way of knowing that he was hundreds of years back in time. An invisible eye was watching and somehow controlling his movements, he felt. It was watching and holding everyone else's, it seemed. He could sense their frustration and contempt. He stayed in the town for many days, watching the people go about their daily activities. He fed himself with wild fruits and berries from the forest.

With time, he realized they had someone in the guise of a nobleman or King ruling them. He had massive property but always seemed dissatisfied and wanted more. He traded with anyone who had anything in order to always have more and more commodities. The singular thing about him was that he never seemed to give anything to anyone. He was like the ocean, always on the receiving end; everything was for himself. Then he died and was succeeded by someone else who took away all the property and owned it. He, too, kept getting more for himself, giving nothing out, and the cycle was running on ad infinitum as Kajere kept watching.

***

It was in the background of these characteristics of the setup that he was approached by one of the men. The said man walked up to him and spoke as if continuing an old discussion: "The Baobab trees have grown to maturity since you first came here. Yet, you've not said a word to anyone. We have not spoken to you either, but we have kept our watch on you going into the forest to forage for food."

"Yes, I've been eating all kinds of wild fruit," Kajere replied, happy that he finally got to speak to someone. However, he could sense fear in the man.

"Yes, we noticed how you've been eating them," Nakanguh replied, happily, for that was his name. "We have been waiting for you to be eaten by the wild animals, but it seems as if they're afraid of you. If any of us entered the forbidden forest, none of us would return alive. So, how do you do it?" He still looked fearful, unable to hide his discomfort from Kajere.

"I don't know," Kajere said. "I did not even consider that a wild animal in that forest could devour me." After briefly hesitating, he asked, "What's the name of this place?" Instinctively, he kept his voice soft and low to avoid attracting attention. Nakanguh smiled in appreciation and seemed to get more comfortable.

"Ngounso," Nakanguh replied.

"So why is everyone so quiet and so badly behaved here? It took you years to talk to me, and everyone looks at me as if I am a trespasser." As he spoke, Kajere searched for other signs of discomfort in Nakanguh.

"It's because we are all afraid," Nakanguh answered quietly, his voice trembling with emotion.

"Of what?" Kajere inquired, leaning closer to listen since Nakanguh spoke in whispers, showing how genuinely scared he was of something or someone.

"We are scared of visitors and their influence," Nakanguh replied, leaning closer to Kajere. "Do you see that house over there?" He pointed in a northerly direction, and Kajere nodded.

Before Nakanguh could say more, some other strong-looking people came up, roughed them up, and took both of them away. Kajere knew he could overpower them but decided not to resist. He aimed at finding out more about the place and its people. If he fought, panic and confusion would ruffle the place and his plan; he would lose his chance of investigating and understanding the area. Moments later, he found himself with Nakanguh in front of the ruler.

"Nakanguh, I thought you were wiser. I told you not to speak to this visitor, but you believe you're cleverer than I am. Since you want to show me how crafty you are, you will face the riddle of the bull." The ruler's voice was as loud as thunder, the ground trembling with its reverberations.

Everyone gasped. No one had ever successfully solved the riddle of the cow. No one had ever succeeded in unravelling the puzzle in a contest. Nakanguh knew his end was near, but Kajere stepped forward and dared to ask, "Why don't you make me face this riddle?" He felt bold inwardly, but pretended to look afraid, making his voice quiver with worry.

"Are you afraid of me?" he asked when he noticed the leader hesitate. "By the way, what's the riddle of the bull?" He challenged the ruler, showing defiance.

There was silence. No one even knew his name, the leader thought. He could be dangerous and a threat. Nonetheless, the ruler decided to go along with the situation, his logic being that the quicker he could get rid of him, the better. Strangers had always been threats and nuisances, bringers of complications. He never liked strangers.

"You believe you are more clever than a king, and you want to undertake a riddle which you don't even know anything about?" the leader derisively asked, laughing and showing up large red teeth that were painted by kola nut. "Ahem, you will soon know. Don't worry. No human has ever solved the riddle of the bull, so after you fail in the enterprise, we will send you and that idiot, Nakanguh, into the forest of demons. There you will forever roam," he said and continued laughing spasmodically, his breath coming out in short rasps. Clearly, he ate too much, which showed in the contours of his face and body.

"And suppose I come out victorious and solve this riddle of the bull, what do I get? Kajere asked confidently but in a subdued tone.

The ruler and his courtiers laughed at him. One in the entourage said, "I don't think you understand what is happening. This riddle has existed from the beginning of time, even before the moon and the sun." He pointed at the sky as he mentioned the firmament. "No human has ever solved it. You will fail." Then he laughed, also revealing teeth stained by the constant chewing of kola nut.

The others also laughed, but in one corner, Kajere noticed Nakanguh trembling. He felt sorry for him and responded to their derision, "I heard you the first time. My question is, what happens if I am victorious? You haven't answered that yet?" He was adamant with his question.

The leader and his courtiers laughed on, but through miffs in his laughter, the ruler said, "You seem to have a thick skull. Don't you realize that no mungang can solve the riddle? The most powerful medicine men in the world tried; they all failed." So saying, he crushed lobes of more kola nut loudly, roaring with laughter while particles of the kola nut shot out of his mouth in all directions.

"I have a suggestion," Kajere said, disregarding the leader's histrionics. "If I don't win, I know what my fate is, and no one has ever come out alive from the forest of demons, as you say. But if I succeed, I require you and all your entourage to get into the forest of demons, and I will confiscate all your belongings. Do we agree?" His forehead furrowed in a deep frown as he spoke.

"What kind of person are you? Where have you come from? Don't you understand what we've been saying? No mungang in all the whole wide world can solve the riddle of the bull. I accept your challenge, even though I did not have to make any deal with you. However, I intend to enjoy this one. After you've been defeated, I will enjoy the sight of you and Nakanguh walking into the forest of demons. We don't like migrants in this country; in any case, you bring a lot of trouble. But if you solve it, I will leave." He roared with laughter and chewed more kola nut. But some minds had a rethink, and one of them was his adviser. He tried to counsel him:

"Tikebeng, can we think about it for a moment?" He was rather nervous. "What if he has a mungang that we know nothing about. We've never had or seen anyone stay here so many years without us talking to him. He could have a mungang that this world knows nothing about." Kajere's quiet confidence was making him think the impossible. He had also secretly watched the gris-gris around Kajere's neck. He was jittery.

"Be quiet!" Tikebeng barked, and the man immediately shut up, withdrew into his shell, so to speak, and quickly returned to the back of the entourage while Tikebeng roared on: "What kind of mungang does he have that we have never seen or heard about in this land?" He brimmed with confidence. "They have been here with all kinds of mungang and could not solve the riddle. None, nobody, not one person in the world can solve the riddle of the bull."

Though sheepish in demeanor, the councilor had not given up. "Look at that gris-gris around his neck, Tikebeng," he persisted, wriggling his way once more to the front. "None of us in this place has seen this kind of gris-gris before; *chei*!"

The ruler detested opposition and now employed the scare method to dissuade the councilor: "Are you scared? Do you want to go with him? Since when have you become an expert in gris-gris? When did you become the expert to tell the power of a gris-gris by looking at it? Get him ready for the riddle," the ruler barked.

Tikebeng's men quickly took Kajere towards the edge of the town.

There stood a large barn. It had been there since his arrival. Nakanguh was behind, crestfallen, his teeth clattering violently against his wish and against each other. Kajere tried to cheer him up.

"I'll solve this riddle," Kajere whispered confidently to Nakanguh, who was convulsing in spasms. He was trembling violently, fearing what he knew would happen, for tradition and culture could not be dismissed by the confidence of the stranger, Kajere.

"Why should I not be worried?" Nakanguh managed to ask. "How do you think you could solve this riddle?" He was incredulous. Kajere's words could hardly measure up against the stack of historical evidence he was used to.

"Don't be worried, my friend. Stay calm. I will solve this riddle and teach Tikebeng the lesson of his life," Kajere tried to be assuring.

Nakanguh nodded after a pause. "I believe you," he said, his voice skeptical. "Go solve the riddle," he added, patting Kajere on his back.

Although Kajere nodded, confidently avoiding betraying any sign of weakness, his heart pounded so loudly that he thought Nakanguh could hear it. However, the drums played incessantly to heighten the mood, which certainly blurred the heartbeat he feared. Moments later, at the sound of a bell, the entire town gathered in front of the barn. Excitement and anticipation overcrowded the air as an announcer detailed the rules to Kajere.

"You will walk into the bull house over there. Once there, you will find a bull. Then, after you fail the riddle, you both will come out on the other side and be sent to the forest of demons. Those are the instructions."

"Have you ever been inside?" "How do you know there's a bull inside and know the riddle which you assume I will fail?"

The announcer acted as if he had not heard Kajere's question and appeared to be looking past Kajere and Nakanguh, his voice rising on that last part of his directives. He laughed dryly just like the ruler and his courtiers. Kajere, however, noticed that much of the audience remained silent. He nodded. Moments later, he disappeared inside. The latch clicked and shut behind him.

Inside, it was so dark that he could barely make out any form. Underneath his feet, dry grass rustled. The darkness was disorienting, and a pungent cow dung smell filled his nose. He tried to get his bearings by pausing, listening, and slowly proceeding. Before long, his eyes were getting used to the darkness. Then he saw the spectacle: a giant bull and a zebu so huge that it looked like it had not moved in epochs. It was installed right in front of him, on his path and chewing its cud, its look one of prolonged boredom.

Kajere sat cross-legged, arms folded across his chest, right in front of the zebu he scanned while Nakanguh fearfully positioned himself behind it. No one said anything for a while, and it was impossible to tell whether it was day or night, for pitch dark glowed into a permanently bleak twilight.

Unused to the power of silence, waiting, or meditation, Nakanguh whispered, "Are we going to sit like this doing nothing?" Kajere simply put his fingers across his lips to indicate silence. Then he rubbed his gris-gris slowly, and Nakanguh slowly fell into a trance-like sleep. Kajere knew it would be a long wait. He closed his eyes in meditative silence and waited for the bull to make its move. When he woke up, he was in a ravine full of rocks and gris-gris of different types. As he tried to tread through the rocks and gris-gris, stones fell and hurt his feet in response to his efforts. The other gris-gris entangled and threw him back down the ravine. He felt trapped, the other gris-gris becoming even more vicious and trying to rip his own gris-gris from his neck. There were times when he got almost to the top of the ravine and to peer over, but the other gris-gris quickly wrapped themselves around him and viciously jerked him back in.

Typically, twilight played between day and night, each trying to overcome the other with various levels of intensity moment by moment. As it were, this was the same fluctuation of force and slackening that Kajere confronted. He fought with magical energy and strength, yet he could not overcome the other gris-gris who seemed to laugh at him each time he was plunged back into the ravine from its rim. Sometimes, the other gris-gris would be suspended in the air as they tackled him. He could sense that they were really tough. At the same time, he knew that his own gris-gris was special.

One long day went by, and the struggle went on. No doubt, his gris-gris had enough power, but he could not lose sight of the fact that it was losing something of it. But, without any explanation, his gris-gris started pulling the other gris-gris to itself. He felt the weight on his neck. Then it started chopping them up, and the sensation of their recoiling in fear was palpable. Some were disappearing upon being slashed open. The proportion of gris-gris that got cut was the proportion of the augmented power of his own. A potency greater than any he had felt before, thrust through him and pulled him from the ravine and jetted him into the air. He gasped for air, shivering from the cold. And all this was within the context of the trial of wills between the bull and himself, in which days passed into weeks and then into months. Slowly, the bull lost patience and spoke.

"Are you the Neanderthal they sent this time to come and interview me?" It was a calf, low, slow, but steadily strong voice, but it did not interrupt the champing of the cud.

Whatever Neanderthal was meant to convey, Kajere nodded and returned the bull's boring stare. Then he asked, "Why do you think I am a neanderthal? Aren't you more likely that it has occurred to you that you could be the neanderthal? You do realize that you are dealing with something smarter than a king, don't you?" he asked, feigning nonchalance while returning the bull's stare as he awaited the riddle. His attitude and self-assurance seemed to flabbergast the bull.

"Maw-maw-maw," it drawled. "This is the first of its kind; a human has come and heard a bull talk, but does not get scared or get going in fleeing fear! The world is surely near its end!"

Nakanguh was still in the trance of sleep.

"What manner of man are you? What mungang or gris-gris gives you that audacity? Let's see.... What are you wearing around your neck?" It plodded wearily closer, peered at the gris-gris, and instantly went wild white with fright. "Never! Never! I have never seen a gris-gris like this. It's impossible! Cheii!" it exclaimed, agitated and angry, perhaps more scared than agitated. Then it looked even closer at the gris-gris, shook its heavy head left and right. Eventually, the bull gasped: "My my! Yes, indeed, you are the one. You are the one sent to find it. Cheii, I've got to run now before it is too late. Your mungang is the ultimate. It is the space of earthly mungangs."

It was like the devil or an evil spirit speaking of the power of God. "What kind of power do you see? And what have I been sent to find?" Kajere asked.

"You are trouble, man. I'm gone."

Before Kajere knew what was happening, the perplexed bull quickly got to its feet and bolted through the rear door. The bull's message rather baffled Kajere. After stalling for a moment, he came to himself and woke Nakanguh up from his trance.

It was as if he had been in a long sleep. But as his mind relocated itself in the context, and seeing no bull, Nakanguh exclaimed, "My mother!" He had thought they were both done for, but now the danger seemed to have vanished. "What did you do?" he asked in total bewilderment. "What kind of mungang! What gris-gris is this?"

Kajere ignored his bewilderment, and they stepped out of the hut to the unspeakable shock of everyone, particularly Tikebeng. He was paralyzed with trembling confusion, and his knees gave way. He crumbled to the ground.

Kajere pontificated: "Your confidence was your downfall. Now, your punishment is ripe." As he spoke, Kajere approached Tikebeng, who lay quivering on the ground. He kept nodding sheepishly, and his assistants were totally confounded. The one who had warned against taking the risk with someone they did not know now spoke boldly,

"I told you to be careful, but you refused to listen to me. See what you've done." So saying, he turned to Kajere and pleaded for himself and the rest of the entourage: "He forced us to join him."

It was a reversal of roles which amused the crowd. They began to laugh, a sense of liberation intoxicating them. They beat the drums louder than anyone remembered hearing in the land. You could hear their reasons in the compounded messages that erupted from among them: "You all will end up in the forest of demons with none but yourselves to blame. You have used us like your latrines for centuries; now it's your turn to answer!"

Excitement was in the air. But there was also anger, particularly from Tikebeng's assistant, who said, "Tikebeng, do you see what's happening? If we enter the forest of demons, I will kill you with my own hands. Believe me!" His rage was fiery. "You thought you knew everything on earth. Clearly, you don't. You were mistaken and it's too late to take it back!"

Kajere, ignoring the loud exchanges, turned to Nakanguh and said, "Lead me to Tikebeng's house."

Since he was totally enjoying the heated mockery of Tikebeng, Nakanguh was jerked to his own status by Kajere's request. He fumbled somewhat in his reaction to it: "Oh, yes, sir." But he needed no further encouragement. And they walked to Tikebeng's house, the whole town in tow. The tense suspense was thick.

They reached. Camel skin and *phiyen* feathers that Tikebeng had amassed over the centuries were stacked in the house.

"Those are phiyen feathers!" someone in the crowd whispered incredulously at the sight of the feathers of the swift swallow.

"I've never seen them before. I did not even know any of those still existed anywhere on earth," another said.

Yet, another exclaimed, "This Tikebeng is a big thief!"

"Now, you go in and do what you think is right," Kajere told

Nakanguh, behind whom Tikebeng and his courtiers had assembled, melancholy etched on each of their wan faces.

However, a different voice rose from further back: "Who do you think you are?" It was one of Tikebeng's courtiers speaking, his voice dry and hopeless. "You think you can just come here and take all our stuff? If anything, you are the thief, and you need to be judged."

Arrogance is found even in the furnace of defeat. A wiser and placatory voice retorted: "Move over; the man is not even taking anything with him, and that tells you the kind of person he is."

Nakanguh, who still had the terror of the bull puzzle haunting him, ignored them all and said to Kajere, "Sir, we will do anything you order us to do with great pleasure."

Kajere shrugged his shoulders. He was not interested in the garbage that the people sought so avidly. So Nakanguh distributed everything to those present, leaving out only Tikebeng and his councilors.

As far back as memory could recall, no one in the town had been as excited as those who received their share of the treasures from Tikebeng's storehouse. Even Ndom, whom everyone knew had no sense of humor but was nearly always in a cantankerous mood, manifested thrill. He was always thinking of himself as a potent medicine man, even if none of his concoctions ever worked. Today, he laughed as he hugged his gift of camel skin. He even approached Kajere with something of a human disposition, but with dehydrated lips and skin that twitched.

With wry twinkles in his eyes, he said, "You must be a powerful medicine man or you could not have solved the riddle of the bull. I would like to know how you did it." He was persuading Kajere into a quiet corner as he spoke.

But Kajere had no reason to trust him or explain himself to him. "I am not a medicine man," he replied, evading Ndom's prying eyes that could tell it was not the whole truth. For even as he neared

Kajere, Ndom could feel his own mungang going quiet, a sign that it had met something superior.

"We are happy for what you did," he said irrelevantly, but Kajere was uncomfortable as Ndom boasted, "I know everything that happens on earth," an impish but sheepish smile belying his claim. You don't even know yet what you have brought to this world, but you will soon find out. I'll go talk to Nakanguh," he added, an unfriendly smile mapping his face as he edged away.

Turning to Tikebeng, Kajere asked the dreaded question, "Are you ready to fulfill your part of the deal?"

Defiantly, for being unprincipled was the dictator's way of life, Tikebeng said, "No, I'm not!"

Kajere did not wait on him or depend on what he wanted, but pronounced: "From now on, you and your cohort of thieves are banished from Ngoso. Nakanguh, you're the new Tikebeng. I, however, urge you always to remember how you got this position and thereby remain humane and humble."

"He can only end up like me," Tikebeng mocked, behind his mind ringing what he had heard long before: power tends to corrupt and absolute power corrupts absolutely.

"Quiet!" the crowd, which was now dictating, roared.

Kajere counseled: "You are aware of the misfortunes brought on by Tikebeng and his goons. They thought only about themselves. Think of that and don't create fear for your people." Kajere directed his words especially to Nakanguh who kept nodding, clearly still in disbelief.

He, however, managed to grunt somewhat indistinctly and repeatedly, "Thank you. Thank you for everything," and added prophetically, "You will succeed in your search for Kwifon, and you will soon have an ally."

"The Kwifon?" Kajere asked, for he could not remember having heard the phrase before.

"Yes, the Kwifon of Mekan. You will one day find it," replied Nakanguh confidently. He could tell that Kajere had no clue what he meant, though. Beside him, Ndom kept the grin of a smile on his face, coyly seeking to ingratiate himself with the powerful one and saying unnecessarily, "Nobody can come here and solve the riddle of the bull and send Tikebeng away. That person's mungang is not of this world. Your mungang, your gris-gris is too strong. You will surely find the Kwifon of Mekan, and Kwifon will save the world." His adulation of Kajere was evident.

"How did you know about this Kwifon I know nothing about?" Kajere asked frankly, trying to figure out what Nakanguh meant. "I'm trying to return to Tikari."

Ndom, ever seeking notice and the limelight, whispered to Nakanguh, "I told you he knows nothing about his powers. Just tell him what I told you."

"You will soon find out," Nakanguh told Kajere quietly, but with newfound confidence. "And I know that you will find Kwifon." Ndom did not seem to affect his disposition at all.

Meanwhile, around their deeper circle of thinking, everyone else was rushing excitedly to help partition Tikebeng's possessions. Waking to the realization of the new situation coming upon him, and in spite of himself, Tikebeng asked, "How did this happen? What kind of mungang does he have, to have solved the riddle of the bull? I can't lose all that I have amassed all my life."

The collective bully of individual cowards, the cohort of anonymity in the masses ignored his wishful revelries and were ransacking like uncaring pillagers what they saw in the stores. His insults might have reached a few, but there was no evidence that anyone was affected by them: "You're all thieves! I worked hard!" He was desperate.

"I warned you, but you were deafened by your own arrogance," his courtier repeated. "You will see my true colors when we arrive at the forest of demons. That is when you will learn the lesson you ought to have learned long ago and too late."

Tikebeng was impervious to the reality and was still trying to stop his possessions from being divided. No one cared. The time arrived, and the people, led by Nakanguh, escorted Tikebeng and his cohorts to the edge of the town. There, they asked them to leave. The ceremony of exiling was that simple.

Nakanguh searched for Kajere. He wanted to thank him once more for the impossible rescue he had effected, but Kajere had disappeared. Before long, it was dark, and the stars twinkled with excitement not imagined before now.

"Good luck, my friend," he muttered quietly to himself, thinking gratefully of Kajere; "you shall find the Kwifon."

While Nakanguh searched, Kajere was back in the dark green tropical forest. He had no idea how he had been transported away from Ngoso to where everything seemed so strange, with tall trees that made the undergrowth thick and dark. Weird animal and bird sounds came to him from the bulrushes. His lone desire was to return to the land of the Tikari and protect its people from the Ketummites. The Kwifon thing Nakanguh had mentioned did not quite register meaning for him.

At one more strange sound, he stopped and listened hard. He looked around but saw nothing. Instinct pushed him to quickly and stealthily climb up a tree. From its height, he saw a figure approaching. Was it Nakanguh? he wondered at first. But no, it was a woman! And then it dawned; it was none other than Princess Zasheri! He wiped his eyes in disbelief. When she neared the tree where he was, he jumped and stood right in front of her as if to stop her from going past him. Princess Zasheri did not recognize him, however. For one thing, he had grown in size. He needed to identify himself:

"Princess, it's me, Kajere," he said, excited. Slowly waking to the realization, Princess Zasheri said, "May the people of Tikari guide me. Kajere, is this you?" Her mind needed adjustment to his new size. "For ages I've been looking for you," she said. She was cumulatively surprised at finding him and that he had grown slightly.

He unraveled the circumstances of his change in size and how he found himself in the new setup, adding with glee, "I think my gris-gris is quite powerful."

"I am so happy to find you and to find you alive, Kajere," Zasheri said, her excitement now matching his as they hugged for a long time, passion piercing through their hearts and bodies.

"How did you find me? How long have you been looking for me? How glad am I to see you again! I was becoming quite lonely!" Kajere's staccato questions were coming out uncoordinated.

"Many rainy seasons have passed since I started looking for you from the moment you disappeared. A lot has happened, much of which you can have no clue about," she said. She tried as best she could to bring him up to date, although passionate excitement kept heaving her chest excitedly and clouding her discourse simultaneously.

"When you disappeared, Ngounso knew what had happened. Wubangeh had used a powerful mungang to make you drink tringeh and disappear. The condition…, the big problem now is that you cannot return to Tikari without the Kwifon of Mekan."

As the narration evolved into long and more complicated implications, they sat by a tree, from every direction looking like lovers on a honeymoon in nature.

"This Kwifon of Mekan, what is it really? Is it human, spirit, thing, or object? Just what kind of entity is it?" Kajere asked, creasing his brow in a tight knot.

"Did you hear about it already?" Princess Zasheri expressed surprise.

"Yes," Kajere replied. "I have been through many situations and solved a riddle, that of the bull in the land of Ngoso. When I did, I was told I would have to find it."

"You solved the riddle of the bull!" Zasheri was in shock.

"Yes," he nodded, as if it were a natural thing for him to have done. The princess was quiet for a moment, her assurance that Kajere was indeed the savior reinforced.

Then, picking up from where they had diverted, she said, "Kwifon is a mystical, most powerful mungang of the universe, never before seen, but only heard about. As for Mekan, no one even knows where it is." Zasheri was matter-of-fact in her tone. She was stating a fact, whether it was comprehensible or not. It was a metapsychic reality, so to speak.

"And just what has that got to do with me, Princess?" Kajere asked to the bewilderment of Zasheri.

Away from Tikari, and with the reassurance that Kajere was by proven action and legend had indicated that he was no less than the expected one, Zasheri said, "Kajere, please don't call me Princess. Call me Zash, like Yafon does." She mentioned Yafon as a distancing device because a passionate pull to Kajere informed what she said.

"Okay, sure, Princess, oh, Zash," Kajere said awkwardly, and they both laughed.

"We can't return home without the Kwifon of Mekan, and the way it looks, you can never find the Kwifon, and you cannot even find or know the way back to Tikari. Will you keep going around in circles until the moon dies?" A discouragingly severe mood swing was taking hold of Zasheri.

Kajere tried to take everything in, and Zasheri watched.

She explained, "Although I don't know what Kwifon is, my father always talked about it and said that the only way to defeat the Ketum-mites was with the help of Kwifon. So, it is no easy charge. For starters, I don't even know what direction we should go."

"My gris-gris will help," Kajere assured her, brushing his left palm over the gris-gris around his neck.

"According to Wubangeh and his cohorts, there's no way we'll be able to return to Tikari. First, they did not know that the spell of ningreh could be broken with help from other powerful people. That's why Ngounso made me find you. Together, our powers will be enough to find Kwifon," she informed him.

Kajere was somewhat lost, but he hoped to understand eventually. Zasheri explained more: "The long and short of it is that the odyssey we are embarking on is huge, but if we find Kwifon, our troubles will be over," she said, peering into the distance and thinking of how forgetfulness of pain comes with the realization of any objective that brought about the said pain.

The enormity of their enterprise registered in Kajere's understanding, so he asked, "Do you think gris-gris can help?" He followed up by narrating what Nakanguh said and what it now means to him: "Now I see what Nakanguh meant when he said I would find Kwifon, and someone would help me. I did not dream that it would be you. Nakanguh kept mentioning Kwifon. Because I did not know what he was going on about, I thought he was insane."

"And who's this Nakanguh?" Zasheri inquired.

"A man I met at Ngoso who solved the riddle of the bull, and because of it, banished Tikebeng. According to them, the riddle had existed from the beginning of time. It was inconceivable that anyone could solve it, but I did. So, they considered my mungang unsurpassable and strong enough to find the Kwifon of Mekan."

"I see that you have already started," Zasheri smiled

"Did Ngounso say how long it would take us to find Kwifon, or whether we would find it at all?" he inquired.

Zasheri said vaguely, "Maybe three hundred years or more. But with luck, it could be a matter of decades." Zasheri's smile disappeared. The thought of being away from home for so long was unsettling. The enormity of their quest was daunting. Yet, she knew she did not need to show how scared she was to Kajere, which would be discouraging. He needed her encouragement a great deal, she knew.

Kajere whistled at the thought of the duration of their search but made light of it by saying, “My mother, we’ll grow hair on our teeth before we find Kwifon.” He laughed and she returned the laugh, relieved by his sense of humor. “Now, why was it you that came instead of Yafon or anyone else, so you could continue to rule Tikari. Why did Ngounso have to send you instead?” Kajere asked.

Zasheri thought a little before answering. “Somebody else could have come, indeed. But I told Ngounso I wanted to come myself. She tried to protest, but I would not take no for an answer.” She avoided Kajere’s eyes as she spoke. Then she switched focus: “Let’s find the kwifon and show the Ketummites that Tikari are tough people. Kwifon is powerful, the only being that can do that.”

***

So saying, she started walking purposefully into the forest as if on an immediate quest for Kwifon, Kajere in tow. The bowels of the woods swallowed them on their way to the unknown, deep into the heart of the forest for weeks. Strange plants they found constituted food. Then the vegetation around them thinned down and they soon found themselves in grasslands with fewer trees. Frustration was bound to seep in, and it did one day for Kajere after they had had a tough and long day’s walking through rough terrain.

“Sometimes, I feel like we are spinning in circles, though we never pass the same place twice,” he said, and sat at the foot of a tree. He took out some dried nuts, Zasheri cozy beside him.

“No, we aren’t moving in circles. We have a destination,” Zasheri coolly reassured him. “No one said Kwifon would be easy to find.”

“And how do you know?”

“What?” she asked

“The difficulty of finding Kwifon,” he said.

"You have the gris-gris, and that is assurance enough," she said, realizing that her words brought down his morale.

"I don't get it," he said.

"Think of it; there is no way you would have traced your way to Tikari if you were not the one chosen to find Kwifon. You have even forgotten where your home is. That's how Ngounso knew you were the chosen one. Now, fill in the gaps of the other happenings," she told him.

As they forged their way through the thick bulrushes. Kajere glanced intermittently at his gris-gris necklace, and toyed frivolously with it, saying, "I am also beginning to believe what Ngounso said about my gris-gris." He led the way, and Zasheri followed in the temporary path they were creating.

"Why do you say that?"

"Because of everything you say."

"I joined you because I believe in the power of your mungang," Zasheri said, brushing aside leaves that were interrupting her view.

"When I asked if that was the only reason you wanted to come, you didn't reply," he said.

"Why did you ask me a question whose answer you know?" she said, a smile flirting with the corners of her lips.

Kajere did not answer because he was unsure of his emotions and ideas on it. Around them, strange bird songs and animal noises punctuated the otherwise tranquil vegetation. They continued, each buried in their thoughts, but not long after, Zasheri said. "Let's rest," and they stopped. Kajere sat beside her and drank, admiring her, which he had not done since they met. He liked her dashiki and the beads around her neck that glistened with sweat. He also watched her heaving chest as she drank, pretending not to notice his admiring gaze.

It was a nice feeling, so she declined when Kajere asked whether they could continue. "Let's rest a bit more. I feel drained today," she explained, yawning and making herself comfortable at the foot of the tree. Soon, she dozed off, almost as if she had been instantly switched off. Kajere stayed awake, admiringly watching her. He gathered some leaves, forged a pillow with them, and set it beneath her head to make her more comfortable. Several hours later, she opened her eyes and caught him still watching her. She gave him a warm smile and he returned the favor, again, fidgeting with his gris-gris.

"How long have you been watching me?" she asked.

He evaded the question. "I'm happy Ngounso brought me to Tikari and even happier that you decided to come on this adventure with me." There was a tremor in his voice that betrayed his inner happiness.

"Me too," she said. Zasheri did not publicly express her emotions, for she felt that love and emotions were private and interior. She took a roundabout route away from telling her liking for Kajere: "My papa was very careful about whom he chose to wear the gris-gris on, and I am certain he led Ngounso to you." Then her mood changed, becoming more serious. "We've got work to do."

Kajere admired the regal attitude that suddenly took over and could tell she was used to issuing orders and being obeyed.

"Let's go," he said, getting up and adjusting himself, but they were stalled by a sudden thunderous sound. It was as if a formidable crowd was stampeding in a northerly direction. The earth beneath them shook violently, so that they barely struggled to stay on their feet.

"Seems like the earth mungang is angry today," Zasheri managed to describe the experience, but her major term put Kajere off.

"What is earth mungang?" he asked and received a mystique of explanation from Zasheri:

"Sometimes the earth gets angry when its mboma has not been fed."

Perhaps baffled by the details of the esoteric hints, silence reigned. They helped each other climb up a tree, from which vantage point they sought to investigate the source of the noise. Thence, they noted the source's direction and came down. But when they walked towards it, it seemed to recede. They could distinguish the noises of people wailing, others laughing, and others screaming in pain, but many were groaning as if in agony or anger.

"We are in the land of Mukumbi, I think," Zasheri said. "It's a mysterious place we learnt about, but I did not believe it existed."

"Tell me more about it," Kajere expressed his curiosity.

"It's something like a place for the aged," she replied pensively. "My father used to threaten to send us there whenever we did anything bad."

"And how do you know it's the place? What makes you think it is the place your father threatened to send you to? You were never actually sent there, but you think you know the place!" Kajere was not satisfied with her explanation.

Zasheri ignored Kajere's insinuations and explained, "Because of the noise and quaking earth, which we were told is peculiar. What we are experiencing fits that description. We did not even believe it then, but experiencing this now fits the picture."

"Mmm. For me, the value of this is that it proves that we have been progressing, even if it is not clear in what direction. Why do we only hear but don't see it?" Kajere asked rhetorically.

The vegetation around them was actually altering—fewer trees, the grassland becoming more vivid and offering a more distant vision. Mountains loomed in the distance, and the horizon curved to the luminous expanse, but no human life was visible. Still, it was hard to tell from where the sounds came.

"We only have to keep on walking until we see something that makes sense to us, perhaps when we get nearer to the source of this tremor," Zasheri said, adding, "With your gris-gris, we shall get to the source."

"Let's keep going," he said with renewed enthusiasm, taking

Zasheri's hand.

"Looks as if you started loving this adventure," Zasheri said, perhaps projecting her cozy feeling of his possessive hand in hers. Their endless groping for the sound continued.

By way of explaining his liking for the adventure, Kajere explained: "I can't explain it, but ever since I arrived in Tikari, I knew I was brought here by something powerful. With your explanation about the importance of the Kwifon, I think I am sure I will find it, especially in the background of the troubles brought on by the Ketummites and Wubangeh," Kajere said.

Suddenly, the noise and tremors stopped. "What happened?" he asked, a sense of vacuity taking over from the intense noise that had suffused the entire ambience.

Zasheri was also jolted by the void. Both of them paused to listen. There was no sound, and it was not until several weeks later that they heard the same noise and felt the earth tremors again. However, attempts to locate the noise kept routinely evading them for months, and Kajere strongly felt as if they were spinning in a circle of absurdity. He proposed an escape: "Let's try walking away from where we thought the sound came from." The suggestion was not new, but reiterated the effort to escape the endless cycle.

However, Zasheri was reluctant to move away from the sound, which seemed to give her a bearing or sense of proximal relevance.

Kajere objected, explaining, "We've been doing the same thing over and over and expecting different results. Maybe things would change if we chose to behave as if we're not interested." He was pensive.

"I did not think of it that way," Zasheri acquiesced, and they turned around and walked just a few hours back. The source of the sound loomed in an amazingly outlandish sight from behind one of the few trees in the large expanse of grass fields. It was striking – a stretch of thousands and thousands of people, all attired in white, all old, but all possessing energy not usually found in older people. Some were so old, they wondered whence they got the power to keep up with the others. All were angry, agitated, and making the said sounds. The variant was that a chariot rumbled along every so often and dropped off a few of them, working up many to scramble to get in. This was compounded by the impatience of the chariot drivers who would not wait for long. As the chariot drove off precipitately, some fell off while others clung to it for their very life.

The gruesome sight fascinated Kajere and Zasheri, the cycle spinning endlessly. Some people would get on the chariot, but hours later, after they were dropped off, they would go right back and want to go through the pain and suffering of getting on the chariot again.

"It is Mukumbi," Zasheri reiterated. "This is most assuredly what I heard of, but never believed it existed."

"What exactly did you hear about it?" Kajere asked.

"That it's a place of suffering for old people," she said summarily.

As Kajere glued his gaze on the spectacle, he said, "Something tells me we are about to find out more."

"You think so?"

The words were hardly out of her mouth when, in front of them materialized two of the older adults. It was as if from nowhere, for they neither heard nor saw them approach. In the hands of the materialized adults were strange devices. One look told anyone that the devices could bring about extreme pain and much discomfort. Kajere and Zasheri instinctively began to retreat cautiously, the pair advancing menacingly. No word or voice was uttered or heard, although the noise continued in the background like a stampede. The two adults were a man with clear but shifty eyes and a woman who looked slightly older than the man.

The man challenged the young people: "Are you friends of the troublemakers?" he asked, his device ominously held in front of them.

"No, Baba; we don't even know where we are," Kajere replied as if he had read the man's intentions. "We were on our way to Mekan and came to this place. No malice is in us. We greet you, Baba and Mama."

"Liars. People don't just come to this place and claim they are on the way to Mekan. Do you know where Mekan is? And, tell me, just why are you going there?" The woman's voice was strident, and the man was looking at them in a wildly unfriendly manner.

"Who sent you to Mekan?" the woman asked.

Zasheri, curtsying, went for the skin-saving roundabout response: "Mama, we don't want trouble. We came here to find out what the noise and tremors we heard were about. So please accept our greetings."

Ignoring her politeness, the woman asked, "What makes you different from other visitors who come here, gain our trust, and then make friends with the bad people?"

"We are not visiting here. We are only passing, our destination being Mekan just as we said, mama," Zasheri courteously replied.

Seeming to yield but still suspicious, the man asked, "What is taking you to Mekan?"

"We are looking for Kwifon," Kajere replied.

The old people laughed hysterically, still advancing menacingly. Zasheri and Kajere soon could not retreat any further because a tree impeded them. Then, of a sudden, the woman stopped and peered closer at Kajere, turning and whispering something to the man. The man, too, instantly stopped, and both fixed their piercing looks at Kajere. With reverent shock at how he looked, the man asked, "Is that a real gris-gris you have around your neck?"

As Kajere nodded, toying with the gris-gris, the strangers' mood immediately changed into a warmly friendly one. They doubled down on this by bowing and then kneeling in homage to Kajere.

"They are for real, Arumbi," the man said and then explained, "I am Usanko and this is Arumbi, my wife. We are glad to finally meet you."

"We greet you," Zasheri and Kajere replied in unison, relieved.

"Does it look as if you were waiting for us then?" Kajere asked, "Or how did you know we would come?"

"Yes, we've awaited your coming ever since the moon first appeared," Arumbi said, pointing at each of them and saying, "You are Kajere; you are Princess Zasheri." A friendliness suffused her face, and the two nodded, exchanging glances of surprise.

"Just how did you know about us?" Zasheri asked. She could not hold back her curiosity, which provoked Arumbi and Usanko to uproarious laughter that seemed exaggerated and almost hysterical.

They, however, sobered, and Usanko suddenly got serious and said, "You see, we've been waiting for you from the beginning of time. With the long wait, we had started questioning whether you would ever come. We've been waiting for the person wearing that gris-gris on your neck to come and deliver us from the evil we face here. We suffered so much that Arumbi and I became headstrong. We decided to do something about it, telling others to join us in escaping. For this, we were caught and severely punished for daring to go against the establishment. All our mungang they seized, but that was only after Arumbi had already dreamt that someone with the gris-gris you're wearing would come to our aid. That is when we first heard of you and your names."

"There's something you need to know, though," Arumbi picked up as Usanko paused. "Although we heard about your gris-gris and that you would find Kwifon, it does not make sense that you should go searching for Kwifon instead of dealing with the problems right now. For one thing, we don't even know this Kwifon or whether it even exists. We do know anyone with the gris-gris and looking for Kwifon portends our salvation as well."

"The drawback is the mungangs of the chindas, which are so powerful that nothing can move them," Usanko said. "Immediately they see you, their mungangs start to control you and there's just nothing you can do about it. So powerful they are."

At this addition, moods were deflated. Kajere, noticing their initial enthusiasm waning, tried to uplift their spirits. "What exactly happens here?" he asked, and Arumbi explained, pointing skyward:

"The chindas usually come from somewhere up there. We have no idea from where exactly. They tell us about taking us where we would get young again and never get old. That is why you will find us fighting and scrambling to get onboard their chariots for their horses to take us away. We get somewhere, but the journey adds up to nothing because when we return, they use their mungang to make us forget everything, and we start all over to yearn and scramble to leave in the chariot," Arumbi detailed.

"So, it is about the journey and not the destination you struggle?" Zasheri inquired, trying to fully understand the nature of the absurd trip.

"Nothing," Usanko said. "There's nothing to it. We only recall smitherings of it because of the power we still have left. Otherwise, everyone else seems clueless about it; they only want eternal youth. We are the only ones who know that the chindas have manipulative control over us." Arumbi's voice was bitter, and her posture was more overt with each word.

The bitterness stirred Zasheri's royal instinct to help. "What would you want us to do for you?" she asked, and Arumbi pleaded without hesitation, profound sorrow piercing her tone:

"Free us from this unending cycle of trouble and uncertainty. Help us to know what our eventual destiny is." Tears involuntarily sprang out of the eyes of both Zasheri and Kajere as they read in her plea the regret of purposelessness.

"How can we do that, the right thing?" Zasheri asked. The complexity of experience and of life made every option open to questioning and doubt.

Usanko, however, had a hope to cling on: "There's a reason why this man with the gris-gris is here. He's here to save us. It is not by mere chance that you are here," he said, his disposition calm but thrust with determination.

Just then, they noticed Kajere's absence.

"Where's he gone?" Usanko asked, looking around, and they all looked. At first, none of them could see Kajere, but hours later, they saw him approaching the crowd. He had left them and walked towards the public to take a closer look and was astounded by how eager each person wanted to get on the chariot and how brutally the guards pushed them away. They watched him from behind one of the few baobab trees. As he walked towards one of the approaching chariots, one of the guards who saw him instantly recognized who he was. He was trouble. Immediately recognizing the gris-gris, the guard took out a device, a bull's horn, and blew it as loudly as he could, but no one seemed to listen to it.

Before long, everyone started a frenzied dance. They all seemed to be possessed by evil spirits. In the meantime, Zasheri, Arumbi, and Usanko watched from their hideout, perplexed.

"I think they can see him," Zasheri said.

"Yes," both Arumbi and Usanko replied in unison, excited.

"When we first saw him, we knew he had a very strong mungang," Usanko said, truly delighted.

"Now let's see what they've got," Arumbi added, her eyes gleaming at the prospect of what she knew would soon happen.

Meanwhile, the dancers surrounded Kajere, paying little heed to the guards who blew their horns numerous times. As they danced, they lifted Kajere and passed him round to the frustration of the guards. Eventually, the guards, through their leader, Ngia, came to Kajere and asked, "Who are you? Where are you from and why so young?"

Kajere promptly and calmly responded, "I am Kajere, and have come to stop this nonsense you and your cohorts are conducting here."

This stopped Ngia in his tracks, smiling awkwardly, revealing kola-nut-stained teeth, and asking, "So, you are one of those people who go somewhere and want to make a change. What makes you think whatever it is you have in mind will be good for them? Why do you believe your good is what is good for them?" Ngia was menacing in his attitude.

"They asked me for help," Kajere replied. "Gauge from their happiness at seeing me and you can tell that I am their trusted help."

"You think you are Sense pass king?" Ngia roared out with laughter as he referred to the legendary wit who beat the king and his councilors in all tricks and attempts to kill him.

"Judge for yourself from how quiet they've become," Kajere said confidently.

At this moment, the crowd started chanting his name, their voices rising with passion into a frenzy. Deliberately misrepresenting the situation and while pointing at the crowd, Ngia ironically asked, "Is this your own definition of quiet?" He keeled over with laughter, and his accompanying chindas joined him in the vociferous mockery. However, Ngia's voice was in the lead, and he derisively told Kajere, "No matter what kind of mungang you have, you can't break centuries-old traditions. In any case, what is the point in changing it?"

Usanko came in: "Because you see that gris-gris around his neck? It's powerful. It will stop all this nonsense here." With Arumbi and Zasheri, he had stealthily come to the scene unnoticed. His voice and presence surprised and jolted Ngia, who asked and commented:

"You again? I should have known! Katakata man, I will show you what I am made of. I should have known you would be behind this."

"What have I not seen? I can show you mungang power that you cannot even imagine exists?" Usanko mocked, confident in Kajere's forte. For his part, standing at akimbo, Kajere quietly observed his adversary.

"Are you afraid?" Ngia asked.

"No."

"I have seen whatever you have around your neck, but my mungang is more potent," Ngia continued.

"Fear is prompting you," Usanko mocked, a grin on his face.

"You all have no brains, and do not even know how to make decisions for yourselves," Ngia roared, his voice echoing far and wide over the grass fields as if to show Kajere the extent of his power.

"Just how did you come by that conclusion?" Arumbi asked.

"You surely deceive yourselves," one of the chindas scoffed.

"Is it Sense pass king who has deceived you into believing your own lies?" Ngia asked, pointing at Kajere who was still surrounded by the aged dancers. Then he mocked the old dancers too: "Look at them. They don't even know what's going on."

"Allow us to decide whether we know anything or do not. You have controlled us for far too long, providing us even with the names we bear. Our being old does not mean we are sick or stupid. We still have our wits about us." Usanko was bold, so bold that even Arumbi marveled at his newfound strength and admired him the more. "We are sick and tired of whatever you think or want us to be. Thank you," he concluded.

This enraged Ngia: "You can't do anything without me. You have no sense of direction or leadership. You need me. Without me, you all are useless," he roared, sounding rather desperate.

"You are wrong there," Usanko confidently said and pointing at Kajere, added, "We've got Kajere."

"I warn you! This little nincompoop here considers himself 'sense pass king', yet he cannot succeed in any of our tests. If you have that amount of confidence in him, we could test him," Ngia threatened Usanko, his mood becoming nastier.

Now put to test by a challenge, despite what he knew about

Kajere, Usanko doubted a little, looking unsure as his gaze moved from Ngia to Kajere.

Noticing his doubt, Ngia concluded, "I knew you would come to your senses."

But Usanko's confidence quickly buoyed up: "There's nothing Kajere can't do," he boasted loudly, disregarding Ngia's premature triumph. It's time for you and these, whatever you call them, to return where you all came from." As he spoke, he dared Ngia with a fierce look.

This tickled the chindas to laughter and they all looked awkward because the sound of their laughter seemed to come from their ears.

Zasheri read evil in their awkwardness, and pulling Kajere to one side, said, "These people are tough, their mungang strong and evil. They are ruthless." Zasheri's voice trembled as she spoke.

A little disappointed that she doubted his capability, Kajere posited, "I thought you believed in me and my gris-gris." Zasheri instantly apologized. On second thought, however, Kajere understood her doubt. It would be the first time Zasheri would see the power of his gris-gris in the wild world away from Tikari. So, he calmly said, "It's ok, but I have no doubt that you believe in me and in our destiny. How will you and I find Kwifon together? This is only the beginning."

His confidence was infectious and Zasheri smiled, relaxing because he was so focused. But as they spoke, Ngia's piquant ears picked the trail and he exclaimed, "Kwifon! Did I hear you say you are looking for Kwifon? Usanko, you brought people who believe Kwifon exists to enter into competition with me? First, I thought you were stupid. This compounds that stupidity."

Zasheri on the watch, whispered, and tenderly looking into his eyes, said, "Lookout! He's extremely cunning."

Kajere asked Ngia, "You want to enter a competition with me?"

Irascible, Ngia responded, "Yes. I will destroy you for these idiots to know that you are just another charlatan who thinks he's Sense pass king."

"Just for curiosity, may I know why you keep calling me Sense pass king instead of Kajere?" He was not entirely lost to the cynicism in the appellation. His question was submerged in the frenzy of the drumming and crowd expectations as some of the chindas began playing the drums. As Kajere and Ngia prepared for the duel, an intensely festive stir possessed the atmosphere. It was a preparation that went on until the sun rose to the middle of the sky. Then one of the chindas stepped forward and motioned the duelers to come forward.

Ngia was the first to do so and to growl confidently, with teeth clenched, "I will teach you a lesson, little man." This amused the guards, who laughed, like sycophants do, to boost their idol's arrogance.

"Are you ready?" the chinda who posed as referee asked and both combatants nodded. Then he detailed: "There will be two tests. First, you will both run over there," the chinda said, pointing into the distance. "There, you will find two chariots, get into one each and solve the mathematics presented there. It is trigonometry. Next, you will go around that spot," he said, pointing further away, "and come back; the first to come back wins. Simple!" He paused and looked round, stealing a glance at each of them. "When you are ready, let me know," he said, walking away while whispering encouragement. The time would strike for both men as they faced each other.

In the meantime, Zasheri and Arumbi rubbed Kajere with *min-yanga* oil to make it gleam and be challenging to grip. Now, Kajere wanted to know the full terms of the contest: "I know what will happen if I lose, but what will happen if I win?" he asked Ngia.

The latter skirted the question and instead said, "You won't win. That's impossible. No earthling can beat me, not when my power surpasses all mungang."

Kajere would not let him off. "Everything has a price. What's yours if you lose?"

Kajere's persistence held Ngia hostage, and after a moment of thought, he reluctantly replied, "Were I to lose, an impossibility in this case, it would be your decision to choose what to do to my people and me." He was sure to crush Kajere easily.

From where she stood watching, Zasheri rubbed on the seed mungangs tied around her waist and muttered some incantatory words. She knew that there were many battles ahead.

Kajere and Ngia now took their positions, everyone having come to watch. Like the quiet before a thunderous storm, everywhere was deadly still. The chinda blasted his whistle, and off the contestants ran. Ngia disappeared into the distance even before Kajere knew what was happening. Momentarily shocked by Ngia's supernatural speed, Kajere sprinted. Hard as he ran, Ngia kept the lead. Things were worse for Kajere as he was unable to see any chariot. Before long, however, everyone had disappeared. He was all alone and running on, surrounded by thick, high grass, knowing that he could be lost. For a moment, he stopped and looked around, but there was no one and nothing familiar in sight. He was forced to call out to the silence and to listen, expecting a moment's sound or response: "Can anyone hear me?" The sound of grass swaying in the gentle winds greeted him. He had inadvertently stepped on a trap set by a giant python, which now wrapped itself around him and tried to squeeze the air out of him. He fought back fiercely. He was savage; a man possessed, you could say, all to disentangle himself from the giant and robust python. Before Kajere overcame it, he heard someone in the background emitting raucous laughter. True to type, it was Ngia who, to the laugh, added a sarcastic comment: "I told you not to try me; you think your mungang is stronger? You are that snake's next meal. Many moons have passed since it last had any dinner. No one will even know where you ended up." He roared louder, thrilling himself with the spectacle.

Kajere tried saying something back but swallowed the words in the hard struggle with the giant python. The python began to tire, which robbed the smile of Ngia's excited facial triumph. He saw that Kajere could win and decided to run away rather than witness his own discomfiture.

Kajere eventually disengaged himself from the python and continued the race. He had seen the direction Ngia had gone. He followed and heard a thunderous sound; Ngia was already riding his chariot. Kajere now found the other chariot made for it, but angry bees swarmed on him before he could get on in. "Not bees. I don't like bees," he thought, frantically chasing them away. But the bees, too, worked up the horses attached to the chariot, and agitated; they escaped with bees in pursuit.

The bees unsparingly stung Kajere so many times, he lost count but would not give up chasing after the horses. Finally, he caught up with the horses. Then he tore up some grass and made a fire by rubbing his gris-gris together. The fire scared off the bees, but he could hardly see his way. He had been stung so many times on the face, and his eyes hurt and were all swollen. He would not give up. He mustered strength enough to mount the chariot and ride away. He would need some minyanga to heal him of the bee stings. With his gris-gris, he located some minyanga, but it was many days' ride to get it. How he wished Zasheri and Arumbi had rubbed more of it on him! He went for it.

***

Zasheri, Arumbi, Usanko, and the rest of the older people stood awaiting Kajere's return. Many days went by. "Where might he have disappeared to?" they wondered, fearing.

"He will be okay," Zasheri calmly said, hoping against hope and deeply concerned.

Ngia arrived alone, took his mathematics questions, sat on the ground and started working on them. Challenging as they were, he quickly solved them. The calculations were long. The judges and all his guards approved of his answers.

Still, Kajere hadn't come, which raised Zasheri's anxiety levels as, having completed his mathematics puzzle, Ngia quickly got on his chariot and disappeared into the skies, exploding with laughter, the entire crowd silent and tense.

Days later, Kajere arrived, battered, eyes so swollen, he could barely see. The minyanga had helped somewhat. He literally fell out of the chariot as he got out and Zasheri tried to rush to his help, but was stopped by the chindas for it was against the rules of the game. "Any help for him means he has surrendered," the judges said, laughing.

It was not against the rules to enquire, "What happened?" Zasheri asked, panicking.

"I'm tired," was all he managed to say as he struggled to stay on his feet.

"Is that minyanga?" she asked, and Kajere nodded.

"Don't rub too much. Do it gently," Zasheri cautioned.

Kajere nodded and did as she advised, with effort, getting to his feet and limping to the line. Then he set about his mathematics task with grim confidence. Days later, he was still not done. Everyone watched him struggle with them, his enthusiasm and strength slowly ebbing. "These questions are tough," he muttered after succeeding in solving one and before moving to the next. "I hate mathematics." Clearly, he was having difficulty with the mathematics. He labored at one, wiped it off, tried again ad nauseam. The chindas would cross each answer, shaking their heads.

Suspecting foul play, Kajere said, "You're not doing your jobs correctly. Why don't others look at my answers as well?" He was exasperated.

"Sure," one of the judges answered sarcastically. Usanko sauntered towards Kajere and saw what the problems were. He knew the answers and could see where Kajere was going wrong, but he could do nothing to help.

"Even your gris-gris mungang can't be of any help to you this time," one judge mocked. "If you had any water in your head, you would have solved it easily."

Zasheri sensed Kajere was about to lose. She had already burned one of her mungangs in order to be with him. She knew that there were more dangerous obstacles ahead. Like the others, she waited for Kajere to deal with the questions as Kajere pored over them amidst taunts and jibes from the guards. Weeks later, he was at last through and judged successful. He was still in pain and could hardly see, though. He limped to his chariot, got on it, and rode into the skies, words of encouragement shooting up to him:

"Remember what Ngounso said. We'll encounter many near-impossible situations, but we will overcome. Your gris-gris is powerful," Zasheri fired sparks of moral energy at him. Her words seemed to affect him, for he hurled himself into the chariot with superhuman strength and was gone. A few hours later, he was floating in the clouds that rapidly whizzed by. He had no idea where he was going, nor did he have any control of the chariot, which seemed to have a mind of its own. The horses sky-galloped on, and Kajere relaxed, anticipating the next obstacle. In the distance, he heard drumbeats but couldn't discern the message they doled out. The sound got louder as he neared and saw the drums.

"What kind of drums are these?" he asked himself aloud about the talking drums of Mabukor, which soon surrounded his chariot. All he could see was that they were producing music that made him feel like dancing. The drums kept making music on their own, a sweet melody enticing him to dance, but his gris-gris attached itself to one end of the chariot and prevented him from leaving it. His horses, not so disciplined, loved the music and started dancing. He knew he had to act quickly or lose the competition. Try as he did, he could not stop his horses from dancing to the music. The drums belted out the tune, and as the music gradually crescendoed, his horses became hysterical and somewhat delirious.

"How do I stop them?" Kajere screamed out his frustration as the horses continued dancing, the drums in merry music-making.

In the distance, Ngia rode on, shooting through the skies and around the meaningless point, so-called because it was where the older people usually began to realize there was nothing in the skies and wanted to return. Past that point, he headed to the finish line, winning confidently, inflating his ego.

Just when Kajere had almost given up hope of winning, a powerful thrust came from nowhere. Before he knew what was happening, it propelled him to grab the drums. He smiled and screamed his thanks as his horses exited the trance gripping them. The gris-gris, which had become hot on his chest, began to cool, and his horses swiftly sped through the clouds, egged on by a now super-enthusiastic and relentless Kajere.

From where he was, Ngia saw Kajere rapidly approaching him. He saw everyone and the finish line. He spurred his horses to go even faster, shocked to see Kajere, whom he had believed the dancing drums of Mabukor would impede for long. He was soon near the finish line and heard everyone screaming. Kajere had caught up with him and both sprinted for the line, their horses breathing furiously and foaming, steam pouring from their nostrils and ears.

"How did you get here? I thought the Mabukor drums had got you?" Ngia said fiercely.

"You were wrong," Kajere replied, straining his horses to the line. He could see Zasheri, and something inside him shot up. He could not fail her. Extra energy surged, and he pulled up every ounce of energy he needed or had left. He crossed the line a few feet ahead of

Ngia, and along with their horses, the two utterly exhausted competitors collapsed. The crowd bellowed the triumph, stunning the chindas and their leaders who watched, shocked at the spectacle that till now they thought was impossible taking place.

Zasheri, Usanko, and Arumbi ran up to the exhausted Kajere and grabbed him as he came crashing out of the chariot. He still carried a swollen face but managed to smile.

"Did I win?" Kajere asked, his parched lips barely letting the words slide out.

"Yes! You won! You won!" Zasheri exploded in breathless excitement at the same time as he caught hold of him, flailing to fall. Usanko and Arumbi rushed up to her and gave instant help as the people gathered around. The euphoric crowd steamed up and waved their hands in unison, thanking Kajere for their deliverance.

Meanwhile, to one side, stood the guards and Ngia, who was also still exhausted but perhaps more furious than dog-tired. He was dazed by the turn of events, not still believing that the impossible of his imagination had just happened. But he was not the quiet type, or perhaps he wanted his rival's victory explained away to squelch his devastation. So, he approached Kajere with the question that at once spoke his admiration that was being choked by humiliation and the need for justification of what had just happened:

"What kind of mungang do you have?"

"It's a mungang with lots of power," Kajere responded evasively. "I already told you. We're on our way to Mekan to find Kwifon," he added.

"What? You cannot be serious! What a quest!?" Ngia was perplexed. "What kind of fool would engage in finding something that does not exist except as stories? The Kwifon myth is just that, a myth, an allegorical tall tale. You would be sensible if you used your powers to do other things, things that are concrete, palpable, visible, reachable. Please, let me go," he cogently settled. It was the temptation against dreamers, dreams, vision, and visionary thinking.

Zasheri simply interrupted his eloquent goings-on with one statement that was supposed to be the finale: "Kwifon exists, and we will find it."

However, Ngia was not giving up yet and sought to keep his victors busy, "Okay, if you think it does, tell me what Kwifon is?" he said.

Kajere had the mental presence to skip his loop: "Time for you to allow them to leave," he said, adjusting himself.

Ngia directly appealed to the people: "What you're doing is evil, and you will live to regret it. You all don't know what you have been having under me. You all can't take care of yourselves, and you all have no mungang to do anything worth anyone's while for yourselves, much less for others." He could not hide his bitter shock at having lost.

"We will make those decisions for ourselves; the choice is ours now," Usanko retorted, Arumbi by his side, gently caressing his arm and adding in echo of her husband's frustration:

"You've taken advantage of us for too long. It's time we did things for ourselves." Happiness at being free at last rang through in her voice, and the multitude present reflected her mood.

Ngia barely held back heaps of insults and curses on Kajere: "You will face nothing but bad luck in your enterprise, and you will never find Kwifon, something that does not exist. No, it cannot exist! Lamentable that you should go seeking what you neither know nor can recognize!"

Cool, Kajere, let Ngia's own logic handle the line of thought he chose. "So, it boils down to my being either right or wrong, an inconclusive poise. That reads like a fifty-fifty possibility. But additionally, there is the incontestable bonus advantage that these people are henceforth free to decide their own affairs independently. They will not be doing your dictates. They will decide for themselves whenever they face challenges or uncertainties. And that is a huge thing."

"Old and decrepit things!" Ngia spat out, showing absolute

disdain for the people he had been lording over.

"Old, decrepit, or whatever; they've been around here longer than any of us, and that is something to count as well," Kajere replied. "It's presumptuous and disgusting for people to come from without and try to live their lives for them. I see that some of them even bear your name. So, they lost even their names! And in a name is found the substance of the person, I think. Do you consider that fair to them?" Reflections that ran the gamut of sad history and the stranglehold of overlording outsiders vexed Kajere. It was a replay of the Ketumite challenge, he reflected, while Zasheri nursed the bruises on him and the sting bites of bees.

"Banish them forever; we never want to see them again!" someone shouted from the crowd, and others picked up the tone: "When you're leaving, take everything away with you, so we never get to think of you again and be tortured by horrid memories!" The rest of the group took the shout and turned on Ngia and his cohorts, justling them roughly away.

"You have not seen the last of me," Ngia burst out. "A stranger who knows nothing about you, just because he defeats me, you swallow his lies hook and line!"

"We believe in winners! We'll decide for ourselves," the crowd retorted in unison. Some began taking down any representation of Ngia right in his presence; anything, even those that had been in the land for centuries and considered sacrosanct.

They rustled the struggling Ngia and his men off, their excited voices fading into the distance as their receding figures happily and gradually got lost in the surrounding grass fields.

"You will all live to regret this! This land will come to nought, you idiots!" were the protesters' last defiant taunts. Kajere and Zasheri last heard Ngia's delivery as he was shoved away.

With the noise dying, Usanko and Arumbi came close to Kajere and Zasheri. Wise ancients, they said quietly and soaked in the compassionate delicacy of emotions, "We know the time has come for you to continue your journey." Arumbi spoke with a gentle but fully broadened smile bordering on an actual laugh, "We want to thank you for delivering us from this tyrant. I know you will find Kwifon despite what he said."

"Please, return to us when you find Kwifon," Usanko added, the same compassionate delicacy of emotions filling his words.

"We will," Zasheri replied.

As if to encourage Kajere, Usanko tapped him on the back, saying, "Your defeat of Ngia tells me your mungang is not of this world." With gentle emphasis, she added, "You will find Kwifon. No earthly being could defeat Ngia." Kajere squirmed with pain but kept a stoic smile that, on closer look, degenerated into a grim grin. In trusted company now, he was able to speak with genial uncertainty:

"In truth, we really don't know what Kwifon looks like. We could come across it and not even recognize it."

Even in good company, Princess Zasheri was not comfortable with this tone. She calmly corrected, "When we find Kwifon, we will know," and added, as a justification for Kajere's tone, "Kajere is too tired." She was distraught by his tone and words, although she knew that Kajere still had much schooling to do.

"We know you have good intentions," Arumbi said. "When the time is right, you will find and know Kwifon," she said, her eyes gleaming confidently. "Have a safe trip."

Good company was hard to dislodge, so goodbyes and modifications of the same with counsels dragged on for a while.

Six

Bankoh

Weeks after leaving Usanko and Arumbi in the land of the old, Kajere and Zasheri kept to their odyssey of quest. They got so used to each other's company that they were at ease talking about their journey, thriving mostly on wild fruit and vegetables that patterned their way. They would come upon a tuber or legume which they recognized and would make a fire and cook them, but for the most part, they were on the move, burdened by their quest.

"How will we know Kwifon when we find it?" Kajere quizzed as they walked along.

"I don't know," she replied, "but when we see it, we will know," she asserted. It was like saying that such a great dream could not just frizzle or disappear; its presence would be phenomenal and unmistakable.

However, this did not satisfy Kajere: "Is it human or spirit? You surely have an idea of its nature."

Zasheri threw it back at him: "That's where you come in," she said, turning on him and stopping him in his tracks.

"How?" He was in the dark regarding the quest object and her puzzle of a response. In answer, Zasheri pointed at the gris-gris swinging from his neck, saying, "When we find Kwifon, gris-gris will let us know." Then, smiling, she added, "That's the kind of power you have." Her assertion touched Kajere who then paused to examine gris-gris once more as if seeing it for the first time.

"Did you say that your father declared that the person whom Ngounso finds wearing the gris-gris would rescue you from the Ketummites?" Kajere asked, leading the way in a virgin path they were paving through the savannah.

"Yes," Zasheri stated. She was aware that Kajere was still finding his feet in his role.

"Do you have an idea why he did not mention Kwifon at the time?" Kajere drove to where his initial comment was leading. This ponderous query set Zasheri on a blank pause for a moment. Eventually, she spoke:

"Perhaps, what Wubangeh would do or even that there would be an opposition to your presence was not foreseen. Good-hearted people could not envisage an opposition to the deliverance of their own people. Of Kwifon, we all know, at least in myth and legend. What surprised us was the darkness of power and rivalry. Then, too, we perhaps did not think Wubangeh would use his mungang to oppose it. Besides, we certainly underestimated the strength of the said mungang used to oppose you."

The lengthy justification taken up by Zasheri did not break the cloud between Kajere and reality. He was dissatisfied with her answer, surmising she was holding something back. "I still can't understand why a deity as important as Kwifon was never mentioned to me upon my arrival."

"Oh, that? It's because you had not been ritually bathed in the ngumba house. The ngumba would have informed you. I think Wubangeh knew that," Zasheri explained after a pause.

"Ngumba house?" Kajere repeated quizzically.

"Yes. We had planned to welcome you among members of my inner government and those of the ngumba house. That is when they would have told you about Kwifon. So, at least they know something about Kwifon, which even I am not privy to," Zasheri elaborated. "Yes, we all know of Kwifon, but they would have offered you explanations which I am incapable of doing."

Kajere digested this new information and then Zasheri continued: "So, I don't know half of what goes on in the ngumba house, but those insiders there have very powerful mungang. That's why when the Ketummites made members of our ngumba house look like jokers, we knew we needed something more powerful, the gris-gris to defeat them."

"Ngounso never told me that," Kajere interjected.

"As Princess, I am now telling you," Zasheri said, deciding to sound official. This had the desired effect, for Kajere went quiet for a while. She explained further, "When you arrived, there were many people, some of the ngumba house, who felt you were not the real gris-gris man. Wubangeh, knowing their doubt, played on their intelligence." Zasheri knew that Kajere needed both fortitude and the justification for the dangerous journey ahead.

Kajere put the pieces together and asked, "So, part of my role is to marry you?"

She nodded, "Father said that only the gris-gris man would marry me."

Kajere's reeling mind made him lose track of what she actually detailed. The idea of marriage intoxicated him. Not as if he was troubled by the thought, for she was both beautiful and stately. Rather, he stole glances at her and wrestled with thoughts of the eventualities. He decided on a sidling way of getting to the heart of the enticing matter:

"We've been walking for a long time, Princess, and I know I've probably asked you before, but why did you really come to find me? Why did you not allow anyone else to do that job while you stayed behind to look after Tikari and fight Wubangeh?" As he spoke, Kajere paused in his stride.

"My love for Tikari was too strong for me to stay back and hand the important search to someone else," she said. "I had to come to be with you to save Tikari," she added, not the answer Kajere expected as he watched her walk nimbly along, love rising in his heart. But Zasheri went on, "If I didn't come, you would not be able to return to Tikari. It would have been difficult for you to find Kwifon even with the help of gris-gris," she continued, looking away while her eyes betrayed an emotional twitch which Kajere did not miss. He realized that something too was moving from deep within himself. It began to dawn on him that Zasheri had risked and sacrificed much for him. A longing pierced his heart as he received with admiration the impact of her courage and tenacity. To himself, he swore that if it were the last thing he would do, he had to find Kwifon, help rescue Tikari from the Ketummites, and ....

Zasheri brought him to the mundane present by urging, "Let's keep moving."

"Yes, I was thinking about the sacrifice you made for your people," Kajere said, a half-truth since 'your people' really meant 'me'.

"Let's be going; we're losing time," Zasheri said, smiling because she heard what he did not say. And so, they journeyed, getting over strange places. The savannah began to peter out, the trees becoming taller, bulrushes coming on thicker as if in response to the greater prominence and grandeur of the huge trees. Mahogany, Sapele, Iroko, Bubinga and many other trees of majesty loomed, some strange even to Zasheri. Still, they plodded on, guided by the power of the gris-gris, which kept determining the twists and turns of their direction. Soon, the forest was so thick that sunlight barely hinted at its presence on the floor as they walked. It was dense, damp, clammy, and desolate, generating an eerie twilight hue. Night came, and they lit fires to keep off the swarms of strange buzzing insects.

"I would never have imagined that finding Kwifon would be so challenging and multifaceted. We can walk this eternal forest until our feet wear out," Kajere said and smiled through his pain, which provoked Zasheri also to smile and say:

"Even so, we have only just begun. Centuries still lie ahead of our beginning to have an idea in what direction to tilt for Kwifon."

A clearing materialized. Many trees had been cut down there, and their stumps looked rugged and aged. The vast clearing extended as far as the eyes could see. No sign of more trees emerged; just grass fields and the thick undergrowth. The sudden appearance of this area took Kajere and Zasheri by surprise, and a feeling of amiss struck them both. They became sensitive and cautious, deciding to explore how far the area stretched. The more they walked, however, the more tree stumps loomed. Days went by. Their walk, hoping to meet a sign of life, was assuaged by a river that ran close by, its water sparkling and pure. They had a lot to drink and ample food as well. Their companionship was heightened by conversation as they walked, getting to know each other better and planning the best for Tikari.

"What happens when we return to Tikari?" Kajere asked.

"I will unite all of Tikari and bring back my sister, Suliya. If we stay together, that's the only way we can defeat the Ketummites when they come again," Zasheri cautiously said, guarding her emotions.

"Why not attack the Ketummites? Why wait for them to attack before defending yourselves?" Kajere's question surprised Zasheri in an irritating way, instantly changing her demeanor into a silent poise. He noticed this but decided not to break the silence. Eventually, she spoke, showing that she had been thinking about his question:

"We tried. My father spent years looking for them but could not find them. Their mungang is so strong that it dwarfs ours, preventing us from knowing anything about them," she said, and this pleased Kajere. In his joy, he did not notice the changes around them. She noticed the changes first. "Have you noticed how dry it has suddenly become?" she asked. "Look, the stream which we've been following for days suddenly has almost no water."

That is when Kajere took note.

"Oh! And it seems to be getting really drier. It would be wise for us to get some food and water handy before we perhaps see far less of any of these soon," Zasheri said and Kajere could not agree more with her. Together, they gathered as much food and drink as they could, loading water in leather bags and the food in other leather containers they had with them. Then they continued their walk for several days, arriving at a large green forest visible from a distance. They headed towards it.

"Finally, some life!" Kajere exhilarated.

"Indeed," Zasheri echoed.

They walked towards the greens as fast as they could manage, given their load and the barren dryness around them, contrasting with the forest green urging them on. Then Kajere noticed the strange phenomenon, but said nothing yet. It dawned that, although they could see the edges of the forest, these edges kept receding upon their attempt to reach them. Some days later, he brought up the subject in the form of a question, perhaps wondering why his companion hadn't remarked about it:

"Does it look as if the forest is walking? Is it walking backward from us? Or how is it that we saw it weeks ago, and having been walking towards it, we are no nearer than when we first saw it?"

The trigger did not work, for Zasheri was not convinced. "Let's keep going. The forest seemed nearer to us. It is actually further," she said. It was a rather casual response, the kind associated with the know-it-all scientist not buying into non-physicalized phenomena.

Kajere became frontal and declarative: "I think this forest is walking. I am very convinced about it." Zasheri made no comment, and they continued along, silent. A few days later, the forest was still as far away, nay, even further. Zasheri sat down by a tree stump, exhausted. Not wanting to bring up the topic of the receding forest, Kajere struck a chord of basic need: "Let's stop for some food and drink."

By now, Zasheri had noticed the mysterious situation but said nothing. She appreciated Kajere's considerate choice, noting that he would do anything for her, a reassuring thought even as he commented: "Hopefully, we must come across some more food and water; what we have here will last us just a while."

"I hear you," she replied, swallowing her regal pride. "You could be right that the forest seems to be moving, although I have not seen it move. Yet, we are nowhere nearer it than when we started walking towards it," she shrugged, agreeing reluctantly with him. "But how could a forest walk?" she asked half loudly to herself as if to question not the idea but the words he had employed.

"No idea. We will find out eventually. Gris-gris will lead us," Kajere said, and they continued the trek. But many weeks later, they still could only see the edges of the forest in the distance. They were no closer. Hard as they tried, the distance between them and the forest did not get smaller; they could not get to it. They discovered the river had dried up, and that the land was completely barren, save for a few tree stumps.

Clearly, the force pushing away the forest was supernatural or mystical. Desperation was setting in on them now that they had eaten everything they had and had minimal water reserves. With despondency, their steps slowed as they plodded on, mercilessly beaten by the sun, while the greenery of the forest forever remained distant. Repetition is the cousin of disillusionment and delirium. Sure as day yielding to night, Zasheri deliriously spoke up with uproarious laughter, "The Ketummites are here."

Still cool, Kajere asked, "What do you mean? Where are they?" He quickly looked round as he spoke before realizing what was possibly happening to the princess and reducing the confusion by seeming to agree with her:

"That's good. It's high time," he said.

She only got worse. "I am the princess; I should go in front and lead my people. You follow behind me with the gris-gris. Understood?" Zasheri said officiously.

"Yes, your highness," Kajere played along before picking her up and trying to make her walk along. She could hardly. So, he raised her to his shoulders like a yoke and trudged on for a few hours. But he himself was also too weak to go on. He was obliged to put her down.

Seeming to come to her senses away from the attacking Ketumites, Zasheri said, "I don't think we'll survive." The sting was in the despair.

"We will," Kajere retorted. "Don't think about it, Princess. Remember, we have gris-gris, we will find Kwifon, and surely, we will survive." So saying, he mustered all his energy and raised her to her feet. That moment, he heard a sound, stopped, listened, and motioned for her to stay still. She obliged and also listened, hearing nothing at first. He motioned for her to listen further and carefully. He himself lay on the ground, put his ear to it, and listened. She did the same. They heard something, a faint sound.

"I heard it, I heard something," she said excitedly, then asked him in a whisper, "What is it?" She feared that the sound of her voice might betray their position. Something changed in her, and she suddenly became fully alert.

"I don't know," he whispered back to her, motioning for her to stay put. The sounds got louder, and he signaled for her to follow him as he crawled on all fours to hide behind a giant tree stump with her trailing. They sat behind the stump, breathing hard while striving to stop breathing, listening out, their eyes trying to pick up any movements, their hunger and thirst both forgotten as their hearts raced.

Before long, they could pick up a signal that a figure, someone or something was moving towards them. They could hardly see the figure. Then, the sounds got really close and a creature, a wooden puppet materialized, peered at them expressionlessly, something menacing about its appearance. To this moment, not even Zasheri had heard of the country of puppets.

Invisible to them on one side of the forbidden land (for unbeknownst to them, Zasheri and Kajere were in a forbidden land) was Ngoina, the controller creator of the puppets. He was watching their every move, never having seen the likes of Kajere and Zasheri. So powerful was he that none of the puppets had ever seen him and did not even know he created and/or controlled them. They always did as he wanted without realizing it. He actually controlled everything that happened in Bankohland and Ntubiseh. Things had been that way for centuries as he made sure they never met each other. He was the deity of both lands, and the appearance of Kajere and Zasheri spelled trouble and chaos in his view. He planned to nip any such nuisance in the bud, which meant doing away with them.

From his dwelling, he watched them as if through a screen of a calabash vessel full of water, overseeing them and planning to eliminate them quickly. Oblivious to this, Kajere and Zasheri concentrated on the figure of the puppet entity and the receding forest. Ngoina was not in their imagination, nor was his control of their movement anything they imagined. The challenge for Ngoina was their having survived in the forbidden land. Suspecting them of having an extremely powerful mungang, he was working out how else to get rid of them.

In the presence of the motionless puppet, Kajere ventured to ask Zasheri, "Have you heard of this place before?"

She had not heard of the place, "No," she replied, cautiously avoiding to upset the puppet with too strong a voice. Her head shook more than her mouth spoke. "But I think Ngounso mentioned it; not that I paid attention to her when she did."

Their eyes riveted on the puppet that had discovered them; they took in the apparition, a short, rotund figure some four feet in height.

It was stocky, apparently made of hard redwood and camwood. There was something always stocky, taut, or bulging about its parts—solid and bulgy biceps, eyes seeming to be in a jumping motion, popping out of their sockets, hair inflexibly held in place while in other parts of the head it was softly cascading. The hair was a mélange of dark and light-colored. As for its mouth and nose, the picture of these hanging as if hurriedly attached to the front after initially omitting them as part of the face. This facial component gave off a comically grotesque tilt to the sturdy fellow. But you could not laugh without feeling threatened because the popping eyes had a perpetual menace to it, ensuring terror. The bulging biceps contrasted with the elongated hands, which, like the hanging mouth-nose element, seemed disproportionately long and out of place.

From all the bearings, the puppet was androgynous and scantily clad in loose-fitting raffia accoutrements. Kajere and Zasheri could not easily make out its gender, though, particularly as it stood statuesquely immobile with eyes unblinking and mouth unmoving. It just stood there, and you had to decide that it was watching them because it was facing rather than backing them.

The immobility dug the question out of Kajere: "What kind of creature is this?" and Zasheri could only respond with another question:

"Is it human?"

"How can we tell?" Kajere replied, more in jest and insinuating the absence of visible boobs or genitalia. Zasheri missed the insinuation, and he let it go by blandly asking, "We got here together, right?"

She looked at him silently, her thoughts unspecified, before whispering, "What should we do now?" She was on the lookout, her eyes not moving from the figure with its menacing look in front of them.

Tease it out of its shell was the informing theory, as Kajere suggested, "Let's see if it can hear or understand us."

But Zasheri was uncertain and asked noncommittally, "You think so?"

In response, Kajere said, "Let's go." Slowly, rather than cautiously rising from his crouched position, he said, "Follow me." He lent Zasheri his hand as he did, but she sprang up without help. None of this provoked a reaction from the puppet, but as they took a step from it, it rushed at them menacingly, and they froze into inaction.

"Let's be careful," Kajere said, controlling his laboring breathing. "Whatever happens, it was bound to do something," he added. Indeed, their action had teased the creature out into action.

"So, do we just wait?" Zasheri asked, unsure what to do.

Kajere, looking at her to be sure fear did not overpower her, said, "Yes, I think so. Let's find out who's more patient." He sounded like an overzealous youth, and Zasheri did not quite trust his choices.

"I hope you know what you're doing," Zasheri said. "I don't like the way it's looking at us." Her eyes were fixed on the creature.

Taking her hand, Kajere impressed on her that they slowly sit down, eyes on the puppet all the while. Though unblinking, the creature seemed to stare right back at them. The scare was real, and when Zasheri whispered to Kajere, "I'm so hungry and thirsty; I don't think I could last long," it drew him back to mundane needs and realities.

Even so, he hushed and warned her, whispering very close to her ear, "Shhh. Please don't say anything; I think it can understand us. Don't let it know how hungry we are."

And so, for days on end, they waited, neither the puppet nor themselves budging. Then, from somewhere deep within the puppet came a guttural sound they could not initially make sense of. However, when the sound came out again, Kajere and Zasheri heard something but had no idea what to do or how to react. Then, moments later, as if from nowhere, other puppets arrived and stood beside the first one, all motionless. They formed an aisle.

Kajere motioned to Zasheri: "I think it's time we know where we are," Kajere said. "They seem to be showing us where to go." He stood up, gave her a hand, and they marched down the walkway created by the puppets, which immediately closed ranks behind them and followed them. Their walk was most comical. They strained to avoid laughing as the creatures sidled to the right for a few steps, then diagonally leftward, followed by a few steps performed in leapfrog hops forward. Their legs would get entangled, quickly disentangle, and then begin the process all over.

"Strange how they walk; why so?" Kajere asked.

"Do you think it would be easier for them to walk like us?" Zasheri asked, stifling a laugh because they seemed to be dancing rather than walking, the weirdest dance to imagine if it came to that.

"You mean that's how they are supposed to walk?" Kajere asked, and then thinking quickly, he added, "I suppose they would also laugh at how we walk!"

"That sounds sensible," Zasheri said, considering Kajere's suggestion. "That was not funny, though," she said, bemused as she tried to capture the puppets' entire walking choreography, which seemed strong and physically most fit.

Kajere guessed that a new series of adventures would be their next experience, wondering whether someone was controlling the puppets and how that was done. He glanced at Zasheri and noted that she was immersed in thought, her quick eyes taking in everything around them. She caught him looking at her from the side of her eyes and involuntarily smiled. Kajere smiled back reassuringly.

Zasheri brought the assurance face to face with reality by asking the down-to-earth question, "What do you think they will do to us?" Her calm voice did little to betray her inner turmoil.

"I don't know, but I think if they wanted to cause us some harm, they would have tried to do so by now," Kajere answered as boldly as he could. "We'll find Kwifon for sure."

This impressed Zasheri, not only by the meaning of the expression but with his poise and calm.

"And maybe Kwifon is right here," Zasheri suggested.

"Unlikely," Kajere replied, "If it were, my gris-gris would have signaled."

They soon cleared the edge of the forest and could hear wood crashing against each other. The sounds grew louder as they approached what seemed to be a city. Kajere and Zasheri did not wait long to discover what made the loud and irritating sound. The sound came from everyone's walking, like a symphonic cacophony, so to say.

They neared and eventually entered the city, a beautiful and well-built setup with well-manicured stone roads and pavements. They evinced an advanced and orderly puppet kingdom. Other kinds of puppets watched them from their homes in an attempt to figure out who they were.

Various activities were ongoing. There was trade by barter, puppet to puppet and there were soldiers, puppet soldiers marching along. A squad patrolled, apparently in a continuous search for something. They eventually reached and went past the huge city square. They found puppets relaxing in leisurely poses, seeming to enjoy the courtyard. The crowd was still with them, and the stamp of their walking on the paved road made complex, cacophonous, rhythmic sounds. They walked in unison, as if marching to music, which astounded Kajere and Zasheri, the crowd swelling with each step. As they passed by, each puppet stopped whatever it was doing and followed them. You could say that they were all inquisitive puppets of the same age, height, and frame.

A whiff of thought crossed Kajere's mind that their stay would be brief. Eventually, after miles of walking through the city, they arrived at a huge, well-carved mansion. The puppet that first discovered them stopped, and the rest stopped, all seeming to take instructions from the first puppet, a guttural form of communication. When the massive crowd of puppets behind them stopped, Kajere looked back, assessed, and was stupefied by its magnitude. Until now, he had not realized so many puppets had been following them. Zasheri was astounded both by the number and the uniformity of the crowd. The swell was phenomenal and disorienting, which made Zasheri ask apprehensively, "Where are we?"

Virtually ignoring her worry, Kajere said, "This has to be an important person here."

"These people must be super resourceful, having powerful enough mungang to build a city like this," Zasheri said in admiration. "Would that our roads in Tikari looked like this!"

Apart from being of the same stature, the puppets bore the same camwood red body shade and had the same shape of the head. Besides looking so much alike, they had the same guttural sound they made, and walked the same. They looked like clones of the puppet that had discovered Zasheri and Kajere, and it was hard to tell them apart. Whoever had created them was either a genius or an idiot, Kajere thought.

"They all look alike. I can't tell one from the other," Zasheri's words loudly interrupted his thoughts.

"Indeed; exactly my thinking," he echoed.

"Water!" Zasheri said thirstily as if a wave of heat had hit hard at her throat. "Water! I need some water!"

Instantly, Kajere grabbed her hand, and they ran towards a brook with sparkling water. How he located it was a wonder even to himself. But a colossal rattle was heard behind them while they busied about Zasheri's thirst. The puppets were in angry pursuit. They both lunged into the brook and drank thirstily. Coming upon them, the puppets halted the chase, realizing that they were not trying to escape. Even so, they kept observing and were curious. Although there was water in abundance, the puppets did not drink and did not know of anyone who did. It was simply not in their world of imagination. So, they stared, stunned at what was a marvelous performance by Kajere and Zasheri, who drank to their fill.

"Why are they staring at us so? Zasheri asked after she had drunk to her fill.

"It would appear they don't drink water. Perhaps they have never seen anyone who does," Kajere said.

As he spoke, Zasheri quickly assessed their circumstances, noticing a strange fruit. "What kind of fruit is that?" she asked, "Never seen anything like that before."

"Whatever it is, we're going for it. We'll die if we don't eat something," Kajere replied, rushed, plucked, and ate hungrily. Zasheri did not hesitate to join him. The hunger prevented her from appreciating its succulence, but when she had assuaged her initial urge, she savored their delicious tang and aroma.

"Very delicious," she said through mouthfuls.

***

From inside his palace, the leader watched. The puppets brought him the two strangers. He was King Babusa and took his time readying for the encounter with whoever they were bringing, while thoughts about the situation of his kingdom ran through his mind. He had had to deal with his uncle, Chiango, who wanted to usurp the throne; then came the factions of people buffeting him with multiple perspectives and desires. He worried about what direction the kingdom would go. It had for centuries been a kingdom that kept to itself and rose into a mighty empire admired by others far and near.

In the other room sat his wife, the ambitious Queen Nsenseh, whose passionate possessiveness of the accoutrements of power made her desire her husband to eliminate his uncle. To her, the uncle was a recalcitrant rival who additionally heaped coal on the flames of her disaffection by objecting to open trade with others.

King Babusa had opened up the kingdom for others to trade, and the kingdom stood to gain much from this. This contrasted with Uncle Chiango's determination to have nothing to do with any outsiders. His uncle also differed in that he wanted their great deity to create more puppets, whereas King Bubusa did not like that. The king now wondered whether he could challenge his uncle with these visitors. A smile distended his mouth as the thought crossed his mind. For the moment, he readied himself to meet those he thought of as extraterrestrials. Queen Nsenseh came in and they communicated in deep guttural sounds.

"Are you ready to meet our visitors?" Queen Nsenseh asked, her voice doing little to conceal her excitement.

Trying unsuccessfully to maintain the rigid airs of dignity and calm required by his royal status, he responded, "We don't even know what they are."

"I know," the queen said.

"I hear it said that Timshui found them in the forbidden forest?" King Babusa frowned angrily, commenting, "I decreed that no one goes to that forest! Just what took him there, for crying out loud? Evil spirits could start pursuing us if we delay performing cleansing rites. What misfortune are we in for, in this foreboding situation, Eh?"

When Queen Nsenseh began saying, "We will find out," King Babusa would have none of such platitudes.

"After so many centuries since anyone went to that forest, what took him there? Why, just why did he have to go there? What tempting spirit took him there? And these things he's brought back to our land, aren't they bad luck? Just how can we tell?" The king was fuming, and his own words raised his temper even higher.

The queen took a commonsensical line to dowse his anger: "Let's meet them first before you draw any conclusions. Rash assumptions about situations and people are no use. It would be better for you to judge only after you have spoken to them and learned something germane about them. Could it be perhaps that they possess mun-gang that sucked Timshui into the wicked forest? We have to allow for such a possibility." Queen Nsenseh picked her words cautiously, and their effect was instantly visible as the king paused his frown to ponder on them.

At last, he said, "Let's go," shaking his head; then he added, "I'll think about this after we meet them. I can't even make up my mind because I am mad." He walked to the door, the queen following and satisfied that her words had had an effect on him. Even so, Queen Nsenseh knew her husband's fury was justified and that his anger was unstoppable.

King Babusa stepped into the yard and looked closely at Kajere and Zasheri, who, from his comportment, could tell that he was the ruler. All noise and fidgeting among the other puppets stopped momentarily, although a few discernible sounds came through. Kajere and Zasheri came to perceive that this was the sound of their walk. Another stalwart puppet stood beside the king. King Babusa's uncle, Chiango, turned out to be, and was known for being trouble-some. All eyes were on Kajere and Zasheri, who in turn stared right back at the puppets, wondering what step to take next.

"What do we do now?" Zasheri's lowered voice whispered to Kajere, her regal persona admirably coming through for Kajere.

In deference to that admired majesty, and in actual truth, Kajere whispered, "I don't know," adding, "They are puppets. Maybe they need us to control them."

"Let's bow to show respect. That's one way to make an impression of peacefulness," Zasheri said, and Kajere nodded. Just then, the gris-gris on his chest began to blink, a bright color. He noticed and showed Zasheri because he had never seen it that way before. Spot on in grounded interpretation, she knew it spelled trouble, while trying to reassure him about it.

"What does that mean?" Kajere asked and shot glances of alarm at it.

"That is a blink of caution; just means we should be careful about what we say and how it comes out," Zasheri said, and he took a quizzical look at her facial expression. He always knew when she was not telling the truth or keeping the shaded side of the truth from him. But her voice drowned his thoughts.

"Let's bow," she ordered. They both bowed, the puppets watching them closely like a cat watching a trapped mouse. To change or modify this unmerited prison setup, Kajere spoke, and did so as loudly and politely as possible:

"We greet you all!" No one answered, but Kajere's mind was set on moving them. He continued, "We want to thank you for the wonderful reception you gave us and for the permission to pass through your land in our search for Kwifon of Mekan."

The mention of the Kwifon of Mekan had a dramatic effect. All the puppets fretted, sending a loud rattling sound out. Kajere did not miss out on this and asked in a whisper, "What happened?"

"They reacted to the mention of 'Kwifon', which means that they know what it is," Zasheri whispered back.

Ngoina watched the proceedings intently from where he was, growing most uncomfortable with what he saw. Something about Kajere was the matter, and it frightened him. Then, at the mention of the Kwifon of Mekan, even from where he was watching them, Ngoina shivered and said aloud, "I knew it! These creatures are trouble. Why are they seeking Kwifon?" he thought. Just then, the calabash with water in which he had watched the scene broke into several pieces. This betokened trouble; his losing control of his calabash being an ominous sign he could not like. He fearfully wondered who the creatures speaking of the Kwifon of Mekan could be. The Kwifon itself was more elusive than the phoenix of the wilderness around which a mythological history of sorts had arisen about its combustion over the firewood of cremation and then waking up to life after! But Kwifon...nothing seemed clear about its person or exploits except the terror in the name. Now, a creature toting the name had to be a dangerous element.

If he became unhappy with something and then stirred the calabash water, it affected the puppet the way he desired. But with Kajere, the gris-gris on his chest blinking when he spoke was the only sign of any interaction with him. This Kajere creature had to be formidable.

For his part, Kajere sensed that somehow the puppets understood him and the Kwifon's significance. Clearly, King Babusa listened carefully, wondering who the creatures seeking the Kwifon of Mekan could be. He eyed them apprehensively and angrily. They were strange, found by Timshui, of all improbable places, in the forbidden land. Now they compounded their weirdness by declaring themselves in search of an improbable and mysterious thing. He glared at Kajere, who stared back, quietly but confidently, sensing that the king was monitoring all his actions.

In the ensuing silence, the king wondered about Kajere and Zasheri, where they might have come from, why they sought the Kwifon... He surmised that their ambitious goal had to be backed by a superlative mungang force. He had proof already that they had survived the forbidden land. Anyone foolish enough to go in search of something like the Kwifon had to be an unparalleled idiot or a rare genius. No one even knew what the Kwifon looked like or what it was, so he decided to get to the bottom of the matter. Why would these creatures go looking for something so fictional? Then a wave of enlightenment struck him, and he suddenly considered using them instead of destroying them.

Just then, the gris-gris stopped blinking, a relieving phenomenon for Zasheri, who now breathed a little easier upon noticing it.

The puppets did not respond to Kajere's greetings, so Zasheri wondered, "What do we do now?" Silence could be more terrifying than even hateful words, she considered. She felt inexpressibly uncomfortable and unwelcome by their total lack of response.

Kajere believed in the power of time, famed for leveling centuries of life. Confident, he said, "Let's wait; they will eventually react or respond." He and Zasheri missed out on the intelligence of the puppets, who used the silent moments to process and understand their language.

King Babusa spoke first, his deep, raspy, but monotonous voice interrupting Kajere's thoughts: "You seek the Kwifon of Mekan," he half asked and half iterated. This took them by surprise, and Kajere exchanged glances with Zasheri before nodding enthusiastically.

"Yes," he said, happy that the king said, although he was not comfortable with the drawl of his voice.

The king was inquisitive. "Do you know what it is or where it is?" The drawl kept taking Kajere by surprise.

"No," Kajere replied, touching the gris-gris around his neck.

"Do you know what Kwifon looks like?" the King followed up, but Kajere and Zasheri shook their heads, and Kajere's voice came out:

"No, we don't."

"So, you seek what you have no clue about?" the King half asked and half remarked, before leaning forward menacingly.

"If you found it, how would you know?" he asked, looking at them triumphantly. Clearly, he was dead serious, but Kajere and Zasheri exercised a lot of restraint in not laughing, for his voice emitted a monotonous drawl that leagued with his comical face which made them burst with suppressed laughter.

The king, however, focused on the important issue of the nature of the Kwifon. "Supposing this Kwifon turns out to be the biggest mountain in the world, how would you know? And how would you take it back to wherever you came from?"

Although the question was meant to mock the whole quest mission, Kajere replied confidently while caressing his gris-gris: "Gris-gris would help us."

This silenced the king briefly, but Zasheri teased him on the Kwifon phenomenon: "Have you heard about Kwifon?" she asked.

"You say you're from Tikari?" King Babusa asked, instead of answering immediately.

Zasheri and Kajere nodded.

"We know about Tikari, but we did not know it existed. That means you must have traveled for years to arrive here," he commented, and they agreed while all the puppets stood still, watching and keenly taking in the exchange. On the part of the visitors, Zasheri was beginning to feel more comfortable now that there was some form of communication.

"Who are you?" The king asked.

"I am Kajere; this is Princess Zasheri, Princess of the Tikari, from where we left in search of Kwifon." Kajere bowed towards Zasheri as he spoke and then said, "We come in peace," again bowing.

Some form of amicability ensued as King Babusa's tone became milder: "We've heard a lot about Kwifon, don't think it exists. It's only a myth for us. For the Princess of Tikari to go in search of it, we find that difficult to believe, you see."

Before anyone continued the discussion, the king's uncle, Chiango, interrupted. "These are impostors, liars, thieves! Don't listen to anything they say. They are like other liars who have come here. You saw what they tried to do." His croaky voice was deep but also monotonous and had an unemotional twang. But what he said did not alter the determination of Kajere and Zasheri even as they detected both urgency and anger in his words. He was most certainly in trouble. And it would appear that the whole city looked at things in the same way as Chiango. The clattering sound behind them gave them that impression as Chiango pressed on: "Strangers are always jealous of us and our achievements." The reception he was getting made him continue. "Why would you consider them as different?"

Chiango's words were similar to King Babusa's earlier thought.

But encounters transform, and he was way along those transformation lines. He thought Chiango might benefit from a personal encounter, but Queen Nsenseh spoke: "Why don't you talk to them yourself?"

"Let him be; our king has a mouth," Chiango said carelessly. It was not clear what he was specifically targeting. His antagonism was abrasive, and Kajere could sense it tightening into explosive outcomes between them.

The king realized that his uncle had gaps in his reasoning and asked: "But Chiango, have you thought of the fact that they survived the forbidden forest in which no one does? Maybe if we ask, they can explain. And what if they are actually telling the truth?" The king was getting hot under the collar about Chiango questioning his authority in front of everyone, and with strangers present.

As the thought of Zasheri's rulership struck him, the King felt an urge to assert his kingship: "This is Bankoh, and I am King Babusa. Here is my wife, Queen Nsenseh," he announced.

"I have heard about you, but never knew you existed. You were a myth to me until now," Zasheri said, and sounded as if she was speaking tongue in cheek.

"We welcome you to Bankoh," the Queen said, sounding like her husband and perhaps missing the slant of humor.

"We thank you for this gracious welcome," Zasheri continued in earnest. As her exchanges went on, Chiango's forehead and face took on a dark hue of disapproval of the welcome the strangers were being offered.

"Something seems to be going on in the palace; we're right in the midst of it," Kajere whispered to Zasheri

Zasheri nodded. "The signs are shouting," she whispered, too.

"So, how did you get past the bad forest?" King Babusa asked. "Nobody has ever survived that place. How did you get through it and onto our world?" he continued, oblivious of the sounds of wood around him.

"At one time, I thought I was going to die," Zasheri replied.

To ensure he broke the rapport that seemed to be building up as evinced by the conversation, Chiango interrupted, "Who are these people, these most unwelcome people. Their getting scot-free through the bad forest should warn us that they have mungang that could cause us harm. No one passes through the bad forest. Who knows what else they are up to? We saw them plunge into the sacred water and how they drank it and ate the sacred fruit. Does anyone do that and live on? These are not creatures of our world."

That was his version of reality, and it was right. Queen Nsenseh angrily put forth another tenable version of reality: "Do you even let it enter your head that perhaps if they had not eaten of the fruit and drank of the water, they would have died? You bothered to ask them?"

"Do we really need people to come here and drink of our sacred water or eat of our sacred fruit? The actions are an evil sign, a sign of witches whom we ought to destroy quickly."

Chiango must have sounded cogent to many puppets, for a lot of rattling behind was perceived as appreciation for what he had voiced.

From his height, Ngoina spat into his calabash of water, on which had been screening everything that transpired; he stirred it, and the effect was instantaneous. Chiango chose his words for effective prejudice. "Maybe they have been sent here by the Ntubiseh people," he suggested, and knew the upshot of his words on the puppet populace. Before he could finish adding, "You can't put anything past them…," rattling that could be heard miles away erupted among the puppets. They were infuriated, but the king and queen looked calm. Of all that Chiango uttered, one word seemed to have hit that mark for the anger that was being expressed – Ntubiseh.

"Who are the Ntubiseh?" Kajere wondered aloud enough for Zasheri to hear. She looked back at him and only shrugged:

"I have heard about them; nothing more," she said beneath her breath.

"They have quite an effect on these creatures," Kajere whispered to Zasheri, his eyes squarely focused on Chiango.

"Indeed," she whispered back, also looking for what Chiango might pull off. "It will not be long before we find out." Kajere nodded and toyed with the gris-gris, perhaps for reassurance.

King Babusa worried that he was losing the support of the puppets and needed to reclaim it with help from Kajere and Zasheri. He announced, "We will keep them here for questioning," and that ended the meeting. Timshui and some other puppets surrounded and marched off Kajere and Zasheri. Chiango, for his part, sensed what his nephew was planning but could do nothing to stop him.

Days, weeks, and then months passed, and nobody said anything to the visitors, who were, however, allowed to drink from the brook and eat the fruits and other food they found near the stream. There was so much to eat and drink there. They were aware of being watched, but no one came to them.

"What can we do now?" Kajere asked, already being impacted by the absence of any happening.

"They will get tired; they must get tired, and then we will know what they want," Zasheri replied."

"Happily, we own gris-gris," Kajere added, and Zasheri smiled at the fact that Kajere was now appreciating his own worth.

Time went on, Kajere studying the habits and mannerisms of the Bankoh puppets. He noted their well-constructed town, its cleanliness and the industrious spirit. They also desired to make their city beautiful, which caused them to forever strive and work at it with military precision and endurance. Leisure and entertainment did not exist among them; they all seemed programmed for work from dawn to dusk. Some worked on the streets, tilling the soil so others could put wood pulp on it. Others chopped the wood and added a liquid from other trees to create a pulp. Initially soft, the pulp becomes hard and beautiful after being designed. Zasheri was not lost to this and even remarked one day, "I admire the diligence of these creatures."

"Yes indeed," Kajere replied as the puppets zipped past him, forth and back.

"Could they have been created just to work?" Zasheri wondered aloud.

"Perhaps, but there should be other things they can do," Kajere replied.

"Such as…?" Zasheri was surprised at Kajere's stance and needed enlightenment.

"There has to be more to them than we see," Kajere responded philosophically. To get better light, he decided to join the puppets at work after a few days.

Zasheri was sarcastic when he asked, "Do you want to work with them?" She wished he would reconsider the decision.

"If we must find Kwifon, I have to work with them. I am likely to gather much intelligence that could come in handy in the future." He put on a relaxed disposition even though he was actually apprehensive.

Zasheri decided to be more subtle in discouraging him. "These creatures work hard; you think you can cope?"

Kajere had decided. "I will try." He had come to realize that whenever he mentioned Kwifon in a discussion, she stopped arguing.

Before Kajere realized what he had committed himself to, Timshui and some other puppets marched him off to a quarry, where puppets chopped wood or dug the earth, while others carried wood, stones, or other objects. At another site, others laid down these supplies with outstanding mathematical precision.

"Come over here," Timshui instructed. Kajere followed him to one end of the quarries, handed him a machete, and instructed him on how to chop the wood. From this position, he could see blacksmiths at another corner smelting metal. They used the molten metal to bind wood and other objects together. The way the Bankohs walked or ran, their communication mannerisms, and everything about them showed that work was what they lived for. Their work ethic was so perfect that nobody seemed to be in charge; everyone knew what to do and what others had to do.

Kajere was impressed. He worked hard all day, harder than ever before, cutting, lifting, smelting, and carrying wood, metal, and other objects. He found it hard to keep pace with the puppets, which amused them.

"The stranger is lazy," they laughed, watching him stretch himself to his best. He got back to Zasheri that evening, wholly exhausted. He felt that without the power of the gris-gris, he would have fared far worse and, even so, would have perished from total exhaustion.

"You want to go again?" she asked, smiling while massaging him.

"Yes, I will," he replied weakly, too weakly.

With months of practice, Kajere won the respect of the puppets as he became even as skillful as some of them, working as hard as they did. He still had not gathered any intelligence on why they were keeping them that long, but he had guesses.

Zasheri asked, "Why are they keeping us for so long? I wonder what they are planning."

"I think the king is thinking about how to use us. There are serious problems in their palace," Kajere responded, helping himself to a fruit and tossing one to her, which she dexterously caught and they both smiled.

"So, we must wait?" she asked, eating her fruit.

"Oh yes. When they are ready, they will need us, and I have the hunch that we will soon need the strength of gris-gris again. Mentioning the gris-gris makes me think of Ngounso. I wonder how she's doing?" He spoke almost as if to himself, his voice barely audible, but Zasheri heard him. She toyed with her beads and then said:

"She's fine. She can withstand anything," Zasheri answered confidently. "Having brought you to Tikari, she will do anything to conserve the throne for me; she knows I don't trust Wubangeh."

"Wubangeh made me drink ningreh; I can't trust him," Kajere said, wistfully thinking about Tikari as his eyes clouded a little and he tried to hide his tears.

Zasheri noticed his tears but pretended not to because she had to be strong.

Then Kajere told her, "As a princess, you know them better than I do."

"Ngounso is fine, Kajere," Zasheri iterated. "Trust me. Wubangeh could be a problem, but I don't think he can do anything. Nkukanteh is there as well," she corroborated, not wishing to show Kajere any weakness.

Had she known that Ngounso had given her the last of her mungang to protect them both in the adventures and hardships she anticipated, Zasheri would have been less confident about how she responded to Kajere. Instead, she caressed her two remaining mungangs and felt more comfortable.

Kajere figured that as princess, she understood Tikari, its history, and its people better than he did. He was glad that he had been delegated to find the Kwifon of Mekan. The more obstacles they encountered in the quest, the more eager he became. Besides, who could have asked for a worthier companion than the princess herself?

***

Unknown to Kajere and Zasheri, things were hotter and complicated in the palace. A hot argument was raging between King Babusa, Chiango, Queen Nsenseh, and Timshui.

"You betrayed me, Timshui. You betray me," King Babusa snarled. "How could you?"

Complacency and compromise combined to make it challenging to describe King Babusa. His personality was characterized by extreme impatience, formidable drive, and a perfectionist twist. When he discovered that the most trusted of his henchmen, the one expected to know and espouse his ideology and governance perspectives, had betrayed him, his anger and disappointment were palpable.

Queen Nsenseh knew this would be a conversation like she had never witnessed in the kingdom's existence. Furthermore, Chiango's heavenly and sanctimonious presentation enraged King Babusa because he understood Chiango's political intentions and savviness.

"How could you betray me and do what Chiango asked you to do?" King Babusa asked Timshui. "Why did you enter the forbidden forest?"

Timshui looked at Chiango as if to take courage from him before responding. "I knew you would deny me the chance to go there," he said, his voice shaking slightly in fearful uncertainty, while Chiango looked at him encouragingly.

"You know what happens to anyone who disobeys me, right?" King Babusa asserted, seeing Timshui beginning to waver, and pursuing his advantage. Breaking Timshui meant breaking Chiango, but clever Chiango sensed what the king was trying to do and audaciously chimed in:

"Don't you see what Timshui has done? He's brought foreigners to our land. We don't even know who these foreigners are? And they look nothing like us. They look very different. The quicker we kill them, the better. Failure to do that will upset the equilibrium of this land. You are supposed to thank Timshui and not scold him for his actions." A hint of a smile crept up the sides of Chiango's lips as he cleverly cased a deviation in the focus of the exchange, Timshui growing bolder.

"We don't know what happens to anyone who enters the

forbidden forest. No one has ever come out of it, and we don't want to know," Chiango continued, realizing that he was starting to break his younger nephew's will.

"I hope the ngumba house in Bankoh punishes you for that kind of talk," King Babusa quickly interjected. Queen Nsenseh was silent during the entire heated exchange while her mind ran through different races. She watched her husband and his uncle battling it out. Then she came to a decision and spoke out:

"Okay, I think there's a way we can resolve this problem." Her voice stopped them both in their tracks. "Why don't we ask these so-called foreigners what they think of the situation?" She spoke quietly and with majestic calm. "For one thing, we don't know them. Yet, from them we know that the woman was a princess of the Tikari who could not, without a motive, leave her people in search of Kwifon. She has to be a mighty idiot or a most ingenious witch. Long and short of it, I think there is help here we can tap," she concluded. Brief silence followed, and then Chiango cleared his throat.

The proceedings shocked Ngoina, who watched from his vantage point. Asking these aliens for assistance was not something he could encompass. He stirred the water, but the puppets did not respond to his remote control. Clearly, some other being was controlling them, which alarmed him. He went berserk, stirring the water in anger, and it all spilled from the calabash. Nothing happened. The discussions at the scene went on as if he did not exist.

Chiango's scheme to become king was evident in his suggestion: "I still believe we should do as I suggested. We should devise a system where the people in the land choose their king."

King Babusa saw through and warned, "Don't get me mad. First, you made Timshui disobey me and enter the forbidden forest. Now, you accuse me of contacting the Ntibuseh people, and you know that this kind of talk can cause me to send you into the forbidden forest. You have inched your way into canvassing to dethrone the natural king of the land. Is it just power hunger or madness that's taking over your thinking?"

Chiango chose to take a quaint angle on the matter and said, "I agree with your wife for once and let the foreigners tell us about themselves. After all, if they are stupid enough to seek an inexistent Kwifon, their wild search may land a solution." He glowered at his nephew while speaking.

It was King Babusa's turn to hit back with a sarcastic question: "Didn't you say we should eliminate them? Why have you turned completely around to now seek their opinion?" Although Chiango expected some contrary imagination, he was unprepared for the acidity of the king's spewing sarcasm.

"Because ...because...," Chiango stuttered. The right words were not coming, and not noticing this, King Babusa pressed home his advantage.

"Did you ever stop to wonder at the kind of thinking that you do? Have you thought about those who want neither you nor me here? How do you plan to treat them? As king, I think, and it is not every problem that is for democratic decision. As king, I make decisions."

After holding a murderous stare unblinkingly towards the king, Chiango found his voice and remarked, "Look at the trouble we're in for which you should take the blame since you're the decision-maker."

"My wife's suggestion is what I will listen to," King Babusa continued as if Chiango had said nothing.

For his part, Chiango spat out, "You cannot be serious! Has this land changed so dramatically that a king listens to his wife for decisions that affect everyone?" In this question, Chiango eliminated himself as king and focused on the reigning king without seeing the contradiction in his remark.

In one corner in the forbidden land, Ngoina sat, realizing that whatever the strange creatures, their presence was sowing the seeds of discontent among his puppets. The puppets suddenly seemed to have minds of their own and reacted to what the other said without heeding or doing his bidding. Clearly, he was losing control and needed to do something quickly before Kajere had his way.

Kajere and Zasheri bathed in the pristine stream and relaxed in a feast of fruits while talking about Tikari.

Nostalgically, Zasheri said, "It's been a long time since we left home." Images of her realm and possible changes that time might have brought there, tumbled in myriad shapes in her mind. Ngounso would do a good job, she told herself, even if she sometimes nursed misgivings about her protective resilience.

Kajere, staring into the distance and fingering the gris-gris, said, "Yes. We now have a proper mission, even though Wubangeh rather planned trouble. Gris-gris will be our mighty help in finding Kwifon."

Her eyes held a faraway look that Kajere did not miss. Zasheri said, "That's true, although I already feel totally exhausted." But words convey more than they announce, and Kajere understood Zasheri to mean that she wanted to be alone with her thoughts. But before she could respond to him, they saw King Babusa and everyone in Bankoh approaching them. Zasheri was quick to remark triumphantly:

"I told you they would come to us when the time would arrive."

King Babusa's monotonous voice rapped, "How are you?" Puppet voices felt impolite and almost aggressive even when they meant to be polite.

"We are fine," Kajere and Zasheri answered, expecting something ponderously ominous in the pipeline.

"I am glad to hear that," King Babusa said, then hesitated a little before continuing. "We've come to see you about a serious problem in our land." The king lunged into the discussion, giving no room or time for anyone to think. "We hope you can help," he declared to the visitors' surprised glances that the puppets could solicit their help.

"Unburden your heart's load; what do you seek of us, Fon? We are ready to help you," Kajere said, suspending the fruit he was eating in his hand and standing beside Zasheri. Other puppets loitered around them out of earshot, ensuring Kajere and Zasheri had no way out.

King Babusa decided to give an introductory history to his request: "When Timshui found you in the forbidden forest, the first thing we wanted to do was send you away, back where you came from," King Babusa began slowly, leaving out the idea of eliminating them. "The person who found you, however, betrayed me, and it seems as if a force stronger than ours is controlling us now, and my uncle wants to take over power from me."

Kajere and Zasheri heaved sighs of relief as the direction of the help they needed to give became less challenging. They listened on.

"Even though I am the Fon here, my uncle is worming his way up, trying to make everyone vote to decide who should be their king. Some would certainly prefer him as king, while others would prefer me. My worry is what could happen to those who support me, were he to have the upper hand." The king then turned and faced Kajere and Zasheri.

"Princess, can you address that worry?" Kajere whispered.

She whispered back rhetorically, "Is it you or me wearing the gris-gris?"

"I should ask who the princess who's ruled Tikari for centuries is and table the problem before her," Kajere retorted.

The king interrupted their thrust and counter-thrust: "So, how do you see it: should they do my bidding or my uncle's suggestion?" King Babusa's voice brought them back to the present, but Chiango, who had strolled to the meeting unnoticed, interjected at that moment.

Kajere pulled a fast one on Zasheri, saying, "We have decided that she should answer the question." He pointed at Zasheri and added, "She's the princess and would not give a biased response." A smile of quiet victory obtained by cunning played on his face even as Zasheri protested beneath her breath with a scowling smile:

"I told you to answer."

"You will need to think carefully, because what you say will affect you and determine whether you stay among us or return to the forbidden forest," the king said.

"That sounds hard, a hard circumstance and condition," Kajere said.

"It is not as if the good alternative has no downside to it," the king said, ignoring Kajere's mild protest and asserting, "If you are right, you will face this traitor at Mbiseh," he said, pointing at Timshui. "But if you lose, we will return you to the forbidden forest," he glanced at Zasheri again. There was a heavy silence while Kajere and Zasheri took in what the king had just uttered, virtually both heinous choices.

"You forgot to add that if he loses, because he will surely lose to Timshui, we will punish Timshui too," Chiango capped with sarcasm. King Babusa acknowledged what Chiango had just said by nodding angrily.

Kajere inquired coolly, "What are the obstacles of Mbiseh?" Kajere inquired, surreptitiously glancing at Timshui, a look which Chiango noticed, sardonically smiled, saying:

"Let's deal with him. Timshui, for the records and your information, is the best in the world and has never been defeated since the founding of Bankoh. That is why I made him my most important chinda," the king said, walking towards the obstacles.

Wood, boxes, and structures of all shapes and sizes, apparently combined to create different types of systems, dominated the testing grounds. Each obstacle was constructed to be impossible to interlock or fit into the other. Some looked like complicated physics, mathematical equations, or just tangled puzzles, which Kajere quickly decided were unsolvable. Some required swimming, and others required passing through high flames of crackling fires.

Kajere understood that the puppets could easily go through the challenges. Still, the problem was compounded by the fact that the obstacles obliged one to race for long and arduously between blocks, a tough and exhausting race. Someone who walked like the Bankoh puppets would find it easier to take on them, being shaped and walking the awkward way they did. Because his own shape, physique, and gesture were not designed for such obstacles, Kajere could instantly tell that big problems lay ahead for him. There were fifteen obstacles in all. As embarrassment smeared his face, Timshui caught sight of Kajere and smiled in the confidence of defeating the foreigner.

"Show him the stuff you're made of," Chiango expressed his bias to Timshui. "Be merciless," he added, smiling in a prolonged manner that gave his smile the tilt of a grin.

Overconfidence drove up Timshui's adrenaline. He needed no second invitation to get going. He dashed dexterously towards the obstacles and engaged the first one, alacrity adding to the ease with which he picked up on it. Kajere and Zasheri quickly realized that looking like a puppet had an advantage. Puppet gait suited the approach to the obstacles. Puppet legs and walk suited the solutions to the obstacles, Kajere decided. He was thus up for a limping start.

Timshui resourcefully traversed one obstacle and then another, inciting Kajere's imagination to riot. His morale was affected in a manner to see himself as the limping dog in the contest, and no match for Timshui. He wondered how, for starters, he would alter his walking style to overcome the challenges. Until now, he had no idea how fast and far the puppets could run. Timshui was a spectacle. He shot a glance at Zasheri, and she smiled back at him, surely trying to assure and encourage him. Her eyes, nonetheless, had that hollow look he had come to associate with some form of desperation.

In King Babusa's gait, he read discomfort as the king watched. Chiango was in a mood of gleeful triumph already. Yes, there was an air of showiness in Timshui as he furiously attacked the obstacles with such skillful giftedness that even those who had known him for his abilities were stunned, Chiango no exception. He was using this warm-up before the competition itself, this demonstration, as a psychological sledgehammer on Kajere's confidence. So, before everyone could catch their breath, he disappeared far into the horizon, solving each obstacle so efficiently as if it were part of his daily dealings.

Everyone stalled, quietly waiting, and Kajere could not tell how long the pause lasted; hours, it seemed. Then they saw Timshui returning from the other side, having solved each obstacle. True, he got back totally exhausted, but he was smiling.

"Now that you've witnessed the obstacles," King Babusa said to Kajere, "are you ready?"

Kajere stuttered, the sweat on his brow reflecting the hard pounding of his heart. "What was that question again?" he finally spurted out.

"Do I rule my people as is my heritage, or do they decide who rules them?" King Babusa altered the question and asked, looking straight and unblinking at Kajere.

Silence swooped on the entire land. From far and near, all the puppets seemed to have heard the question and waited for Kajere's response. No clacking of their legs as they walked was heard anywhere. This amplified the ponderous moment, and Kajere thought hard, looked at the gris-gris, and almost inaudibly said, "It would be wrong for me to answer that question."

This unsettled the expectant King Babusa, who asked, "Why?"

Kajere only slowly came up with the words, "Even the best cooking pot can't prepare food."

Behind him, Chiango smiled, confidently tapping his feet and raising little puffs of dust in the process.

Wisdom guided Kajere's utterance, his voice quiet as before: "It would be wrong for me to answer because no matter what I say, it would seem as if I were making you see things through my eyes, which would be wrong. You have to see things through your own eyes. Before we arrived here, my princess and I never knew of you or such a place as Bankoh. Actually, in particular, I hadn't. She had heard but thought it mythical. Right here now, what I see is a wonderful place of hard-working people who make the land so beautiful. What you think or your motivation for doing so is hidden from me. Were I to answer your question, I would be taking advantage of you and imposing my perhaps diametrically different worldview on you, which to me isn't right."

All were aghast, wondering what to say in response. Realizing this, he concluded, "If I have ruffled a few feathers with what I have said, I willingly accept deserved punishment from you."

At this point, everyone perceived that Kajere had just solved the question of Mbom, something no one had successfully done. The puppets' discomfort was visible, and Ngoina frowned, frustrated by Kajere's answer, which was compounded by his loss of control over the puppets' actions. Chiango stopped tapping his foot, and his smile ran away from his face. The focus was now on the subdued discussion between Queen Nsenseh, King Babusa, and Chiango.

At the end, King Babusa turned to Kajere, royal poise and dignity swirling the air around him. "We have heard you, Kajere, and we have spoken. You have answered correctly, so we will not return you to the forbidden forest. You will compete with Timshui on the obstacles of Mbiseh. If you are victorious, we shall allow you to continue to Ntubiseh to find out whether it exists. We will inform you when the competition against Timshui should take place."

That said, the king hastily departed. Although Kajere had answered the question rightly, each of the tasks awaited was a suicidal dead-end, going by the expectations and experiences of the puppets. Yet, one victory was worth a clap or a song. Zasheri could not help cheering, hers the only voice as evident disappointment among the puppets prevailed. They had expected Kajere to fail this initial challenge. The future was pregnant, and Zasheri considered the options as she told him:

"You need to start training immediately for the competition; this is only the beginning."

"You are right," Kajere said.

Oblivious to them, Timshui and a few puppets stood behind them, watching their receding figures. One of the puppets told Timshui, "You have to watch out. That creature could defeat you; don't get too confident."

Another puppet countered, "Don't mix up things; we are talking about the world's greatest competitor. Nothing in this world can defeat him. Nothing!" He was emphatic.

"Just what I am saying," the first puppet tactfully picked up. "We just don't know this creature or the kind of mungang it's got."

Arrogantly boastful, Timshui announced a little too loudly, "I'm not going to be careful, and I'm not scared of him. Let him train all he wants; he's not my match. In fact, I have no match in the world over when it comes to the obstacles of Mbiseh. Countless others have attempted and had the same punctual outcome – failure."

The two puppets who had been bothered about cautioning or defending his prowess both shrugged their shoulders and followed him away in silence. They did not look at Timshui close enough to notice the worried expression he was concealing.

Timshui and the puppets walked towards the obstacles and saw Kajere in training. He was so clumsy, so unskillful that, with other puppets, they served themselves the humor of his absolute lack of coordination that was making a fool of himself. They walked away, one muttering, "Even I would effortlessly defeat him," and Timshui laughed, echoed by several others as they retired. The exhausted Kajere contemplated the near impossibility of his ever conquering each obstacle and the impossibility of doing so with the lightning speed Timshui had demonstrated. Days mounted to several weeks, and the day arrived.

Kajere and Timshui faced each other in the obstacles of Mbiseh. Kajere's weeks of trying to master the various obstacles had been no mean feat. The barriers were as physical as they were mental and required too many emotional and psychological requirements. Practice revealed to Kajere just the depth of the challenge, and he wondered at his own readiness. Yet, strength surged from the gris-gris into his body, diffusing through his entire person.

Zasheri boosted this inner forte with encouragement. "Don't worry; you will be victorious," she said.

To suck in more of the external push-up from Zasheri, she asked, "You think so?"

"Now is the moment for you to witness the gris-gris power and be assured that we are destined to find Kwifon; this won't stop us," she said with confidence and clarity, which encouraged him.

As the competition day closed in, however, Kajere's confidence waned, Ngoina watching on and aware that Timshui would defeat Kajere and send the strangers to roam in the wilderness of the forbidden land. He already looked forward to making their lives thoroughly miserable there. A sardonic smile crossed his lips as his sinister anticipation played up his feelings. In confident expectation of Timshui's victory, he put water in a different calabash solely for Timshui. Around his room, the hanging amulets and mungangs testified to his power and desire to control everyone in Bankoh through his mungang.

The festive atmosphere of the day of the competition rang with drumming far and wide as the ferocious sun lashed down. Since arriving in Bankoh, the visitors had not had such sun brightness or intense heat. Putrid humidity from the forest beyond emitted more potency, and the air was heavy with no breeze. You would not think it an ideal day for such a competition, not, in any case, for someone unused to the climate like Kajere. A constant drip of sweat poured down his face in rivulets as he strove to take in copious amounts of air with each breath. Yet the heat did not seem to affect the wooden puppets, least of all Timshui, who seemed even to prefer the conditions as they were, even hoping for the weather to be more severe. The weather odds were against Kajere.

A once-in-a-lifetime competition, all Bankoh puppets came out to watch. The anticipated competition stirred vociferous arguments with vehement declarations and gesticulations of how and who has to win. For the most part, and naturally, they tipped their hero Timshui for victory.

Zasheri stood by herself and cut a quiet, lonely figure, tensely fiddling with her seeds. To one side sat King Babusa, Queen Nsenseh, Chiango with other dignitaries, while the puppets that had come to enjoy the spectacle occupied another part. Around the lonely Zasheri, the puppets postured and loudly discussed the coming event until the sun was straight overhead. Then arose King Babusa to the applause and hoots of the crowd. Members of the king's ngumba house, all embalmed and bearing various mungang on their bodies, walked past amid excited claps of the crowd.

The king spoke: "We welcome everyone to the arena of the obstacles for Mbiseh today. Our very own man of power, Timshui," (Timshui's name stirred rattles and noises to erupt from the crowd in crescendoes). "Our very own Timshui," (the king repeated) "will compete against the foreigner, Kajere." The crowd went dead silent at the mention of the name 'Kajere'. It was already a psychological disadvantage they were impressing on him.

The king continued: "We know the rules. No assistance from anybody to either competitor. If Timshui loses, he will be banished to the forbidden forest." The noise started again from the crowd when they heard this, but King Babusa maintained a dignified poise. From his demeanor, it was hard to tell who he preferred to win.

"I will pepper you this day," Timshui snarled, whispering to

Kajere, who declined to respond because he was too tense already. Interpreting Kajere's silence as disdain or a show of overconfident know-how, Timshui pursued: "You think you are Sense pass king?"

Kajere said, "Why do you think I am Sense pass king?" he asked.

"Are you not? Ever since you answered the question of Mbom, you are making *nyanga*," Timshui explained.

"Are you sure about that?" Kajere asked.

"I will show you the *ngomsong* that you've never seen before," Timshui said and smiled.

"I guess we should just wait and see instead of you announcing what I might see," Kajere replied and sat down.

One puppet got up to commence the proceedings. He bore a long horn made from the trunk of the raffia tree, which was well-decorated and had symbols of the strengths of Bankoh. Upon seeing the puppet, Kajere and Timshui took their places at the start of the race, Timshui being super-confident and adorned with various amulets and mungangs.

The crowds knew it was time for action, and each person was a fan of one or the other contestant. The arena went dead quiet in tense anticipation. It was a historical moment, for not since Timshui had taken on Wobgi, that most dreaded man the world over, had there been such anticipation. Wobgi was now seated near King Babusa and Queen Nsenseh, anticipating the spectacle as Kajere and Timshui took their places to kick off. The drums stopped; the crowd sat, deep in anticipation. Then the horn was sounded. The competition began.

Timshui attacked the first obstacle enthusiastically but calmly. Practice, skill, and understanding buoyed him up. Though he kept pace with him, Kajere labored. His efforts did not promise completion of the course. Certainly, there could be little hope of his finishing before Timshui.

The first obstacle was to carry heavy logs of various sizes and try fitting them into designated holes. Here, Kajere realized that perception was not the same as reality. Whenever he took a trunk to a spot he thought it would fit, the hole would turn out to be of a different shape as he got close to it. The effort of carrying the logs without being able to fit them soon wore him down.

Timshui could anticipate and knew how to get to a hole within a few minutes, while Kajere took more time fitting the logs into the holes. But it was clear that the crowds were for Timshui because each time he worked a log, the crowd rattled and cheered. It was not so for Kajere when Kajere succeeded. Only Zasheri cheered for him when he succeeded. Yet, he plodded on, only completing the first obstacle when Timshui was already beginning his fourth and diving into a muddy lake. He could hear the taunts and laughter of Timshui:

"I don't think you will survive."

"We shall see," Kajere replied, more out of keeping with the tone of his earlier replies than from confidence. He got to the fourth obstacle when Timshui was at the tenth. And this fourth felt like the toughest so far, with him having to dive into the muddy lake, which had almost nonexistent visibility. Here, he had to string together various animal skulls found on the bed of the lake in order to create a figure akin to a puppet. Several puppets stood by, ready to dive in and examine his work.

Timshui had long passed this stage. Kajere took several deep breaths. Amidst the clatter of the puppets, he could hear Zasheri's encouraging voice. The skulls were strewn over a large area, and he had only about four minutes of air in his lungs. He needed to work extremely hard. Zasheri worried that he had been underwater for nearly five minutes. When still she could not see him come up, she ran to the King and begged hysterically, panic-stricken:

"Please stop this now; Kajere will die."

"If I stop this now and he gets out alive, you will end up in the forbidden forest," King Babusa said, leaning back on his seat. "Is that your wish?" The king, who secretly wanted Kajere to win, was disappointed that Zasheri was giving up on her hero that quickly.

Toying with her mungang and wondering if she could use one, Zasheri hesitated answering King Kabusa. Ten minutes later, bubbles surfaced from the lake, and Kajere had not yet come out. Zasheri's fear crystallized into tears running down her face. She struggled with whether to use one of her seeds or not. The crowd in the distance cheered Timshui on. He had commenced the twelfth of the fifteen obstacles. Zasheri was about to give up when Kajere resurfaced, breathing hard and looking spent. The inspector puppets dived in, checked, and confirmed that he had done right. King Babusa looked at Zasheri, and she smiled with relief.

Kajere reached the fifth obstacle. The contrast between him and Timshui was demoralizing and Zasheri already felt that Kajere was unlikely to make it. She would use one of her sacred mungangs to help him, she decided.

Ngoina watched on, cheering Timshui on, his hands loaded with a powerful mungang which he caressed in the process. His complacent poise was jolted by the expected appearance of an arachnid in the calabash water serving as his visual screen. He stepped back, embarrassed at the tarantula he thought he saw, but it disappeared without a trace. He peered and stared at the calabash, horrified, quickly refilling it, but a hollow feeling sucked up his confidence.

Timshui started the thirteenth obstacle, Kajere still on the fifth. The obstacle required Timshui to tie one end of a string twice around his ankle, the other end knotted to the top of a tall palm tree. Then, he had to swing himself high into the palm tree, cut some coconuts, dive back down, and race with the coconuts to another structure. There, he would place the coconuts, pull up the whole system to the top of a hill, lift it, and then run a good run away to the end. A little mishap happened, for as he tried to go up the palm tree, his feet tangled in looped ropes. Hard as he tried, the tangles would not dislodge.

"I am stuck!" he screamed in pain and frustration, to the hearing of everyone in the arena.

"Use your mungang!" someone shouted back from the crowd. Nothing but trial and error for Timshui ensued, and the crowd worried. Zasheri screamed, encouraging Kajere, who, slowly, scaled one obstacle and then the next, tired, but forging on. Around his neck dangled the gris-gris, and he got to the thirteenth obstacle and found Timshui still dangling, entangled, so worn out and frustrated, barely moving any part of his frame. Much as the crowd screamed to encourage him, Timshui could not help himself.

At obstacle thirteen, Kajere strapped the rope around his ankle in preparation to swing into action. Then he stopped. The crowd wondered what he was up to. Even Zasheri was lost, although she still cheered him on. Kindliness in a do-or-die venture was the least expected from the crowds. Kajere undid the rope from around his ankle, went over to Timshui, and helped untie the rope around his ankle, thus freeing the puppet in the process. This stunned Timshui, who asked the expected questions of disbelief:

"What are you doing? Why are you helping me?"

Kajere did not hurry to respond but eventually did: "Because you are good. It will not be good to see someone with your will end up in the forbidden forest. It's no place anyone should get stuck in," Kajere said, calmly undoing the twine around Timshui's ankle.

"Don't you know that if you disentangle me, I will beat you in the competition?" Timshui asked, still in disbelief.

"Why not? I know," Kajere replied, struggling with the tangles of the twine.

Everyone in the arena went stiff and confused, unsure of how to react to the selfless action in dire circumstances. Zasheri paused in her encouragement to Kajere. Disbelief held her hostage. Ngoina, too, couldn't believe what unraveled, and he had no idea who was in control of Timshui's entrapment and associated happenings there.

Not just embarrassed, Chiango burst out: "What's that fool doing?"

King Babusa heard Chiango's question and smiled. He realized that Kajere and Zasheri were super-powerful and indeed needed to be made his friends.

Kajere undid the twine, freeing Timshui. In return, he helped Kajere and together, they completed the final obstacles of Mbiseh. It was clear that there was mutual respect and indebtedness. For Kajere, this featured in his trying for them to cross the touchline simultaneously. For Timshui, admiration for Kajere's unexpected demonstration of gentlemanly love needed to be acknowledged in extreme. So, when they arrived at the line, Timshui refused to do what Kajere was trying to bring about. Instead, he tricked Kajere, making him cross first.

The crowd was joggled into ecstatic hysteria, King Babusa totally out of his depths. How could he banish Timshui from the land, given such a heroic gesture that made Kajere victorious? Kajere himself had done a most heroic service in freeing Timshui rather than hurrying up to victory. Queen Nsenseh, beside the king, smiled, while Chiango's rage seethed because it was clear that he had lost the popularity contest with King Babusa. An exhausted Kajere, with Zasheri by his side and a most appreciative Timshui, approached King Babusa at the dais, bowed, and stood waiting for his verdict.

"That was an excellent performance, Kajere. How you showed Timshui that winning is not everything is a superlative lesson," King Babusa said with admiration. Then, turning to Timshui, he said. "You did a most impressive thing today. Even though you knew that not winning meant ending up in the forbidden forest, you respected this foreigner for his magnanimous deed to you. You lifted the stakes and raised the pride of Bankoh by doing so."

"Thank you, *Mbe*," Timshui quietly responded, still worried about his fate.

"Kajere, you won the biggest competition Bankoh has ever witnessed, greater than when Timshui defeated Wobgi." Nods and loud rattling indicated the assent of the crowd; even Wobgi agreed to it and interjected excitedly:

"That's true, Mbe; this was surely the greatest competition this land has witnessed." For his remark, the crowd cheered even louder, and the king picked up from where he had ended, a little irritated.

"Kajere," said the King, "continue your search for Kwifon, elusive though it be."

"Thank you, Mbe," Kajere replied gratefully, exhaustion taking away enthusiasm as he leaned on Zasheri's arms.

"You may leave anytime you like. You no longer need to visit Ntubiseh and return," the King added.

"Thank you, Mbe," Zasheri replied.

Then, turning around, he said, "Timshui, you made us proud; me especially. You are reinstated as my chief chinda once more; you will never go to the forbidden forest."

Timshui sank to his knees in gratitude. "Thank you, Mbe," he said, and kissed the King's feet.

The crowd, until now dead silent, rattled with excitement. Ngoina, at the edge of the setup, could not contain his frustration. Losing the power of control was something he could not hold, yet he knew he had lost the puppets forever.

Chiango, for his part, made peace with the situation and joined in cheering King Babusa for his suggestion. Queen Nsenseh, watching him cheer, nudged the king, who smiled in response, motioning to Timshui. Then Timshui hurried nearer to the king who whispered something that made him stiffened and shocked. Seconds after, his face broke into a huge smile, and he nodded enthusiastically.

Once more, turning to Kajere and Zasheri, the king said, "We want to thank you most profoundly for your bravery and wish you good luck on your journey." Then the king splashed a panoramic look over the horizon and the puppets before speaking: "I have asked Timshui to get Shengah for you." So saying, King Babusa dispatched Timshui.

At the mention of 'Shengah', the crowd of puppets rattled, their excitement wild. Ngoina listened to those words and was maddened, asking himself why the king would give them the core symbol of Bankoh. While he puffed, Timshui returned with Shengah. Kajere and Zasheri were dazzled by its look, and so were the puppets. Although most had heard of Shengah, far fewer had been privileged to see it. All stared, mesmerized.

Shengah was actually a giant bird, one that Kajere and Zasheri had never heard of or seen. It was so huge, and on its head grew horns, its legs quite like a bull's. It was a marvel. Timshui ordered it to fly high and far. It did with supernatural speed and grace and landed with such elegant softness despite its size.

Of course, the strangers needed to know more about the creature even as they were surprised by its size and comeliness. "What is this?" Zasheri exclaimed as the edges of initial shock got blunt with time. Yet, the surprise of the creature as a gift to them was unimaginable. "You want to offer this to us?" she asked the king.

"It's yours if you please," King Babusa nodded with a look of satisfaction, and Kajere exchanged glances with Zasheri.

Zasheri, in particular, was nervously eager to try it. "Can we try it?"

"Of course, it's yours," King Babusa said, adding, "Timshui will teach you everything you need to know about it – how to fly it, what it eats, and anything else." He motioned for them to join Timshui, who helped them on and climbed up beside them. When he whispered something to the creature, it took off and flew high, so high that they disappeared into the clouds. Kajere and Zasheri clung hard to the creature for their dear lives.

Timshui noticed their tenseness and tried to set them at ease, speaking above the winds that whizzed past them: "It's a gentle bird, as you can see. I'll tell you everything you have to know about it. Please, don't worry," he added, smiling at them as he spoke. The next few weeks, he spent teaching them Shengah ways. As he told them, the creature was docile and understood that Kajere and Zasheri would be its masters. It would be doing their bidding.

They were soon ready to leave. Every Bankoh puppet came out to wish them well. Ngoina still grumbled about them, but he was irrelevant since no one knew him or even whether he existed. Besides, Ngoina could only watch and had no influence, having lost his controlling forte. He had become redundant to the puppets he had created. They had become masters of their own fate, something he knew would happen to those in Ntubiseh, through which Kajere and Zasheri would pass.

The thousands of well-wishers were enough to swamp any contrary spirit. Music and dance everywhere provided a befitting farewell from puppets who were clearly not musically talented. Kajere and Zasheri readied to mount on Shengah, smiling. They waved back to the swirl of waving crowds.

"Have a safe trip, and if you find Kwifon, let us know," King Babusa shouted in his guttural voice, smiling back at them.

Kajere climbed, helped Zasheri on, and they attached themselves to Shengah. For the first time, Kajere looked into the eyes of the creature, and there was something vaguely familiar about it. He could not quite place his finger on what it was, however. But there was just something about the creature that made him think there was some familiarity he had had with it before.

As everyone waved at them, Kajere coaxed Shengah, which sprang up immediately and started flying. Moments later, they had left Bankoh far behind and were flying high and swift.

Seven

Tikari Jitters

Back in Tikari, jitters began to build up. Ngounso, assisted by Nkukanteh and Yafon, maintained peace in the land for several months. Then Wubangeh became restless. He wanted to take things into his own hands. By his reckoning, since Kajere and Zasheri were out of the way, leadership devolved to him by default. Together with his cohorts, he reasoned, he could take on and overthrow Ngounso. Her resistance would stand no chance in the absence of Zasheri, he decided.

So thinking, he brought together his close friends one evening and told them he wanted to challenge Ngounso to a duel. But they were noncommittal, even downright resistant to his suggestion, expecting him to wait for Kajere's return.

Kamesu spoke up hotly, "You already challenged Kajere; why can't you wait for his return?"

"Because they will never return," Wubangeh shot back confidently. "Kwifon does not exist and there's no place called Mekan. Myths all!" he said, trying to sound convincing, but they would not buy in.

"Mmmm. I think you might be making a mistake, Wubangeh," Asabuna said cautiously. "You do remember what Kajere did to you when you threw him up into the air, don't you? You remember how he returned unscathed. His gris-gris is incomparable to any other."

Kuriyango, who had said nothing during the conversation, now looked squarely at Wubangeh. "What I want to ask is why?" She was slow and thoughtful. "Why do you want the throne when Ngounso has given us everything? If she has done anything that has made Tikari a worse place to live, I would understand. I would be the first to support you in that case. We all helped you to make Kajere drink ningreh. Now, when people become too ambitious, when they get drunk with something they want and fail to listen to others, they make grievous mistakes. I sense that you are about to do something foolish if you move to fight Ngounso for the throne." She retook her back seat. Everyone went silent, deep in thought.

But Wubangeh would not let anything like defeat smear his arrogance. With rattling force and anger in his voice, he responded with an accusation, "Kuriyango, why did you use your mungang to make Zasheri disappear in search of Kajere?"

"Hahaha, I wanted to see what stuff the great Wubangeh is made of," Kuriyango answered sarcastically, further infuriating Wubangeh.

Yet Wubangeh found it wiser to sound analytical. "The time has arrived for us to do something. We cannot wait for things to happen. We must be proactive. If we don't initiate action, nothing will happen. We oversee our own destiny," he managed to explain, breathing hard. He decided to talk to Kuriyango later and let her know he was the one in charge. His brazen quest for the throne came clear: "We have to make Ngounso know of our plans for me to ascend the throne of Tikari, whether she likes it or not."

Wary of the kind of reply Wubangeh might spit out, Kamesu ventured gingerly, "Do you think we have to do this?"

Before Wubangeh could answer, Kuriyango came in, also speaking quietly, noticing the subtle but visible creasing on Wubangeh's brows: "What are you afraid of?"

"No! Nothing!" Wubangeh was defensive.

"Then why don't you wait for his return?" Kuriyango asked, maintaining her quiet but disturbingly calm poise while insinuating that Wubangeh dreaded the return of Kajere and Zasheri.

Not prepared to be upstaged by Kuriyango, Wubangeh projected his ego in a threatening manner and dared her to test his resolve in public: "I am Wubangeh. Lest you forget, I have defeated anyone who has dared me. My mungang is not challengeable." Scowling as he surveyed them all, he asked, "Who's coming with me?" The tremor in his voice betrayed an inner turmoil. He, too, could not oppose any wrongdoing on the part of Ngounso and her caretaker leadership.

They all looked at each other, undecided. Wubangeh had done a lot for them in previous times, and they could not just let him down. Yet they did not know why he would want to challenge Ngounso. Only the vaulting quest for power, the desire to usurp her position and become the new lord of the land, could inspire such an action. And that was a travesty, Zasheri being alive somewhere still. The only acceptable excuse to have a new ruler would be the Ketummites visiting and taking away the designated leader. As far as they knew, the Ketummites did not have Zasheri. Kurinyango, however, had her own ambition. She considered this the chance for her to take over Ngounso's position in Tikari. So, Wubangeh's open ambition found favor with her own.

Asabuna saw through this and asked, avoiding the looks in the eyes of the two power-thirsty ones, "What do you want us to do?"

Kamesu quickly took his cue and repeated the question, "Yes, what do you want us to do?"

Wubangeh unraveled the plan: "Tomorrow, I'll pay Ngounso a visit. I want you all to come with me." He had recovered some of his poise at finding them willing participants in his resolve.

Not as if they gave in willingly, for Kamesu and Asabuna only halfheartedly nodded, avoiding each other's eyes because guilt was written there. Kuriyango had been studiously staring at them all, the displeasure on her face quite evident. She asked, "How about Suliya?" This was not just a sly introduction indicating the unseen threats they had to watch out for. She was introducing her own notebook of ambition and rise to power.

This flustered Wubangeh, who immediately threatened Kuriyango, "You won't dare mention this to her or anyone else. Dare, and I will challenge you myself."

Kuriyango knew she had gotten Wubangeh where it mattered, and she wanted him to recognize both her role and new position. Not willing to let the opportunity slip past her, she clinched her position: "We have a system of rules and rituals in this land, Wubangeh. Don't make me regret helping you to make Kajere disappear. I did so because he was a foreigner whom I didn't want to have any power in our land or be associated with our deities. You, better than many, know that his mungang is strong and has a powerful gris-gris. You can't achieve much without my help." She bold-facedly confronted Wubangeh.

Cornered, Wubangeh realized that progress lay in compromise. "Okay, I heard you." He needed her on his side. "Tell me, what do you want?"

She was reluctant to share her desire to hear all that moment. "We'll talk later," she said, eying Asabuna and Kamesu, and Wubangeh nodded. He was still seething, but knew he could not sidestep her in the scheme.

Days later, Wubangeh, Kuriyango, Asabuna, and Kamesu visited Ngounso and Yafon. Ngounso had already known of this visit because Yafon had informed her, and she had steadied herself. Feeling so guilty about the trend the meeting with Wubangeh took, Kamesu could not keep his mouth shut. He spilled the meeting details to Yafon, who, in turn, informed Ngounso promptly.

Relying on custom and the value of precedence, Ngounso did not think that Wubangeh could take any step forward without proof that the Ketummites had abducted Kajere and Zasheri. These thoughts ran through her mind as she watched him approach. As soon as he got to her, Wubangeh wasted no time announcing his intentions upon her and leading them into her inner chambers.

"Zasheri and Kajere are lost, we know," Wubangeh claimed. "It's been a long time, and no one has heard anything about their whereabouts. They cannot find Kwifon, we know. I will take over rulership of Tikari." Confidence oozed from his voice and bearing.

Deep silence seized the scene as Yafon looked at Ngounso, wondering what she was thinking. She did not wait long.

"Did you come up with this brilliant idea?" Ngounso asked Kuriyango. "Because only an idiot can come up with nonsense of this height and depth."

"Who do you call idiot?" Wubangeh asked, indicating to Ngounso that she was up against a legion.

"You. What do you think of yourself when you know the laws of this land but choose to torpedo them?" Ngounso was self-possessed enough; she would not be rattled.

"I know the laws and rituals of Tikari more than you do," Wubangeh replied. Kuriyango had thoughtfully kept silent, knowing that they were treading on thin ice, safety being in cautiously calculated speed.

"You do? I don't think so from your action and words," Ngounso said calmly but firmly. She looked at him directly in the eyes and posited the challenge, "Where's your proof that the Ketummites have abducted our princess?" She knew no proof existed, and indeed this stunned Wubangeh, who was suddenly tongue-tied, at least briefly, for Ngounso to continue with her momentary upper hand:

"Indeed, I could guess. There is nothing to show, or can you show proof of the Ketummites having abducted Zasheri? Without that, there's really nothing you can do unless you choose to shatter the centuries-long laws and culture of this land. That you know, at least."

The lull of bafflement over, Wubangeh came on, catching her off guard and from a perspective she had not been considering: "We don't know how long they will be away – a few months, a few years, decades, or centuries? We cannot tell. While we are in that dark, I want to oversee Tikari. I challenge you to it as well as anyone who thinks I am stoppable."

Sensing that Ngounso had not expected his angle of approach and so was startled by it, Wubangeh pushed his luck even further, inching in with a speculative claim. "There's too much chaos in the land, and it needs someone strong to stop it."

Ngounso did not let the hint lie go unchallenged. She shot back, "I don't see any chaos in the land. No one, not even those in the ngumba house, have raised concerns."

Truth was not what could stop Wubangeh's rampaging run for power. He applied the fallacy of induction, glossing over details and claiming, "No law in the land stops a successful man like me from becoming ruler. No law that says only Zasheri and no one else should be a ruler." He spoke facts with a sly tilt of the opportunist's crudity, the sides of his lips twitching to hint at a sarcastic smile.

Ngounso stuttered, referring to pristine tradition and legitimacy while trying to regain her composure: "Zasheri put me in charge. You know that, and I swear only to her, a thing well known to Nkukanteh as well."

Her composure came too late, Wubangeh having sighted her weakness. He drove hard at it. "Trash! Where's she? Is she here? Nkukanteh, what does he know?" Wubangeh heaped derision on sarcasm and then took a seat and relaxed to give the impression that he had all the time in the world. Kuriyango keenly but surreptitiously watched the proceedings, a smile on her face. As for Yafon, who had been standing with Ngounso, this was an unbearable attack on pristine proceedings: "Who gave you the right to come to this palace, in the first place?"

"Who's squeaking?" Wubangeh mocked. "You?" Then he burst out into a loud laugh, almost alone. Asabuna and Kamesu were with him, but their faces only carried mirthless grins that barely concealed their discomfort with the goings on.

Wubangeh laughed so loud that he missed out on Ngounso's words and she had to repeat herself: "I challenge you to Tchongwa arena." It was a momentous pronouncement that stopped Wubangeh's laugh instantly as he looked at her in disbelief. Then he shook his head slowly, realizing the enormity of her challenge and the entailed seriousness. Kuriyango stiffened at this unexpected blast from Ngounso.

"You cannot be serious!" Wubangeh exclaimed, his surprise spinning his mind. He felt insulted, but Ngounso was not backing out.

"Do I look like your clown?" she asked. "I am dead serious. Meet me at Tchongwa." Her calm reaffirmed her earnestness.

Ngounso's declaration shocked even Yafon, whom Wubangeh's shenanigans had rebuked. She, too, had not expected it, and so she whispered to Ngounso, "Do I hear you well?"

"You do. This idiot must not do just what he feels like doing in this land," Ngounso declared.

Yafon could only be encouraged by her strength of character and fervor to acquiesce. She turned to Wubangeh. "You have heard her."

Asabuna and Kamesu were dumbfounded at the gauntlet Ngounso threw. Asabuna made a mental note, promising himself to become her fervent supporter if she were that serious and could beat Wubangeh in any obstacle. He secretly prayed for her to win, but Wubangeh's loud voice interrupted his thoughts.

"Set the day! Make it sooner rather than later! I'm not patient!" He was in an irascible haste, trying to outdo himself in his own self-confidence. Then, he pulled, almost dragged Asabuna and Kamesu out of the room, Kuriyango in tow.

As they left, Ngounso's words lashed at their back: "Kuriyango, if you think your mungang can help him, you are grossly mistaken. It is clear that you are behind all this, but Tikari is bigger and stronger than your petty quest." Ngounso was actually screaming at the departing figure of Kuriyango and her cohorts. To give the semblance of unconcern, Wubangeh emitted a loud, husky laugh, which Ngounso and Yafon could still hear echoing far away, moments later.

Left to themselves, Yafon returned to the question she had already asked, "Ngounso, are you serious about this?" The impact of the decision was hitting her harder anew.

"Do I joke with matters of such magnitude? Tikari cannot be left in the hands of a mad fellow; no, not without a fight. All my powerful mungangs are with Zasheri, and Kuriyango knows. Tikari is headed for a bad place if Wubangeh ascends the throne." Ngounso stopped talking and looked past Yafon and the other attendants who had entered the room silently.

Far away in Kumbat, several walking days away, in a far corner of Tikari and away from Princess Zasheri's house, lived Princess Suliya with her adviser, Prophetess Nabangua. Suliya ruled there, Nabangua by her side, always making the people do her bidding. Her iron rule was unopposed, and the people believed that as princess, she had both the knowledge and wherewithal to make them do her dictates.

Kumbat was many days away from the area of Tikari where Zasheri and her courtiers lived. The setting there was the same, but it was also blessed with the same tranquility and serenity as the other part of Tikari. Like everywhere else in Tikari, the Kumbat lived on vegetables, fruit, and legumes. They were also young and suffered the anguished consequences of visits from the Ketummites. Suliya surveyed her territory; it was beautiful indeed, serenity augmenting its appeal. She strolled out and about and saw her people at work, foraging. Prophetess Nabangua, her advisor hurried towards her, breathing hard; then bowing and curtseying at the same time, she said:

"Your highness."

"Yes, Nabangua," Princess Suliya responded and looked directly at her, her eyes becoming hard as she watched Nabangua muster the courage to speak. When she delayed responding, Suliya acidly asked, "What is it?" Judging that hardness might not be helpful, she tried to sound light-toned, making light of the situation, without missing out on the possibility that something gravely wrong was brewing.

Nabangua retrieved her voice and stuttered, desperately searching for the right words, "Your sister."

"Yes, my sister…What has she done this time?" Suliya inquired, her furrowed look slightly in a frowning mood. "You already know that I don't like talking about her," she spurted, but her voice was both flat and impatient.

"Many moons have passed since she was last in Tikari. We heard she went on a long journey. Ngounso hid it from us," Nabangua informed her, her gait gaining in confidence when she noticed Suliya's anger was not erupting quickly as was usual in moments of this nature.

Suliya was infamous throughout the land for how her anger manifested. People expressed terror when she got angry. No one would willingly dare to make her angry, except, of course, her sister princess, Zasheri, who took on her even at the peak of her anger.

"Times before, she disappeared for years and always returned. What's special about it this time? Just what's different now?" Suliya was beginning to lose her temper.

Nabangua did not answer immediately, a thing Suliya was not used to. In previous instances, Nabangua would jump to answer her question. Now, she struggled to find the right words to report the problem.

Sensing that this might indeed be a different and perhaps more challenging situation, Suliya became more cautious. "Do you know where she went?" she asked. But even though she was careful, she had all the marks of anger held in check, for her eyes squinted dangerously. She was clearly having difficulties holding herself in check, but was containing herself remarkably by her own standards.

Hesitating and looking everywhere except at Suliya's face and dreadful wrath, Nabangua said, "We heard that Wubangeh made Kajere drink ningreh, which made him disappear. Zasheri went to look for him, and Wubangeh cast a spell on them, saying they could not return without Kwifon." She spoke as if trying to glide over the words, but the princess heard everything.

A moment's silence after, Princess Suliya's wrath came tumbling out, entirely blown away by the information. "Zasheri went to look for Kwifon?" When Nabangua nodded, she asked, "This Kajere, who or what is it?" and took a deep breath, still having difficulty staying calm.

"It's the small man Ngounso returned with after her sleep journey," Nabangua informed her. After that, there was silence during which Suliya digested what she had just learnt.

Then, fearing that even more was going on behind her back, she asked, "When did you know all this?" An angry storm was rumbling in the background of her controlled question.

Nabangua was lucky she hadn't kept the news long. "Just now, your highness," she said, cowering under Suliya's catty stare.

"The Kwifon of Mekan… the Kwifon of Mekan… Kajere," Suliya repeated aloud to herself in a ruminating manner. "Nobody even knows if Kwifon exists," she muttered, her anger rising. Ignoring or having forgotten that Nabangua only learnt of the happenings that moment, she asked, totally enraged, "You knew all this, and you kept it to yourself? Why did you not inform me immediately?"

"I swear, princess, I only knew it this moment," Nabangua replied, cowering beneath Suliya's gaze.

"They will never find Kwifon!" Suliya pronounced. "No one knows if it exists. It's only a myth. They will fail. They will never return to Tikari." She talked to herself more than Nabangua, though her anger was still evident.

After some silence, Nabangua ventured, her eyes averting Suliya's, "That is not all, your highness." Suliya understood that that kind of eye-aversion meant much was out of order. She waited for the worst and for her to continue. "The said Kajere claimed to have the gris-gris that will free us from the Ketummites; he already won some supernatural competitions."

"What? Who? Like what?" Suliya asked. Restlessly unsure of what she wanted, and angry at her own anxiety.

Nabangua was less fearful now and informed her, "We heard he defeated the drums of Mabukor."

"Are you serious?" Suliya asked, shocked.

Progressively, Nabangua felt freer to speak. "Your highness, that's not all," she said, seizing her chance to say everything before Suliya could get mad. "This same Kajere solved the riddle at Ngoso, and all saw that it was a cow in the shed. So maybe his gris-gris is the real deal." Nabangua was glad to have gotten everything off her chest.

Anything that had to do with her sister got under Suliya's skin, but was much worse. As she digested the information given to her, her face darkened with angry frustration at the realization that Zasheri was getting the better of her.

"How can you know all this without telling me?" She asked again, ignoring what Nabangua had just told her. Nabangua had never seen her so inflamed and looking for someone to blame.

"Princess, you know whenever I know anything, I let you know immediately. I can't keep vital information from you," Nabangua strove to explain herself, avoiding any hint that the princess was to blame for inattention.

"So, how did you know?" Suliya asked, her gaze fixed on Nabangua's.

"From Kuriyango. She also said Kajere and Wubangeh competed.

That because Wubangeh was afraid of the power of his gris-gris, he played on their intelligence and made him disappear. But Ngounso found a way to help because of her mungang and made Zasheri go to look for him," Nabangua narrated.

"And how did Kwifon get into the issues?" Suliya asked.

"Wubangeh became clever and said they should not return without Kwifon. As you know, anyone controlling ningreh can do that," Nabangua added.

"Wubangeh wants to mount the throne of Tikari," Suliya illumined the stakes. "But, he can't! It's not possible, not with me around! The fact that we don't know where my sister is does not mean she's been abducted by the Ketummites, and even if they have, Tikari should be mine, not his." She became more restive.

"That's my thinking too, as soon as I learnt of it," Nabangua found room to be ingratiating.

"Hmmmm…A lot is going on in Tikari right now," Suliya remarked thoughtfully, and her brows creased. "This Kajere, who exactly is he?"

"Ngounso brought him after her long sleep journey to free Tikari from the Ketummites," Nabangua informed her. "And she made Zasheri follow him to seek Kwifon because they believe in the prophecy of your father." Nabangua was pleased to be able to include an idea or two.

There was no time to lose. Suliya ordered, "Gather all the mungang in Kumbat and inform my ngumba house immediately. I want to locate them to make sure they are not lost," Suliya said, pensively calm to Nabangua's momentary surprise. "There's a good chance I may take over Tikari now that she's gone. Do you understand me?" Suliya added, and Nabangua nodded as she looked at her with the awareness that something was really going wrong. The prophetess usually scuttled to obey her commands, but now, she just stood watching her. She had to ask, "What is it? Is there anything else you want to inform me about?"

Indeed, there was a darker fact behind the scenes.

"She told me this because she wants us to make you disappear and join our sister wherever she is, and then she and I can rule over Tikari and Kumbat. She also said that we would then join our mungangs and make Wubangeh a symbolic leader, while in fact we would have all the power," Nabangua opened up.

The surprise for Suliya was unspeakable. Nabangua studied her, waiting to see in what direction she would tilt towards. First, she made Nabangua repeat Kuriyango's plan, and her respect for Nabangua rose.

"She thinks you are friends, and can both take over the whole land, right?" Suliya asked, and Nabangua nodded.

Suliya thought hard for a long while. It was the first time Nabangua had seen her princess almost lost in thought and at a loss for words.

"Thank you for standing by me," she said quietly. She needed Nabangua's total support and trust. Then she did what took Nabangua by surprise. She went down on her knees: "Nabangua, thank you for trusting me. I will never let you down."

"Princess," Nabangua stuttered, too shocked to do anything.

"Get all members of the ngumba house immediately as I said. Also, find out more about this Kajere and his gris-gris," she said, rising to her feet.

"Yes, your highness," Nabangua replied, still embarrassed. They continued their walk to the palace, both deeply absorbed in thought.

Eight

The Lure of Ntubiseh

Shengah flew so fast that Kajere found it hard to control it. It was exciting, which showed in the way it flew. Days after they left, they flew into a powerful thunderstorm, so powerful that Kajere and Zasheri had to hang on for their dear lives. Lightning flashed across the skies, and rain followed hard on its heels, with large hailstones. Still, Shengah flew on, unaffected. Around his neck, Kajere's gris-gris dangled and he smiled, looking at it. It was his strength and the source of his strong sense of purpose.

"Can we survive this storm?" Zasheri asked from behind him, clinging to him and Shengah for dear life.

"Of course, we will," Kajere replied, exuding confidence. "We've been through worse." His calm contrasted with the chaos of the weather around him, which surprised and gave her courage.

Shengah continued, and the storm soon passed. They flew into sweltering humidity that was so hot and putrid that it was hard to breathe. Even Shengah showed the impact of the heat and flew slower, sweating profusely.

"Can't we land somewhere to allow this weather to pass before we continue?" Zasheri asked. She worried about her own health and that of Shengah.

"I would like that as well, but remember what Timshui said," Kajere reminded her.

Zasheri nodded in spite of herself, remembering that Timshui had told them of Shengah's supernatural qualities and that whenever it felt ready, it would land unbidden. He had also said that they would find problems where Shengah dropped them off, but that they would always surmount any obstacle they met, and always know how to continue their journey. That in the back of their minds, they clung to Shengah in flight. Days blended into nights and back into days; they kept flying.

Many days later, Shengah started descending to Kajere's excitement. The first glimpse of land again, land so beautifully lush with green forests, thrilled him. Shengah landed on the tallest tree and helped itself to some fruit before flying down to a grassy patch.

They dismounted and looked around. No sound was within earshot. It was a mix of eerie tranquility and pristine peace.

"Where can we be, I wonder?" Zasheri tried to figure out their location as she made her way into the field.

Then Kajere suddenly became alert and warned, "Let's not get too comfortable. This serenity is eerie and ominous." He tried to harness Shengah, and Zasheri gave him a hand, but Shengah got irate. Before any of them could realize what was happening, it flew away, leaving them floundering after it.

"Disastrous! What do we do now?" Zasheri exclaimed as they watched Shengah fly off.

"I think Shengah wanted to drop us here, or else it would have taken us along," Kajere tried figuring out and convincing himself.

"You think so?" Zasheri asked for reassurance.

"I think so," he said, his eyes surveying the new land while his mind told him there was no harm in looking at the bright side of things.

"Shengah looks so majestic in flight," Kajere said, and they both watched it slowly circling them. "How can we go about with it if we need to discover this land?"

Seeming to understand his last phrase, the creature cawed aloud, flew low one last time over them, and dropped something. Then, quietly and slowly, it flew into the distance, becoming a little speck. Kajere waved at it as it disappeared. He had the satisfaction that if they faced any challenge, Shengah would return.

Zasheri lacked that total confidence. "You believe it would return if we had problems?" she asked, a look of doubt over her usually serene face.

Kajere did not respond to her. He found a well-used path, and they decided to follow it. For days, they followed the trail, which seemed to lead nowhere. They felt like they were going around in circles while failing to recognize anything they had seen from previous days. Yet, they continued in silence, feasting on wild berries and other legumes they found.

"Aren't we going round in circles, even I can hardly recognize anything?" Zasheri asked at last when exhaustion and frustration came over her.

"Very likely," Kajere mused. "Even my gris-gris doesn't seem to know any better."

"Again, no one ever said that finding Kwifon would be easy," Zasheri mused.

"Very true," Kajere replied.

At such moments of doubt, their thoughts and conversations reverted to Tikari, and they wondered how things were going on there.

"I wonder how Ngounso is doing," Zasheri said aloud as they walked on.

"Fine, I should guess," Kajere replied, although he really did not know. It was his duty not to alarm Zasheri, he felt. He knew Ngounso would be too weak to face anyone with strong mungang.

"Suliya is likely to have figured out everything by now. She might even try to take on Wubangeh," Zasheri continued thoughtfully, knowing that Kajere was only trying to be encouraging.

"What makes you say that?" Kajere asked.

"Being a princess," she replied, laughing at how taken aback he was at this reminder that she was a princess. "I understand people and their thirst for power, especially power games related to Tikari. Yet, Suliya can do nothing, unless she is sure that we have been abducted by the Ketummites."

"What would happen to Ngounso or Wubangeh if that happened?" Kajere asked.

"Ngounso would have to cede my throne to Suliya, but Suliya would have to choose her chief assistant, and that's where Ngounso could find problems. For Suliya would probably choose her assistant, Nabangua," Zasheri mused pensively. Kajere noticed the change in her mood and tried to enliven the conversation.

One evening, as they rested at the foot of a palm tree and Kajere made sure Zasheri was comfortable, she leaned on him, her head on his thighs, totally exhausted, and quickly fell asleep. He stayed awake and studied her beautiful features for a while. He thought of her beauty and how they would make a wonderful couple. He fell asleep later, holding tight to her torso.

***

The Dream

In this lovers' posture, they slept. It was hard for Kajere to tell for how long. Hours certainly flew by, and he dreamt. In the dream, he was bow-legged and found it hard to run. Hard as he tried, he could not run. He shuffled and floundered from side to side without progress. In the dream, Zasheri had disappeared, and he found himself alone in a strange place, the gris-gris not around his neck.

"What kind of place is this?" he wondered in the dream. Then, suddenly, the wind started buffeting him from all sides, almost pushing him towards a door he could perceive in the distance. From the door came a powerful beam of light. Somehow, he knew he did not have to go towards the said door as there would be no turning back. He only waddled in his attempt to run away. He made to grab anything within reach, but nothing substantial could be found. Desperate, he tried to scream for help but realized that he had lost his voice.

The wind seemed to be laughing in a deep guttural voice, pushing him more forcefully towards the door. His waddling did little to help his cause. Just when he neared the door and was about to be hurled in, he felt himself falling and jolted himself awake. He looked around wildly, recognizing almost nothing and no one for a moment.

Seeming to realize that it would not get Kajere through the door, the wind said in a deep voice, "You will forget this dream."

"Why? And why do you think I am dreaming?" he heard himself ask in response.

"Who do you think you are? Sense pass king? You are nothing," the wind retorted.

"If I am nothing, why did you wake me up from sleep and bring me to this unknown place?" Kajere asked.

"I told you he's headstrong," he heard a voice in the vicinity whisper. "If we have to do anything, now's the time. Let's take him," the voice continued.

Then he felt himself being pushed by the wind. So formidable was the force that it blew away everything in its path. Kajere found himself hurtling again towards the door, trying desperately to stop himself, but knowing it was inevitable. Yet, as he was about to be hurled through the door, he heard someone scream his name.

"Kajere! How can you be walking around without your gris-gris? Are you crazy?" Although he could not make out whose voice it was, it was somewhat like Ngounso's.

"Here. Take this," the voice said, and he saw the gris-gris sailing towards him. He grabbed it and felt its power as it brought him to a screeching halt.

"Never you move around without it," the voice admonished.

The last thing he heard was the voice trailing away as the wind left him.

***

"Kajere, wake up, wake up!" It was Zasheri. "Kajere, can you hear me?" She whispered.

"Yes, yes!" he said and jumped up. Zasheri was tugging him and whispering. He wondered what was happening. All she did was point, and he looked in the direction she was pointing. It took some time for his foggy mind and eyes to get the picture. There were puppets, puppets again, and of all sizes and colors. There were big ones, little ones, large ones, circular ones, rounded ones, tall and slim ones, short and squat ones, kinky ones, and sleek and spritely ones. Their colors were pink, blue, orange, black, purple, and others in colors and shapes that Kajere had never seen, nor could he describe.

Some had lots of hair on their heads, others had none. Some had stiff, prickly hair sticking in all directions; others had long, pliant hair that touched the ground as they walked. Later, from the sounds they made, he was sure they spoke different languages. Amazing, however, was the fact that they had the same characteristics. Each had two arms, legs, eyes, ears, a nose, and other features like their other mates. They all had the same intellectual capacity to understand quickly what he and Zasheri said, the same as those of Bankoh. They also believed in the same deities.

Hundreds and hundreds of them watched Kajere and Zasheri silently.

"Where are we?" he heard Zasheri whisper.

"This might be Ntubiseh," Kajere whispered, his eyes observing them.

"I thought so when I first saw them," she whispered back, too afraid to say anything else.

"Let's try to walk and see how they react," Kajere suggested in the same whispering pitch. "Let's see if they know anything about Bankoh," he added.

"What if we waited to see what they do instead?" Zasheri suggested.

"We've got to see how they react," Kajere pushed forth.

"Are you sure?" Zasheri was not convinced.

"I now see why Shengah left us here," Kajere said, joking about their circumstance, but Zasheri was not up to his levity, not under the present circumstances.

"What should we do? Stand, or walk?" Zasheri asked, a silent yielding to Kajere's preference.

But Kajere reverted. "I think you are right. Let's wait and see what they do first."

Hours went by, and the crowd made way for some dignitaries to walk through the colonnade they had formed. The said dignitaries walked the same way the Bankoh puppets had done and made the same guttural sounds when they talked.

"We're about to get an answer to your question," Kajere whispered to Zasheri as the dignitaries came up. "They read us the same way those in Bankoh did," he whispered, his face not for once leaving their onlookers.

"How do you know?" she whispered back.

"I think we're in Ntibuseh. They are different, but have many similarities. A puppet is a puppet and will always be a puppet, no matter where you place them," Kajere asserted playfully despite their circumstances. He had hardly finished when the puppets approached them.

"Seems like you know what we're thinking," one of them, probably their leader, said by way of introduction. "Who are you, and how do you know you're in Ntubiseh?"

"I am Kajere," Kajere said with a bow. "This is Princess Zasheri, princess of the Tikari." First, he bowed to Zasheri, and then they both turned to the Ntubisans.

"Tikari?" one of them muttered. "That's very far."

"Yes, indeed. Took us decades to get here," Zasheri said with the poised dignity that befitted the princess of the Tikari. Kajere stole a glance in her direction and felt proud.

"We heard about you at Bankoh. We are in search of the Kwifon of Mekan," Kajere informed them.

At the mention of Bankoh and the Kwifon, the crowd of puppets gasped and stiffened. Disbelief was in everything they manifested, followed by complete silence. As Kajere and Zasheri soon realized, the Ntubisans and Bankohs had similar characteristics but starkly different philosophies.

"The Kwifon of Mekan," one of them whispered. "Does it exist that a princess would go in search of it?" Sarcasm thrust the question, Kajere and Zasheri looking on.

The leader and his entourage were attired differently from the other puppets. After hearing Kajere, they quickly got together and whispered among themselves. Kajere was still amazed at how different and how similar they were. He could tell that they were whispering in various languages, yet they seemed to understand each other very well. Meanwhile, the other puppets talked excitedly among themselves, glaring at Kajere and Zasheri.

"I wonder what they are talking about," Kajere whispered to Zasheri, who looked tense.

"Me too," she echoed, touching the mungangs in her clothes and remembering that she had not mentioned them yet to Kajere, which bothered her. Yet, she hoped that one of them would come to good use now to save them. At the same time, she hoped that the power of the gris-gris was enough for the moment. Then her mind also drifted to Ngounso and she wondered how she was doing. Recently, she became worried because she remembered that Ngounso had no powerful mungangs of her own. She had given Zasheri all her mungang. Despite hoping that no one would notice Ngounso's weakened self, she also feared that the secret could be out. She pined for them to find the Kwifon as fast as possible. She was jolted out of her reverie by the puppet leader's voice.

"I am Makenji, Fon for Ntubiseh," he said with proud authority. "My wife here, Queen Ewusa, and these here," he said, indicating a group of puppets around him, "are members of my ngumba house. Together we rule this land."

"We are glad to make your acquaintance," Zasheri replied.

"Where's Menago?" Makenji asked.

"Right here," several voices of his ruling council members answered. A puppet stepped forth, looking very masculine and well-carved.

"This is Menago, the medical head of the land. He performs all major rituals." He turned to Menago: "Say hello to them," he told him.

"I knew you were coming," Menago started, startling Kajere and Zasheri with his feminine voice, contrasting with his masculine look.

"You did? How?" Zasheri asked, seeming to aim at inflating his pride, and indeed, Menago rose to the occasion with an exaggerated sense of his own importance.

"My mungang informed me." Menago was proud to show everyone else how powerful he was. "I informed the Fon and members of the ngumba house about your arrival, and that you are not troublemakers," he said, conscious of their reactions to his voice. It seemed he liked to hear himself talk, for he continued to prattle until the Fon interrupted.

"Let them rest, Menago. Let someone show them the way to their home."

The crowd laughed, rattling excitedly, as they made way for the Fon and his council. Kajere and Zasheri were directed to follow them, and everyone else followed. Kajere observed the new land, discovering that the Ntubisans were nowhere nearly as orderly as the Bankohs. Their pathways were not as developed or as well-structured. Nevertheless, the countryside was stunning, Ntubiseh being beside the sea that stretched far into the horizon as they walked along.

What they lacked in development, Ntubiseh had in manners. They were open and talkative, and had miniature puppet kids who clung to their parents as they walked along. Their walk was like that of the Bankohs, and their manner of speech was similar, too. They spoke a little faster, though.

"Although they look alike, these puppets are different from the Bankoh," Zasheri said, interrupting Kajere's thoughts.

"Just what I was thinking," Kajere replied.

Hours of trekking led them to the palace, where Makenji and Ewusa sat on the throne, the council round them. Before them stood Kajere and Zasheri and the high priest, Menago, managed the proceedings.

He was totally at ease and felt free to do as he pleased. He cleared his throat loudly and spat out particles of kola nuts that dislodged from gaps in his teeth. Full of himself and wishing to sound profoundly wise, he said, "When grasshoppers fight, birds are happy." Kajere sensed that the puppets had turned more warm-hearted, ululating after Menago shouted. Then he bellowed a few more times, and they also ululated after him. Menago's body shook each time he shouted, the mungangs and amulets adorning him also shaking with him. Then he turned towards the strangers:

"We have heard that you are seeking the Kwifon of Mekan. We wish you luck, even though Kwifon is a myth in our own understanding.

A puppet that knows nothing may yet know, and others may know what yet others have no idea about," he said, smiling.

"You don't believe Kwifon exists?" Kajere asked, trying not to get him angry.

Menago burst into raucous laughter before responding with a series of questions that seemed to be fashioned to make him sound intelligent: "How can that which does not exist, exist? You can't ask about the impossible when the impossible is not possible." The others looked at him, confounded, conjecturing that he might have powerful mungang.

"Kwifon does exist," Kajere insisted, "and we are seeking and will find it."

Menago took off with the rambling characteristic of sophists, repeating himself in different words: "You can only find that which is intelligibly considered possible and meaningful. Kwifon is neither, but abstract," he said definitively and Kajere decided not to pursue the conversation after Zasheri nudged him to be careful.

Menago lit a small fire, breathed in its smoke, and gently heated the horn of a bull until it warmed enough. Then he passed it to King Makenji to sniff and passed it over to his wife, Queen Ewusa. She smelled it and handed it to a council member, who passed it to the next and then the next councilor until all had sniffed it. Menago took the horn to Kajere and Zasheri last, completing the sniffing ritual.

The sniffing over, Kajere took a closer look at the puppets and noticed the strange look of some of them in the evening. With the sun setting, these seemed to turn greenish, which, with their original blue look, created a turquoise hue the likes of which he had never seen before. Apparently, those who became turquoise had something about them which Kajere could not yet comprehend. He decided to find out, especially as Zasheri also noticed and whispered in alarm, "They are changing."

"So I see! Unbelievable!" Kajere said.

Although there was no difference in how the puppets interacted with each other, despite the change in some, Kajere felt there was something sinister associated with the color change. He wondered why they said a fight between grasshoppers is a feast for the crow.

"You are passing through Ntubiseh on an important but useless journey," Menago said, eyeing them comically. "It will be nice for you to spend some time here before continuing," he suggested, a slight undertone of bitterness coloring his voice. When his last words came out, lightning and a distant rumble of thunder were echoed as if on cue, and the puppets cheered and clapped; the rattling sound they produced reminded Kajere of Bankoh. Menago interpreted the thunder and lightning: "Our ancestors have heard and accepted our prayers."

Menago spoke with passion and as if accentuating what he said, a juju sprang out of the blues and danced, a skillful leader controlling it. It had powerful mungang, for its feet did not touch the earth when it danced. Then, even as it had appeared from nowhere, the juju disappeared suddenly.

Then, all the puppets pitched forth and started dancing, advancing into passionate gyration as if they were getting possessed by the minute. The priest, king, and queen were in the lead in the dance, which Kajere learnt was praise and thanks to their makers. He perceived some of their faults, but wondered at their magnanimity. They instantly trusted them upon merely encountering strangers like Zasheri and himself. What made them thrive as a community, he wondered. Even while he wondered at this, one of the king's chindas blew a horn a second time, signaling Ewusa to come down from her throne and meet Zasheri, who immediately stood up and ululated. Loud ululations followed in response, and women puppets joined the queen, who led Zasheri away. Kajere watched them unafraid. His inner hunch did not suggest any harm in wait for Zasheri in their custody. He also realized that he had become close to her enough to be sensitive to what could befall her. Concealed from him was the immediate future that he would only be seeing Zasheri intermittently and sometimes in extraordinarily harsh conditions until they would leave Ntubiseh.

Evening was descending while they took Zasheri away. Kajere noted Ntubiseh dwellings. They lived in different clans spread out in different parts of their land. As Ewusa left with Zasheri, Kajere watched them go away to their various abodes, sensing that their stay in Ntubiseh would be exciting.

Kajere woke up the next day, determined to study the Ntubisans and their daily habits closely. Soon he realized that the more he saw and learned their ways, the more days he wanted to spend there. Creatures of the most relaxed disposition, they had what Bankoh lacked. Their children, the miniature puppets, had the same characteristics as their parents, he noticed as he walked around the community watching their every movement. They liked the entertainment and playing around but lived in different clans spread over the different parts of the community. Although they looked different in appearance, none of them seemed to take much notice of their differences. There was no sign of interclan conflict. However, their dwellings were not as clean, nor were they as developed as Bankoh. So, they lost in efficient hard work ethics what they had in warmth of heart, generosity, and amusement.

Exhaustion from Kajere's sightseeing walk was exacerbated by frustration with not having seen Zasheri or knowing where she was. He had no premonition of her being in any trouble, though. In his exhaustion, he sat in front of his abode and took in the sights and sounds of the setup to comfort himself. That is when Makenji surprised him without an entourage.

"Don't be afraid," Makenji said upon noticing his demeanor.

"I am only taken off guard by your unaccompanied visit," Kajere said.

"You think I must always have someone beside me? I am the Fon and known to them all. They do what I direct, and I don't need them around me all the time. Is it different where you're from?" he asked.

Kajere skirted the question and asked instead, "Are you not bothered that someone might be mad at you and try to take away your throne?" Kajere ventured.

The idea was not in the functional ethos of his environment and so Makenji thought about it for a moment before responding, "Look around you," he began.

Kajere took a panoramic look at the miniature puppets playing and the bigger ones having fun while some toiled on the fields and others engaged in odd jobs. He wondered what the fon was leading to.

"Have you noticed anything that could make anyone mad at me?" Makenji asked, and when Kajere shook his head, he went on, "My secret is one word, Kajere. Respect. If you respect yourself and your people, they will respect you. That's how I see it, and centuries of experience tells me that disrespecting others invites madness at you."

Kajere nodded slowly, "I see." He was imbibing wisdom in spite of the power of gris-gris.

Makenji then returned to the raw beginnings of Kajere's quest: "So, you are seeking the Kwifon?" he asked.

"Yes," Kajere replied.

"That is something many only talk about; no one knows if it exists. What impels or propels you and your princess to go searching for it?" Makenji inquired seriously.

It was the question he had had to answer several times before, yet he paused for a moment because Makenji was the first Fon to directly coin the question. Most of those who wanted the same answer did not ask the question but expressed shock at his quest. The idea of Kwifon being non-existent always came up. Instead of an answer, Kajere inverted the question and threw it back at Makenji: "What makes you believe that Kwifon does not exist?"

"Nobody has seen it," Makenji replied.

"We have not seen all there is, and that does not prove non-existence," Kajere put himself in an argumentative mood. "I have circumstantial and situational buttress. Ngounso spent centuries to find and know that I am the gris-gris man destined to help the Tikari and others from the wrath of the Ketummites," he added.

"You mean she spent all that time to get you so you could find Kwifon because you have the gris-gris?" Makenji asked, stupefied.

"We are not to return to Tikari without having found it," Kajere informed the fon.

"There are all kinds of rituals in this world," Fon Makenji murmured to himself, smiling.

"When we find Kwifon, we will stand up to the Ketummites. Kwifon is the most powerful being in the universe," Kajere informed him with confidence, as if to say that the process was a ritual.

"You don't need Kwifon to free your people. If you want to enjoy freedom, ask your princess to bring Tikari people here," Makenji said.

The convoluted pattern that had brought him and Zasheri to these parts made Kajere consider Makenji's words a joke. Upon noticing the expression on the fon's face, however, he saw seriousness. So, he processed the insinuation for a while, wondering whether Makenji was right, and instead of seeking the Kwifon, he could convince Zasheri to bring her people to Ntubiseh to enjoy the kind of life there. Almost immediately, the absurdity of the thought pushed forth, it being clear that he barely understood the superficial components of the Ntubisehs. So, out of politeness, he told the fon, "I'll think about it."

"That is okay for me, but right now, I have a ritual to perform; come with me," Fon Makenji said. His mood changed significantly from lazy to somber.

"You arrived here at the right time," Fon Makenji continued, "and that's a sign of good luck."

"What do you mean, exactly?" Kajere pursued the silver lining hint from the fon.

"Today is Tsintoh," Makenji replied, leading the way. "It is the day we celebrate a thousand moons in honor of the happiness of being alive and of work."

Makenji brought Kajere and Zasheri into his company of spectators. They were his guests of honor, and the best among Ntubisans, went to guests. Kajere was a keen observer and saw that from all community sections, they gathered at the huge outdoor arena.

Makenji and Ewusa walked forward, the whole community behind them, along with members of the ngumba house. Kajere could not believe everyone suddenly went silent in such a short time. At this point, Menago stepped forward and, starting with a trembling voice, he became louder as he spoke on:

"Ntubiseh people, welcome oh!" he said.

Everyone replied in unison, "We thank our creator!"

"People of Ntubiseh," he continued as solemnly as he could. "Welcome. Here we are again, a thousand moons after, to remember who we are and what is important for us." His voice volume, pitch, and tempo swelled. "My people, let's remember we are one in everything."

"Yaa, yaa!" everyone responded and rose as if in ovation. Then, as if on cue, the earth trembled, slowly at first. Feeling the ground shake, assured them that their prayers were taking effect. Kajere also noticed a concurrent eclipse taking place. The sun was in the middle of the sky, yet darkness was slowly descending on the arena. These Ntubisans must have very powerful mungang, Kajere thought.

Makenji and Ewusa sang, their voices loud and clear and the earth continued to tremble, getting stronger as darkness came down. Some of the puppets started turning turquoise, the same way Kajere and Zasheri had seen them do during the first sunset they saw upon their arrival at Ntubiseh. The earth was shaking but no rumbling or noise was heard except the singing voices of Makenji and Ewusa.

Kajere perceived three puppets spring up from the ground as if hurled by a formidable but invisible force. From the darkness above, too, descended one puppet, and all four met in front of Makenji and Ewusa. At this point, the entire assembly joined to sing in unison with Makenji and Ewusa.

A few minutes passed, the earth stopped trembling, and the darkness slowly receded. More minutes later, everything returned to normal, the turquoise hue disappearing and the singing coming to an end. Silence and stillness held sway as everyone fixated on the four puppet emanations standing beside Makenji and Ewusa. One of the apparitions hugged Makenji and the other clutched Ewusa. Kajere studied them all. They looked like the Ntubisans, but an ethereal, mysterious, mystical, and powerful aura marked them out. They walked, their gait was different, and their feet did not touch the earth. They floated but gave the appearance of walking all the time. As they hugged Makenji and Ewusa, their bodies seemed to fuse into them. They were ghostlike, yet clearly solid, and Kajere wondered how they combined the palpable and the ghostly simultaneously. He was awed.

When the beings spoke, a distinct tenor of dignity was carried over from their unearthly personalities. He thought of their voices as hollow and echoing, yet there was nothing of a scream or shout, even though they were perceived by all. They could whisper, too, which hinted at their human habits, yet their unearthly qualities astounded Kajere and he instantly knew that he would be in for more.

"My child, how are you?" the unearthly emanation asked Ewusa.

"Doing even better now that you have come to see us," Ewusa replied, smiling and embracing her back. There was a connectedness between them that went beyond familiarity. This emanation was Gwasamba, the goddess of carving and mother of Ewusa, it turned out. She had been reluctant to give Ewusa in marriage to Makenji until the whole community and the deity intervened. So, she always liked to return to see how he was treating her daughter, happy and smiling, when she found Ewusa in such good spirits.

Hugging Fon Makenji was his own father, Mvum, god of leisure and fun, who saw to the elimination of stress from the land.

"Welcome, father," Fon Makenji said reverently.

"What have you been up to since I last visited?" Mvum asked, looking at everyone and smiling but directing his question at Fon Makenji.

"Not much; same as you know," Fon Makenji replied. "But we have some visitors," he continued in the same reverent tone and posture.

The casual and relaxed manner of the conversation surprised Zasheri and Kajere. There was no superimposed unearthliness to indicate the weightiness of the one-in-1000-moon event. They must have special mungang to have this kind of relationship, Kajere thought. His thoughts were interrupted by one of the gods.

"And who is this?" she asked, looking at Zasheri, her smile switching into a suspicious scowl.

"Princess Zasheri," Ewusa replied, "She is of the Tikari and that is her guide, Kajere. They are going to Mekan in search of Kwifon," Ewusa spoke, mockery coloring her last comment. All four emanations went pale and transitioned into startled looks at the mention of the Kwifon of Mekan. It was not a look of disbelief but of curiosity.

"Seeking Kwifon?" Muhvi, goddess of the sea, asked.

Kajere nodded, and Zasheri did the same. The gods and goddesses buffeted them with prying questions; they were keen on knowing why the strangers were seeking the Kwifon.

"It does not exist," Muhvi said.

"It does," Zasheri and Kajere both replied at once, their confidence aided by the affable nature of the emanations.

"Impossible," Muhvi laughed.

"Kwifon exists," Kajere asserted stubbornly. "This gris-gris here is very strong mungang," he added, indicating the pendulum hanging from his neck.

"Our puppets can see us, which is why they believe in us. They also know we rule over their affairs," Muhvi said quietly, the severe look in the eyes of Kajere and Zasheri not escaping her.

"That is what we see," Kajere replied.

"How come you hold fast to an idea you have no clue of its existence, a thing you know nothing about?" Muhvi asked.

"We do not lack the clue that Kwifon exists, and is the most powerful being in the universe," Kajere replied. As he spoke, a gong sounded.

"We have a ritual to perform before Tsintoh starts; let's go," Muhvi said. "We'll talk more later." So saying, she walked away.

The crowd made way for the gods and goddesses to walk through and towards the edge of the sea. The general public followed, led by Makenji and Ewusa. From the edge, Muhvi slowly walked into the ocean, disappearing from view. Silence returned with absolute assertion as the crowd waited breathlessly, anticipating the next thing. Kajere felt the tense atmosphere without knowing the reason for it. Eventually, Muhvi emerged from the sea and carried a live chicken in her hands. The crowd exploded in wild joy, indicating that the ritual had begun successfully, and Kajere bathed in the warmth of the spectacle. Yet, he wondered how all the puppets from different parts of the community could come together with no hint of conflict, disagreement, or dislike. They did not even seem to show any sign of differentiation, even when some changed hue as the sun went down. They were one.

The ritual entered the second part with everyone seeming relaxed in what involved Menago, Makenji, and Ewusa together reporting the achievements of the past one thousand months.

Kajere and Zasheri managed to sneak in and meet at this moment when the puppets concentrated on the reports. It was one of the few times they had done so since they arrived at Ntubiseh. Zasheri was excited in a rather chaotic and inexpressible level of eagerness.

"How are you?" she asked, her eyes brimming with joyful eagerness. I've never been this happy in my life," she continued, unable to retract her eyes from Makenji and Ewusa, who were still deep in their reports, which were being given in chants.

"I'm fine," Kajere replied, excited but watching Makenji and Ewusa. Then he added, "Let's spend the rest of our lives here; we don't need to look for Kwifon any longer."

Zasheri did not hear what Kajere said, but agreed with him in her excitement as Makenji and Ewusa completed their chants. Menago reassembled the crowd of motley color differentiations.

Zasheri remarked about how remarkable the puppets' united differences were, but Kajere could not hear her above the din and excitement around them. "They are all different, yet they act like one and don't see any differences," Zasheri repeated her remark in different words. This provoked Kajere to look at the crowd again as if for the first time. It seemed they were gathering for another event. Their differences and their oblivious attitude to it struck him anew.

Zasheri made a quick comparison with the Tikari situation. "Back home, my sister and I argue; Wubangeh wants to seize the throne; the Ketummites keep invading us… and we all look alike. These puppets are so different, but they are so much of one mind and well organized!" she mused, regret coming up to the surface of her consciousness despite her excitement.

In different words, Kajere now repeated what he had said and Zasheri had missed because of the noise: "I won't like to leave this place. It's better than anything I will ever want." He was emotional, and her declaration had a touch of finality. Then Zasheri stole a glance at him and saw the determination in his eyes. Her mind suddenly became clouded, and compelling euphoria swept over her. It was a serene sensation and coursed through her body, causing her to shiver from the intensity. In that brief instant, she knew what Kajere felt.

Deep inside her still, she heard a voice calling her, which she ignored.

Around them, the crowd got more and more excited. Soon, the sound of drums was heard from afar and then it got closer, the puppets responding more frantically. Then the emanations sat on the dais and were flanked by Makenji and Ewusa. Behind them were Menago and the ruling council. Everyone was soaked in happiness and deeply involved.

Nvum whispered something to Gwasamba, who in turn whispered it to Ewusa. She nodded and whispered to Menago, who grinned diffusively and then quickly left the scene.

As Zasheri was voicing her concern to Kajere, some puppets came in, led by Menago. Then too, a group of dancers came towards them, lifted Zasheri, who squealed in excitement, placed her on a chair, and carried her towards the dais while others hoisted Kajere up and also took him to the dais. They sat Kajere between Nvum and Muhvi, while Zasheri sat between Etombe, the goddess of nature, and Gwasamba. Sitting between these emanations during the festival was considered a distinctive honor. Menago construed to bring this to the attention of Kajere and Zasheri, even though they already understood it and were most grateful and felt humbled by the recognition.

Dancers and masquerades stormed the arena, the spectacular performance they brought forth with skillful gyrations bearing witness to the conjecture that their lives were about dance and music. They were so impressive. The masquerades had different animal heads carved from wood that came in all shapes and sizes – cow heads, snakeheads, buffalo heads, lion heads, elephant heads, hyena heads, eagle heads, squirrel heads, and the heads of strange animals and birds which Kajere could not even envisage. All sections of the community had representative dancers and masquerades in a cacophony of colors. The masked puppets adorned with the heads of the various animals and birds danced, flanked by dancers from the different sections. The musical instruments used were the likes of which Kajere had never seen or heard before, and they produced the most delectable music he had heard. Not only Kajere but Zasheri was also entranced, which Ewusa noticed and moved to chit-chat with her about it.

"What do you think?" she asked.

"Is this how you live daily?" Zasheri asked, fascinated by the show.

"No, we are honoring our deities for overseeing us, especially as they are here today," Ewusa replied, smiling. We do have a weekly festival that involves everyone, though," she proudly announced.

If she had been sent to convince Zasheri to stay, she was doing an excellent job. As Zasheri watched the spectacle unfold in front of her, her eyes grew misty with extreme joy, girded with deep peace.

Kajere stole a glance in their direction and smiled, but stayed focused on the spectacle before him, which was quickly reaching a crescendo. The masquerades started dancing with greater vigor; dancers and the crowds erupted into paroxysms of laughter, tears, and total engrossment and talking in tongues. These were clear signs that the festival and the visit of the emanations were successful. Before Zasheri and Kajere could come to terms with the extraordinary potency of the dancing masquerades, they rose into the air, floating high above everyone, and transfixed the crowd, while their voices rose in unison, chanting and dancing. The emanations joined in while the floating masquerades maintained their rhythms, effortlessly dancing in the air.

Caught up in what was going on, Kajere found himself up and dancing, striving to imitate the puppets. It was awkward, and he certainly did a bad job of it, for laughter echoed from one part of the audience to the other, along with praise for his efforts. Zasheri joined him, and ululations burst out from many puppet corners. Kajere now danced more vigorously, the laughing crowd joining him, and he found himself close to Zasheri. They were literally captivated by what they were doing and by the spectacle.

"I will remain in this land, and I want to learn to sing and dance like these puppets," he said, breathing hard.

"Me too," she answered, also lost in the thrill of the rhythm.

A whiz of thought came to Kajere about the dancing drums of Mabukor, but that music paled into insignificant crassness when compared with what he was having right now.

Makenji and Ewusa put up a show for everyone, given their walk and gait. Eventually, the floating masquerades came down but continued dancing. The musicians strummed the instruments in slower but harder hits as the crowd was silenced to watch their king and queen dance and sing in alternative solos.

Makenji sang, great thrill and total expression in his voice:

Welcome to the land of love and life!
Welcome where music never ends!
Welcome where happiness lives!
Welcome where joy is core virtue!
Welcome where boredom is foreign!
Welcome to the forever land of life!
Welcome to Ntubiseh perpetuity!

Taking over with equal passion, Ewusa sang:
We will dance to the rhythm of njang,
Dancing the dance of everlasting joy.
In Ntubiseh happiness we delight
Spinning as we stir joyful bliss
In the best place in all the world
Where all selfishness is eschewed
And mutual respect is permanent.

Each line of their solo was taken up by the crowd in a repeated boom. At Ewusa's finale, the crowd exploded in applause and hailed the king and queen to their seats.

Unwavering, the masquerades danced, crooned by the crowd and the music. At last, after they had floated down and danced a long while, the masquerades took off, rising once more above the earth, continuing to dance. Then dusk fell, and some of the puppets started to turn turquoise. Kajere came to an understanding of what turquoise meant. For the puppets that turned turquoise took up another level of dancing and singing, along with the masquerades that had also turned turquoise. The thick dust in the arena was like fog as puppet feet shook up the particles of broken earth for so many hours. Darkness set in. The emanations departed for the evening, heralding an end to the proceedings amidst ululations, song, dance, and ritual pageantry. Makenji and Ewusa also left, and the arena slowly emptied out, many hours after, returning to a quiet, lonely place.

In the wee hours of the morning, Kajere sneaked into Zasheri's abode, something he knew was not allowed. After much convincing and help from Ewusa, Zasheri came to meet him, wondering what emergency had made him look for her so early in the morning.

"Are you okay?" she asked, concerned.

"Yes, my princess," he replied as solemnly as he could. At once, Zasheri sensed that there was trouble brewing.

"I have decided to remain here," he said. His enunciation was slow but firm.

Zasheri was already awaiting this moment and was not surprised at him. She was ready. "You have surely thought this out carefully; have you also thought carefully about our quest for Kwifon? Choices need balancing," she added after the stress on Kwifon.

Alacrity and levity were on Kajere's mouth and response, although he spoke slowly and avoided the eyes of the princess. "Yes, and I don't think we should waste our time looking for inexistence, which is the essence of Kwifon."

Zasheri had to be diplomatic and empathetic in order to tackle the crisis. “Kajere, I love it here also…” she began, but Kajere cut in, interrupting what she was about to add:

“Then let’s stay here. Let’s forget Tikari. Let’s forget all our troubles. We can start a new life here with these puppets,” he rattled on, still avoiding her eyes. He had caught an expression in the middle and converted it to nonsense in his intoxication with remaining in Ntubiseh.

Zasheri had to come forth more forthrightly: “I can’t do that. Tikari awaits us, expecting us to use the gris-gris to find Kwifon, a mission planned ages ago. We need to leave this place, and you are coming with me,” she said, attempting to use royal firmness on him, but she felt she was pouring water on a duck’s back.

Kajere spoke back. “All we seek in life is happiness, princess. We found it here.”

Zasheri had a hell of a time trying to show the loopholes of the situation. “These are puppets, not humans, Kajere. Can’t you see that? They are not us and not like us!” Her voice rose. The mention of the word ‘puppets’ seemed to strike a chord, making Kajere turn and face her for the first time. Zasheri saw this and doubled on her advantage: “These are puppets, mere puppets! We can never be like them.”

Kajere still tried to reason the matter out. “If puppets can be this happy, should we not be with them?” he asked matter-of-factly and, easy as the question sounded, Zasheri found it challenging to refute.

“We’ve got work to do, Kajere; we’ve got duties to fulfill,” she stuttered. “We owe it to Ngounso and the gris-gris.” Zasheri was getting desperate and knew she had to use an argument to unwind and win him over. How was she to make him know that happiness was not about a dog chasing its own wagging tail? How was he to know that what really mattered was duty in process and not gyration at the end, which can only be an effect rather than the cause of happiness?

Apparently, Kajere had totally forgotten about the gris-gris, for at its being mentioned, he yanked at it, trying to rip it off his neck and fling it at her. He tried really hard, but did not progress. It stuck to him like the duty against mere pleasure, which Zasheri was trying to impress on him. Totally exhausted because of the struggle with the gris-gris, he collapsed, foaming at the mouth, but not giving up just yet.

Although Zasheri had heard of it before, she had never seen anyone affected by *nshua*. She was sure now that it had Kajere by the throat. It was an ailment that attached you to the place and circumstance you found yourself in. It was not an initiative, impulse, or propellant, but more like gravity, the absence of resistance, something you kept going by, unresisting, inertia. From the look of it, nshua is not abrasive or harsh. Like the pliable softness of water, however, it penetrated to unimagined zones and corroded the hardy resistance or resilience of diamond-hard rock by sheer passive persistence. It was hard to handle because it was not confrontational or argumentative. It was just there with its inertia of indisputable presence. The gris-gris and the mungang of her seeds paled before this placid nuisance. Patience alone could be of help, Zasheri decided.

Kajere briefly paused, smiled, and then said, "I'll wait, but you cannot move." The smile on his face as she looked directly at her communicated nothing. It was like sound and fury that said nothing, a fool's paradise showing forth.

Zasheri was beside herself with the discomfort of indecision. Before she could regain composure, a group of puppets came by and were excited to see, who in turn got excited at seeing them. There was some chemistry between them that Zasheri found difficult to interpret.

"We are going to the farm. Care to come along with us?" one of them asked. Kajere looked at Zasheri and, wishing to have enough time to think something out, simply smiled wanly and nodded.

"Oh yes," Kajere responded excitedly, forgetting everything he had just discussed with Zasheri.

She had never seen him that contented. Gris-gris would have to work overtime to get them out of this brainless bliss. But at that moment, sudden dizziness came over her and persisted. She tried walking away but only stumbled forward. Her mind was getting numb, foggy, and forgetful. Much as she tried, she could not remember who she was or anything for that matter. She only felt a strong, impulsive desire to stay on in Ntubiseh. At that thought, warmth enveloped her entire person, and a swirl of joyful contentment wrapped her. Hot tears of joy ran down her cheeks as she floundered to her quarters. Not even when Kajere first came to Tikari with the long-awaited promise of freeing them from the dreaded Ketummites had she felt this overwhelming happiness. She, too, was in the grips of nshua now.

Nine

Turmoil in Tikari

Yafon woke up to the noise outside and the cold gusty morning, which she read as an ill omen. The hard wind was unprecedented, rustling through the leaves of all the trees, scaring birds and animals to shelter. Morning bird sounds were muted and made the environment eerily hollow. In league with this fierce silence of usual morning sounds, lightning flashed across the skies, and the earth rumbled in thundering echo. This day, Ngounso and Wubangeh would combat each other, the single day Ngounso needed her most.

Yafon woke up and started getting ready when a rustle behind her announced Ngounso's presence. This perplexed her because Ngounso had never come to her quarters unannounced.

"Nangie," she said, a little out of breath: "Are you okay?"

"I am trying my best; it's hard," Ngounso replied, trying to stay calm but Yafon saw her vulnerable feeling beneath the composure.

"Any message or sign from the Princess yet?" Yafon inquired, Ngounso's vulnerability catching up with her as well.

"Nothing," said Ngounso, her voice flatter than Yafon had ever heard.

"That doesn't sound good," Yafon said. "At the least, they should be aware of what's going on here."

"They are in some kind of trouble. Otherwise, this could not escape their notice." Despite her own circumstances, Ngounso was concerned about Zasheri and Kajere. It had to be something grave if the gris-gris did not react.

"Everyone knows your mungang can defeat Wubangeh's, and even Wubangeh too knows this," Yafon tried to be reassuring. Even as she said so, she was worried about what could happen to her, too. She quickly added, "There must be something we can do. We can't allow Tikari to collapse without a fight. It worries everyone." Distress rang in her voice.

Ever considerate and an encouragement, Ngounso firmly encouraged, "Yafon, you have to be strong; we have to be strong and not make ourselves the object of his mockery. Listen to me closely," she continued as calmly as she could afford under the circumstances.

Encouraged by Ngounso's reassuring words, Yafon continued "Nangie, you have not even fought yet. You will defeat him."

"I will lose, Yafon," Ngounso said with melancholic calm.

"Nangie, you cannot say such a thing? You cannot lose. You are Ngounso, the one who traveled away for centuries to bring Kajere, the man with the gris-gris to save Tikari. You will defeat Wubangeh, no matter the mungang he boasts of?" Then, she paused for breath, breathing hard and transposed to another realm by the sounds of her own words.

A mother, Ngounso smiled and held Yafon's hands. "Thank you. I am not surrendering, but Wubangeh will have Kuriyango to help him." Her words brought Yafon back to Tikari.

"You have the most powerful mungang in the land. Wubangeh cannot win."

Yafon was unprepared for Ngounso's grim revelation: "When the princess left, I gave her all my powerful mungang."

Shock silenced her for a minute before she spoke. "You mean you have nothing other than what I know you have?"

Ngounso nodded.

"Oh! Oh! Oh! Cheiiii! What shall we do now?" Yafon threw the words to the universe and knew the answer could not even blow in the angry winds.

"This I need from you," Ngounso began and said, "Continue working until the princess and Kajere return." Then, she drew Yafon closer and made her reluctantly kneel.

"Nangie, but even the mungang you still have can defeat Wubangeh. Please, hear me."

Ngounso cut her off sternly: "You will do as I say." Her cutting-edge tone told Yafon that compliance was the only option.

"Wubangeh may defeat me, but he must not sit on the throne for long. Suliya will not be long in coming for it. Only stand fearlessly firm when I lose to Wubangeh. Be strong till Suliya arrives."

"Suliya knows nothing yet, not even about Kajere, his presence or absence with the princess seeking the Kwifon." Even with the foreboding and challenge pushed forth by Ngounso's unquestionable utterance, Yafon's confidence grew as she felt privileged to be privy to major secrets of the land.

"Even so, I am inclined to think that Kuriyango has whispered a thing or two to Nabangua since they both despise me."

Yafon on her knees on the floor, Ngounso rubbed her hands, spat on them and placed them on her head, saying, "If my mungang fails in the fight with Wubangeh and I am forced into the forbidden forest, let your word be strong until our princess and Kajere return." Then she rubbed Yafon's head and face, removed the cowries around her neck, and put them around the still startled Yafon's neck. While she did this, the wind decreased in violence and virtually ceased as the morning sun rose. Near the arena, the crowds began to gather, and the two women heard the crowd's excited expectations.

In Wubangeh's camp, while Ngounso endowed Yafon with all the power and authority she still had, Wubangeh impatiently paced around his quarters with Kamesu and Asabuna in attendance. There was no chance of his letting an iota of his authority, power, or possession drop. With disproportionate loudness pitched on hoarse impatience, he roared, "Where is she? I told you that I wanted her here?"

Kamesu and Asabuna cowered. His very presence, even without the hoarse roar, was intimidating. Kumesu's voice quivered as he said, "We told her you wanted her here. Something must have cropped up to hold her back."

Wubangeh gathered his thoughts. As a few minutes passed, Asabuna ventured as before to ask, "Do you really want to fight Ngounso?"

Wubangeh's arrogance would not process the weight of the question. He roared so loud that the earth vibrated and retorted rhetorically, "What question is that? Wubangeh I am, unconquerable and Ngounso will not even begin in that direction." He puffed out his chest and strutted around with the arrogance of a cockerel among hens. At this point, a rap at the door announced Kuriyango, who stepped in silently.

The welcome she got was hard and loud: "Where were you?" he thundered.

"I had to get myself ready. Do you underestimate the magnitude of this fight? There is great potency in a fight after which Tikari will change. You ask me where I was? Can you be so small-brained as to miss out on the full scale and impact of what is about to happen? We are talking here about Tikari and the dramatic change it will soon experience." As she spoke, Kuriyango was looking at him, eyes not batting. Wubangeh was staring back, eyes bloodshot, but that did not frighten her. In critical times, little intimidations are wont to lose their pristine value.

Kuriyango pursued, "Tell me or name a single place where a non-entity like you ever overthrew a fon and his inner chambers?"

She paused to let her insult sink in. Wubangeh said nothing, seeing rather the narrow possibilities before him. Clearly, the prospect of moving from his sublime quest to ridiculous rubbishing was one false step away. "You have no inkling about the implication of your actions, engrossed as you are only in ascending the throne without the preliminary requirements. You are gunning for privileges without the willingness to sacrifice. It is hard to tell whether you can even guess the requirements or the kind of work you have to do as a leader. Your ambition does not bring to focus the perspectives of other people, far or near, and how you will impact them!"

Wubangeh did not answer.

"If I speak amiss, point out the fault." Kuriyango would have liked to provoke him to utter a more incriminating word. Barely concealing her wrath, she stared at him, and he returned the favor. A few minutes passed, their eyes locked in this unfriendly mutuality, watched by Kamesu and Asabuna, who waited to see the first flinch. Her mind full, Kuriyango soon batted, and the umpires justly or unjustly decided that Wubangeh had outdone her. As if to corroborate their unannounced verdict, Wubangeh smiled and coaxed, a conciliatory demeanor doing the rest as his face broke into the smirk of a smile with the words, "You know how important you are to me." By crook, force, or plea, as by friendliness, Wubangeh got the upper hand even if Kuriyango did not return the smile as she acknowledged it with a nod.

Wubangeh needed time to gather his broken ego. He looked at the three present and thought deeply. He planned to change the course of Tikari's history, whatever else he did. He wanted to make history and, for the first time, pass leadership of the land into the hands of someone other than was designated by Zasheri's ancestors. He was breaking new ground, or so he wanted it to look, given that as far as history went, only Zasheri's ancestors had ruled in the realm. He did not need to go sampling opinions on the necessity of his action.

His desire for the throne came from deeper designs than he had time or ability to analyze.

He had tipped himself as best qualified to handle the crises when the Ketummites abducted Fon Azunga and his father. In his view, his physical and mental capacity could figure out the Ketummite hazard. But there was the gris-gris with Kajere, which he would have liked to have. He suggested to himself that perhaps he could do without it. Yet, a shiver ran down his spine at the thought that Kajere and Zasheri were still loitering somewhere. Without news of their capture by the Ketummites, they remained a threat to him. But that was no holdback on his designs, for he had made up his mind that his destiny was to lead the Tikari. He was going to prove this by getting rid of the vestiges of the leadership of the land, in the person of Ngounso. Outside, the wind had died down. He could see the sun rising brightly above the trees.

Wubangeh believed that he had gathered massive support among the Tikari; that he had convinced many of his supporters to lead them against the foreign intrusion, especially by the Ketummites. He even told some that the Ketummites would never come again, and knew this was a risky assumption. Those were campaign promises, which he would deal with after defeating and exiling Ngounso.

Kamesu cleared his throat to attract Wubangeh's attention. He looked back and asked, "Everyone is going to the palace to watch the competition. Are you ready?"

"A moment, Wubangeh," Kamesu replied.

"I have told you that from today, how any of you must address me. I am the leader, no longer Wubangeh. What did I tell you to call me? Or have you already forgotten?"

"I'm sorry, your highness general," Kamesu replied.

"Remember that and always," he said, glancing across the rest. "The people of Tikari will learn from you."

All nodded, including Kurinyango, who added a cynical smile

to the nod and commented: "Now you are beginning to understand what it means to be a leader." It was difficult to see whether Kuriyango was being sarcastic or just commenting. Those were not niceties that Wubangeh dwelled on at that moment.

"I have been waiting for this competition for ages. I have been ready since before the sun was created," he added with a mirthless laugh.

"Thank you, your highness, general. Let me summon the chindas and the musicians," Asabuna said, going out. "Follow me when the drumming starts," he added.

Ngounso's tension mounted as she struggled to fit into her competition attire, her maids not believing she could lose. Yafon had a tough time keeping cool as she dished out instructions to the maids. Ngounso's calm did not moderate the emotional chaos. Centuries before, Azunga had chosen her as the prophetess because of her ability to be a cool thinker with lucidity even under extreme pressure. Such times were certainly rare, but here was one and in extremis.

True, Tikari was not the perfect land, for troubles came as they went, not least the Ketummites invasions. Yet, you could not classify it as a land of woes. In fact, things were always great, and under Zasheri, things had been serene and pleasing.

Troublemakers like Wubangeh and Suliya were always lurking, but they were not invasive, always under control.

Ngounso watched Yafon and her other maids prepare her for the competition; she knew she had to maintain a posture of calm dignity. Without, they could all hear the excited crowds walking past, arguing among themselves on their way to the arena. The perennial topic was about who would be the victor in the combat.

"Everything is alright," Ngounso said with as much authority in her voice as she could muster. "I don't want to hear anything. But Yafon, as I told you, you are to be in charge." The attempted authority in her voice carried a hollow ring in this slightly coded reminder to Yafon about taking control, short of announcing the result of the temptation against her favor.

"We can't just let them heap insults on you and those of us supporting you," said Ngunini, one of her maids. "Is that the new Tikari down-road of decay?"

Although everyone was beginning to think about what would happen, they did not want to dwell on the possibility of Wubangeh exiling them all.

"Wubangeh does not have the heart to do that," Yafon said, making final touches on Ngounso's readiness. Where could their Princess Zasheri be at this moment? Yafon wondered. With her and the command of authority she had, none of this nonsense would be happening.

Ngounso had the same thoughts as Yafon. She was convinced that Zasheri and Kajere must have found themselves in deep trouble. That was how she explained why neither the gris-gris nor the munging she gave Zasheri seemed to be working. Her focus, away from her own plight, zoomed in on the well-being of Kajere and Zasheri.

She wondered what exactly was blocking them from sensing that there was trouble in Tikari. As if to find an answer, she looked fixedly at Yafon, who had completed her task and was admiring Ngounso's perfect, ready look for the competition. Her garments stuck cleanly to her body like a second skin. She liked how her amulets hung around her waist and clung to her body. If only everyone knew they were almost powerless against the better and stronger charms that Wubangeh had. Yafon had ensured they were visible to make Wubangeh think her mungang was powerful. They had some power, but not enough to rescue Ngounso from Wubangeh's.

Ngounso knew it was time for her to walk towards the arena as a loud shout from outside heralded the sound of the gong. It was loud and exciting outside. Inside her quarters, everyone became quieter at the sound of the gong. It was as if the gong had just informed them that there would be a competition, as if they did not already know that. There was fear in all their eyes, but it was time.

"Are you ready?" Yafon dared to ask, trying to appear cheerful and robust, her voice puncturing the silence that hung like dark, pregnant clouds, heralding a stormy rain.

"Yes, I'm ready," Ngounso said, not losing her calm and trying hard not to scare her own people.

"Now, let's teach that idiot a lesson," Yafon said, with false confidence in her tone. Then, she began ululating as loudly as she could. Music and dance followed, and the maids created and danced in a circle with Ngounso in the middle. The song encouraged Ngounso, and she bellowed in an ecstatic verve that transported her to a liminal place. They were glad to see how ready she looked for the challenge.

Seeing this exhilaration in her mistress, Yafon whispered with delight, "Nangie, don't ever give up. Wubangeh does not know what will hit him. You will be victorious."

"Don't overthink, Yafon, but I am Ngounso. I will give it my all," she whispered back, smiling wanly. "Remember that if I don't win, you have to wait until you are sure of what has happened to me before you do anything. I know Wubangeh will want Kuriyango to take my position, though he is selfish and wants all the power to himself. Watch out for Iamba; she's a green snake in green grass."

"Yes, Nangie," Yafon whispered reluctantly, sensing the tone of deathbed wishes in her words. She adjusted Ngounso's costume and amulets as they continued to the arena. There, Ngounso danced wildly, sweating profusely, urged on by her crowd of supporters who also knew what her victory would mean to them. The land had become divided, and not since Suliya took some clans away to Kumbat to form her territory had Tikari been so divided. While she acknowledged them for supporting her, Ngounso felt deep melancholy. She knew she had to buy time and do everything she could until Zasheri returned.

As she examined her supporters and well-wishers, Ngounso wondered how and why everything had become conflict, division, and chaos. She regretted that she had not been allowed to reach an agreement with Wubangeh that would benefit the land and its people. Tikari did not have to go through with this, she thought. Yet, even as she saw the eyes and faces of those clapping for her, she knew Tikari was about to be dramatically altered and remain so until Zasheri returned. She wondered whether all the people were really going to fall under Wubangeh. Would they accept him? How did he manage to sow such seeds of hatred among his people?

In his quarters, Wubangeh also heard the gong. Asabuna and Kamesu had done an excellent job in readying him. His outfit also clung to him like a second skin, showing his bulging muscles. Around both his wrists were layers of amulets; around his waist, he had layers of charms and mungangs as well. He was superbly ready for whatever Ngounso was up to. From her corner, Kuriyango stared at him without uttering a word.

Wubangeh watched the guides and herald take their positions to lead him to the competition, thinking of how far he had come in preparation for the moment. It had been a distant dream until now. A dream which he was not too sure of was happening in real life and conveniently earlier than he had thought possible. Kajere's appearance had been a major hurdle, but now the world was at his feet. Nothing could stop him from taking what he considered was rightfully his. He was the lawful ruler of Tikari, soon to be proven in his defeat of Ngounso.

The gong sounded, and Wubangeh sprang up, literally bouncing up and going out. At the sight of him coming out, his supporters shouted loud and long, joy intoxicating them. Thrilled by their loud salutation, he made a few dance turns to show his readiness for the competition. Not as if his assurance was without blemish. He was aware of the land being in a chaotic state, a period of uncertainty and change, a time of necessary and transforming pain and metamorphosis. The entrails of the culture that had governed the land for centuries were in paroxysms that would issue in establishing a new era. It was destined to be led into the future by him.

Sly Suliya sent some spies to Tikari to report on the competition to her. They infiltrated the Wubangeh camp as well as the Ngounso side of supporters. Master planner Nabangua had encouraged them to sow seeds of confusion among the supporters of each base. Thus, they would weaken them in readiness for Suliya to take control of Tikari in the absence of Zasheri if Wubangeh won the fight.

An august and memorably rare event, even flora and fauna felt the rhythms of change affecting the land. The birds were rather in a languorous flight mood, sluggishly slow, so to say, in a bid to participate in the proceedings right from their vantage aerial positions. The grunting field animals paused to watch and hear, unaccustomed to a frenzy of this vibrancy among the people. The only distant comparison to the frenzy was when the Ketummites raided. As far as it was visible to the beasts, none of the Ketummites were visible in the vicinity at that moment.

Time tumbled by, and the moment arrived for Wubangeh and Ngounso to arrive at the Tchongwa arena, which was teeming with expectant spectators. Everyone who could, was there. It was not a spectacle to sit behind and get secondhand feeds from those who would see it happen firsthand. In front, in the very first row, sat the leaders, patient in wait but restless in anticipation. They sat symmetrically in groups of bird feathers, each with those they affiliated with.

The curiosity was to the right, where sat the new ngumba house members, brought in by Wubangeh. He had handpicked them for their unflinching support of his schemes. As far as he was concerned, all members of the traditional ngumba were irrelevant and banished. His new picks had not even gone through any initiation process. Wubangeh claimed that his mungangs were powerful enough to cleanse and ready them for their roles.

The drums rumbled while the xylophone emitted a non-resonant, precise, penetrating melody. The blend of the two was resonating melodiousness with an atavistic tinge to which dancers and musicians from both factions nodded as they slowly made their way to the arena. Tailing them were Ngounso and Wubangeh, whose entrance the crowd saluted with hoots that told of their sides and expectations, name-calling according to support inclination being part of the noise.

Then the gong boomed, and dead silence squelched even creaking sounds. Bare-chested and attired in a ngwashie that loosely hung down, Ntukenteh of the Bakunteh clan rose. Smudges of various shades pockmarked his body, signifying the multiple mungangs on him, his eyes large and red as if he had ingested some over-peppered concoction. Long before the competition, when the Bakunteh clan announced it would come, those who might have been lackluster realized that the matter would be unprecedented. Not only were the Bakuntehs the farthest Tikari clan, but they also hardly ever participated in the festivities or ceremonies of the land. Their distant location must have partly accounted for their rarity. But much might have had to do with Nkukanteh, a hardliner, albeit a consistently fair and just person in every situation and whatever he said or did. He was dependable and of the higher value beings whom Zasheri never troubled with anything unless absolute necessity dictated. He was one of the few who escaped the last Ketummite rampage. He had been closely associated with Azunga and Wubangeh's father, Cheikah. Wubangeh, who was now threatening to break the land in two by facing Ngounso in competition, had been with him when the Ketummites last appeared.

Legend grew around Nkukanteh that the Ketummites were too afraid of his powers, which is why they had not captured him. As with most reputations of heroism, the truth was less glamorous:

Nkukanteh had been nowhere near the Ketummites when they had been gathering and taking away everyone. His mood at the moment was one of regret and anger at having to preside over a competition between two people of the Tikari clan. It was easy to think he was sympathetic towards Ngounso's cause, yet he had not shown any bias or support for either contestant.

A rugged man of gritty pastoral toning and attitude, he cleared his throat loudly and spat out phlegm nearby. Straight from that gruff action, he went straight to the core of the day's matter. "We are here today to witness something I never dreamed I would ever encounter since Tikari was created. Two important people in our great land have decided to compete against each other for the throne. I don't know if craziness has descended upon us." His bloodshot eyes glared at everyone, glowering in suppressed anger before continuing. "I did not want to be here, but decided to come and be a witness to how low Tikari has fallen in fact. I came in order to personally witness the depravity and to know what to report to Princess Zasheri upon her return."

It was clear that the enterprise they were engaging in went against his spirit and desire, whether he sided with one side or the other. While one side of the crowd cheered him on, the other shouted him down and out.

Wubangeh certainly had no patience for his discourse about depravity. "Can we start? Do not waste my time," he spurted as loudly as he could, and the area of the crowd supporting him, laughed and cooed. The rest were stony silent, seeing in the very response to the great Nkukanteh, one proof of the depravity he detested. And in truth, no one had ever dared interrupt Nkukanteh, certainly not in an open arena and in public. Confident about winning the competition, Wubangeh wanted to let everyone know who the strong man and ruler was. His way of illustrating this was to challenge the one whom everyone in the land held in awe and great esteem.

Evidently distraught and barely holding back boiling fury, Nkukanteh paused for a moment, looked piercingly at Wubangeh, and kept his cool. Not every battle was worth the fight of a man of any substance; it seemed to have been the ultimate argument for his calm.

The shock of Wubangeh's words and attitude absorbed, a few whispers ensued. "You heard what he said to Nkukanteh? He lacks respect. That's what will descend on us if he wins – chaos, decadence, depravity, as Nkukanteh prefers to say," Yafon whispered to Ngounso as a way of steeling her.

"I know what he's trying to do," Ngounso whispered back.

Nkukanteh's assistant, just then, dashed for and brought some water and palm wine in giant gourds. These he placed in front of Nkukanteh, who, kneeling and spreading his outstretched arms and hands over, mumbled some incoherent incantations (in tongues, it seemed). He was hardly through with the mumbled words when a giant bird flew down from nowhere. Nkukanteh sprang onto its back, and his assistants handed him all the guards. Immediately, he was airborne far into the sky. Then, it started somersaulting stunts, with Nkukanteh clinging to it and clinging to the gourds in acrobatic fashion for a few minutes. Nkukanteh did not fall; neither did a drop of water or palm wine spill from the gourds. The mesmerized crowd sang and stamped its feet because Nkukanteh and bird actions had decreed the competition valid.

The bird then slowly descended to barely above the competition arena and the crowd. At that point, Nkukanteh opened the gourds and spilled water and palm wine over the area as well as on Wubangeh and Ngounso. The public, particularly Wubangeh supporters, went ballistic, excited anticipation multiplying the noise in pitch and volume. The bird eventually landed, and Nkukanteh got off it, returned to his seat, and the loud gong proclaimed the presentation of the competitors. Ngounso and Wubangeh marched forth and stood before Nkukanteh. He brushed them both with a sacred leaf which he had inserted into the calabashes. Then he declared the competition started.

"You both understand the rules," he said firmly. "To win, you must pass all ten tests. The first to finish wins. Any questions?"

No question forthcoming, he took a few minutes to climb up to his seat high above the arena, the contestants watching. From their vantage point, he and his assistants could watch everything. The moment arrived, and he signaled for the horn to be sounded.

The first test was wood splitting, two thousand firewood logs. Whoever finished splintering them first won. Wubangeh smiled and got himself ready at the starting point. Ngounso stared at the logs of wood. She knew she could do it, but had less confidence in her speed. She noticed the confidence and amulets as he stole a glance at her competitor. A deep and sinking feeling at the bottom of her stomach made her feel as if something was dropping off from her womb.

The until-now noisy crowd hushed. Not since Azunga's fight with Vetsem many centuries before had anyone dared to take on these obstacles. Tikari's future was staked in the fight. Legend had Vetsem as an imposter who tried to usurp the throne, leading to his epic battle with Azunga. So, when Wubangeh proposed the test and Ngounso accepted it, the importance of this competition was generally understood. While the winner stood to gain a lot, the loser's loss was colossal.

They went to it with all the engaging drive of a do-or-be-outdone target. Their sinews strained against their outfits. Even before the first test, sweat was already pouring down their faces and bodies as they waited for Nkukanteh to give the signal in the late morning heat. Nkutankeh, his look fixed on the guide with the horn, raised his hand and nodded. The guide blew his horn loudly, and the deep blast heralded the beginning of the competition. Both Wubangeh and Ngounso attacked the wood ferociously. The crowd screamed in excitement, each side urging their hero on. Yafon was surprised at Ngounso's vigor, and she shouted her encouragement. But Ngounso felt her arms and shoulders tensing painfully by the time she had fragmented shy of two hundred logs.

Ngounso wondered why they used wood from the iroko tree. It had the hardness of black rocks and was the hardest tree in the land. She took a side glance and was sure Wubangeh had shattered perhaps twice as many logs as she had done, and his fan club was urging him on. Her own palms were beginning to blister, but she knew she had to save Tikari and do so with all the energy and endurance she could muster.

Yafon urged Ngounso on, telling her how brave and powerful she was. She smiled to herself at Yafon's unyielding loyalty, which soothed her pain and discomfort. It was also a psychological test, for when the focus was on the hardwood, defeat filtered into her psyche. She focused on other things rather than the wood she was breaking. She was hoping that this tactic of diversion would take away the pain. It did some good, as she found herself attacking the wood with more ferocity.

Wubangeh complacently smiled to himself after shooting a quick glance at his opponent's state of things. He could already feel his destined role as the next Fon of Tikari. Suliya and Zasheri, being both away, was to him an indication of his illustrious fate, all obstacles obliterated even if only circumstantially. The sole but weak obstacle now was just Ngounso, and the way she went about the wood blasting was promise enough that he would have an easy ride. From his gauge, she was unlikely to outlast even this very first of the nine tests. How else would he find himself in this situation if the deities had not destined it that way, he reasoned.

Around his waist, scores of amulets shook and dangled. He could feel their power pumping into his sinews. He knew that Ngounso's mungang and charms had little more than aesthetics about them. He attacked the wood wildly, shattering and letting them scatter in all directions.

On and on they went and by the time Ngounso was about two-thirds way through, Wubangeh was approaching the last few logs. He had no sign of pain and no blisters on his palms. He felt his amulets were doing great in boosting and in protecting him.

Meanwhile, Ngounso seemed to gain some invigoration, repelling the pain from her blisters. Although she was trailing him, he could not dismiss the fact that she was still in the competition, which drove him on even harder.

When Ngounso heard a section of the crowd roar, she knew Wubangeh had completed the first task. Indeed, he had. She stole a side glance in his direction and saw him kneel in front of Nkutankeh. Her section of the crowd, Yafon in the lead, was urging her on. Then, from nowhere, a second surge of tremendous inner strength pulsated in her, powering her to quickly complete the task to her own stunning surprise. Even Wubangeh was jolted, and by the time he began the second task, she was not far behind him. Her section of the crowd became vociferously encouraging.

Noticing that she was still a serious threat to his ambition, Wubangeh sought to wilt her spirits by demeaning her success so far, "I see that you have survived the first one," A mischievous smile caressed the sides of his mouth as his aides rubbed him down, preparing him for the second challenge.

"Yes, I also see you survived it," she replied, echoing his derision. She knew his aim at intimidating her, but she would take none of it.

"We'll see how you do with the second," he said, the grin still etched on his face.

"Why don't you focus on yourself? When Zasheri and Kajere return, they will take over Tikari," she announced, smiling. She knew the confident mention of the absent strong people was a blow to his arrogance.

"So, you too believe that fiction of Kwifon's existence?" Wubangeh mocked before continuing, "Your princess and that little foreigner are gone forever. And if you ask me, good riddance." Ngounso's brilliant completion of the first test made him wary of all his mockery of her rival. He anxiously began in earnest to get ready for the next. Their guides were still massaging them while awaiting the next test. Although Yafon noticed the exchange, she held her tongue and, pretending not to do so, caught Kuriyango surreptitiously staring at her.

The second endeavor was about chicken catching, a hundred free-ranging and wild chickens having to be caught and put into each prepared *kenjas*. Having grown up in the wilds and being many years old, the chickens were energetic. They had survived countless attempts on their lives. They were thus super athletic and so mischievous that some people thought the chickens had mungangs of their own. This supposition was difficult to outargue because of the creatures' self-serving and mesmerizing running and flight skills. They could take care of themselves against most of the danger in the vicinity.

The gong sounded; Wubangeh and Ngounso gave chase. The crowd roared, their noise mixing with and getting lost in the sounds of music tearing the air. The drummers and other musicians strummed and beat the instruments with total abandon, accentuating the festive tension that rocked the atmosphere.

The chickens rapidly took to flight, as if on purpose, in all directions, being not only worked up by the chase, but frightened by the explosive festivity. Danger so loud and near, they raced with determination never to be caught or even closely approached by their pursuers.

The determination of the chickens was nothing compared to that of the contestants. Ngounso knew that everything she had ever known or lived for would be in jeopardy if she gave up. She knew that she had to show Wubangeh that, despite the help he was getting from his amulets and that she had given her own powers to Zasheri to go after an even more significant cause for the land, he was not really her match. The chickens seemed to sense the stakes and did not make anything easy for her. By the time she had filled her first kenja of five, Wubangeh already had caught over thirty and was again about with her mocking laughter. His dexterity in catching chicken after chicken was superlative.

"You ought to have joined and aided me to take over the governance of Tikari instead of accepting my challenge," he mocked. "Only those with powerful mungang can do what I do. You can see for yourself. I will make you regret this."

Wubangeh had no monopoly on spirit-dampening mockery. Ngounso returned the favor with acidity. "What did you do when Kajere defeated you?" she asked to deflate his ego. Her intention worked a little, as a scowl crept from the sides of Wubangeh's mouth and enveloped his entire face, laughter momentarily leaving him.

On and on, they went, each exhibiting skill and talent in the chase and entrapment of the chickens. Ngounso showed why Azunga had chosen her to be the prophetess of Tikari. She would not give up, a woman of enduring resilience. High above the competitors, from where he sat watching the proceedings, Nkukanteh was impressed with her combativeness, though he felt she would lose because she had no help. His mungangs had already indicated that to him. These were also mean chickens, for after they were in kenjas, they fought to free themselves, fiercely pecking Wubangeh or Ngounso. Both contestants exhibited great skill in avoiding these attacks.

Although Ngounso came second once more, her effort made Wubangeh think. She finished closer to him than he had thought possible. He had to expend more energy than he had expected, and now knew for sure that it would not be an easy ride. It was not going to be an easy competition, he realized, but he tried to derisively smile at her. She was aware that his purpose was to try breaking her slowly.

"The real competition is yet to begin," he told her. "We will see if you can find *tuffih*," he mocked.

"Nobody has ever seen tuffih," she said, "and maybe if you see it, you will tremble like a child," she laughed, walking away because she did not want to see the dark look that enveloped his face. She knew she had touched a raw nerve.

She wondered if she could do the unthinkable and beat him without help from the amulets, and he, too, pondered the chances of that happening. While they caught their breath for the third endeavor, the crowd quickly shifted its focus and position to tuffih, the disappearing animal of the labyrinth. They had been waiting for this. Most of them held that it was the most difficult of the tests. The maze had hundreds of rare tall trees as its construction material and was rumored to be dark and eerie inside. Tuffih was the elusive animal that few had ever seen. It could only be detected using some supernatural powers. Finding it with the tuft of its hair was the endgame of the third endeavor. This was compounded by the fact that while it was a tall order to find the animal, the maneuvering of one's way out of the labyrinth was a most challenging puzzle. Many of those who had gone in got lost and never returned. Even those who claimed to have seen it could not give an exact description of what it really looked like, not even Nkukanteh, who was reputed to know everything about Tikari.

Ngounso was aware of these challenges, and before this third trial, Yafon confided in her. "I am certain that no matter where they are, Princess and Kajere are thinking about you. I can't believe you almost won the second competition," she said delightedly, which was her way of encouraging her. "He's started to doubt himself. He's scared," she continued, confidence bristling on her as she rubbed Ngounso's muscles.

"I am exhausted," Ngounso said. "Let's focus on tuffih. Any ideas?"

"Focus, Nangie, focus. Think of Tikari. We are all behind you." Yafon did not like the feeling that her mentor was losing the fight. She determined not to show Ngounso any weakness to hang onto. She wondered what Tikari would look like without Ngounso.

Ngounso knew that at this third trial, Wubangeh's amulets and mungangs could play a significant role in determining who would win the contest. It was extremely dangerous, and everyone knew it. She needed some help to complete the endeavor, and the battles coming after this were cranked higher with danger. Yet, the future of Tikari was at stake, and much depended on what would happen in the contest. Strangely, Wubangeh left his own camp and walked over to where Ngounso was. Then he gingerly and quietly sat beside her. This shocked Yafon and the others, who kept their eyes on him. Ngounso motioned for them to leave, for she sensed that he wanted no publicity of what he wanted to communicate to her. As soon as her maids left, Wubangeh went straight to the point:

"I no longer want us to compete," he said in an extraordinarily quiet voice and submissive mien.

Everything, from his manner, gesture, words and tone took Ngounso by surprise. The humility, or what seemed like a humble approach, was not the kind of thing you associated with Wubangeh. He gave what sounded like an explanation for his proposal, "I realize something must have happened to you. Your mungang has no power to survive tuffih; we both know that. If you enter the labyrinth, you will never return," he added.

Wubangeh was not to be trusted easily. "What are you trying to say?" she asked guardedly, instantly suspecting some deceit or trick.

"I am suggesting that you surrender and I will not exile you. Instead, I will allow you to live here and, even though I will make Kuriyango my prophetess, you will take orders directly from me," he said, and a moment of stiff silence ensued.

That witch, Ngounso thought, when he mentioned Kuriyango.

She should have suspected her motives. She decided to go to the roots and demanded: "What of Kajere and Princess Zasheri? At which point or position do they fit into your plans?" she asked, unblinking. For her, taking the throne by stealth, cunning, or violence was on the same plane.

"They are lost and will never return here. Forget about them and focus on the now, the new Tikari taking off soon," Wubangeh's reply was quietly stern.

"You are obviously sorry for me and want me to become one of your toothless, obsequious chindas at your beck and call, cringing at your feet everywhere, right?" She expected her sarcasm to enervate him; instead, he nodded, naively or cunningly ignoring the acerbity in her question.

Both their camps nervously waited around them, not knowing what outcome to expect from the encounter. Nkukanteh watched them from his high position and could guess what the result would be. In the background, the crowd continued in noisy anticipation, the musicians and drummers strumming disorderly and jarring discords of pace and tune.

In his affected or ignorant lack of understanding, Wubangeh began speaking, "Now you started to reason with me…"

Ngounso angrily interrupted him, "You always lack vision, Wubangeh, which is why you can never be a ruler, only a bully. People like you have always been bad luck anywhere they are found." She was so furious that she found it hard to breathe.

Her reaction stunned Wubangeh not only because of the content but because of the fiery way it was delivered. She heaped more on him:

"You heard me! You've already brought nothing but confusion and division into Tikari. Look at what you've done," she said, pointing at the divided crowd, some of whom supported him, and some her. "Tikari has lost its luster, thanks to your greed and reckless desire for dominance. We were the envy of others far and near. Now we are torn into pieces by your divisive and selfish insensitivity. Your father must be cowering in shame at what you have turned out to be and are doing now. Do you have anything else to say?"

"Ingrate! Churlish woman!" Wubangeh snarled, gasping for breath because it was as if Ngounso had slammed shame on his face. Besides himself with fury, he screamed, "I will teach you a lesson," storming off. Deeper than the façade of his lost self-esteem, he admired her for her steadfastness and loyalty. It was loyalty to a lost cause, according to him. He only wished his own lieutenants could show him that much devotion.

Nkukanteh knew what had happened. The drumming stopped, and the crowd anticipated in suspense as the assailants got ready.

Yafon and her assistants got Ngounso ready. "Nangie, we are waiting for you on the other side when you get out," Yafon said, a wan smile telling of her deliberate effort to be cheerful even amidst gnawing fear. Her effort was lost to the tense atmosphere.

Ngounso motioned the other assistants away; only Yafon stayed with her. "Now, listen to me carefully and don't try to interrupt me," she told her sternly, and Yafon swallowed hard.

"I will not return. That is decided already. You may let Wubangeh ascend the throne, but never become one of his chindas."

"But, Nangie," Yafon began, forgetting Ngounso's initial warning not to be interrupted. Ngounso would not allow her to speak. Instead, she ordered, "Now, kneel!"

She hesitated a little and then slowly went on her knees. Ngounso spat on her hands and rubbed them on Yafon's head, murmuring indistinctly. Then she added, "Whatever happens, make sure Nkukanteh is informed, even though he will not have the power or mungang to help you. That does not take away the imperative for her to know whatever you have in mind. Now, stand up."

Yafon stood up and uttered no word.

The sound of the horn having been heard, Ngounso marched out and walked towards tuffih, avoiding the eyes of the beaming Wubangeh walking beside her.

At the entrance, they stopped and Ngounso took one last glance at everyone. The cold breeze from inside hit their faces as she and Wubangeh entered tuffih through the left and right entrances respectively. It would be the last time she would see him and everyone else. She shivered as she stepped in. Minutes passed, and she disappeared into the entrails of the labyrinth; the sounds of the drums and the excited crowd rapidly receded. Then the sounds all died to her, yielding dead silence and darkness that was lighted enough for her to make out the time of the day as still daytime. The long fingers of the sun's rays thrust through the branches of the tall trees and she anticipated that she wouldn't be able to do much at the onset of darkness and hoped to be out before nightfall. She shivered from the cold breeze. She was glad Yafon had insisted that she take along the warm wrapper. She quickly wrapped it around her body.

In the loneliness and eerie ambience, she thought of calling out whether Wubangeh could hear her, but her sense of pride would not let her do so. She pursued her lane. On and on she went. Hours later, she was surprised to notice that the trees seemed to be moving; whenever she turned and tried to return from where she came, she met a dead end; new trees stood in her way, and she had to forge a new route through another new furrow between a new set of trees. She was a little lost as to whether it was her imagination playing with her, or the trees were indeed moving.

Dead silence reigned on, and she had so far encountered nothing or creatures apart from the trees. She tried to figure out how to find the elusive tuffih. Then she heard a sound, which at first, was like the loud thumping of her own heart, causing her to stop, hold her breath and listen. The sound came again, but was distinctly like a waterfall. She walked towards it, the sound receding as he approached, and a strange light was visible. She followed the light. Days went by with her in a vain and intelligent pursuit of the sound. Totally exhausted, she had to rest. She fed on seeds and berries from the trees, some of which contained a sweet liquid she drank to quench her thirst.

Then she resumed the pursuit of the sound of the waterfall through trees that were sometimes so close together that she had to force her way through with much difficulty and sustaining bruises. Still, she kept on. She did not notice when the sound of the waterfall petered out. Total silence accentuated the darkness and it was hard for her to tell whether it was daytime or nightfall. It was like a suspension of time and light hue, for everything seemed to have reached a standstill. She groped down some steps, but kept running into more trees to the right and the left, depending on where she felt she could go.

The unrelenting dark was monotonous and caused an angular disorientation that made her lose track of spatial, directional, and temporal bearings. She continued her shuffled search for the elusive tuffih until she heard a sound and stood still. The sound kept rising in pitch and volume, like the voices of people singing with a determinedly expressive crescendo rising with great forte to the sound of some musical instruments. Not long after the emission of the sound, she saw the source. She saw people for the first time since she left Tikari. They walked in Indian file, women in front, men in the rear, bearing coffins. Their destination was a cemetery of sorts. Some men and women had plants that they kept dipping into calabashes of water and sprinkling on the coffins with the coffin bearers. These had on expensive-looking ngwashies, the likes of which she had never laid eyes on. The male folk wore a green-dominated color while the women wore a dominantly red color.

The women would pause intermittently, bringing the procession to a stop with loud ululations of mourning for their lost ones. At the same time, the men grunted in response before the procession resumed its movement. Ngounso joined them in a bid to blend in for some kind of security and company, even amidst these total strangers. They were of mankind, she argued, because she had heard of them or their likes, the Atimkoh people. Her joining did not disrupt the parade, for they continued as if they had not seen her; she seemed invisible to them.

As she had been told, the Atimkoh people had been in that procession in search of where to bury their past kings and to create a new establishment for themselves. Centuries had caught up with them in this search. When she first heard of them, she considered them pure imagination, not people who had come through Tikari. She sang and walked with them for days, deeper and deeper into the unknown, until they started climbing flights of steps unending. They walked on, not stopping to rest, eat, or drink. From sheer exhaustion, she lapsed and gave up, letting them continue without her. They did not miss her.

She fell asleep while catching her breath but woke up to the sound of horse hoofs, the sun shining so brightly it almost blinded her. She had not seen sunlight for a very long while. The horse rider screamed, "Look at where you are going, you troublemaker! I could have crushed you. Do you plan to bring me ill luck?" Behind him, other riders came to a stop, peering at her. The lead rider wore a colorful and finely woven attire, a scarf, and a cap. Weird-looking mungangs hung or stuck on various parts of his body. They were such mungangs she had never seen or heard of before now. His horse, too, was braided with amulets all over its body. The horse calmed down, and after looking closely at her, he did not recognize who she was and, suspicion rising, the leader asked, "Who are you, and where are you from?"

"Ngounso from Tikari," she answered fearlessly, her confident demeanor catching his attention.

"Never heard of a place called Tikari. How did you find yourself here? What brings you here?" he asked quickly, his suspicious look not abating.

"That's the same question I wanted to ask you?" she said, looking at him squarely.

This was daring, he thought and then laughed uproariously. The others joined him in the laugh. Of a sudden, he stopped laughing and became stern. "You come to my home and ask me who I am?" As he asked, he turned and looked at his men and added, "These lunatics walking through our land always beat me the way they behave." Scorn and contempt braced his voice. "If we did not have laws here, I would have beheaded you," he declared angrily.

"Who are you, and where am I?" Ngounso asked, understanding that she was somewhere alien even to her who had been to many faraway lands.

"I am Dobunji, and you are in the land of Wingo. I am fon here."

"I am Ngounso from Tikari in search of tuffih. Are you tuffih?" she asked with genial indifference. They all stiffened and went quiet at the mention of tuffih. Fear descended on them as they looked at each other for clues and support.

"Did you say tuffih?" Fon Dobunji asked to ensure they were not mistaken about what they had heard.

"That is my quest, and it's been ages since I left Tikari. I have no idea how long I have been on it. I entered the labyrinth and only saw the sun again in your land," Ngounso detailed, taken off guard by their stiffening at her mention of tuffih.

"A bad omen!" Fon Dobunji said. "Here, tuffih is a bad omen, a place where murderers are sent. Is that your quest?" he asked.

"No, no! In Tikari, it is where we go to have strong mungang to help others," Ngounso informed them.

The implications of content and context and the pragmatics of usage set them in distant, divisive camps. "Fon, I believe this woman is bad luck. Let's let her go her way," one of the men said. "Getting involved can only bring us trouble. Let her go her way and not loiter here," he said, reining in his horse.

The speaker was seconded by another of the men, "Your highness, he's right; people of her type have mungang that can only bring trouble upon us. They don't seek peace. Let's send her away."

The horses, too, got agitated at the word tuffih, or so it seemed, for they all started neighing and shifting anxiously.

"Point taken," Fon Dobunji remarked and pointed north, saying, "We don't want your kind of foreigners here. If you stay on, you will pollute our land with foreign habits and bring us bad luck. Anyone who came seeking tuffih here only brought trouble. Please, continue your odyssey," he said sternly.

Ngounso was not eager to stay there either. She told them, "I heard you and only need you to please show me the way to leave right away? One favor first, though – water. I am so thirsty. Please, give me some water to drink."

When it came to kindness, they were not in want. Their fear related mainly to harboring someone with the kind of mission to the cursed place Ngounso mentioned. One of them immediately offered her a goatskin full of water while the fon hastened to direct her away.

"That is the way," Fon Dobunji pointed in the direction for her to follow. "There is a path there to enter the forest. Follow it," he added. Their horses kept shifting, and they had a hard time trying to control them.

Ngounso thanked them and started walking towards the forest as directed by the fon, followed by Dobunji and his men on their horses. They were anxious to make sure she actually left their land and did not loiter or turn around and get to some other part of it. At the edge of the forest, she saw a path and pointed at it. Dobunji nodded, saying, "Follow that," his tone neutral but underlined with a feeling of relief.

She ventured in. Moments later, she had disappeared. From a

leather pouch pulled out from inside his gorgeous clothes, Dobunji sprinkled a powdery substance along the path Ngounso had walked on and then lit a fire. The fire only burned the areas her feet had traversed.

Rapidly disappearing in the forest, Ngounso soon found herself again in the labyrinth. Days spun their endless yarn of recurrence; still, she found nothing but exhaustion and reached a corner among the trees to rest in. Sleep followed swiftly, but she woke up to the sound of people singing close by. In the murk of near sleepwalking, she ventured towards the noise but reached a blocked end, the trees so tightly knit that she could not get through. She found no second route and so reverted to the first. With great effort, she forced her way through onto a stunning site. She had spent centuries looking for Kajere to come wearing the gris-gris; she had spent ages looking for tuffih; now, she was struck dumb by what she saw.

The sounds she heard were the singing and dancing sourced from Tikari. For, as it turned out, the Tikari people, at one point in the history of their land, had all left in search of tuffih. They never returned. She recognized them all. Some of those she thought had been taken by the Ketummites could be seen there. The inexplicable reality of it was that they had not realized that they too had disappeared in search of tuffih. She edged close to them, unbelieving what was materializing before her very eyes, until they saw and recognized her.

"Is that not Ngounso?" one of them asked as much in disbelief as Ngounso herself was, and squinting to peer into her face. "Ngounso? What are you doing here?" he followed up after being assured that she was the one and barely able to contain himself.

After her initial shock, Ngounso became excited, hugging and embracing everyone present. At first, she was so excited but dumbstruck and lost for words, only acting, while tears welled up in her eyes. When eventually she was able to speak, she had a volley of questions: "Where am I? Is this a dream? Is this possible? Am I indeed in the presences of my people again? Impossible!" she screamed and she began calling them each by name: "Kwanya, Njalawi, Tisap, Abangong, Mumbi…," each embracing her or being embraced by her as she called out their name. Then, hours later, after she had told them everything that had happened, they reacted angrily to what had befallen her.

"That is not unlike him; that is typical of him. How dare he! I always suspected that Wubangeh would try something like this," Kwanya growled. "If only we could get out of this place and teach that scoundrel a lesson! He's lucky that when we were there, his father was a good man."

The others noisily voiced their acceptance of this perspective, adding other comments of disappointment with Wubangeh.

"And Nkukanteh can do nothing about it?" Mumbi asked.

"What can he do?" Kwanya asked rhetorically, and they all understood his drift.

"There must be something they can do," Njalawi said, wishing to keep the options open but fully aware that, as it stood, Nkukanteh could do nothing. It was frustrating, but hope could be lit by keeping openings for the unknown.

Their anger was heart-warming, but there was the actual and present circumstance that needed a way out. "How can we get out of here without finding tuffih?" Ngounso asked, refocusing on the present predicament. The others burst out laughing, to her embarrassment.

"Ah, you are a new arrival, and we were almost missing out on that. That's tuffih over there," Mumbi said, pointing.

"Where?" Ngounso looked in the direction where she was pointing, at first, seeing nothing.

"Over there," they all said. Then Ngounso saw tuffih. She burst out laughing.

***

Meanwhile, after a few days, Wubangeh returned to Tikari. He had not found tuffih, but decided to return home. He was battered and bruised but happy to have returned after the ordeal in the labyrinth. He did not tell anyone that he had not gone very far in or that he had turned around and quit the search. Instead, he made everyone understand that he had found tuffih and Ngounso had been taken away by tuffih, and never to return. It was a convenient lie that served his uncompromising quest for the throne.

Most of the people had not left the arena. They would do their chores and come back over the next few days, waiting for their hero. So, upon his reappearance, Wubangeh had lots of his supporters to hail him. They sang his praises, convinced that his mungang was indeed super powerful and overcame tuffih. Wubangeh was comfortable with their belief and did nothing to dispel it.

Nkukanteh watched Wubangeh receiving the adulations while Yafon and her aides looked crestfallen. The land was not far from trouble now and, as if they read his mind, various birds began flying away in droves. The birds were leaving, a thing unknown in the history of Tikari. Everyone watched them fly away, bemused. Wubangeh was too tired even to notice the anomaly, and Yafon and her aides had to eat the humble pie of watching his excited supporters carry him to his abode.

"I don't think Nangie will ever return," Ngunini managed to say, uncontrollable tears streaming down her face.

"That's true," Andoshie said. "It is perhaps the time for us all to leave this land before we become victims of the worst," she added.

Both speakers stared at Yafon, awaiting her verdict or hint. She spoke after a brief hesitation: "Don't be scared. We will be fine. Let's see what Wubangeh will do. Ngounso will return, and Kajere and our princess too." No one said anything, but they all looked at her.

Although deep in her she knew all was not fine, she did not want to show them how worried she was as it would affect them disastrously.

Ngounso had not returned for several weeks. The stage was set for Wubangeh to claim that his narrative was valid. He visited Nkukanteh. "It is time for you to crown me as fon of this land. I will broker no more delays," he said.

"I can't do that," Nkukanteh protested. "Ngounso has not returned, and she needs to return to complete the rest of the competition. We can't go against the rules. You know all the laws. Why are you asking me to break them?" He knew what Wubangeh would say.

"She's not returning, and our laws have to change. You will all learn to follow the new laws I will create," Wubangeh said, his tone haughtily pontificating. "We know for a certainty that Ngounso will not return, so don't try to deceive us with phantom laws about things that don't matter," he added, smiling mischievously triumphant.

"What proof do you have to show that you saw tuffih?" Nkukanteh asked, looking directly and with bristly confrontational courage at Wubangeh.

"I am here, and she's not," he said lamely and then asked, "Doesn't that count? How many people have returned from the tuffih search? How many? I am the only one!" Wubangeh answered, impervious to corrective modification of his desire. He struggled to return Nkukanteh's condescending gaze.

"No matter how much rain falls on a leopard, it will not wash away its spots," Nkukanteh said in an attempt to draw the ire of Wubangeh. Whether he succeeded in doing so was difficult to tell since Wubangeh maintained a bland total lack of response to the snide comment.

Simply continuing as if he had not been interrupted, Wubangeh indicated that his absolute control was already taking place by offering an inconsequential concession, "I want to be fair; I will add two more market days. If she's not back by then, you will crown me Fon;

no ritual can stop you. If you produce any, I will create new rituals."

Two markets later, Ngounso still had not appeared. Instead, Kuriyango had visited her quarters and made herself known to Yafon, with her aides who had received her as civilly as they could, though she could sense that she was not so welcome. It was about power and control, which Kuriyango went about without apologies:

"The time has come for things to change in this land," she announced.

"Today's your day; tomorrow will be mine," Yafon replied defiantly.

"We'll see about that," Kuriyango dared her.

Yafon knew things would not be easy for her from that day on. Yet, she cherished Ngounso's last words in her mind.

One hot day with many people in the market and the sun high in the sky, a few droplets of rain began to fall. Many did not leave the market because they felt it would not rain since they could not see any clouds.

Before anyone could react, a series of incredibly bright and treacherous flashes of lightning lit the sky, the likes of which no one had ever seen. Before they could react, the loudest thunderclap in memory crackled and rumbled. The lightning and thunder pulled Nkukanteh out of his house, many miles away and threw him naked in the middle of the marketplace. Everyone knew Wubangeh had something to do with it, a presupposition that seemed to have been at the back of what took place the next day. For the following day, Nkukanteh anointed Wubangeh as the ruler of the land.

Ten

The Nshua Clasp

A few years after they had been living in Ntubiseh, Kajere got up and looked outside. It was as beautiful a morning as he had ever encountered. In the distance, he could hear the roosters crowing to announce the morning. All around him, he could hear the Ntubisans going about their daily chores. He simply lay back in bed and smiled.

Even the Ntubisans had forgotten that Kajere and Zasheri were strangers. They treated them as their very own, Kajere having become one of the best dancers, one all clans wanted to watch or pair with in dancing. There were arguments sometimes about who should dance with him. He was the darling of the dancing stage.

Not only was he on the stage for dances, but he also worked on the farms, being considered a great tiller of the soil. He understood physics and mathematics and helped to solve scientific challenges that had frustrated Ntubisans for centuries.

On her part, Zasheri became friends with Awusa, helping her in matters of the state to arrive at far-reaching decisions for the land. Fon Makenji sought her advice on serious issues affecting the land. For instance, a few months before, Fon Makenji sought Zasheri's advice regarding some boulders that had been in Ntubiseh for ages. They were in a dangerous position and could crush any puppet who lived in the valley below. No clan wanted the boulder in its territory. Makenji consulted Zasheri on the quandary: "What can we do? Nobody wants the boulder in their land."

Zasheri pondered for a while and responded: "You are fully aware of the problems if that boulder falls, right?"

Makenji agreed and explained: "This problem has been going on for centuries. No one has been able to do anything about it. Now they want me to solve it. What am I to do?"

Zasheri could feel his frustration and helplessness. "Well, Fon Makenji," she said, after thinking about it for a while, "You've got to make them understand what each of them stands to gain if the boulder stays in their land and how they have to be proud of the benefits it brings to them."

Ewusa listened silently to this exchange, chipping in a word or two when necessary. It was she who had advised her husband to seek Zasheri's advice.

"Your people are hardworking but also like to have fun and be entertained," Zasheri said. "Why don't you get them to work together, have a part of the stone in their territory, then create a ritual and festival that will commemorate this work. The ritual should involve the ngumba and a cult they believe in?"

Makenji thought about it for a while. "I will bring that to the attention of the ngumba house," he said pensively, afraid to reveal how excited he was at her suggestion.

"Do that and these two clans will have a ritual as well as a form of entertainment," Zasheri concluded.

Behind them, Ewusa smiled with satisfaction. "I did not hear you thank her for such a brilliant suggestion," Ewusa said with a smile.

"Thank you, princess," Fon Makenji said, still trying to avoid showing much excitement.

Some days later, Makenji took the suggestion to the council. He did not tell them that it was Zasheri's suggestion, and support for the idea was overwhelming. Many wondered why they had not thought about it in the first place. That is how Zasheri became the confidant of Makenji and Ewusa, helping to rule the kingdom with the wisdom and political savvy of Tikari.

On his part, beyond being a fantastic singer and dancer, Kajere, with the power of the gris-gris, was an excellent teacher. He taught them to do many things they had not previously imagined, his understanding of the sciences, mathematics, and writing equaling his ability to transmit to the puppets.

Makenji was so appreciative that he called a council meeting without informing Kajere and Zasheri. It was a crucial meeting at which he proposed that Kajere and Zasheri become official council members and play a part in the official government of the land. He told the council, "I have asked you here today because I want us to discuss something vital. I want Kajere and Princess Zasheri to join our ngumba house. What do you think?"

The immediate response was prolonged silence. Then Nganga, the council leader, declared firmly but respectfully, "I will speak for myself. This is not a good idea at all. It's a terrible idea. I have always supported you in everything, but I can't support you on this."

This embarrassed Makenji, who had not expected any opposition, and if any drawbacks, not from Nganga, whose ideas he had high regard for. He decided to play cool and invite opinions to dampen the shock he just received: "Is there anyone else who thinks like Nganga?" Makenji asked. A few puppets mumbled something about being on the same line of thought as Nganga. Perhaps he was missing out on something Nganga knew or suspected. He turned to Nganga and, leaning back, asked, "Why don't you want them to join our ngumba house?"

Before his answer came, music floated from outside, Kajere's voice careering to them in waves of intermittent croons. Nganga found himself tapping his foot on the earth floor to the rhythm of the music in spite of himself. Catching himself off guard, he quickly stopped because Makenji and the others had their eyes on him. A mischievous smile beamed on Makenji's face, and this maddened Nganga to spurt out: "They are foreigners. They are not one of us. They don't even look like us. How can we make them members of the highest authority in the land?" His voice was flat, humdrum, and dull.

"Is that any reason for them not to become members of our ngumba house, really?" someone ventured. He was immediately countered by a different member who was at pains to prove Nganga right:

"Let's hear what Nganga is saying," the member said. "They are not of us. We have welcomed them among us, but that does not mean we should also make them privy to the highest secrets of our land. They look different from us, and how do we know if they would one day leave, taking our secrets with them? How can we make the puppets respect us if we accept foreigners into our ngumba house?" His voice slowly rose with full of spite as he went on, generating murmurs of acceptance from a section of the council

Makenji kept quiet, but Nganga was baited by the flattering speech of the councilor. "You are right," he said. "How can we explain that people who look different from us even get into our ngumba house?" After looking confidently at the assembly in front of him, he continued, "Soon, they will change everything here, making us do what they want until eventually taking over our ngumba house. Do you know what that will do to us? Do you know the kind of puppets we will become?"

He allowed the rhetorical questions to blow in the air, instilling silent thoughtfulness. Makenji had not looked at things in that light, and he allowed his surprise to show on his face. Quickly realizing that he had hit a sore nerve, Nganga pressed his point further: "What will happen to us? Eh?"

One member of the council found room to speak. "Yes. Our

own ways might end up in the background, become obsolete, and become extinct if we pursue what they bring. Is that what we want?" he asked, and again, silence came down and lingered in the room before another member of the council spoke up:

"I agree with you. Before you know it, we will be made to wear the same kind of clothes they wear, eat what they like, and then we will be peopled with their people."

Logical as these expositions were, there were gaps that Makenji needed to bring up. "Do you remember when we resolved the problem of the boulders?" he asked, and they all nodded. Do you know Princess Zasheri came up with the idea?"

It was the turn of those who opposed the inclusion of the guests into the ngumba to be embarrassed. They looked at each other, scratching their heads in disbelief. Yet, Nganga would not give up. "We have allowed them to stay in our land, and we have taught them a lot," he said, playing down their input and instead emphasizing what the guests gained from them. "We do not need to make them join our ngumba house. It is unnecessary, and they could use their knowledge against us," he ended furiously.

Nganga had never opposed Makenji in public or anywhere else. Usually, Makenji made up his mind about a thing and only informed the council of what he would do. He was not in the habit of asking them for their opinion before making decisions. But because they knew this was a crucial moment in their history, they all wanted to be a part of it.

***

Ewusa and some of her attendants, unknown to Kajere and Zasheri, stood close by and could hear them conversing. They hugged each other awkwardly, and Kajere complimented the princess, "Princess, you look good."

"Thank you, and you look great as well," Zasheri replied, looking into his eyes.

Ewusa noticed this, but before she could do anything, the dance group appeared in front of them. Makenji was in the lead, and Nganga was noticeably at the rear.

Not having seen Makenji dance before, Kajere was surprised at himself that he had not known of it before. As he processed this, some masquerades came along, intensifying the dance, and he and Zasheri were about to join in, but were restrained, which surprised them. The masquerades danced and began to fly, and many puppets converged in the marketplace, filling it up, virtually everyone being present. Kajere and Zasheri found themselves at the center of attention, but were not bothered since this fitted the usual dance procedure. However, there was something the matter with the arrangement this time around. Indeed, there was something strange, for on Makenji's cue, the flying masquerades descended, and everything suddenly stopped, followed by an eerie silence.

Stepping forward, Makenji held out four gold-colored bracelets, putting Zasheri at a complete loss. The crowd cheered with understanding, for only rulers wore such bracelets. Ewusa made her entrance, and then Makenji spoke: "We, the puppets of Ntubiseh, want to thank you for everything you've done for us," he introduced and then the oldest puppet in the council, one who hardly ever spoke, stepped forward. Called Tishom, this puppet had compelling respect from all, and no one could mess with his mungang. So portentous they were that he could tell what anyone was thinking.

"When the fon has a good ngumba house, his rule is peaceful," Tishom began in a slow but loud and powerful voice. All in the arena could hear him clearly. "Today, we welcome Kajere and Princess Zasheri as two of our leaders, and Fon Makenji has asked us to give them an area near the stream. Any puppets who live there will come under their leadership." Tishom was solemn, his pronouncement received with loud cheers that seemed to last forever.

Makenji swung the bracelets in the air, their powerful mungangs no secret to the puppets. The crowd seethed with joy and lifted Kajere and Zasheri up into the air and sang and danced with them to their new abode.

In the quiet of their home that evening, Ewusa and Makenji talked. Ewusa quietly introduced the matter: "Why don't we make Kajere marry Zasheri?" causing Makenji to stop what he was doing and look at her because it was a high-level matter.

"Is that possible? Zasheri is his princess and we don't know their culture, and whether a chinda there could marry a princess," Makenji commented, unsure of anything in that direction.

"Did you see how they looked at each other when Tishom said we were to come together as one, and when you gave them the bracelets? There's something there." Ewusa decided not to consider her husband's reluctance. She looked at them with the savvy of female intuition.

"Their long time together is because they are in quest of Kwifon. There is nothing to suggest that they should marry, something they ought to have done long before now, don't you think?" Makenji knew that Ewusa was always trying to get puppets together.

"Maybe he's afraid to ask her?" Ewusa said.

"Or maybe in their land, chindas don't marry royalty. How can we know?" Makenji suggested.

"We shall see," Ewusa said. She was determined to plan the Kajere and Zasheri union.

"Have you considered the possibility that we might end up maddening them instead of pleasing them? Is that advisable?" Makenji asked.

"What culture thwarts two lovers from getting married? Can you hear yourself, Makenji? Talk of that kind invites trouble," Ewusa challenged.

Makenji pretended to relent. "If anything should go wrong, don't say I did not warn you. Just what do you have in mind?" He knew that his wife always had something in mind before raising issues of that nature.

Instead of answering him, she nodded and smiled knowingly, which shut up Makenji. Without Kajere and Zasheri knowing it, their fates had been sealed. Were they really?

They stayed on in Ntubiseh, marveling at the new roles they had to play, roles they embraced with passionate enthusiasm and went about it with total abandon. A time came when neither of them could remember when they came or how they even arrived there, their roles in the ngumba house being uppermost in their mind. They were admired by the Ntubisans, especially at the ease with which they solved problems and resolved situations considered difficult or even impossible. The power of Kajere's gris-gris awestruck them, and before long, he and Zasheri were regulars in Ntubiseh, no longer considered strangers. They got comfortable and complacent in their new abode and roles, and without their knowledge, Ewusa began to plan their wedding. Everyone in the land got to know about it, except the concerned. It was a guarded secret, which they considered as a way of thanking them for the new lines of reasoning and renewed enthusiasm for life they had brought to the land.

In the background of this euphoria and plans for compensation of the strangers, Tishom was walking along a path one dark night in the absence of the moon and stars and pitch darkness. Though unable to see his way right in front of him, he was used to the path and could always tell when someone was close. When he bumped into someone, he was surprised that he did not feel the person, for he could always tell when someone was around, even in total darkness like this evening in Ntubiseh. For this, he was known throughout, his extraordinary sense of detection heralded.

"Who is it?" he asked.

"It's me," Nganga replied.

"Ah Nganga, where were you hiding? I could not tell who it was," Tishom asked.

"To be honest with you, Tishom, I was indeed hiding," Nganga said.

"Hiding in the dark? Why?" Tishom asked suspiciously.

"Your question is the answer for why I am here," Nganga replied mysteriously.

As he pondered the words and the joggle of ideas of Nganga, Tishom took out a pipe, fumbled through his bag in the dark, got out some tobacco, filled the pipe, and lit it. Nganga did the same.

"So, what's the problem? You are not the type to come out here at this time to talk about something good," Tishom said, chuckling.

Nganga hesitated, cleared his throat, and took longer than usual. Tishom waited patiently. Finally, they felt some tree roots that crossed the path using their feet and then sat down there.

"Those foreigners in our land," Nganga said.

"I thought so, what about them? I thought you had forgotten about it," Tishom said pensively.

"I did not forget," Nganga replied. "See the kind of changes we are already having in our land!" Nganga prodded, wondering whether Tishom was on his side.

While Tishom smoked his pipe, pondering Nganga's words, Nganga saw this as hesitation and pursued his cause. "We still have some mungang that we could use. I think it's time for them to continue their quest for Kwifon," he added.

Tishom thought about it for a while. Decisions are not a thing to jump into without proper thought, he said, standing up to mark the end of the discussion, "I will think about it."

The conversation was over and Nganga felt somewhat encouraged that the older man was to think about it. He then stood up too, and both of them walked away, each deep in thought.

***

Kajere Awestruck

A few days after this meeting, Kajere was doing a dance routine with some puppets in preparation for an upcoming festival. He slipped and fell, hitting his head against a stone. He went unconscious, causing Zasheri, who was with Ewusa, to rush to his side and was distracted with worries and demanding to know the circumstances of the swoon.

"When he fell, we considered it a joke, given his penchant for jokes. It is when the swoon prolonged that we sent for you," a crestfallen attendant puppet explained.

Zasheri had no time for words. She rushed Kajere home and applied some water on him, trying in vain to revive him. He was wandering in the shadows of dreamlands, so to speak, an arid desolation in which tiredness and thirst were compounded by hunger. It was a complete wilderness with a little child there playing *tabala*. The child stopped playing and stared, her eyes so bright that Kajere could barely look at it without shading his own eyes from the brilliance.

"Who are you and what's your business here?" he asked.

"That is what I should be asking you. I live here," the child replied, looking straight at him.

"I don't know where or who I am," Kajere replied.

"If you don't even know who you are, how did you get here?" the child queried.

Still trying to figure out his bearings, he said, "I don't know, but I am starving and thirsty. Where can I find food and drink?" He was barely able to conceal his own embarrassment as the child laughed, asking:

"Are you an idiot?" the child insulted.

Hardly able to contain itself, Kajere was momentarily stunned by the child's answer. Though a little upset, he tried to conceal it. "I don't think so," he stuttered in reply.

"How do you find yourself in a place like this without food or water?" The child indicated, pointing around, just how dry and desolate the place was. "Only an idiot does that. Do you even know where you are?" the child asked, holding back a guffaw.

Kajere responded after hesitating a little, "I don't actually know who I am or where I am."

Kajere's serious look caused the child to stop laughing and to think for a moment.

"How you got here, hmmm…. It beats my imagination!" the child mused, becoming empathetic. Then he tossed a leather bag that had a leather string tied around it at Kajere. In it was something. Kajere caught the bag but was unable to open it, and he was unable to undo the string no matter his efforts. He even murmured some chants, trying to use the power from his gris-gris to no avail. He guessed that the bag contained food and water. After tossing it in every direction and employing all his skill to no avail, he asked for help from the child.

"Can you help me undo this?"

"I can't believe what I just heard," the child replied sarcastically. "First, you come here and ask me who I am; then you tell me you're hungry and thirsty. I gave you food and drink, and now you want me to help you to eat and drink? How far will you go with your ridiculous demands? What kind of person are you? Can't you do anything for yourself?"

"As you can see, I have been at it for hours, and failed," Kajere protested. "Can't you see it?" He gave a last unsuccessful try.

"What kind of man are you that you can't even take care of yourself?"

"You can see how hard I am trying," Kajere replied, desperate.

"It's been a long time since I met anyone from where I come from," the child continued. "Anyone who has been here was able to feed themselves, know where they come from and where they are going. I will ask you again, who are you, and where are you from, and where are you going?" As the child spoke, his eyes got frightfully brighter and Kajere had to turn away.

"Don't turn away from me when I am talking to you," the child ordered, looking angered. "You are not showing respect to the person who gave you something to eat and to drink." Then he burst out laughing and started to walk away.

"Wait, wait. Where are you going?" Kajere asked, trying to follow him, but discovered he could not move.

"Hey, help me, please," he said, desperation taking hold of him. "Please!" he yelled, and the child stopped, slowly turned and walked back to him. And before Kajere could assess the circumstances, the child jumped up and smacked him hard on the jaw. It was quite a heavy spank, coming from a child that tiny. Kajere felt the weight of the slap throw him yards away and onto the hot sandy ground.

"What was that for?" Kajere asked angrily, not knowing what to say or do. But the child did not reply. That aggressive turn, compounded by hunger, thirst, and anger, made Kajere attack the boy. Yet, hard as he tried, he found himself unable to move, stuck. No wonder, fatigue wore him out in his attempt to reach the child. He eventually fell down from exhaustion.

"Who are you, and what kind of mungang do you have?" he asked, apparently enraging the child with the question.

"Remember who you are and what you left Tikari to find," the child said. "Have you forgotten what you have around your neck?" the child asked, and Kajere felt the gris-gris around his neck as if for the first time, as the child continued: "You left Tikari in search of Kwifon, but on reaching Ntubiseh, you abandoned the quest, right, Kajere?" The child looked wildly at him, and he stared back, stupefied. "Remember who you are and your mission. I'm gone." So saying, the child turned and walked away, disappearing into the distance.

Desperate, Kajere tried to follow the child's receding figure. Yet, not even the power of gris-gris helped him out of the body heaviness he seemed to have been plunged into.

The child's words lingered in Kajere's mind, obliterating the hunger and thirst momentarily. The hunger and thirst soon returned with added weight. He writhed, making his body take all forms of tortured looks. Then, without any logical explanation, he found himself screaming in Zasheri's arms.

"Are you okay? Are you okay?" Zasheri asked, distraught, and Kajere looked around wildly, trying to remember where he was.

The hunger and thirst still in his memory, he asked, "Where's the bag? Can you open it?" Then he looked wildly around, not recognizing where he was. Zasheri and the puppets were worried, joined by Makenji and Ewusa.

"It's me, Zasheri. Can you hear me, Kajere?" Her attempted poise was disastrous, and she soon turned and motioned for everybody to leave the room. When they did, she heard Kajere request:

"Please give me the bag so I can try to open it. I must open it. It contains all the food and water." He looked wildly around as he made the request, which was an embarrassment to Zasheri.

"What bag are you talking about, Kajere?" she asked. She feared for him and worried that he might be losing his mind. She had known him for many years now, and they had been through numerous adventures. She had never seen him this caring. She could tell that he did not know where he was.

"Can you hear me? Can you hear me, Kajere?" she called out, her voice combining fear and hope.

Oblivious of being in Zasheri's arms, Kajere asked, "Where am I? Did you see the bag? Let me have it, please."

"Let me get it from the start, Kajere. What bag are you talking about, really?" Zasheri asked.

"That bag that contains food and drinks you gave me! I am

starving and thirsty!" he exclaimed, still frantic, a hazy mist circulating deep inside his head. So thick was the fog, he did not know how to get rid of it. It got thicker, the more he tried to understand his circumstances. But the mention of food and thirst set Zasheri in food mobilization mode. She dashed out and returned with an assortment of food and drink for him. The puppets, including Makenji and Ewusa, clamored to know what was going on, but she gave no answer to their prying questions.

"Here is food and drink," she said, offering them to Kajere. The wonder was that Kajere refused to touch and kept asking for the bag, to the total bewilderment of Zasheri.

"Where's the bag? I want that bag! Give it to me!" he kept saying, his voice rising. Saliva started dribbling down the sides of his mouth as he spoke.

Zasheri's lame response was only a mild expression of her frustration: "I don't see any bag."

Eventually, Kajere calmed down and slept off. After holding him for a while, Zasheri stepped out to talk to Makenji, Ewusa and the puppet members of the council who had arrived upon hearing what happened. Among them were Nganga and Tishom, both trying to make themselves as inconspicuous as they could. They loitered in the background.

In Zasheri's absence, the gris-gris around Kajere's neck began emitting a brilliant brightness, and then a deep and loud flatulent sound that woke Kajere up into full consciousness. The stench from the gris-gris was unbearably harsh and caused him to moan. At his moan, Zasheri quickly reentered the house, and he asked, "Zasheri, is that you?" He moaned and tossed, still in an effort to get away from the gris-gris.

Zasheri was glad to hear the question, which indicated some level of normalcy now, but her concern bordered on paranoia as she answered, "Yes, it's me. Are you awake? Can you hear me?" she asked, her concern bordering on paranoia.

Kajere looked around, seeming to recognize his circumstances. "I am fine. I am fine," he said, which relieved Zasheri. "What is that pungent smell?" he asked, his face contorting with discomfort and his palm and fingers closing his nose. The stench was, however, his private preserve, for Zasheri did not sense it.

"What smell? The food I brought you does not have a strong smell," Zasheri said, poking her nose in the air.

"Don't tell me that you can't smell it!" he exclaimed, stifling a smile in spite of himself. "It's like rotten flatulence," he said.

She shook her head, announcing to him, "I can't smell anything," which set Kajere on a worry trail.

"Fon Makenji and Ewusa are outside," Zasheri said. "They want to greet you. Maybe they will be able to smell it when they get in," she said and stepped out.

The smell was like a shaft of radiation going right into Kajere's head. No attempt to eliminate it yielded any fruit. When they came in, Makenji, Ewusa, and the other puppets looked worried.

"How are you, Kajere?" Fon Makenji asked. "We are glad to see you okay. Just what really happened?"

"I don't really know," Kajere replied, a wan smile in league with the pungency making him twitch his nose while Zasheri gently massaged some plant oil on his still throbbing head. "I was practicing some new dance moves, and then found myself here. Zasheri has told me that I went unconscious."

"We are happy to see you okay," Ewusa echoed her husband, relieved. "Zasheri, please let us know if we can offer any help," she volunteered before Kajere asked the question that was bothering him.

"Do you smell anything here?" He made a circling indication with his index finger to locate the place that was almost causing him to puke.

Makenji and Ewusa held up their noses in the air, smelled nothing strange, and shook their heads. "I smell nothing," Makenji said, and after winking as a way of affirming his wife's own verdict, he asked Kajere, "You smell something bad?"

"Yes, a horridly pungent smell," Kajere replied, unable to disguise his repugnance as he turned his head in all directions in an attempt to escape the smell.

"Can you describe the smell?" Ewusa asked.

Many thoughts ran through Kajere's head about how experiences were generally nondescript; how, even when attempts were made to describe anything, the attempt remained a far cry from the experience. Now she was asking her to poke into the mess he was sensing in his nostrils and give her a graphic presentation of something so obnoxious. He was too embarrassed to reply.

Noticing his reluctance to bring forth the nastiness to the hearing of a queen out of respect and politeness, Zasheri broke in: "It's like flatulence, an aggressively foul stench."

Ewusa stifled a chuckle because of the reproachful look Makenji gave her at the unpolished statement from Zasheri.

"Has anyone here messed the air?" Makenji asked, looking round. Everyone shook their heads. Then, going outside, he loudly summoned and requested any of the puppets gathered in the courtyard if they could help, but since none of them smelled the said foul stench, none had any offers to make. He returned, bemused, in a pensive mood, trying to figure out how to help. Coming to Kajere and watching him walk around the room in an attempt to get rid of the pong, he once more posited, "Is there anything we can do?"

"Don't worry. I'll see what I can do," Kajere said. Nodding at Zasheri, Makenji filed out with his entourage, leaving the pair alone. When they left, Kajere told Zasheri that he wanted some time to be by himself, politely requesting that she give her the time to be alone.

Zasheri was half-protective and half-precautious as she asked him, "Are you sure you want to be by yourself after all you've gone through? Then there is the smell you're talking about as well," she inquired.

He tried smiling and said, "I am fine, princess. I just need a little time to clear my mind. I hope you understand?"

She smiled, quietly walking out, leaving Kajere to examine the room as if he were noticing it for the first time. The smell still bothered him, and on his chest, he felt the gris-gris getting cold. He attempted to wrench it off, but he knew in advance that his efforts were futile. Even so, he tried hard, propelled by the unbearable coldness the gris-gris generated. The icy discomfort did not leave, nor did the rottenness of the stench abate.

Zasheri heard and noticed him trying to pull off the gris-gris. "What is happening?" she asked from her respectful distance from the irate man.

Kajere, in an irate retort, answered, "Can't you see that I am trying to get rid of this thing?" Frustration added abrasion to the quality of his voiced response.

He was truly in need, and Zasheri thought it her duty to help him. Together, but to no avail, they tugged at the gris-gris.

"Are you feeling how cold it is?" Kajere asked her.

Zasheri felt nothing and said, "No. It has a room-temperature feel to me," she said, again worried as she added the worrying smell to the coldness of the gris-gris.

"What's happening to me?" Kajere cried out as they both tugged at the gris-gris.

"Nothing's happening to you," Zasheri tried to console him, though she could tell that he was not listening to her. "I think you hit your head and it affected you. You are fine," she said as reassuringly as she could.

"Aiieee, that thing's very cold!" Kajere shouted. "Could you remove it for me? Please remove it!" Kajere requested, his voice screeching with agony, and this loudness brought the puppets to the door.

Zasheri, however, told them to go away. "Please leave! I can help him," she said loudly so that her voice could be heard above the din coming from the outside. She was also losing her nerve and getting angry to be in such a predicament. Then she again tried to help him pull off the gris-gris, but the more they tried, the harder it proved to be. Besides, Kajere was still greatly bothered by the pungent smell. "Do you still smell the nasty smell?" she inquired.

"Yes," he answered, and nodded and then said, "Please, leave me alone," his voice impatient. She sensed it and left immediately, and he heard her instructing the puppets outside not to visit him, but to leave him alone until he was ready to see them. The inconveniences aside, Kajere felt relieved to be alone, a condition he needed in order to gather his thoughts.

Information about Kajere's malaise was all over, and there was concern for him, with puppets taking turns visiting him in his quarters. This went on for an entire month, with Kajere staying in his room and unwilling to see anyone. But solicitous Zasheri kept leaving food outside his door for him to take in and eat when no one was around.

The smell persisted and got worse for him, even beginning to seep into his mouth and produce a putrid taste that altered the taste of any food he tried to eat. So, he lost his appetite and had to force himself to eat. Still, he kept away from everyone, even Zasheri, which was very frustrating for her because she had no idea what was really happening to him.

Unable to endure forever, out of sheer frustration, Kajere burst out of his room, stunning Makenji, Nganga and some other puppets as he ran wildly into the nearby stream. The puppets rushed after him, Nganga keeping his distance and critically on the watch. Makenji called for Zasheri, and she hurriedly arrived with Ewusa accompanying her.

In the stream, Kajere was excitedly splashing around and muttering words that could not be understood by anyone, not even Ntubisans with their knack for making meaning of most languages. The interpretation of many was that Kajere had gone delusional, a scary thought for many.

Hours later and already evening with some puppets turning turquoise, Kajere stepped out of the stream. He was a sight to behold as he was also turning turquoise, unknown to himself. The expressions on the faces of onlookers directed him to himself and to his own shock. This was an extraordinary and frightening thing for Zasheri.

At this point, Nganga whispered to Makenji that something had to be done about it, and Makenji agreed, requesting to know what exactly needed to be done.

Instead, Nganga speculated, "I think he's been attacked by a very powerful mungang. The kind of mungang we know nothing about."

Makenji noted that Nganga had a critical point which he could not disregard. The issue was what steps he needed to take. Kajere was changing right in front of their eyes. Not that he had ever had anything against those who became turquoise. The turquoise puppets danced, sang, and worked best. Kajere becoming like them was a quandary. "Is there a ritual that can cleanse him?" he asked Nganga.

Nganga went straight to his initial plan and declared, "The time has come for us to expel them from our land. They come with trouble and more trouble. She will also start having these signals, and then, who knows, we all might. We cannot know the end of this strange start."

Nganga was cogent, elaborate, and deliberate, but his shock was that Makenji repudiated his proposal with a threat: "If I hear you talk that way once more, you will be summoned to appear before the ngumba house. Do you hear me?" Makenji stressed severely.

"Yes, fon," Nganga replied, embarrassed and made to hear the elaborate rebuke from Makenji: "So, after everything they have been and done for us, you harbor these thoughts about them, Nganga?"

Nganga bided his time and kept his distance from the fon. He had noted how doubt had crept into Makenji's eyes at the mention of the possibility of Kajere being affected by a mungang yet unknown in Ntubiseh.

Meanwhile, Kajere slowly metamorphosed, talking loudly to himself. Hard as Makenji tried to conceal it, he was deeply troubled and perplexed as he walked back to his quarters. Later that evening, he discussed his perplexity with his wife, his face deep-furrowed. He asked her for suggestions, but she had nothing in mind.

"I don't know what's going on, but Princess Zasheri, too, is confused and has gone quiet, not knowing what to do either," she explained, excusing her own lack of ideas.

This sank Makenji's heart because the two people who usually had answers for him had none. Ewusa's lack of a suggestion was the erasure of the last vestige of hope for him, and he felt as if the ground beneath his feet had been violently pulled away. He tried another way to draw out a suggestion from his wife:

"Nganga says we should expel them from the land because their presence is ominous and will bring us bad luck. Can you imagine that?" he asked, looking at his wife for any reaction.

On Ewusa's face, Makenji saw that rarely visible look, accompanied by the question, "How dare he say that?"

Makenji needed this supportive question and heaved a sigh of relief. He had not missed out that after Kajere and Zasheri became council members, Nganga showed signs of losing empathy, along with a few councilors who had become rather cold.

Kajere was still restless. Then his gris-gris, still very cold, began to vibrate, the putrid smell getting even more potent and slicing into his head. Something inside him gave way, and he fell, wriggling on the floor with paroxysms of words spurting out. The puppets outside had been warned not to enter his quarters, so they only heard noise but could identify one word – nshua – but had no idea what it meant. Then the gris-gris stopped vibrating, ceased to be cold, and the smell still hanging around him became less abrasive.

"Nshua!" Kajere muttered among the many other words as his head lightened and got more coordinated. "Nshua!" Nshua had caught him; he came to a concluding thought and looked around, seeing everything for the first time, as it were. He heard the puppets muttering and casually walked out and saw them, again, as if for the first time. They looked at him suspiciously, even though he was no longer showing signs of hallucination. They did not take long to realize that he had recovered. They smiled at him, and he reciprocated without knowing the reason for their smile. He wondered where he was and where his princess was. Slowly and painfully, he began to recollect himself, forcing himself to focus on what was in his environment and the circumstances. That is how he noticed his turquoise body and was scared, but he was also returning to his normal color, things fitting into their sensible places eventually.

Bankoh came to his mind, as did his flying with Zasheri into Ntubiseh on Shengah's back. He remembered meeting the Ntibuseh puppets, watching them dance, and meeting their gods. Nothing else immediately came to mind, but he soon understood himself and why he was where he was. 'Zasheri' was the word that popped from his mouth, and the puppets quickly went to get her. When she appeared, Kajere heaved a sigh of relief.

It did not take long for her to heave her own sigh of relief as she read a return to normalcy on his face, even as she asked, "Princess, are you okay?"

"I am fine and worried about you. How are you?" His wits were obviously back, which greatly pleased her, but before she could speak, Makenji and Ewusa had arrived, smiling broadly. Kajere saw them, although for a brief moment he could not tell who they were and asked Zasheri, "Who are these?"

"Don't you recognize them?" Zasheri asked, alarmed that he might have a relapse.

He quickly recognized them, however, and paid them his tributes to Zasheri's relief.

"We are happy you are back," Makenji said, extending a warm hand and shaking Kajere's, smiling.

"Did I go somewhere?" Kajere asked, amusing those present.

Makenji explained, "You were unconscious, and recovered only to say you were smelling something which no one else did, and that your gris-gris was extremely cold."

Kajere knew he had to think quickly and avoid antagonizing his hosts, who seemed so nice to him and Zasheri. He asked everyone to leave him and Zasheri alone. Then he stuttered, "Do you know anything about the Kwifon of Mekan?" Although he had hope in his eyes, his heart was thumping so loudly that he imagined she heard it. Her answer would determine what he would have to do next, but her words confirmed his worst fears.

***

"Kwifon of Mekan? What is that?" She asked, a frown on her forehead, shaking her head. "No, I've never heard about it. What do you call it again?" she reiterated.

"Kwifon of Mekan," he said. She only shook her head, a little confused.

Kajere's heart sank, for he realized that nshua had also afflicted her. The challenge before him was how to break the curse and continue their voyage in search of the Kwifon. He tried to stir something or a memory in her. "Have you ever heard of Tikari and the Ketummites?" An affirmative answer would be a loophole for progress, he hoped, but again she shook her head:

"Why all these strange questions? Are you okay?" She was now worried that something more inimical had taken hold of him, even though he seemed to have returned to normal. "Who are these people you are asking me about?"

Kajere realized the situational irony facing them. She was worried that something was wrong with him, whereas she was the one with the ailment. He thought hard, planning to act fast. "Okay, I need to rest. We'll talk more tomorrow," he said. He needed quiet time to think out the next move and was happy that she readily agreed and left. He now paced around the room, absorbed in thoughts about ifs and whens and hows, what strategy to employ and how to get around Zasheri's oblivion and make them leave. All concept of time disappeared, and how long they had been in Ntubiseh did not register in his mind. Afflicted by nshua, Zasheri too had no concept of time; in that blanket of timelessness, she was thrilled here. No urgency featured if time was lost. She would surely vehemently resist any attempts to dislodge her and take her away, worse, if the puppets took her side and encouraged her to stay on. On that question and in the dark, he lay down to rest. A clear mind needed rest and no congestion.

Nearly all the puppets had gathered near his quarters before he was up. They sounded excited. The rotten smell had gone with the coldness of the gris-gris, which was a mighty relief for him. Now, he needed to figure out how to get Zasheri away. Zasheri walked in, beaming and asked, "How was your night?"

Uppermost in his mind was how to raise the subject worrying him as she excitedly rattled on, failing to notice his silence: "All the puppets are outside waiting to pay you their respects. Some of them want you to teach them the new dance moves," she informed him.

His mind wrapped around how to leave Ntubiseh, he did not know how to answer her. She added, "Also, Makenji wants you to help him decide a problem at the palace." His silence and racing mind had not struck her yet.

Hearing her, he surmised that he could dance and that he was a decision-maker. He decided to try his luck and to go for the jugular. "My princess," he gingerly introduced.

At this, she noticed his mood and guessed something was amiss. Instantly, her excitement quickly shrank.

"We have to leave now," he declared, avoiding anything that would tempt him to postpone the precision of their instant need. "We have to continue on our journey in quest of Kwifon," he added, attempting to read the expression on her face.

She went blank and silent, a smile escaping her mouth from the sides with the loaded question, "What is Kwifon? Have you lost your mind? This is home," she said calmly. "Because you hit your head, you might think strangely for a while, but you will recover with a little more time."

Kajere saw how much more complicated the matter would be than he had thought. Who or from where could he get any help? Clearly, if his gris-gris had been strong enough mungang, they would not have been caught in here in the first place; whoever inflicted nshua on them must have had stronger mungang.

He wondered whether nshua precluded proper reasoning as he spoke with Zasheri, "You have to listen to me, your highness. You have been afflicted with nshua, just like I was." As he spoke, he tried to hold her hands, but she withdrew them and retreated slowly and with fear.

"Please, stop this insanity," Zasheri said.

Kajere had to use other tactics, but where to begin bugged him. He stopped advancing towards her, adjusted himself, and walked outside instead. When he emerged, everyone cheered, Makenji and Ewusa beaming with pleasure and simultaneously calling out, "Kajere, welcome."

"Thank you," Kajere replied, uncomfortable about extricating himself from them.

"Are you ready to dance again?" a voice shouted from the crowd. While he was still baffled by the attributed dancing, which he could not remember, everyone started shouting, "Yes! Yes!" Although he did not know he could dance, apparently, everyone believed he could. He decided to go along with the charade.

"So, I know how to dance?" he asked, much to the merriment of all the puppets who thought he was joking. He too laughed, wondering where this would lead him.

"Yes," Makenji replied, playing up the fun. "You are the best dancer in the whole world, and everyone wants to learn from you." A little exaggeration did not expose the reality Kajere was strange to.

As he talked, his mind zipping and zapping for ways to Zasheri and himself out of there, he saw Zasheri emerge from his quarters slowly, taking a nondescript posture and position among the crowd.

"Show us your latest style!" someone shouted.

This embarrassed Kajere, and he asked, "Right now?" scared of disappointing them.

But the enthusiastic crowd screamed out, "Yes! Yes!" Zasheri suspiciously and silently watching from her niche. Immediately, they formed a circle around Kajere; some drummers and other musicians started playing on their instruments. The music was so good and outstanding, and Ewusa decided to be the lead singer, everyone waiting for Kajere to dance. He yielded and took a couple of steps in rhythm following the beat, but nothing spectacular followed. The crowd was disappointed.

Suspicious but lost in the crowd was Nganga, who sensed that something was wrong and very wrong, although he could not place a finger on the exact spot. This world dancer ranking stranger could not so suddenly and casually have lost his skills. Meanwhile, a yell from one of the puppets smacked every ear: "Maybe we all have to forget like he is pretending to do. Maybe that will make better dancers of us all." No one seemed to understand the situation, but the puppet's voice echoed, and they all developed amnesia to be like Kajere. Kajere, Zasheri, and Nganga were taken off guard by this. This pretentious collective hypnotism included even Makenji and Ewusa. The puppets behaving as if they had forgotten everything about their lives created a spectacular scenic situation.

Kajere was lost in the act, and understanding only came afterward. But he rose to the situation and thought it a golden opportunity to abduct and run away with Zasheri. He did not have an idea about what direction to go. But Nganga did not fall for the melee and followed everything with suspicion. He approached Makenji later that day and expressed concern: "I think something is wrong with Kajere."

"What again?" Makenji asked defensively.

Nganga had a pack in his suspicious quiver. "Kajere was the best dancer before he fell unconscious. Now, he does not know how to dance, or so he wants us to believe. Isn't that strange?" he asked guardedly.

"You and evil ideas, eh Nganga!" Makenji retorted, incensed. "You are like all cynics, knowing the price of everything and the value of nothing. Why don't you think he was trying to teach a new style?"

"Is that how you see it?" Nganga asked. He did not like Makenji's exaggerated trust and value for Kajere.

Makenji delivered the killer snipe by asking, "Are you so jealous of him for transforming us into puppets? Is the fact that we learn styles so obnoxious to you? Don't you want to change, which is the only constant that is self-renewing?" Makenji plied Nganga with incensed, rhetorical, snide remarks.

To Nganga, Makenji was driving his attachment to the strangers to a ridiculous extent. He almost laughed but caught himself on time, volunteering only to ask blandly, "You really think I am jealous of him?"

"You are! It has been established," Makenji replied, unable to conceal his dissatisfaction. "It started manifesting when I suggested they become members of our ngumba house." Makenji continued.

"You miss out on something," Nganga protested, "That something is a reality happening right now under your nose. Think about it!"

"You begin to upset me, Nganga. Your sickening complaints tire me out. Why do you hate these people so much as not to want them to live with us? A word from you against them once more, and you will be on exile," Makenji said with finality.

Nganga could not explain the attachment of Makenji, Ewusa, and everyone in the land to these strangers. Were they hypnotized or bewitched by Kajere and Zasheri? He decided on a one-man offensive to stop Kajere. He had suspected him from the moment of their first encounter. He was convinced that his suspicions were now being proven to be true. He was indeed facing an enormous challenge, being the only one with this interpretation, a loner in a big field of opposition, compounded by the fact that to achieve this magnitude of bewitching, Kajere had to have very powerful mungangs. Just why had the puppets been so quick to abandon their ways for those of the foreigner who looked and behaved so differently? This power of mind-control was surely sourced in great power.

But Zasheri, too, unknown to Makenji and Nganga, was troubled by Kajere's behavior. There was something the matter with him, but her misfortune was that she could not share her worry with anyone else since they all idolized him, seeking to be like him and to copy his ways. That is how, with the unfolding of the day, he felt that something good was happening. But first, from her distance, she watched what at first seemed to indicate that Kajere was making a fool of himself until her mood swung back from seeing the genuine faith of the puppets. She jumped into the fray and danced so well that Kajere's jaw dropped in disbelief. She leaped around the arena with the lightness of a winged creature, her feet lightly caressing the earth, and everyone screaming in ecstatic thrill.

Kajere noticed that Nganga did not seem interested in what

was happening. Somehow, he had the conviction that if he had to leave, Nganga was the only puppet who would help him do so. For something, Nganga told him he could be an ally in his escape plan. That night, therefore, he stole himself into Nganga's quarters. Nganga was not asleep. He heard his footsteps.

"Who's there?" he asked, concerned but not afraid that someone was visiting him that late at night. To his surprise, Kajere, the very person he was plotting to get out of the land, made his appearance. His mind raced in all directions to make meaning of the visit from him.

"Greetings, my father?" Kajere spoke.

"Greetings," the puppet replied, trying hard not to sound or look suspicious.

Kajere was quick to unburden himself. "You are certainly surprised to see me here at this hour. Let me not waste your time with preambles. I saw the way you were looking at me earlier today when I tried to dance. Suspicion was in your look."

This preamble put Nganga on the alert and confirmed his suspicion that Kajere was using powerful mungang to influence the puppets. How else could he have read him that exactly, he wondered. Nganga shifted in his seat, a little cowed, but offered Kajere a seat, wondering what trap the powerful man was laying for him. Yet, he ventured to tease out the truth, for he would gain nothing if he did not venture anything.

"What made you think so?" Nganga asked.

"You could not have been more direct by your look at me," Kajere said.

Nganga did not know what to do or say. He kept quiet. He had no idea where Kajere was leading. Kajere simply embarrassed him with the truth that he felt the pressure to leave as soon as possible. So urgent was the pressure that he felt it would be good to do so as soon as was possible. That very night, he declared, was as good a time as any. He was not padding about Nganga's hate. The sarcasm in Nganga's voice and looks indicated that he would be glad to see him and Zasheri gone. He pleaded, "Nganga, listen to me, please. We need to leave Ntubiseh as soon as possible."

Nganga wondered whether he had missed out on something. Was it possible, or was Kajere setting a trap for him? Evil and good could be housed by the same plant, house, or setup. He hesitated because of this quandary of determining the intention behind Kajere's plea, while Kajere considered his hesitation as a ploy, fearing that he could raise the alarm. Nganga interrupted his thoughts.

"I may not have heard you well. Did you say you want to leave us? You and your princess?" Nganga asked, and Kajere nodded slowly, his defenses on the alert. Nganga's own defenses were also on full alert and he needed to test the genuineness of Kajere further. "Hmmm, are you crazy? Why would you want to do something like that? And why are you telling me? Why don't you tell the fon?" He emphasized the word 'fon'.

"I don't want him to know, so just trust that I could let you know," Kajere replied, still guardedly.

Nganga wondered whether to let his guards down now, trusting Kajere. Could he be straight with him and tell him how he felt, or should he take the part of him that saw the thing as a charade? He took the risk, knowing that trust generated trust.

"When Makenji wanted you and your princess to become members of our ngumba house, I vehemently opposed it," Nganga informed Kajere.

Kajere ignored the implications and said, "I only came here to ask you to help me and my princess escape, if possible, tonight."

For Nganga, this information was too good to be true, and Kajere sensed his uncertainty.

Then, pointing at the gris-gris on his neck, Kajere asked, "You see this?" and Nganga nodded.

"Do you know what it is?" Kajere asked, to which Nganga shook his head in negation.

"This is my gris-gris, the mungang that is showing me what direction to go in search of Kwifon," Kajere explained.

Nganga nodded, squinting in the dark to have a better look at the gris-gris. A friendship of sorts was building between them, for they had a mighty focal commonality now. "Are you really that serious about seeking Kwifon?" Nganga asked in stupefied half-admiration of this dreamer of the impossible.

"Yes," Kajere asserted with a firmness that left no doubt. Then he added, "We journeyed long to get here."

It was a ponderous moment, and Nganga remained silent.

"When I fell and hit my head, a vision cleared my head of the affliction of nshua. My princess is still under the aegis of it as we speak, but I know it's time for us to leave," Kajere explained to the incredulous Nganga.

"I've heard about nshua as an idea, but not that it actually exists," Nganga said, visibly more relaxed, seeing that Kajere was neither a threat nor a trap for him. "So why don't you simply take your princess and leave? Why do you need to inform me about it?" he asked.

"As I have said, she is right now afflicted with nshua and would not listen to me. She thinks I'm mad for telling her about her situation and if I try to force her, she will tell the fon. That is not a risk I want to take," Kajere said.

Nganga nodded, thinking quickly about what he should do. "We have a bit of a problem because if you leave, he will think I forced you out, and that will be big trouble for me," Nganga announced.

This took the wind out of Kajere's sail for a moment, and after a brief silence, he quietly asked, "Is he right in thinking you want us out?"

Was this the initial trap, and had he fallen for it? Nganga thought. He did not answer but nodded slowly, saying, "Yes, but now I see your side."

"Nothing to worry there, Nganga. You loved and wanted to protect your land and your people," Kajere consoled, and another stretch of silence ensued.

The silence issued in resolve as Nganga felt obliged to be cooperative. "So, do you have any ideas?" Nganga asked.

"Yes, but risky," Kajere replied. "If you would go to Zasheri's quarters now and tell her Ewusa wants to see her, that would give us a head start. She will surely be surprised to see you there, but she will surely oblige. When she gets out, hit her on the head for her to swoon. At this stage, I will take her away," Kajere exposed the kidnap scheme.

As Nganga thought and delayed, Kajere interjected, "Do you think you can do me that favor?"

Nganga was in no haste to respond. He needed to weigh the pros, cons, risks, and sequences. The urge to make Makenji look stupid pumped his blood up. He contemplated the scene during which he would gloatingly make him see and say that he was right. This overwhelmed all the other options of his SWOT analysis. He yielded, held out a hand, and Kajere took it.

"Even though I did not want you to become members of our ngumba house, we learned a lot from you," he confessed. "I can only wish you luck in your search for Kwifon and cooperate to get you going," he said, gentlemanliness suddenly flooding his puppet face.

They held their greeting hands for a long time, cementing a loyalty bond as they gently jerked the interlocked hands up and down.

Kajere was most grateful. "Thank you," he solemnly declared, and Nganga nodded, a smile and relief defining his puppet look.

United in purpose, they could execute their plan to perfection later that night. As projected, Nganga lured Zasheri out and hit her head. Kajere was ready, and she fell into his arms unconscious. There was no mediation time to lose, for an alarm could ruin the expedited plot this far. And so, before Nganga could wave them goodbye, Kajere was off and running with Zasheri swinging limply in front and behind him from his shoulder. Given the weight, his speed was supernatural, not to say supersonic, which stupefied Nganga, who now felt a pull of loyalty and attachment towards these people whom he had detested at the start.

Hours later, a great distance away from the kidnapping scene from which he had raced at breakneck speed, Kajere heard a noise above and looked up. It was Shengah who soon landed. No time to lose, Kajere hauled the limp Zasheri across the bird and climbed up to position himself to support the princess. Not finding it secure enough to support her, he firmly strapped her up, making sure her face pressed against the gris-gris. This he did in the hope that when she regained consciousness, she would know that she was safe in his arms. Then Shengah made a preliminary walk, then a short, quick run, and flew off high in the air with its load.

Eleven

Ventures in Bunejeh

I felt myself emerging from the never-ending darkness and wondered where I was. Again, I thought I was slipping in and out of consciousness. I could not seem to focus, and what was that smell that would not go away? Then, again, I felt conscious once more, and it seemed I was flying.

I decided that I was in a dream and would soon wake up, but the dream felt very real. When I finally regained consciousness, I discovered that I was actually in the air and flying at a supernatural speed. Yet, the smell would not leave, and I had a thumping pain at the base of my head. I looked for Ewusa and Makenji, but could not see them.

The sun was so bright that I was almost blinded by it. The sky was an intense blue. The only person I saw was my faithful companion, Kajere. I tried to smile at him, and he smiled broadly back at me. I could not move when I tried to. I was heavily strapped, my face close to his chest, with his gris-gris almost covering my whole face. Where was I, I wondered? What was happening? And why was I so tightly strapped to Kajere and the gris-gris, I wondered as we flew on. And what was that strong smell that would not go away, but was rather pinging deeper into my body, particularly my lungs and head?

It was acrid and kept penetrating, creating distaste and discomfort. The strapping was worsened the discomfort. I appealed to Kajere.

"Where am I?" I asked.

"Hello, my princess," Kajere said, happy she was recovering. "How are you feeling?" he inquired at the same time, feeling some qualms about the pain he inflicted on her. His steering the flying object did not distract him from being caring.

"Fine," I replied, but hastened to add, "Can you undo me?" I wriggled to get out, but Kajere would not help, which rattled me at first.

While trying to steer Shengah, he explained, "Princess, I can't undo you now."

"You can!" I retorted acidly and threatened, "If you don't, I will make sure Makenji and Ewusa are informed about it." Kajere's look scared me at the mention of the two names.

Then, as if to calm the dread on my face, he explained, "My princess, you know I respect you, and whatever I do is for you and Tikari."

"What exactly is Tikari?" I asked, my ignorance of the word Tikari seeming to tick him off. He looked at me strangely, but his words were soft and reassuring:

"I love you and Tikari," he said, striking me on the head.

I must have been unconscious for a really long time. When I began to regain consciousness, we were flying through a massive thunderstorm in thick darkness, with heavy rain clouds. The deep rumble of thunder belted across the skies after intermittent lightning flashes. The heavy raindrops pelted my face, giving me a pleasurably caressing feel. However, there was the unyielding stench whose source I could not tell. I opened my eyes by a fraction and saw Kajere steering what I discovered was a bird across the dark sky. I wondered whether it could be Shengah, but the stench was distorting my perception.

"What is that smell?" I muttered loud enough for Kajere to hear me.

"You are awake, my princess," Kajere began.

“I’ve told you to call me Zasheri,” I said sternly. “Just what is that smell?” I asked without a pause.

“No idea,” he said casually, explaining, “I can’t smell anything.” He struggled to control the bird through the wind and the rain, and I sat silent for a moment until curiosity made me speak:

“We are on Shengah, how come?” I asked as softly as I could against the torrential rainfall. He heard me, and a smile beamed across his face.

“Yes, this is Shengah,” he answered without hurrying to explain how we came by it. The smell still bothered me and was still seeping into my body. Kajere continued leisurely, “It carried us as I ran with you. It has always known where to take us,” Kajere smiled sincerely as he spoke.

I soon started focusing. Then I groped for the strong belt I always had around my waist, containing Ngounso’s mungang seeds. It was still there, remarkably intact.

Kajere interrupted me with the question, “Do you know where Tikari is?” I was surprised and a little angry at the question, wondering whether he thought I was still unconscious or had lost my mind. Perhaps something is the matter with him, I surmised and confronted him with his own mess:

“What kind of stupid question is that?” I spouted out heatedly. “You ask the princess whether she knows her own fief? Or have you forgotten?”

Kajere leapt for joy, almost forgetting we were in the air; he nearly fell off Shengah.

The smell evaporated without warning, and I felt better and lighter. Kajere’s hands were undoing the strings that bound me to him and the gris-gris. Had anything I had said caused him to be so positive, I wondered?

He spoke, “You’re back, Zasheri, you’re back!” He called me Zasheri as naturally as I had ever heard him call me and went on,

"Do you remember anything that happened recently?"

I settled myself on Shengah's back and thought hard, trying to remember what had led to the present situation. My mind was foggy, unable to focus. Yes, I did remember that we had landed in Ntubiseh and met puppets and their king and queen. But that is as far as I went in clear or sensible focus. Beyond that, I knew next to nothing; I could not even tell how long we were there.

Kajere laughed. "Nshua caught you and me," he said, and I took it for a joke. I knew Nshua, the forgetful disease. Upon contracting it, you begin to love intensely and become attached to where you find yourself. No one in my memory ever recovered from it after contracting it.

"Nshua!" I pronounced incredulously. He nodded, and I went quiet for a moment to digest the enormity of what he had just said. "So, how long were we in Ntubiseh, and how did you break the spell?" I asked as we buffeted against the wind, the rain, and the darkness.

He touched his gris-gris and said, "I had a dream."

Although I had always been thankful for the gris-gris, never had I been this grateful for it. We kept flying rapidly, and I fell asleep. When I woke, the sun was up in the sky of a brightly beautiful day, Kajere still controlling Shengah. I expected Shengah to drop us off sooner or later and then leave until it was ready for another journey with us. I wish it would drop us this time around somewhere in the neighborhood of the Kwifon of Mekan so we can take it and return home. Nights and more days caught us in flight, my mind straying off to Tikari and how people were wondering about our whereabouts. Ngounso, in particular, was my focus, and I hoped she could keep Wubangeh and my sister under control. Her mungangs being with me meant that her powers were greatly diminished. I didn't expect Nkukanteh to be of much help, being someone with certain strong traditional biases.

Casually looking down, I noticed some changes in the topography of the land we were flying over. More mountainous and grassland features showed up, and it felt much colder. I wrapped myself up to keep warm. From my wandering thoughts and then to the topography and weather conditions, I burst into whatever might have been Kajere's thinking:

"Can you feel how cold it is?" I asked.

"It is quite cold," he confirmed, maneuvering Shengah. "I hope it gets warmer," he continued. Then Shengah cowed. It was a sound I had heard before and remembered that it signaled the beginning of another phase of our journey. Indeed, that is how it was, for Shengah flew gently down and landed. When I stole a glance at Shengah and Kajere, I read something inexplicably odd in the eyes of the bird. I made a mental note that I would bring the matter up with Kajere after we landed and understood our bearings better.

Immediately after shedding us, Shengah flew away, a sign that we would be in the new place for a good while. It dropped something, which Kajere picked up and scrutinized. It wasn't something familiar to us. We hadn't even heard of its likes. A hard, transparent wooden object on one end; it had a leather string, which suggested to Kajere that it could be tied around his waist or strung around his neck. But he needed my input for better understanding.

"What's this?" Kajere half asked me and half murmured to himself.

I shrugged my shoulders, saying, "I don't know," and we took a while trying to understand the object and its possible functional application.

Probing for possibilities, Kajere said, "If Shengah leaves this for us, we shall be needing it in our search for Kwifon."

The logic was unimpeachable, and I agreed with it. Kajere soon figured out with excitement and relief what the object really was. Looking through it, he screamed and jumped with delight.

It was a good thing, I decided and asked for precision, "What is it?"

"Here. Look!" he exclaimed, handing the object to me. As I hesitated, he teased, "It won't bite! It won't eat you. Look here," he pointed to a hole at its base. I took a peek, seeing nothing at first. Then Kajere adjusted something on it, and I screamed and jumped, leaving him laughing empathetically. "This thing makes what is far look close," he said, examining it carefully. Then he looked through once more.

"Incredible!" he said. "The message is clear. We can use this to see people before they know we are there."

I also took my time to examine it meticulously. The wooden part had intricate designs of various animals and birds carved on it. While I studied it, Kajere took the time to look at where Shengah had dropped us off. In our excitement about the object, we had not yet looked at our surroundings.

"Just where are we this time? I hope we're in Mekan or very near it," Kajere said, looking around and gauging our position.

I peeped through the object, seeing far, but, at least for that moment, there was not much I could see that naked eyes could not. For convenience, I called the object, *lieshih*. Perhaps from the excitement of having this strange object, my optimism peaked, and I said, "No matter where we are, we are certainly closer to Mekan and Kwifon." I tried to sound casual, but I was scared. Kajere was my bulwark; having spent so much time together in our journeys, I had come to trust him totally. I gave him lieshih and we explored the new place, wondering what new adventures we would encounter. Again, I felt for the mungang around my waist and developed qualms for not telling Kajere that I had received help from Ngounso to come after him. I managed to keep back the worry and to trust that Kajere's gris-gris would lead the way. It did.

In the distance, we heard some animals. I could not tell what they were since we could not see anything. The thoroughfare we were passing through was unlike anything I had seen before. Leading the way, I was the first to see it. Kajere was behind me as I uttered a low scream. Kajere quickly overtook me to see and face whatever had caused me to scream. I only pointed at the scary spectacle—a man walking backwards.

We looked closer. It was not an act. It was a natural thing, and he was actually walking normally. However, it seemed he did not know where he was going. We stood still as he came nearer. He got near enough for me to hear him muttering some incomprehensible sounds, walking past us, eyes wide open and hands outstretched. He did not see us; if he did, he did an excellent job of acting like he did not. A natural spectacle in my view, he was the object of my glaring stare.

Cooler-headed, Kajere quickly formed a plan. He allowed the man to go a few paces away, then beckoned to me and half whispered, "Let's follow him."

Unlike Kajere, I had no formed plan, but expressed my doubt in a question, "Are you sure?" whispered back to him. He nodded, and we followed the man for what felt like hours, and when we got to the top of a hill, we saw him begin the descent. From the hilltop we looked through the lieshih down a vast valley below that extended as far as we could see and disappeared far into the horizon. From it rose a noise, monotonous and unending, wind-wafted up to us. We stood staring down a massive river snaking through the valley. It separated the setup into two settlements, each on either side. We would later discover that, though they had many similarities, external forces had forced specific differences on the two camps, making them look different.

Everyone we saw seemed to be roaming, compounded by the unrelenting irritation of the deep hum coming from there. So deep was the sound that I could feel the pit of my stomach rocking in consonance with it. It is Kajere who made me have an idea of the sound source.

"They look like somnambulists," Kajere said surreptitiously about the roamers.

"What does that mean?" I asked, unused to the idea and word.

"They are sleepwalkers," he said, altering the expression and smiling.

"Are you sure about that?" I asked because they were awake and normal except for not noticing each other and their routine activity.

"I think so, and they seem to converge here from somewhere else," Kajere said studiously as we slowly descended the hill.

"And how do you arrive at that piece of detail?" I asked. As far as I could see, there was nothing to suggest what he just said.

"If you observe well, they are not blind, don't walk into each other, and do nothing sensible. Let's take a closer look," Kajere said without clarifying his source of the information, that they came from elsewhere.

Memory lit up and I said, "If you're right, this place must be that which is called Bunejeh, land of sleepwalkers."

"Am I missing something here?" he asked and I sensed he had not heard about Bunejeh.

"Bunejeh," I said again, and he repeated the word after me for exactitude. It took a few attempts to get it right, and I laughed at his gaffing.

"Which means you've heard about them before!" Kajere exclaimed, briefly focusing attention on me.

"That's right," I said. "Father told us about them long ago, but we did not take him seriously or see the relevance of what we considered a mythical place to Tikari." We were awed as we took careful steps down the steep side of the grassy mountain.

"Your father knew better, then; the place is right here," Kajere whispered, pausing on his track so as not to trip or slide to a fall.

I whispered back, "Why are they gathered here? What attracts them here?"

"I don't know, but we will not be in doubt for long because a solution to a challenge is always within the ambit of how the thing operates," Kajere said wisely as I kept close behind him. I was afraid of one or several of them pouncing on us.

"Can they attack us?" I asked, fear pushing me to instantly finger the mungangs in my belt in case their potency needed to come in handy.

"Not likely," Kajere replied casually. "I even wonder if they can perceive our presence now."

Kajere's explanation paled before the awkward walk performance of the people. I was as scared as I had been from the start.

We also noticed that they seemed to be in an undetermined number of groups. We made our way gingerly towards the foot of the mountain, absorbing as much of the thoroughfare as we could in spite of the noise and the somnambulists. Additionally, there was a putrid stench emanating from the valley below. It was intermittently wafted to us by the direction and strength of the wind, but there was no escaping from the stench, for I sensed it in every direction I turned my head. Kajere also felt the stench and asked more to himself than to me, "How can anyone live in such a putrid atmosphere?"

Although the stench preoccupied me, I felt our stay would be exciting while simultaneously hoping we would not be there long. This was undoubtedly not Mekan, and the Kwifon could not be in this place. Even the beautiful trees and plants we found on our way down were tainted with the stench.

Arriving at the foot of the mountain and walking its vast plain, we saw the gathering of the somnambulists from everywhere imaginable. Thousands arrived just as thousands left, their movement being eternal. We could not establish how long they stayed before departing, and it would take us a great deal of time to understand the goings-on there. A feeling that something strange was about to happen came upon me as we made our way through Bunejeh, choosing to start exploring the settlement to the left of the river and to explore the other side later.

We traversed the vast dwellings but no one saw us. They trooped past, engaged in various activities, not bothering how their actions affected others. They indeed lived in communal groupings, but each was independently doing what they were destined to do.

"It's getting dark," Kajere said, "let's find somewhere to rest." We found a place where the stench was minimal. It was a little way off from the settlement and I could tell that Kajere was unsatisfied with it. We pitched camp there, none of the inhabitants seeming to be bothered by the smell. I got the feeling that they had no sense of smell.

The following day, we explored Bunejeh to the left of the river. It took us the whole day to walk around the establishment and kept walking into people. Perhaps it is better to say that different people kept walking into us, a scary discomfort at the start, until I got used to it. They hardly walked into each other, however. But we were pretty much observers and not interactors with these folks. Shengah probably dropped us here to cultivate our abilities to observe and not to be a part of the settlement. Among themselves, the harmony and precision they had seemed to evolve from the apparent chaos, an organized chaos, so to speak.

I counted some fifty-four settlements, about twenty-nine to the west, some seventeen to the north, south, and east. Just four were to the south, a great distance from the seventeen. Kajere's curiosity pushed him to investigate the reason for the arrangement and the differentiating factor among them.

One way of doing this was to attempt to interact with the Bunejehs, which was both complex and comic. After a few hours of walking, we sat by a large tree, the species of which I was not familiar with. There, we rested, dead tired after walking around the settlements. We were joined by one man who came, sat beside us, and started talking, all to himself, as it turned out. But the discovery that he was speaking to himself came after attempts to interact with him.

"Money is no medicine against death," he drawled.

"Are you talking to us?" Kajere asked, tilting towards him.

The man simply said, "Speak less and carry a big stick; you will go far," again with a drawl, adding, "If the cockroach wants to gain power over the chicken, it has to hire the fox for bodyguard."

"He can't hear us," Kajere resolved, surprised at the man's disconnected pronouncements.

It was quite puzzling and I asked, "What should we do?" It was hard to be an observer in that environment.

The man got up and tried to climb the tree under which we sat. It was a massive tree, and I knew he could not climb it, at least not in his state. Nevertheless, a twisted convergence of comedy and seriousness followed as we watched him try. To watch, we shifted from where we had sat. He would take some steps backward and make a brief run, then try to climb. He punctually fell back each time and would mutter what to us was gibberish. Before long, he was foaming at both sides of the mouth, but not giving up. His garb would get attached to the tree trunk and he would fall in the attempt to extricate himself. Then he would start all over, all the time muttering. Around him and us, life for the other Bunejehs was without any change, and no one noticed the other.

It was not as if he only made statements and stopped there. There was continuity in what he said, albeit in images. The main abnormality was the drawl and punctual repetition: "Money is not the medicine against death. If you speak softly and carry a big stick, you will go far. If the cockroach wants to rule over the chicken, it must hire the fox as its bodyguard."

"Is he insane?" I asked Kajere, and he laughed before responding:

"No way!" but he did not miss the funny side of the man's words and actions. "Rather, he's asleep," Kajere said laconically.

I felt the total weight of what Kajere meant and began to look at him in a new light. His wisdom was more obvious, making me see why my father and Ngounso had chosen him to lead us against the Ketummites. This cast the odyssey into a new light. It became increasingly obvious that, beyond the direct search for Kwifon, it served as a learning process.

A changed expression from the man followed a brutal fall in the attempt to climb: "If someone is well-mannered, then anything ugly turns beautiful, and anything beautiful turns ugly." It was tempting to attribute the change in the wise enunciations to the hurt from the fall. Drap platitudes replaced what he had been saying.

"Happiness can only happen when we all understand each other; my bosom friend can become my worst enemy." This seemed like a cue to Kajere, who immediately motioned for us to leave.

"Let's go to another site and maybe learn newer things," he suggested.

"Where should we go?" I asked as we were already walking around the settlement.

"No idea," Kajere said. "Let's find the source of the smell. It's unbearable."

Before we knew it, the weather had changed. Dark clouds covered the sun; deep thunder rumbled in the background, accompanied by flashes of lightning. It got eerie.

"It's going to rain," I muttered.

"I doubt that," Kajere said with unaccountable assurance to my surprise.

"How?" I asked, stretching out the single-word question.

"I see the sunlight pointing in that direction." He pointed north. He was right. It was bright, but not a good omen, then, I saw it. And indeed, we hardly had started walking away from the man when a spectacle made me rethink our being among the Bunejeh. What appeared to be a mother and her child were walking northward away from us, and we decided to follow them. That was the first mother and child together we had encountered, and they seemed to be communicating with each other, but they had the same glazed look everyone else had. They did not seem to look at each other directly while speaking, which was perhaps my perception, given their glazed looks.

"I've always told you to stay beside me. Why are you always running away?" the mother asked the child, her tone brisk and mechanical.

"I'm playing," the child replied. Its tone was also mechanical as they waded through one of the muddy slimes near the river. "I'm looking for anyone who wants to play with me and my toy."

At this point, I noticed that the child was carrying what looked like a puppet or totem, a tiny thing. It was hard to tell whether it was an animal or a human carving. Its black-and-white stripes suggested animal skin.

"What a toy!" I commented to Kajere, who then took a closer look as the child walked.

"It does not seem to be a toy," he said.

Instead of responding to Kajere's suggestion, the glazed look triggered my interest, and I commented and laughed a little, "I don't think they can see you."

Kajere did not echo my light spirit by turns severe, intent on examining what the child carried.

His attitude aroused my curiosity, and I asked, "What do you think it is?"

"I cannot tell yet. Looks like some mungang or object of worship. It could possess strong powers."

"How do you come by that?" I asked, the child having tarried to play with some insects near a muddy pool.

"The way the thing looks suggests that it has some power and can tell who we are," Kajere said softly and rather cautiously. Just then, as if on cue, the mother called out to the child again.

"Don't stand there playing; come and help me look for food," she said dryly and they promptly got up to rejoin her mother. Just then, drama started as a group of Bunejehs, all clad in white, materialized, quickly approaching the woman and her child, one of them making for the totem to which the little girl was tightly clinging.

One of the men spoke out angrily, "We've warned you against bringing that thing here; you never listen. How do you think you and your child can be like us if you walk around exhibiting this thing about which we have warned you many times?"

The others were struggling to wrench the totem from the child as he spoke, but the child clung to it, crying hysterically. I made to intervene, but was restrained by Kajere, telling me, "They can't see us, can't you see? What might happen if you join that fight is not known to you and I. Let's keep watch and be alert in order to see what happens next or eventually. Understanding the place and its people is of primary importance," he cautioned and I knew he was right.

One of the persons in white, the one who had spoken before, ordered, "Take that thing away from that child! If they want to be like us, they have to take our orders."

Much of what was going on made no sense to us. The woman turned around, swiftly snatching her child's totem and throwing it into the fast-moving river. The child cried and ran towards it as if she would dive after the totem, but she stopped short and came back to her mother. She was crying and pointing at the river, and her mother picked her up.

Gruffly speaking, the person who seemed to be the leader of the men in white said, "That's how it has to be," which made me so upset that I wanted to punch him, forgetting the wise counsel Kajere gave. He restrained me once more, saying, "Patience, my princess. Justice is your heartbeat, but we need patience in this strange environment."

He spoke right, for justice is also a function of context, and we were ill-informed about our circumstances.

"Are you happy now?" we heard the mother ask them.

"Yes," said the leader, adding, "That's the only way to become one of us. "His voice was slightly less gruff this time. With glazed and hardly blinking eyes, the mother and daughter walked around as if propelled by an external and powerful force. The glazed look was typical of the Bunejeh denizens.

As the woman walked away scolding her child, the others laughed among themselves, also going away.

I could not contain myself as I asked Kajere, "You see what happened?" He was about to reply when the same woman and child with the totem returned and were harried by the same people in white. Again, she threw her daughter's totem into the river, received the comments about their satisfaction from the men in white, and the circle went round and was repeated yet again. I found it difficult to get my head around it. It was hard to know why the mother so desperately wanted to be one of the white turbaned people at such emotional cost to her daughter. Kajere's suggestion for us to wait patiently was most valid in the circumstances.

We spent time among the settlement of about twenty-nine clans, trying to get to the source of the smell and also inquisitive about the criteria for the partitioning of Bunejeh. There was remarkable order undercut by phenomenal disorganization. The astringent, paradoxical nature of the clan was evident in the grouping. It showed up the remarkable construction and deconstruction talent. No obvious reason accounted for either action. This lack of logical cause for action showed in multiple ways.

Thus, we watched one woman mount pumpkins to form a huge triangle, after which she walked to a nearby ridge recently made by her, it seemed. From that ridge, she brought a pumpkin and carefully placed it on the mound of pumpkins, muttering rapidly and incoherently to herself, foaming at both sides of her mouth in the process. Then, another woman came and walked on her neat mound of pumpkins, bringing everything crashing down without a word.

"What made her do that?" I asked Kajere, but he simply put his fingers across his lips and pointed for me to watch. This time, it was a man building another mound, then a woman brought the mound down, and the process was started all over. It made no sense to me. And around the woman, other Bunejehs engaged in different activities that simultaneously seemed meaningful and meaningless. The differences were in who did what. For the woman who brought down the man's mound, she also built her own, and the man walked through it, bringing it down for the process to start all over.

It seemed that the entire scenario was leading nowhere, so I told Kajere, "Let's stop here."

"Not yet," he replied with customary calmness, which made me mad at him.

"Why are you so calm, witnessing such chaotic behavior? Such frustrating nonsense! Can't you use your gris-gris power to stop it?" I asked him heatedly.

"Relax, princess," Kajere said, refusing to be flustered, but in a calm monotone that had the quality of Bunejeh voices, explained: "We don't know how long they've been here, and we don't know how long that woman has been doing that. Maybe both sides must do that to each other. How do we know? Let's not judge by that which we see."

"What, in other words, are you trying to say?"

"I can't use my gris-gris when I don't have to, and when I don't believe they are in any danger, or if it is stopping us from finding Kwifon," he continued, his look glued to the woman at work.

I decided to act without consulting him. After the woman constructed the mound, I made to run up to the man who was about to walk into the mound. Just before I was to push him off, Kajere caught me and carried me away, angrier than I was.

"Suppose you wake them up? Then what? Do you know the kind of confusion you can create?" he asked as he eased me on the ground. I had not thought about that.

"But how can we accept such injustice?" I protested, but Kajere pulled me away.

"Let's not confound our investigation with intervention," he said. "Multiple-tasking usually has to do with doing similar things at the same time. Contraries must be set apart. No intermingling of opposites. No yoking of contraries. Remember that we are only at the beginning and more might happen that may resolve or further confound us," he lectured.

Despite my inhibitions, I agreed to go along with him, glad that he suggested that we walk around. In the process, my eyes opened to other hard-to-understand activities. When we rounded one corner, twenty-nine warriors were seen being led in marching, all attired in short leather skirts and with no shirts on. They were wielding thick cudgels, their leader a strange-looking figure. Whether the leader was male or female, it was hard to tell as white turbans covered the figure's entire body. It was both fascinating and scary to watch the warriors marching with great precision. They synced their actions with the masked figure's orders. Then they would stop and reenact a duel for some minutes, all with great precision. It was hard to believe they were not seeing each other in real life, but Bunejehs reacted subconsciously. It turned out that they were one source of the stench that permeated the setup. Yet, it was hard to tell whether their outfits or bodies emitted it. In any case, the pungency was so harsh near them that Kajere shifted away and sat beneath a tree, motioning for me to join him. I was loath to leave where I stood since I wanted to watch what was unfolding better, but the stench also deterred me.

The leader in a deep baritone called out to the soldiers, "You want to be like me, and you want to know where I'm from?" It was virtually a singsong or incantatory tune to which the warriors responded in unison.

"Yes!"

"You want to be like me, and you want to know where I'm from?" He would ask again.

"Yes! Yes!" they would reply.

"Then do as I say," he would say.

Then, two fighters would face each other in a mock wrestling match for a few minutes before walking randomly among other differently engaged Bunejehs. They would carry individuals, throw them in the air, catch them, and then march the unfortunate Bunejeh away. Upon returning to the military fold, the said duelers would be tossed white garbs to wrap themselves in. However, putting on the apparel was futile because it would keep falling. Eventually, it tangled the attempting wearer and would be cast aside. Then the leader would say, "You are not ready, you see! You cannot be like me if you can't do a simple thing like wearing those clothes. Only the strong can become a fighter like me," he would say, his tone a combination of anger and mockery.

All the warriors unsuccessfully tried to become like their leader and angrily dispersed among other Bunejehs. They would be shoved and viciously cudgeled while the leader gathered away their cudgels and other items. Following that, he would march the failed soldiers around the clan and then restart the whole process once more. The precision and dumbness of the Bunejehs were mind-rattling.

"Why don't they leave?" I found myself asking. "Why do you follow his instructions and obey him so slavishly?"

"They call that blind loyalty," Kajere said quietly, and I noticed that he was deeply quiet, troubled by the corruption of practiced suppression and victim cooperation.

I boiled with the desire to do something about it and said, "We have to do something." In reaction, he only nodded and I could see that he stuck to the idea that we needed to explore the camp further. We still had a lot to learn about Bunejeh. Our knowledge was based purely on what we had so far observed, and that did not seem to be enough data.

"Do you have any plans on what we need to do to be better informed?" I inquired, half believing he knew the answer.

"Time, the leveler, as some people categorize it, will help," he said, and added, "We will definitely find out about it." Then, he thought aloud, "Something to find out is why they only come to this place? What is it about it? What attracts them here?"

This is when this line of thought occurred to me. And indeed, as we traveled throughout this first camp, there was a lot we did not know about. We knew nothing about their objectives, why they were there in the first place, or why they were only at that spot. The twenty-nine clans in the locality were also a puzzle. Specific numbers like one, three, five, seven, ten, twelve, twenty, twenty-five, thirty, and forty, as well as many related numbers and round figures, had gathered significance. Twenty-nine was not in their number. I was, like Kajere, determined to get to the root of the matter.

Another section of the camp lay in a sizeable quagmire, to which we wondered. There sat some Bunejehs, mainly women and children, all working, weaving raffia bags in various colors. The fiber bags were so attractive that I would have touched them had Kajere not restrained me.

"Touch nothing yet!" he said in a somewhat strained voice held back by respect for me as a princess. When things were a bit rough, like now, he restrained himself, influenced by his awareness of our social ranks.

"Why?" I asked blandly. Although I saw his wisdom, I felt he needed to be more deliberate in his choices, declarations or instructions.

"Supposing you woke them up, can you predict their reactions? Fear of the unknown should temper our inquisitiveness." His firmness was tempered by expressed wisdom. Watching him so desperate to control himself put me on the brink of raucous laughter as we strolled through the camp, silently observing the sleepwalkers at work. Some of them lifted their heads and looked in our direction as we approached, but they were looking with unseeing eyes. The same glazed look characterized them all. The warriors would come leaping through the camp and intermittently splash dirty water from the quagmire onto everyone present. No one responded to the obvious humiliation, but they would wait until after the warriors departed before quietly resuming their work.

Righteous anger surged from deep within me at the sight of such injustice, pushing my frustration to a boiling point. "Why don't they do anything?" I asked Kajere.

"There is surely a reason why," he replied caustically, but when I looked at him, he quickly looked away, knowing I was mad at his acerbic tone. Then he said, "Just a joke; no harm meant. I withdraw the sarcasm." I could tell that he was genuinely contrite, and I accepted his apology. We continued watching the happenings in silence as was propitious.

"The water is so dirty, yet the bad smell does not come from it," he said, twitching his nose.

"The entire place stinks, yet the one place the smell should arise from has no pungent smell," I partially concurred, suspecting that he could not smell, especially as he still had the cloth over his face covering his nose. To prove him wrong, I walked closer to the quagmire, leaning over it with none of the Bunejehs looking in my direction. Kajere was right. The faint smell I sensed was definitely not from the odorless quagmire, where the general odor was least.

I walked back to Kajere in disbelief and asked, "How did you know the smell was not from the quagmire?"

"I see it through the innocent manner in which these people are making raffia," he said studiously. I did not see the connection between the innocence, fiber, or Bunejehs at work, but chose to keep quiet as we lingered around. We watched the Bunejeh weavers at work before Kajere signaled that it was time to move on. What we were seeing and how to remedy the situation and bring justice preoccupied my thinking.

As we rounded the corner, we came face to face with the wise man we had met before, the one who had been tiring himself with loud muttering. He was still at it, new words and ideas falling from his mouth: "The one who thinks himself a leader with no following is only walking," he said.

"Do you hear that?" I asked Kajere.

"He is still at it. It seems this is his way of life, unbending and unyielding. Let's follow him," Kajere said as if he had just received lucid light on the way forward. "A lesson or an idea might fall from his mouth to instruct us about this place."

"The ear that does not listen will also go when the head is chopped off," Wiseman said. "People should not talk when they are eating pepper, lest the pepper rush down the wrong road," he added, causing Kajere to laugh involuntarily. I also laughed, in spite of myself.

We followed him to another section of the camp where a woman was talking to herself. She was giving very clever instructions but to no one in particular, and I named her Wukitoff, or the wise woman. She was royalty in dress—colorfully and beautifully woven clothes, many layers of neck beads and chains, some gold, beads around her wrists, layered bracelets and other forms of body ornaments. Apart from talking, she was wailing loudly. Amidst the wails, she interjected quotable snippets.

"When hunting, be rubbed with *Banga oil*, so you'll be shining. Prey dread the shine. That is what I always told you, but you never listened because you said you were cleverer and that you would respect nothing I said. See how you ended up." Then she stopped talking, looked up at the sky, and raised imploring hands as if to a superior entity above for help. "Now, you've left me to suffer alone. Why did you do this to me?" she wailed and paused and began to cry in a voice so sorrowful that it brought tears to my eyes. Her wails rent the air while her body shook in spasms as she cried and switched to talking, still crying.

"You told me I was your world when we were together, and you praised my teeth to be as white as melon seeds. You teased me to laugh so that everyone could see my teeth. Now I want you here, but where are you?"

Hers seemed to be a lost love story, and it so moved me that, before Kajere could notice, I went to console her. I approached her, noticing her glazed eyes fixed on me directly. I held out my hands and tried to embrace her softly. What happened to me next was so swift and shocking, I barely had time to think. For, instead of melting in my arms the way I thought she would, she grabbed me, and I was surprised by her strength. Her strength was superhuman, swift and fierce. With lightning speed, she flung me to the ground. Luckily for me, Kajere, though taken on the spot, pushed her away before she could attack me again. Then she continued as if nothing had happened, clearly unaware of what she had just done to me.

I tried not to look at Kajere, but his face was saying, "I told you!" even as he asked, "Princess, are you okay?" and added, "There must be a reason she reacted that way, and we'll soon find out."

Without a pause after her violent action, Wukitoff continued, "Our home was a place where everyone was fine, a place where there were no fights until those people came who made us believe we were horrible people, that we must change and be like them. I told you not to go, but you insisted you wanted to leave with them. You never listened to me."

While we focused on her, the warriors kept on with their charade. They were still splashing muddy water at the ever-quiet weaver Bunejehs behind Wukitoff who seemed to be evolving a story: "You decided to join them, saying you would return a much better person than before you joined them; that you would know everything about the world upon your return, and make our people better. But where are you now? Why did you do this to me? Why did you do this to your people?" she lamented what sounded like lost love. "Why did you go with them? Why? Why? You said you wanted to be like them. You wanted to look like them because it was better that way. You were wrong. Wrong! Wrong!"

She spewed the last words out of her mouth with venom, her eyes getting even glassier as the words jetted out. Lost in the story, I was brought to the present by a hand I felt on my shoulder. It was Kajere's, and when I turned and stared at him, I saw he was in tears, the first tears I ever saw him shed. This was shocking because he hardly showed strong emotions, let alone so in public. He quickly tried to wipe them, and I pretended not to see that he was crying. He held my hand, squeezed it gently, and without looking at me, said, "Let's continue. There's more to see here."

"I can't retake any of this," I told him, my voice becoming too emotional. Unaccountably, I thought about my dad and thanked him for getting Ngounso to bring Kajere to me, to Tikari.

"Let's go," Kajere said, leading the way, my hand still in his, not letting go of it. As I smiled at him, he smiled back. Looking at me, he nearly collided with two other Bunejehs who suddenly came upon us. They were about the strangest sight I had seen there and, based on what they said, I was sure there was something concerning with the camp. The first was huge, scantily clad, and the fattest man I had seen this far. Just white goatskin was wrapped around his waist. He was virtually neckless, the place where the neck ought to have been having disappeared beneath his large face, huge chest, and massive layers of fat around the chest and abdomen. Prominent was his enormous forehead, which protruded threateningly. The size of his thighs and legs approximated the baobab tree in girth. From his right hand, he was eating an enormous mango fruit, its juice all over his mouth and face, and dribbling between his fingers. It was an indulgent nastiness as his large teeth tore into the fruit and the juice from it dribbled down the sides of his mouth and fingers, accompanied by slobbering sounds of grunting and munching that could be heard far away.

His left hand held a rope, pulling another man behind him. The man was so lean. I was surprised that he had the energy to walk. He was wearing goatskin accoutrements, black goatskin around his waist. He bore a bag of mangoes from which the fat fellow intermittently took out a mango after finishing one mango.

In a small, feminine voice, the fat man asked, "You want to be fat like me?" The thin voice coming from his massive frame was strikingly odd.

The petite man replied in a contrastingly deep, rich, and powerful voice, "Yes!"

"Why?" the bigger man asked through mouthfuls of mango.

"Because I want to be as big as you; I want to gobble mangoes as you do. I want to be like you because you are wealthy, and anything you've done, you've been successful at it," the petite man detailed eagerly.

"Are you ready to forget your wilderness and follow my elegant ways?" the bigger man asked, pausing between mouthfuls of mango.

"Yes," the petite man, enthusiasm in his tone, "My way has no value, my mores old and no good, in fact, no longer meaningful or leading me nowhere. Show me the right path to become like you," he said, his eyes set on the bigger man like the eyes of the slave on its master.

The bigger man threw away the mango seed and gestured for another mango from the bag the little man carried. The little man responded with practiced subservience and speed to the fat man's demands but was courageous enough to request, "Teach me how to eat mangoes the way you do."

"Tell me why," the bigger man requested between mango fruit

mouthfuls.

"I grow the mangoes, but only you have taught me the right way to eat them," the petite man responded.

The spectacle enacted by the huge and the petite fellows whose eyes bore the same glazed and faraway looks of the Bunejehs was surreal. Our nearness brought us into grips with uncomfortable details like the putrid stench emitted from the big man's mouth when he spoke. How a petite man withstood such a horrid stench was difficult to understand. Incomprehensible is the fact that it seemed to attract him. As it turned out, whatever spewed from the bigger man's mouth was contributing to the odor of the place. Having had his fill of the spectacle, Kajere dragged me away. Actually, he did not need to because I already wanted to leave as quickly as possible myself.

"This is most bizarre!" I said as we walked away. "Is there anything we can do to change things in this place?" The tenor of the place, its justice and general way of happenings went against my understanding or concept of how things ought to be in order to pass the test of sanity and justice.

Kajere was still in the discovery mode. He said, "Around every corner, something awful seems to be waiting to surprise us. Looks as if we have to tune ourselves in readiness for real trouble. The way things are going, trouble is near and soon," Kajere said guardedly as we set for the mountain where we had first arrived days back.

At sunset, we arrived there and found a nice grassy patch close to the forest. The patch contained lots of good food, and I could see potatoes, yams, cassava, corn, lemon yams, huckleberries, and many other types of food we already knew and had in Tikari. We correlated this with the machetes and axes, which we had noticed in one of the camps. We had helped ourselves to these, and now Kajere applied them to hack down a tree and to cut some grass. The grass and the branches constituted a kind of bed as well as what should be considered a comfortable lodge. I gave him a hand the best I could, getting so tired by early evening that I could barely stand or keep my eyes open. Perceiving this, Kajere told me to go to bed.

Before my head touched the makeshift bed, I was drowned by sleep. I woke up later to the sound of thumping, which at first felt like a throbbing headache. Getting accustomed to my environment, I realized that it was Kajere who was already awake and chopping wood. I sat up and watched him. He had no shirt on, which was the first time I had ever consciously perceived him without the top of his *ngwashie*. He sweated as he worked, the morning sun on the pouring sweat of his oily skin glistening his sinews. The morning was beautifully warm, the rising sun spraying its rays on everything, and the sky above was deep blue and almost cloudless. Just a few clouds drifted sparingly and lazily across the morning sky.

Near Kajere lay yams, cassava, potatoes, different tubers and vegetables which he had harvested. Not knowing I was awake, he was poised to make a meal. To this end, he split a fair amount of firewood and paused to take a breath, still thinking I was asleep, and I did not disillusion him but pretended to be sleeping as I saw him saunter over to where I was. Through half-open eyes, I saw him take a long look at me, smile to himself, and then set about making food for us.

First, he dug a hole and used a stone to spark a fire, in which he proceeded to roast yams and some other tubers along with some vegetables, including garden eggs, my favorite. To one side, Kajere stowed chewing sticks, which struck me as meticulous, and I thought it appropriate to stop the pretense graciously. So, I stretched out and acted as if I was only then waking up.

"How are you, princess? Did you sleep well?" he asked when he saw me stir.

"I did. You are up already?" I asked, watching him handle the roasted potatoes.

"Yeah, I'm up," he answered, stopped what he was doing with the potatoes and sauntered towards me. When he was close enough, he got a chewing stick, knelt in front of me, and placed it in my hand. I considered this most considerate, looked at it and looked at him. It was a virtual pantomime of courtliness, a wordless solicitude. He had never done a thing like this before, and I noticed he was somewhat nervous.

All the same, I slowly took the chewing stick and chewed until one end was soft. I brushed my teeth, rinsed my mouth, and then gave back the chewing stick to him. He did like me and handed it back to me. We kept passing the stick between us this way, chewing it each time the other gave it to the other until we were satisfied. The message was clear to both of us; our innermost feelings were known to each other.

We ended the pantomime dramatically as he bit the end of it one more time, and I bit the other. We kept chewing at the opposite ends simultaneously until our lips came close to contact. It was a unifying action. The ground beneath me moved, and all happened so suddenly and swiftly. I found myself drawn to him in a way I had never felt before. Then, he took me up in his arms and offered me food and drink. We did not talk about how we felt towards each other, even after such a powerful experience; all was internalized.

I didn't realize how hungry I was until I had started eating. "This is delicious," I said, avoiding his eyes.

"Thanks," he replied. I noticed the monosyllabic response as an indication that his heart was too full for words. We focused on the physical reality of the food before us and devoured it in silence, but the chewing stick moment replayed in my mind with emotional tickling again and again.

It was the first time Kajere had expressly shown a passionate emotional pull towards me. Although I could not stop the pounding excitement of my heart, I knew that my regal dignity had to be maintained.

We ate silently, scorching and spicy pepper lying on one side,

Kajere knowing that I liked peppered food.

"What do you think we should do?" His words interrupted my thoughts just when I was about to swallow, and I nearly choked on the spicy food. The question was innocent but suggestive. For, uppermost in my mind at that moment was the just-ended chewing stick game, whose impact could not be ignored. He could be referring to it or to our situation in the smelly setting and skewed justice of the setup.

"Are you asking me for my opinion?" I asked, surprised because Kajere avoided trouble like a plague, and I was rather on the careless and risky side.

"I don't know yet," I replied. "We certainly need to do something," I said lamely, wondering which way his mind was tilting. He came to it immediately.

"I've been seriously thinking about it," he continued. "We need to get a full grasp of their habits, rituals, their totems or worshipped animal, and how they all got to this place." He was speaking and looking at me in a way that indicated that he was asking my opinion on the matter. The idea was that he was approaching me the way one would approach his/her ruler, whether the thinking was in the right direction, politically correct.

Because our position kept us away from the pungent smell that seemed to be everywhere the Bunejehs were, we decided to spend a few more days there. Our task for those days included finding out why there were twenty-nine groups there. So, the hearty meal over, we readied and braved the odds. We covered our noses and made it to the punkie section. Our quest was derailed as right there and then, there was general commotion. The last few days had been beautifully warm and humid; the commotion now raised dust and noise everywhere.

"There's nothing so chaotic in a most idiotic manner and yet as thrilling as watching Bunejehs arguing among themselves," I heard Kajere say as he attempted to figure out what was happening. I was about to respond to his remark when he powerfully pulled out of the way of some ferociously charging Bunejehs. They were in pursuit of some of the white robed fellows who had for years tormented them.

"At last, they've had enough!" I heard Kajere exclaim, an excited thrill in his voice. The thrill was not to last long. Some of the white-robed fellows stormed in on us, pulled me a distance, and then carried me away. Although I yelled at the top of my voice amidst the chaotic noise, Kajere did not notice that I was gone until he accidentally looked in my direction and then gave chase.

"Help! Help! Help me, Kajere!" I screamed in panic.

"My princess! Princess!" I heard him shouting and racing after us, the man carrying me running as if he were winged, and the others, too. Yet they all still had the glazed look.

"Let me go!" I screamed to no avail, my abductor not perceiving the sound I made and not aware that he was carrying me. He stank foully, in spite of being so cleanly attired. More white-robed people poured out in support of their fellow, white-robed runner, scaring the Bunejehs who were giving chase. Then, they stopped and walked back.

Eventually, my abductor set me in front of the big man who had been pulling the little man. In the background, I heard noises from other Bunejehs and did not find Kajere, but was sure he would come.

"You have to be clever how you deal with these fellows," the big man started. "You can't make them do what you want unless you have self-respect," he bellowed, his massive nose twitching as he walked past me. It was inconceivable that he had not seen me.

"What wrong did we do in doing as we always have done? Yet we were attacked this time," one of the men tried to explain, giving me the impression that although I was their captive, they were oblivious of me and could not see me. But when I tried to wriggle myself out of the arms of the man holding me, I realized just how powerful his grip was. For, hard as I tried, I could not budge from his phenomenal strength. I decided to stay put, biding my time and worrying about not seeing Kajere yet.

Angry sounds came from the crowd of Bunejehs as they tried to figure out how to approach the white-garbed fellows. One of the white-robed fellows, having something significantly reverent about him, stepped forward and everywhere went silent, including the big man. The reverend man knelt down and muttered. He was at prayer, it seemed. His words affected, constraining them to all kneel down and pray along with him.

Apparently, the prayer emitted some spiritual power that empowered them to quickly become remarkably robust and agitated.

It was time to act, but I was still in the solid grip of this white-robed Bunejeh and knew that even if I were to extricate myself, the other Bunejehs would not let go. Though still a victim, my mind was already on what Kajere and I would do to bring change to this land. First, we needed to wake them up from their slumber to realize who they were and what was happening to them. My reverie was broken into by the voice of the big man:

"Now that we've been blessed," he shouted, "tomorrow we have to deal with them. They seem to be gaining in cleverness, meaning that they will soon become headstrong. That has to be stopped. Understood?"

An ecstatic response reverberated among the white-turbaned Bunejehs. It made me wonder why Shengah might have brought us to Bunajeh, and whether it was for us to instigate change and balance among the people. Just then, the one holding me suddenly flung me in front of the crowd, a powerful shove that set me flying before landing at the feet of the big turbaned man, who looked and scoffed at me. I fidgeted as I looked at him, finding around my waist the mungang Ngounso had given me. I held back myself from using its power because I felt it would serve me better later. While I did so, sudden silence palled the place as the big fellow picked me up and looked into my eyes. For the first time, I had the impression that he did not have the glazed look I associated with all Bunejehs. But the shock from the fly-landing I had enacted might still have influenced my perception. I was probably not seeing or thinking clearly. Yet, even if the big man had the glazed look, he seemed to know what he was up to, or so I thought when he leaned closer to me and started talking, almost in a whisper.

"Who are you?" he asked, his whisper stern.

I promptly replied with as much dignity as I could muster, given the undignified treatment I had received so far. "I am Zasheri, Princess of the Tikari," I said, watching him ponder for a moment. But if he knew anything about Tikari, he did not divulge it.

"And what are you doing here so far away from your people?" he whispered fiercely.

For the umpteenth time in various circumstances, I had had to respond to this echoing question, and the answer was simple: "I am seeking the Kwifon of Mekan." I was deliberate, telling him the truth in a bid to find out if it would elicit a reaction from him. Although it did seem to affect him, he valiantly tried to suppress the exposure. There was a slight movement of his eyebrows, enough to say that he understood I was from another world and therefore a threat that could expose him and the others for the charlatans they were.

He grabbed me by the throat, almost throttling me, and then very roughly threw me to the ground. Then, seizing a flailing whip, he proceeded to lash me hard, the whip slicing the air with a hiss and ending with a smashing thud against my body that directed searing pain to course through me.

"You are a traitor who came here to sell me!" he shouted.

"No," I managed to say as my heart raced from the terror and the pain of the lashes. "I have come here to reveal you for the thief you actually are!" I twirled and tossed from pain as I spoke. What I said affected him, and he stopped whipping.

Then, leaning closer to me threateningly, he spoke in a cold voice that was hoarse and low, "If I hear you say that again, I will kill you with my own hands." Before I could add another word, he viciously smacked me across the face. Instantly forgetting his might, I decided he had no monopoly on slaps. I angrily gave him a slap that was as hard as my female softness could muster. It was hard enough to embarrass him, it being possible that no one before now had ever challenged him and applied his own crude violence against him. His instant reaction was to give me an even harder bash across my face, causing blood to gush into my mouth while he muttered close to my ear for me alone to hear, "You won't leave here alive." Then, looking up at the crowd, he loudly yelled, "This woman is a thief and wants to sow confusion here."

Immediately, the white-turbaned fellows rushed at me and surrounded us. They were clearly the ringleaders and core members of the gang, with eyes that blinked all the time.

"Kill her! Kill her! Kill her!" they all shouted, a hellbent mob of unthinking murderers. Leering and leaning closer once more, the big man sarcastically grinned, announcing, "They can't hear you! Only I can." Then, he exploded in a loud laugh, the crowd of cronies shouting in rhythm:

"Kill her! Kill her! Kill her! Kill her! Kill her! Kill her!"

The times were desperate enough for me to employ the last option, the desperate remedy for an extreme circumstance – the mungang that Ngounso gave me. Before it became too late, I managed to squeeze the mungang, but a familiar voice cut in with my name.

"Princess, let's go." It was Kajere on a horse. Where he found a horse was too much of a detail to require at this moment. Before the big fellow could react, Kajere alighted from the horse, grabbed and seized the whip from the stunned man's hand, and mercilessly whipped the fellow. Everything was happening so fast, him beating up the huge man as I had never conceived a person could be beaten before and asking with a scream, “You lay your filthy hands on my princess, eh?” All the arrogant pose of the man disappeared as he writhed in agony, and the rest of the Bunejehs only watched and were stunned or too petrified to react. They were so stunned because none of them had ever known the big man could succumb to anything or anyone or whine like a terrified stray dog.

The big fellow was still in shock when Kajere stopped whipping him, picked me up, and in a flash, we galloped away from him and his cohorts, who now worked up and were in hot pursuit of us. But their hot pursuit only went that far, for they came to a screeching halt and would not cross a certain point. Noticing this, Kajere also stopped, and we watched them make a turnaround.

“Why did they stop?” he asked in wonderment.

“I don’t know,” I replied, but the torture I had undergone was uppermost in my mind. “You took so long to come?” I commented, half in anger.

“Sorry, princess,” he said. Whenever he called me princess, I saw contrition behind the address. He explained, as a follow-up, “I was looking for horses.”

“That is alright,” I said. “I was worried, fearing something bad might have happened to you,”

We rode along, and as he turned to look at me, the horse lunged a little and neighed, surprising me by its sudden movement. After he calmed down the beast, I told him: “When the big fellow looked me up close, I did not see the glazed look of the Bunejehs in his eyes. Then, when I told him I was searching for Kwifon, his face changed, even though he tried to hide it from me.”

“Are you serious? What did he say?” Kajere asked, a little overexcited.

“Not much, but that no one except him could hear me,” I told Kajere. “So, I told him I knew he was not a Bunejeh. That angered him to start threatening me.”

Kajere digested the information in silence and then said, "That is a most dangerous fellow, then, but we will not be daunted. Let's go to the other side of the river and see what kind of Bunejehs live there. We can come up with a strategy after that."

I nodded, and just then realized that the horse had no saddle, just some leather protection. I smiled and leaned on its back, also realizing that I was seeing Kajere riding for the first time. "You didn't tell me you could ride," I said.

"You never asked," he replied. We were nearing our abode and the putrid smell forced us to wrap the cloth around our noses even tighter.

Twelve

The Middle of Nowhere

Following a hard day's ride, we reached our abode when it was dark, in spite of the starlit sky. As I tenderly lifted Zasheri off the horse, she yelled in pain.

"That hurts," she said painfully.

"Ashia," I replied, trying my best to be careful as she looped her hands around me, warming my heart and saying tensely:

"Be careful!"

That was when I knew she was in much discomfort. As I gingerly placed her on the bed of soft grass and branches I had made days earlier, she squirmed, pain defining her forehead and knitting her brows as I laid her down. I lit a fire to examine properly and tend her wounds and bumps, glad that I had arrived when I did to avert a worse situation. Even so, Zasheri was severely bruised, which awoke anger and vengeful feelings in me as I attended to her bruises. In shards, I heated water with which I rubbed her cuts and bruises tenderly. Luckily, there was no broken bone, and there were abundant plants that could heal her injuries quickly. The drawback was that I had to wait till morning to find them. My impatience bit the dust because it was impossible to go searching for the healing grass in the dark. Until dawn, I had to sit duck.

"Watch out," she said again in pain.

"Okay," I replied while carefully sponging her bruises, some of which looked really bad. Then, I served her some food, and she was fast asleep before long. I had the leisure to briefly watch her before going to bed as well, but all night long, she moaned in pain, making me wake up again and again to tend her. Eventually, she slept for a few uninterrupted hours, but I slept lightly because I had to be attentive to any restlessness she manifested.

Before sunrise, I was up and out to the forest to harvest healing herbs for her injuries. I found *kekeng*, *njah*, *mtombo*, and lots of *ntsam*. As it turned out, there were many healing plants here, accounting for the perpetual health of the Bunejehs, none of whom looked sick, even if it was clear that they were subjected to sufferings.

My search led me to a surprising find of herbs in addition to those with healing properties. There were plants with supernatural qualities in a locus that had the potential to create powerful mungang for anyone adept at such skills. The sheer plush of plant variety was amazing, igniting thoughts I needed to share with Zasheri as soon as her health became less of a worry. For now, her health was paramount.

I took quite an abundance of herbs back to our abode and found Zasheri still sound asleep and predictably still in great pain. I set about preparing her treatment, grinding some on wood and cooking some. Zasheri awoke just before I was through, but noticeably, she was still in much pain and barely able to talk. So, I lost no time in administering the drugs to her. I began by making her drink some water before anointing her entire body with the ointment I had made from some of the herbs. Noticing that she was also weak from hunger, I tried to make her eat, but she could only take a little food on account of the pain she was feeling. Then she went back to sleep again. This became our routine of activities for about a week, and the nights were sometimes quite dramatic as she would wake up so hysterical, fearing that she had become a Bunejeh or call up some bizarre matter.

One night, for example, she woke up looking strange and shocked me by angrily asking, "Why are you squeezing my neck?"

"No, not me. I'm not!" I stuttered, confused.

"You squeezed my neck and told me we had to return to Tikari," she said, protesting ardently and angrily.

"No, not me! I said no such thing," I objected.

"Oh, oh, so you are trying to make me stop looking for Kwifon? You have failed," she went on.

As I watched her, wild with an indescribable look on her face, it began to dawn on me what could be happening to her; I asked, "Where are we?"

"Banda," she replied, and almost immediately went back to sleep, waking up only hours later for me to nurse her bruises. The bumps were much improved, and we got into a more realistic conversation. I was mute about her bizarre outings, and only a few days later, she was back to her buoyancy, waking up even before me and doing some stretching exercises. Her health had improved so much that I considered it time to discuss a plan with her. That was after I had offered her an assortment of herbs that made up her healing breakfast.

"The whole forest is full of herbs," I began and moved to sit beside her. "What is more, some could be used to make powerful mungang." At this, she paused and looked thoughtfully at me, suspending her medicinal drink. When I signaled her, she drank for a while in silence and then spoke between sips:

"What next?"

I considered her field experience of what I saw to be an inspirational booster and asked, "Would you like us to go back there and see what we can do or explore the other side?"

She simply responded, "Let's go to the other side and see what's there," and I quickly obliged.

To her nodding and smiling, I suggested the time and the direction of our expedition: "At dawn, we will ride to the riverside and try to cross to the other side."

I had prepared roasted yam and *egusi* soup with tomato, *nja-ma-njama*, and some spices, which I hoped she would like to eat. She tasted and nodded enthusiastically. "Very delicious, Kajere," she appreciatively said, smiling. Then she called, "Kajere," in a tone that suggested that she had something important to say.

I was preoccupied with her health and did not think much of what she wanted. Nonetheless, I stopped applying the ointment on her and looked attentively at her.

"Would you want me to show you something?" she asked pensively, and I wondered where this was leading. I did not need to wonder for long, for she immediately pulled a chewing stick from inside her top and began chewing on one end. I trembled and melted like wax at her gesture, an initiative of passionate love. I had until now always been the initiator of overt advances in love, leading in showering her with affection. Now, it was her in the lead, my body quivering in a melting manner as she chewed slowly, tenderly, and seductively at her end of the chewing stick until it got soft and desirable. Then, she swallowed and meekly handed it to me. I needed no second invitation to look into her eyes while taking it. I, too, chewed the other end and swallowed before handing it back to her. She took it, put it in her mouth, and moved closer to me, using her mouth to offer me the other end of the stick. As I slowly took and chewed it, her hot breath against my mouth and face evoked unspeakable sensations all over me, our eyes fixated on each other as I took her in my arms. Deep within, I knew the time was not yet right to be with her wholly; that if we went beyond this, we would compromise a beautiful thing and the power of the gris-gris, making me powerless and losing the cause and search for the Kwifon of Mekan. The stakes were too high, including allowing the Ketummites to invade

Tikari again and to capture and enslave Tikari. Although I teetered on the brink of the chasm of total passionate immersion, and the overwhelming push almost swept me away, my masculine analytical frame of reference held fast.

From this state of mind, Zasheri woke me with a seductive whisper, "Kajere, is there anything wrong with me? Am I not beautiful for you?"

I was stalled, totally disarmed, and could not proceed without unraveling the truth to her. I groped for the right words to assuage her distressed question that was inflamed with a passionate but languorous look. "There's nothing wrong with you, Zasheri," also pronouncing her name seductively to avoid traumatizing her with a feeling of rejection.

"Then why do you hold back every time we get close?" she shot back at me.

I was in a fix, having to contend with my passion and knowledge of the reality imposed on me at the risk of total failure. Why had Ngounso restricted me, knowing that I would fall in love with her princess? Why hadn't she warned Zasheri about it? Why hadn't she told her to stay off and away from me?

"Zasheri," I replied as emotionally as possible, "My heart is beating to breaking point for you, and there is nothing I cherish more than being yours forever." I must have sounded really crass, yet, that was the best I could do without betraying Ngounso or divulging anything, plus I knew I risked her anger. Zasheri's reaction surprised me, however, helping me out without me breaking any eggs.

"I know we have work to do for Tikari and us," she replied. She had so much love for Tikari, even at personal cost and in moments of personal passion.

So disarmed by her words, I could not help but hold her tenderly close to me, and she obliged with unspeakable tenderness that told me she was willing to wait for love. In my arms, even so yielded, I realized she was the Princess of the Tikari and would do anything, including sacrificing herself for her people. The storm of passion was over, and we spent the next few hours gathering different spices and roots, most familiar to us. We knew we would need them. Then we rode to another part of the forest where I showed her the plant zephua, whose roots, when dried and pounded into a powder, would make enemies weak if blown at them. If done in a significant quantity, it could cause paralysis.

The information overwhelmed Zasheri so much that she went quiet; she steadfastly assisted me in digging up the roots, which I sliced into bits and encased with others in our leather sachets. That done, we rode to our abode and rested on that dry and warm night, which we decided to spend in the open. It was our last night there, and crickets, other insects, and bird sounds whispered to each other all around us, as well as our relaxed minds and bodies. The starlit sky was illuminated by the full-blown moon, which enhanced its bright brilliance and heralded the mating calls of other animals.

Around us, the forest noises continued with increased urgency, or so I thought. I could make out all the stars in the sky, and the warm heat rose from the ground, telling me that dawn would bring us a beautiful day to go to the other side of Bunejeh. Zasheri, breathing steadily, was fast asleep beside me.

When morning came, we prepared some food, ate quickly, gathered our scanty belongings, mostly herbs and supernaturally imbued plants, and rode to the top of the hill from where we hoped we would look down the valley for one last time. Through lieshih, I saw the Bunejehland to which we had just been and the large river that snaked between both lands.

It was time to get going. We rode down the hill and made our way towards the river and to the uninhabited part of Bunejeh. We aimed to depart quietly, attracting no attention even as the putrid stench once more came in wafts that made my insides revolt.

But Bunejeh was never without adventure, for as we rounded a bend, we nearly rode into the man we had come to know, the talking man. This time, he was not trying to climb a tree, but to jump over a muddy pothole about the length of his arm. Hard as he tried, he could not leap over it. We stopped for a moment to watch and listen to him, his eyes maintaining the dazed look characteristic of all we had met there, except the big fellow and his accomplices.

"Until the lion tells the story of the hunt, the hunter's story will always glorify the hunter," was the wiseman's voice, and I recognized it. No matter how big the sea is, it can always be crossed," he added and rattled on. When you tell a foolish person a proverb, you have to explain it."

Even though we had met him several times and fed on his characteristic verbiage, he still fascinated and moved us. "Why does he talk so much?" Zasheri asked.

I tried to relate his words to his actions and then urged Zasheri, "Let's go."

We did not move one step. In front of us stood Big Man and his cohorts, white-attired and spotlessly clean. Zasheri nearly fell off the horse, looking at the river in the distance while the talking man continued his rant:

"Anyone who is clever but has no wisdom is like water on the sand." He couldn't care and did not notice that Zasheri and I were in a big circle, surrounded by Big Man and his cohorts.

Big man noticed and heard him, however. Apparently, Big Man did not like whatever he was saying, and so he barked out, "Can someone take that idiot away from here, now?" Serviceably at Big Man's beck and call, some of his men immediately rushed forward and led the inveterate talker away.

As he was being hurtled away, he flung out blurts of memorabilia: "If there are many of you, you can cross the river. A goat is never innocent when its judge is a leopard."

The big man faced us and said the obvious veiled threat; his grinning face flushed with fury: “We meet again.”

“Is that what you think?” I asked almost in a scarcely audible whisper.

Nudging me, Zasheri whispered, too, even less audibly, “Let’s use our mungang.”

“Perhaps, not yet,” I whispered back while keenly observing our chances. “We may need it for something else.”

She persisted. “If we don’t defeat him, we cannot so much as step away from here,” she said in alarm because our foes looked really threatening.

Big Man, thinking we were already his prey, decided to parley. “Hey, why are you here?” he bellowed arrogantly.

I began reconsidering Zasheri’s advice to use some mungangs to fight our way out. The urgency rose as Big Man, from beneath his white garbs, pulled out a large and gleaming machete while advancing towards us. We had not a moment to spare. We had to weaken him and prove to his cohorts that we were more powerful. No sooner thought than done, I quickly undid one of the small leather pouches and took out a pinch of zephua powder while he advanced and boasted:

“I have been the fon here for centuries. You can’t walk in here and disturb a system I have spent my whole life constructing. I will send you and your wife to a place where you will die in pain.” He bellowed because he wanted to show off to his stooges. I took advantage of his loquacity to buy time by responding to him:

“First of all, this is not my wife but the mighty Princess Zasheri of Tikari. You have to treat her with respect,” I said, the zephua in my hands making me confident and emboldened. Zasheri, too, was emboldened, I noticed.

“Respect?” the bully asked angrily, seemingly on the verge of vicious action.

"Do something now," Zasheri whispered to me with urgency, and indeed, I made ready to throw the zephua at him when he blew something at us. He, too, had come prepared with his mungang, which cleanly threw Zasheri and I from our horses and suspended us in midair, defying gravity. Worse, I felt energy rapidly draining from my body, and Zasheri was experiencing the same depletion. There was no doubt that his mungang was strong, really strong, and I wondered whether zephua would be any good at counteracting it.

Further, Zasheri screamed in fear, and I tried to help her, but found out that I could not do much. Suspended in midair, we were trying to adjust to not having our feet on firm ground. Big man had his time of glory and bellowed with laughter as he gloated, "When you want to fight against strong people, you must always come prepared." His men, who surrounded us, guffawed.

I stole a glance beyond them and saw Bunejehs doing their regular activities, ignorant of what was going on. Big Man was not done yet with mocking us, however: "I will teach you to respect me," he said, seeming to think of something different from slaughtering us. He now put his sword back in its sheath. Then he pulled out a long whip, the same one I had seen him use on Zasheri, which incensed me.

Overconfident now, he made the singular mistake of coming closer to me. That was his doom, for with the last ounce of energy I could still muster, I threw some zephua at him, stopping him in his tracks.

"Huh, you also have something?" he looked at me, disbelief in his eyes. He could not comprehend the sudden shift of power and the consequent shuffle from victor to victim as he slowly sank to his knees, his strength rapidly draining from his body. Now, the weaker he got, the stronger Zasheri and I became, which frightened his men, scaring them because they were wont to see their leader only in power mode. They were too embarrassed to know what to do as we finally had our feet on the ground. While they fretted, we went for our horse, quickly mounted it, and rode towards the river at breakneck speed.

"You think he will come after us?" Zasheri asked anxiously.

I could not answer because I knew he was already pursuing us. We rode past Bunejehs going about their business as if nothing were happening, the pungent smell still harassing the atmosphere, and I hoped the other side would be stench-free. The greater worry was Big Man and his cohorts in pursuit. But just before we reached the river shore, Big Man and his cohorts suddenly stopped. They watched us reach the river and get down from our horse. They had halted at the same place as before, when I had rescued Zasheri.

"They probably know something we don't. Let's leave before they change their minds," I said, and we left the horse and approached one of the two canoes in the river.

"They are not moving at all," Zasheri worried about Big Man and his gang. "There's certainly something the matter. Use lieshih to survey the area."

I focused lieshih on them and could not hear what they were saying, but I saw Big Man laughing, pointing at us and mouthing something to his cohorts. Zasheri also looked through lieshih and handed it back to me, her expression more worried, saying, "Something's not right."

Trying to calm her as best as I could, I said, "Let's talk about it as we cross the river."

We got into the canoe and paddled towards the other side. The weather was good, the water serene, the sun high overhead and surrounded by a deep blue sky. Cattle egrets and other birds lazily hovering in the sky proclaimed the peace of the river. We could see fish in the water too, unhurriedly moving about. Even in this calmness, the image of Big Man laughing and pointing at us as we got into the canoe stuck relentlessly on my mind.

Zasheri made herself comfortable and we coursed along. Seeing the egrets made her smile unaccountably in my view, but before I asked, she burst out singing:

Cattle egret, cattle egret,
Welcome home.
Here, take my fingernail and give me yours
Cattle egret, Cattle egret,
Welcome home.

I watched her sing, and when she ended, I was impressed. "Nice song," I told her.

"When we were kids, we sang whenever cattle egrets came, believing that they would change the color of our nails. Of course, I never knew what color their nails were," she said, smiling like a child. Her eyes twinkled with nostalgia, and I paddled along, happy that she was that relaxed.

Moments later, I looked across the river using the lieshih but saw nothing. Puzzled, it was the best I could do to avoid panic. I looked a second time. Still, there was nothing but water meeting the skies on the horizon. I turned and focused on the direction we had just left. Nothing was there. I swallowed hard and tried to maintain a certain degree of calm.

Zasheri had noted my hidden alarm, and nothing ever escaped her notice. "What's wrong?" she asked, her anxiety suddenly returning.

I had no words for her. Quietly, I gave her lieshih, and she looked and saw nothing. She looked again and again; she saw nothing. She put lieshih down and looked at me.

"There's nothing," she said, applying great effort to sound calm.

"That is what I see, too," I said.

As if the fault was with lieshih, we both looked through it several times in turns, but nothing changed. We were rowing into a bright wilderness. I tried to turn the canoe around to paddle back whence we came, but the canoe would not be turned around, hard as I tried; it kept doggedly, like a stubborn pig, pointing its prow to and going in one direction only.

I looked at Zasheri and announced, sounding casual, "I think we have a little problem."

"I know," she replied, also sounding slight about it. I had to look at her a second time to make sure I was not misreading her.

"When I saw Big Man and his cohorts stop and laugh, I knew something was wrong," she continued.

Continuing the casual mood, I tried to laugh it off. "Nothing we can't handle," I said, but realized that I sounded so foolish in the light of the actual weight of the challenge. I laughed at my folly and Zasheri also laughed. Even this false laugh was something I clung to, for it meant that both of us were still in our strong spirits, enough to maintain the sense of humor.

The unexpected horror started like a little tremor, which I barely felt, but Zasheri did and asked, "Do you feel that?"

I did not get what she was aiming at, so I looked around and saw nothing. I certainly felt nothing. "No," I said. A second tremor occurred and I could not pretend that I did not feel it.

"That's it again," she said.

"Yes, I got it," I replied, half giving the impression that I understood what it was, and in a bid to stay calm and keep her from panicking.

"What do you think?" she nudged.

"Just waves, what else?" I replied to assuage her fears.

"It feels strange," she continued and peered into the water fearfully.

My own alarm was shown in action as I once again tried unsuccessfully to reverse the canoe's direction. Nothing changed. Then, far off, we heard the low rumble, which did not resemble anything in our previous experience. Then it came again, a bit louder, and felt somewhat like a storm. But how could that be when there was no rain, no wind, and everything looked so serene? The birds in the sky still lazily hovered and basked in the midday sun.

"Feels like a massive storm," Zasheri said again, looking around strangely.

"A storm is impossible in the present atmosphere," I declared, but also looked around suspiciously. Before the words were out of my mouth, a huge wave could be seen coming towards us.

"Hold on, princess, hold on," I shouted, and we clung to the canoe's sides. The waves lifted us so high I could almost touch some of the cattle egrets flying above, and they scrambled away.

"May my people of Tikari bless me!" Zasheri screamed in terror even as we came crashing down and almost immediately swept up again by another mighty wave.

I heard myself screaming out, and in the brief suspension on the high wave, I heard Zasheri scream at the top of her voice, "I don't think we will survive this one," and I felt the same way.

The waves kept lifting us and bringing us down with brute force, each time higher up and then lower down. I wondered how the canoe withstood the brute pounding this far. My imagination did not wander for long because after crashing down from the peak of another wave, I saw a massive crack in the middle of the canoe.

"This way! Come this way!" I screamed at Zasheri and half-dragged her to my side of the canoe just as the canoe crackled and split into two, with us clinging to one.

"This must be the reason for Big Man's last laugh," she said, clinging fearfully on for dear life. Her sense of humor at a time like this made me wonder. Before I could return the favor, we were again hurled into the air. The marvel was that the tumultuous river did not affect the calm weather and the serene sky. No thunderstorm or lightning, no disruption of the leisurely twirls of birds in the tranquil sky. Another thing was that after the rumble we had heard from afar, the waves were not noisy. Not even the soothing swash of their ebbing was heard. A quick interpretation is that we probably had disturbed the tranquility of the waters. My gris-gris pressed against my chest, and the lieshih and our tiny amulets had been firmly tied around our waists and torsos. I felt ready to battle against the elements. Looking at Zasheri, I knew she, too, was ready, and what she said between plops of water on her lips assured me of her status as the Princess of the Tikari.

"Kajere, any plan they have against us will fail."

I smiled, and the waves seemed to have heard us and rose with more fury, slamming heavy tons of water at our feeble frames, lifting us even higher and plunging us lower and much rougher while we clung to the broken piece of the canoe for life. We continued like this, buffeted left and right by strong waves until it got dark. I started feeling energy sapped from my body, and I could guess that Zasheri was having the same effect on her, but she would never let me know unless she was near the point of expiration.

The waves waned a little with the darkness, but remained strong enough to keep us alert and awake.

"I'm hungry," I began.

"Me too," she answered, and we both laughed.

Now, the river water did not look so clean, but it was not salty. We drank generously. Filling the stomach in whatever way was the illusion of fullness we were trying to achieve. Yet, hunger did not go away but kept gnawing on our entrails.

"I did not think it could take long to cross this river," I said.

"It does not look like a crossable river. If we look through the lieshih, we cannot see the other side," Zasheri said. "The wonder is how such calmness can generate such harshness. There have to be cruel mermaids in this river," she said.

"I don't think anyone has ever crossed this river," I said.

"Perhaps not, and maybe there's nothing on the other side," she said.

"But that can't be. I know what we saw," I replied, frustrated but not daring to reveal my frustration.

"There is likely to be a powerful mungang in this river," she said, shifting from the idea of mermaids.

"We shall most certainly have a lot of work to do when we reach the other side," I said, assuming that there is the other side and that we shall get there. It was a statement of faith, so to say.

"If we get there," she replied, drawing attention to my presumption before becoming dead silent.

Around us swam lots of different kinds of fish, but neither of us had ever eaten fish before. Much as hunger was maddening us, we instinctively knew that we had to stay clear of them. Before long, we drifted to sleep, a delicate risk, for our lifeline lay on a curved half of a canoe. Tiredness imposed its natural rhythm irrespective of circumstances. How long I slept, I cannot tell. I only heard Zasheri's voice, which woke me up.

"Kajere, help!" she shrieked to the complexly high waves, which happened not to be as furious as the day before, or not just yet. Zasheri had let go of the piece of the canoe and was only clinging on by the rope attaching her to one of the amulets caught on one end of the broken canoe.

I quickly grabbed and pulled her towards me as hard as I could. We were lucky because just then, the piece of wood broke off, dislodging from the rest of the canoe's half. Only my hand was stopping her from being swept away.

"I got you, princess!" I shouted as a way of assuring her of safety amidst the chaos. "I got you!" I said and tugged and hurled her up, using all the strength I had left.

"Kajere!" she screamed as I got her on, "I don't think we can last long like this. Do something!"

I brought her close and piggybacked her. The river seemed to be awake and watching, for the massive waves of the day before, chose that moment to attack us again.

"Whatever happens, hold onto me," I shouted between mouthfuls of water.

We were again tossed high in the air, nearly colliding with the birds in their relaxed flight modes, which were oblivious to our predicament.

"Help us!" I screamed desperately to one of them before we were brought down and swallowed by another giant wave that pushed us very near to the floor of the riverbed. It was so darkly ominous there that I could only see within a few feet of where we were. Zasheri's arms were firmly around me. She tried to say something, but I could not hear her. I clung to the piece of the canoe, knowing it would bring us back to the surface. Sure enough, it did. We were thrust back and thrust high in the air.

"I can't take it anymore!" Zasheri shrieked.

"Yes, you can, my princess!" I shouted back, but we were in such turmoil that none of our positive or negative declarations seemed to hold water.

The next wave crashed so low down that my feet felt the riverbed, and I also saw a mighty fish approaching. It was absolutely massive and seemed to be after us for a meal. From its size, it could easily swallow us and seemed intent on that.

Zasheri panicked, but I fought the fish off, running out of breath when it finally gave up and departed. Then, somehow, we found ourselves thrust up to the river's surface, and as suddenly as the storm had started, it stopped. Everything went still. But we could not trust anything anymore. I clung still to the little piece of the canoe, Zasheri still piggybacking on me.

"How are you?" I asked since I could not see her face.

"Tired," she whispered right in my ear and laughed lightly.

"Good, because I think we have another problem," I said softly so as not to jolt her worries.

"Not another one and not now!" she said.

"If you have noticed, we have not moved from this same place for a long time now."

"Yes," she nodded.

"We need some shade. It's getting too hot." I knew we would not last long without any shade.

She was silent for a moment, and we swam around lazily, trying to shield ourselves from the burning sun, whose heat was now merciless. I knew we would not last long if we did not have something to eat, and, at this sun's fury, we would not only get burned but also become delirious too. Even so, nothing changed. Energy was sapping away from me, and Zasheri was losing the staying power to stay afloat. She was willing herself beyond the extraordinary, stuck to the same piece of wood in the same place in a river, hungry and extremely weak. By the third day, I had reached breaking point and cared little about whatever might happen.

"Say hello to Suliya," Zasheri said.

"Suliya?" I asked, perplexed.

"Yeah, say hello to her."

There was nothing and no one around to see, except Zasheri herself. She was in extremis of tired weakness, her eyes now glassy. I had seen that look before and knew its entailments.

"Suliya, how are you?" I replied, speaking to no one in particular. "Fine," I heard a voice say, but it was like Zasheri's. Had I not been looking at her when I heard the voice, I would have sworn that she had answered me herself.

The voice continued the conversation. "Zasheri told me about you. I hear you are seeking Kwifon." Suliya said, more a remark than a question.

"Yes, we will find Kwifon of Mekan," I replied. Was I talking to myself? I wondered

"You should know that I now own Tikari," the voice continued.

It was becoming complex. I reverted to Zasheri and asked, mesmerized, "What is happening? What is Suliya doing here? How did she get here, by the way?"

Though weak, Zasheri was coherent. "I don't know. I only woke up and saw her," she said.

"How did you get here?" I asked Suliya.

"You and my sister do not imagine that you can easily get rid of me, do you?" she asked and laughed sarcastically.

"What did you do to Wubangeh?" Zasheri asked.

I looked at Zasheri and noticed that she no longer looked tired but seemed truly energetic, though angry, as she spoke: "When I left Tikari, it was because I went to look for Kajere, who had been made to disappear by Wubangeh. He had to meet Kajere at Tchongwa arena; instead, he used Ningreh on Kajere."

Suliya laughed rather uncontrollably. "Ah, is that where you still are stuck? Well, I exiled him centuries ago. My job at hand is to deal with you and this Kajere person," she said, addressing herself to Zasheri.

"And what about Ngounso? Where's she?" Zasheri asked. "What did you do to her?"

"Don't worry about her. You should be worried about yourself. I know she gave you all her powerful mungang, but I have something much more powerful," Suliya said, again laughing sarcastically, almost hysterically.

An unbridged gap worried me, a piece of a missing link about a powerful mungang with Zasheri. I asked her, "You have some powerful mungang?"

"Of course, how did you think I found you?" she retorted.

"But you never mentioned anything like that to me before," I persisted.

"I was thinking of a good time to tell you. So, please, don't be mad at me," Zasheri replied, regretfully.

"You see," Suliya said, laughing. "Now you see why she's not popular among her people. She's a liar and has always been like this."

"She's my princess," Kajere protested protectively. "You can't talk to her that way."

"Why are you here?" Zasheri asked her.

"I came here to make sure you never return to Tikari," Suliya replied, her eyes hate-filled. "You have caused too much trouble. Time for you to leave," Suliya announced dismissively.

"And how will you confront the Ketummites?" Zasheri asked.

"I have my ways. Even Kajere's gris-gris won't help you this time," she said, still hate-filled.

"And just how do you intend to do it?" Zasheri asked. "We are looking for Kwifon, and will find it," she announced.

"If I have anything to do with you, you will never return," Suliya said as if to clinch her own advantage. "Your journey ends here," she added with a blood-curdling laugh.

"Father made me his successor. If he wanted you, he would have put you in charge," Zasheri said with as much authority as I ever heard from her, adding, "You tried everything, but nothing has ever worked, and none of your tricks will ever work. I am the princess of Tikari. The sooner you accept that, the better for you. We can work together to expel the Ketummites whenever they come again," Zasheri said, a conciliatory tone of finality in her voice, before adding, "You came here to cause trouble; you better leave now!"

"Wake up, Zasheri, wake up!" I said in order to bring her back from the delirium in which I was a participant. The glassiness of her eyes immediately disappeared, and she asked, "Were you worried?"

I thought the new line of words was off the hinge of continuity from what we had just experienced, and I asked, "Why?"

"Because you will be more worried when you see that," she pointed out.

"What?" I asked, directing my gaze at where she was pointing.

"Over there," she iterated and shook her index finger to indicate the spot where a creature was swimming lazily towards us. At first, I could not make it out.

"What is that?" I asked.

"No idea," she replied, "But it looks menacing."

The water had calmed down, so I managed to extricate lieshih from my back and focus it on the creature. My jaws drooped, and Zasheri caught my terror.

"What is it?" she asked, extremely distraught.

"It has the shape of a frog, the biggest frog, bigger than a cow!" I rattled in disbelief.

"You are surely joking," she said. "I've heard about frogs of that dimension, but always thought they were fictitious creatures," she said in alarm as I gave her lieshih to peek into and make her own judgement. She did and very slowly returned the gadget to me.

"What do you see?" I asked, no less scared than I expected her to be. Instead of answering me, she went dead silent. A little later, I heard her mutter something.

"Did you speak?" I asked.

"Kensoin! That's kensoin!" she said, really terrified.

I guessed I had to start with the worst-case scenario, so I asked, "Do they eat people?"

"They do," she said, tremor in her voice.

"Kajere, do something! We must leave this place! Use your gris-gris! Now!" The urgency in her voice was poignant and rose with each statement or phrase.

By now, we were splashing in the water. She was off my back, and we swam but covered very little distance even as the kensoins were gaining on us. In fact, I could even hear their yawns and knew we needed some help. Yet, I had no idea when such help would arrive. I instructed Zasheri, "Hold tight, my princess, hold tight. I've got an idea, but we must wait for it to attack us first."

"Crazy! Are you crazy?" Zasheri asked incredulously. "Did you not hear what I said? They eat people! They are mighty!" She was virtually screeching the way she screamed.

I was cool and told her, "I know. Let's just wait." In spite of her natural inclination to fruitlessly try to swim away, she acquiesced, not without dread, though.

"Don't move!" I barked sternly. "Stay close to me," I followed up as the kensoin that looked like the leader of the school leaped towards us. The stunning immediate note was the distance it covered in one leap, a giant leap literally. One moment it was in the air; the next moment it was on us, the great distance we were away.

Despite its surprising giant leap, I was alert and side-swam it for it to land a few feet away from us. In one move, I swung over to its back as if it were an easy horse and then beckoned for Zasheri to join me. She piggybacked on me, and I clung to kensoin's back for all it was worth.

The amphibian had tremendous energy, and I could feel its strident muscles rippling beneath me while I struggled to stay on its back. It kicked, frog-jumped and swam with big, mighty strokes in a bid to dislodge me, but I stuck to it like a tick. Our lives depended on the desperate clutch, which indeed compared me to an ectoparasite. For in a different light, we were to live off the life of the kensoin.

It croaked loudly like a roar, perhaps to terrorize us with the aggressive sound, and the other kensoins came as if to help it, but could do little. Daytime became night. Still, the kensoin was in a rage to dislodge us to no avail. It failed. I clung on, digging my fingers into its flesh, which was quite soft for such a powerful and frightful creature. Two days went by with none of us relenting. Since the kensoin was the active actor and we were more passive and employing its own energy against it, it got exhausted and went unconscious. It must have meant a lot to the other kensoins that their leader could come to such a dismal fate at the hands of midgets like us. So, perhaps fearing for their own lives, they left, and the waves pushed us. We could not say how, but before we knew it, we were on land.

What relief! I stepped off the floating monster, half-dragging, half-carrying Zasheri to the shore. We collapsed in a heap, besieged by hunger and too exhausted to know our whereabouts, but glad to be out of the water at last.

Our quest for Kwifon, the Kwifon of Mekan, was still on, and the adventures to come were yet unknown. We had no idea what to expect and did not know that what lay ahead paled in comparison to what we had been through.

Acknowledgments

This work is dedicated to my wife, Lucie Belola, who has stood by my side and always encouraged me. To my kids, Akumbom, Lema, Tita, and Nahnine, for always being there for me. And to my mother and father, Grace, and Andrew Fusi. Special thanks to Dr. Tony M. Ndifor.

To everyone who contributed to making this work possible, including family, friends, my editors, Mr. Patrick Tata, and Dr Jude Fokwang and his team, thank you all. Lastly, I give thanks to God.

About the Author

Martin Fusi is a storyteller whose work bridges myth, memory, and imagination. Born in Babanki Tungo in the Northwest Region of Cameroon, he draws from a rich cultural heritage to craft narratives that explore African history, spirituality, and identity in inventive and cinematic ways.

He holds a PhD in African Literature and an MA in Theatre and Media Production from the University of Hull in the United Kingdom, following earlier studies in English at the University of Yaoundé. Over the years, he has shared his passion for storytelling as a professor of creative writing, screenwriting, and film production at leading institutions, including George Washington University, Kentucky State University, the University of Southern California, San Bernardino, and the College of William and Mary.

An accomplished screenwriter and director, Fusi has written

several screenplays, two of which were produced as feature films under his direction. Quest for Kwifon: Book One is his debut novel—a sweeping work of fantasy and magical realism rooted in ancient African traditions, set several centuries ago.

Martin Fusi lives in Los Angeles, California.

To inquire about booking Martin Fusi for a speaking enagement, please contact Spears Media Press at info@spearsmedia.com

About the Publisher

Spears Books is an independent publisher dedicated to providing innovative publication strategies with emphasis on Africana stories and perspectives. As a platform for alternative voices, we prioritize the accessibility and affordability of our titles to ensure that relevant and often marginal voices are represented at the global marketplace of ideas. Our titles – poetry, fiction, narrative nonfiction, memoirs, reference, travel writing, African languages, and young people's literature – aim to bring African worldviews closer to diverse readers. Our titles are distributed in paperback and electronic formats globally by African Books Collective.

Connect with Us: Go to www.spearsbooks.org to learn about exclusive previews and read excerpts of new books, find detailed information on our titles, authors, subject area books, and special discounts.

Subscribe to our Free Newsletter: Be amongst the first to hear about our newest publications, special discount offers, news about bestsellers, author interviews, coupons and more! Subscribe to our newsletter by visiting www.spearsbooks.org

Quantity Discounts: Spears Books are available at quantity discounts for orders of ten or more copies. Contact Spears Books at orders@

spearsmedia.com.

Host a Reading Group: Learn more about how to host a reading group on our website at www.spearsbooks.org

www.ingramcontent.com/pod-product-compliance
Lightning Source LLC
Chambersburg PA
CBHW020605310726
48979CB00008B/1360/J
* 9 7 8 1 9 5 7 2 9 6 7 1 5 *